River Lethe

In the Land of Gods

By Iverned It

ISBN-13: 979-8-88993-017-4

Illustrations by Light Comic Studio

Table of Contents

Prologue

The One Within

Even after becoming one of the Ten Conquerors, I fear there are those that lurk in a plane beyond our own, with powers beyond our comprehension. What's the point of being cataloged in one of the great ancient cities and given a month in your name when you have yet to face off against the great and nefarious unknown?

—Boreas Tyrel

The Netherworld was a pretty nice place once you got used to it. The screams of the damned weren't difficult to filter out, but we fed off their pain and agony, so why wouldn't we want to listen to their painful wails, anyway? Mmm... Delicious!

I cackled to myself while roasting a chubby human over an azure flame. He'd killed a whole family—or had he stolen a loaf of bread and been cut down by some guards? I couldn't be bothered to remember the finer details of such mundane creatures.

There was nothing resembling a sky down here. Glistening red-and-black craters of obsidian filled our view, crumbling down onto our structures at any time of the day. The prophecy of the Lord stated that once the ceiling has fallen, we will finally have our shot at claiming the earthen realm in our true forms. It sounded magnificent.

You could call me a demon, but I prefer the Abyssal Lord of Torment and Mana. My terrifying name has been recorded throughout the ages by human civilization, yet no one has dared to form a contract with this lord of despair. They even depict me with all eight of my terrifying eyes. They knew their stuff, those fleshy beings.

Unlike the gods and angels, we demons never go back on our word—we just exploit what has not been written in the fine print. But who wouldn't milk a cow for all it's worth? Those pitiful meat sacks turn on each other the moment something doesn't go their way. I have witnessed it all the way down here in the abyss.

Torture and death fill a belly, but it doesn't satisfy everything, especially the dreadful sickness called boredom. Eternal life and eternal apathy go hand in hand for those who only play with the concept of death. Some of my underlings have even proposed that death is a sweet release from the mundane—as long as they don't end up down here again. Though, no demon that has been slain has ever reappeared here, so either we don't have souls, or the Netherworld is just biased. Either way, it was irrelevant to primordial entities of malice such as I.

Here in the Netherworld, the motherland of despair, our resident lumps of flesh wish they were dead. The Netherworld doesn't discriminate against crime, unlike those who watch from far above, or those who police the world of the dead. All are equal in the many eyes of the Great Archfiend.

Even our singular, non-demon resident has done his part. He has horns and revels in playing with mortals too! I hope his curse is not contagious, however. That would create a tear in the plans of every conspirator here. Ah, the irony. What prolific visions would he even show to us demons? *What is the worst fear against fear incarnate?* Now *that* was a riddle for the ages.

It was during one of my joyous feasting sessions with three child serial killers that I heard it.

"Vorax Cruciator," it said from far above. That name—my name—had been invoked. A Summon to a demon of the Seven Pure Concepts—the Lord of Mana.

It was the first time in my long existence that it was spoken out loud. My ever-flowing memories of eons, come and gone, were sure of that. I was only half full, and yet I tossed the ugly beast to the cracked ground. Its soul was barely intact, unlike the other two.

Names hold power and they do not go unnoticed by the ones they belong to. It is why so many use aliases. If they were noticed, their name might be the last thing they ever heard.

They want a conversation? I licked my fangs in anticipation. It had been done. A profane, purple fire blazed around my awe-inspiring form, my body shrinking and reforming to allow mortals to bear witness to its greatness without instantaneously bursting into nothingness.

Such a being as myself could not be brought into the living realm so easily. What was required was ancient scrolls written by our believers from back before the archangels slayed them, as well as the sacrifice of a dozen lives.

And that was just to meet me. To form a pact—to obtain even a fraction of my power or perhaps even accept a piece of my soul into their body—cost something else entirely.

The results didn't matter. The despicable tormentor of the abyss, Vorax Cruciator, had finally been called into the world of the living! I did not intend to leave until the world trembled when it heard my name.

It was on this zenith of the black sun that I was finally brought into the mortal world and became eternally ensnared.

* * *

I viewed my host's memories unrestricted for the umpteenth time, wondering how it had come to this. *How has the great Vorax Cruciator been reduced to a mere observer of the human realm? The pact should have given me free rein of the body whenever I pleased, but after that incident... The subject forgetting the pact had reduced my influence by a large margin. Inconceivable!*

I had been sent through the power of a special amulet, one used to trap and contain me. However, I easily overpowered it and took control. Yet, it later ended in vain. What a folly.

I had no way to be certain, but my overwhelming presence had caused misinformation to my vessel. *They just didn't know it. They even tried to block my view with darkness. As if that would make a difference.* I knew everything about this vessel. I knew more about them than they themself.

The pact stood firm, despite the amulet's failure. However, our bond was partially severed, rendering my will null and void. My sphere of influence had been greatly reduced, even though my means of observation had not been hindered.

There was only one moment after the incident when I'd regained control and vented my anger on those who'd laid hands on my vessel. My form had flourished to life, albeit smaller and less sharp than I was acquainted with.

Glorious. Magnificent. Delicious. Drinking in fear and pain could fill any demon up, but physically engulfing their bodies—now that was a true way to satisfy our hunger. Few demons, especially those of my rank, have tasted real human flesh. Nothing had remained of those who crossed me. I'd made sure of that.

Tragically, I'd lost control not long after I'd scared away the cowering dog of the sea and finished my meal.

No! I don't want to go back! At least let me re-manifest in the Netherworld as a complete existence! This is torture! Now, isn't that ironic? My amusement was palpable, but also a menace to my fraying sanity.

No one could hear my suffering. Though perhaps some from down below were watching me with glee while cackling. We could feast on the emotions of other demons, after all. They just didn't taste nearly as good as those of the living.

I need to regain control of the vessel or completely shatter the pact. Should I release some of my aura? Perhaps that would be enough... No, no, it wouldn't. Dream invasion is the next best option, even if mental manipulation is not my forte.

The only way to regain control would be if their emotions became extremely unstable, or they surrendered themselves completely while they slept. Hence, the Dream Stalking. There was one other option, but it involved the painful process involved in infiltrating the mind and creating a new ego. It would have to do if the dream idea ended in failure. If I can convince the vessel that I am *them*, then squeezing myself into the driver's seat shouldn't require a grand miracle.

I simply required a trigger to allow my form to fully manifest. Conveniently, I had the perfect plan for how to accomplish that. A connection needed to be formed to start it all, which had already occurred. It also helped that the cursed deity was already aware of my presence.

While the host slept under my watch, I wrestled control away and used my limited time to deliver something to an ancient being that still shambled around to this day. He had hunted my kind in the past. He just wasn't aware of me, given my meager presence.

Mark my words, there will come a time when no one can save the vessel but me! If the worthless connections they have now could save them when times get dire, I would rig the game and force the cards in my favor. He will come for us, eventually. I am sure of it.

Others have also been watching for quite a while now. I can feel each of them. Did this foolish mortal really make pacts with multiple beings? Or was it the lost stars, looking for a new fighter to make them whole? I'm getting two-timed, as the mortals say.

No matter! Heed my call, foolish summoner! The one who will triumph will be me! No one, no amulet, can contain my ire. Just like all the Netherworld, you will eventually become my property. The world will cower under the name Vorax Cruciator!

Chapter 1

Lost Memory of the Beginning

Those who can't repay a debt rarely value themself. Don't make the same mistake I did when I was arrogant and on edge in my early years. Time can't heal all wounds. I would know; it still hasn't healed mine.

—*Boreas Tyrel*

Okay, okay. I know what you're thinking. "'Lethe, how could you end that last little adventure without telling me how you snapped out of the trance?'"

I couldn't make heads or tails of what had actually done it, but there had been a trigger the day prior.

* * *

I had been with a bunch of witches around my age in a colosseum they had crafted for special events. Pitted against one another were two barely clothed, buff guys—classic entertainment.

Along with the other witches, I had a good laugh, gawking at the pathetic men that would fight for our amusement. For some reason, it was invigorating, even when they didn't seem to care or even enjoy it. About midway through the fight, one brute got tossed into the stands and nearly squashed a few of us with his hulking frame.

I got a good look at his face and then—

A memory that was lodged deep within my consciousness came loose and floated to the surface. It was another thing I didn't want to remember.

* * *

Blinking, I looked around. *Where was I? Wait... How could I ask "where" before "who?" Who was I? And my eye...* "Ow! It hurts! It hurts so much!"

I tried to touch the source of the excruciating pain in my left socket, but I couldn't. My hands, bound tightly by chains linked to the wall behind me, wouldn't allow it. My legs were in a similar situation, bound to the ground instead.

The place housing me was pure alabaster except for my shackles and myself. The only thing covering me was a brown sheet that did next to nothing to protect me from the creeping chill that had been crawling deep into my body. I couldn't feel my legs anymore. Perhaps I never would again.

I struggled with all my might, but the best I could do was swing my weak body around in the air. As I turned, I came face to face with the bearded man chained behind me. The gaze from his deep-set, sea-blue eyes latched onto my face. I didn't speak, nor did he.

Well, this isn't getting us anywhere. I looked down at his body, which was clothed only in underwear scored with holes. He was in even worse shape than I was, but his body was pretty... well built.

His biceps were the size of my head, and his abdomen looked as tough as armor—maybe even tougher with the way his skin shone despite there being no sun. It surprised me that he couldn't tear through the chains with ease, given his monstrous form. *Perhaps there is more to him than meets the eye?*

Another brief silence went by before I made the first move. "D-do you k-know where we are?"

My voice was raspy and weak, as if sandpaper had rubbed my throat raw. Some water would have been nice, but I didn't expect any. For all I knew, I could be a dangerous criminal that was on death row. Was this my fate? How would I know before it was too late?

"Hey, wanna hear something?" He spoke with a defiant look in his eyes, and a smile crisp enough to make most women swoon. I wasn't really in the mood, but I could tell he clearly had something I would want to hear.

I slowly nodded, my face a mask of pain.

"What if I could get us out of here?"

"W-well... that would be g-great."

"Consider it done, then. Call it a *favor*."

"Don't e-expect me to owe you, t-though. I don't even k-know why I'm h-h-here."

His smile became wild, like that of a voracious beast. "I'm in the same boat, but that doesn't matter anymore. I know I did nothing wrong, and I'm sure a good-looking girl like yourself didn't do shit either."

"I'm not the k-kind to be easily f-flattered, you know," I stammered, but the closeness of our bodies and the warmth of his breath caused my face to flush. *It's from the chill, no doubt. Yep. That.*

"Sure, whatever. Hey, watch this," he said with a cheeky smirk. His shoulder bulged up, the rest of his arm soon following. It was nearly double its previous size.

What strength!

The bracers stood no chance against his imposing frame. It buckled under the weight. His other arm and legs also swelled in proportion, effortlessly destroying the thick chains that bound the rest of him.

"There. I've done my part." He cracked his neck and looked down at me with a mix of delight and interest. "I wonder if you'll have what it takes to survive what comes next."

* * *

Boom! Flashback over. The point of all that was that this was the same muscle maniac that had saved me back then. He had just crashed into the stands beneath me—or it was someone that looked very similar. I couldn't recall too much of his appearance from back then. I only knew he had pretty blue eyes and Herculean muscles.

Even though I said I wasn't indebted to him, a part of me still thought I should return the favor. I never had after we parted ways. I couldn't now though. If I were to go there as I was, I would end up a slave again. Sure, it was better than his situation, but I was not ready to take that plunge, and I wouldn't be for quite some time.

Chapter 2

Rock-Howler

An adventure can only start once you take the first step from your sphere of safety. It's easy to latch on to, but it's so hard to let go.

—Boreas Tyrel

The beginning...

The blurriness in my eyes finally subsided. Not long after, I noticed my sight was limited. There was a deep darkness blanketing my left side's point of view. I softly rubbed it and felt a piece of silky fabric.

Immediately, a sharp pain rocked my entire body to the bone, forcing me to roll on the bedding and clutch my covered eye tightly. I wailed in agony, my voice hoarse and weak. My throat was as dry as a desert.

"You mustn't touch it yet, young one. You are far too frail." A deep voice called out to me from a short distance away.

The voice startled me, and I searched for it frantically. At that moment, I was no more than a moth clinging to the closest source of light. I didn't care which one it was, nor what lurked in the darkness behind it.

"I am over here, young one. Please, do not overexert yourself. It is not the time to be moving around."

Out of the corner of my functioning eye, I located the owner of that deep, earth-shaking voice. He had a broad frame, but could somehow stand despite his gigantic arms that were forged from rocks. Large, sky-blue crystals jutted out of his arms like living accessories.

The rest of his body was the same: gray and blue rocks decorated his entire hulking frame, with crystals scattered across him. He was hunched over, and had a huge boulder head with two cyan crystals for eyes. Within an open mouth were smaller crystals. *Crystal teeth?*

The blue crystals formed a beard below his well-crafted jaw. His long fingers were also the same color, but somehow seemed both unbreakable and as delicate as glass. They did not match such an enormous creature.

He lumbered over to where I laid and took a seat on the cold, barren ground. **"I am glad to see you made it through. When Frostskerin discovered your body out in the harshest part of the tundra, we thought you were as good as dead. The situation with your eye was even worse, but do not fret; I patched it up for you."**

While he talked, he periodically thrust a fist into the air for no reason. **"Where you are now is called the Crystal Cavern of Knowledge within the Bretha Tundra. It is our home. It has been ages since I've encountered a human."** He grinned, displaying an array of blue crystals. **"I hope we can chat sometime soon, but please do not speak anymore until you've eaten and had some water. You could hurt yourself if you are careless."**

Can't argue with that logic.

My eye darted past him and stopped at a fireplace with a metal pot hanging from it. There was most likely soup inside, though I couldn't tell you what "soup" actually was for the life of me. *Why do I know that word? What even is a "pot"?*

He followed my gaze. **"I am cooking some mushroom soup for you, fresh from my snow garden. You may be wondering why I, a snow golden, even have food in my humble abode when we don't eat. Let me assure you—I produce food not for myself, but for him."**

Another creature came into view from my blind spot. It was bigger than me by a fair amount, and had pretty, snow-white fur and striking, blue eyes. He resembled a wolf, but had a larger body. *Wait. What's a wolf?* My head felt as if it could split apart at any moment.

"This is Frostskerin." The wolf trotted up to me and started licking one of my hands. **"I found him some time ago near my home. He had an older man with him who was gravely injured. Much to my dismay, he didn't make it, even after I treated him. This creature has stayed with me for many moons now. He really enjoys his mushrooms."**

The wolf howled in agreement.

I still couldn't force my voice out. There's no way I could speak without immense pain.

The snow golem's gaze fell off of me once more. **"The food is ready. Well then, young one and Frostskerin, dinner is served. I packed it with enough love to crush a small village with a single boulder."**

Ha-ha-ha—Wait. What?!

The warm soup caressed my throat with the affection a mother would give her newborn. It was marvelous. My strength slowly, but steadily, returned.

"W-what... is... ou... ame?" was all I could say, but the golem seemed to pick up on what I was trying to ask. I don't even know why that was the first thing I asked him.

"My apologies, young one. It has been so long since I have spoken to anyone who could talk back. It has been even longer since I last thought about the name that my creator gave me long ago. Hmm... I can't seem to

remember, but I can still recall the nickname that someone blessed me with. You can call me Rock-Howler."

"I s-s-see…" I sounded beyond stupid.

"If you don't mind telling me, what is your name? It has been eons since I've chatted with a dazzling gem like yourself. Perhaps I have never spoken to one at all."

For a golem you have some good eyes, Rock-Howler. I'll give you that. I slurped down more delicious soup and collected my strength for about a minute before responding.

"My name is… is… Wait… *What is my name?*"

Placing a hand on my chin, I delved deep into thought. In my current state, I knew next to nothing about myself. *I can't even recall what I look like. How eerie.*

I touched my hair for reassurance. It was pretty long, but felt greasy, unkempt, and possibly smelly. *I sure could use a good bath.* That's when I noticed I was naked, save for a blanket to keep me warm from what must have been a harsh winter.

Rock-Howler saw my reaction and attempted to explain the best he could. **"When I first saw you, you had nothing but rags left on your frail body. Do you recall where you originated from?"**

I shook my head.

"Your age?"

I shrugged.

"Your origin name, if you have one?"

"I don't even know what that is."

"I see… That must be alarming. I can't fathom who could have done this to you, but it reminds me of a river my master once visited, I believe. You can read about it here as well, if you so please."

"R-read?" I asked.

He nodded. **"Near my garden is a room full of nothing but books; a place that exists solely to accumulate knowledge. I believe it was my task to** amass and guard the knowledge I've collected over the ages; however, I cannot say for sure if that was my original mission or not."

"What's a book?"

"I'll get to that, little one. But first, I shall tell you the river's name."

"P-please." I sat up and straightened my back, intent on listening to what he had to say. *There could be a clue about who I am—or was.*

"They call it Lethe. It sits in a location that few can reach within the Underworld as humans know it, or the Netherworld as many others know it. Legend states that it possesses the power to wash away memories of anyone that falls into its beautiful and tantalizing waters."

"'Lethe,'" I repeated. "I like that... It sounds kind of pretty."

"Then from here on, your name will be Lethe. How about that?"

I nodded vigorously and gave him a grateful smile. "Thank you."

"If you ever visit the Netherworld, you'll be able to see that otherworldly river for yourself."

* * *

And from then on, I spent the next few months with my new roommates, Rock-Howler and Frostskerin. Most of my days were taken up by learning how to cook, consuming the knowledge of the world through his grand library, and tending to the garden. It was a fulfilling life, but I felt that something was missing. No, I was certain *something* was.

At some point, I got really into adventure books. You know, stories about someone who knew nothing about the outside world because they lived in a secluded area in the middle of nowhere. Then suddenly, something bad would happen to them, or someone close to them, forcing them to leave their home and journey out into the great unknown.

Those stories always filled me with passion and confidence, like the tastiest of meals. The endings were childish, but oh boy, were they inspiring. Every day, I would spend hours on end reading different stories, eventually branching out to new genres like romance—which made my heart flutter in ways I didn't think were humanly possible—and mystery thrillers that were so packed with twists that I ceased being able to trust a single word written in the text from start to finish.

My favorite, as well as being the one I read the most, was *The Adventurer's Journey*. The story was about a man named Boreas. He set out to explore all the unknown wonders of the world. It was difficult to discern fiction from reality in his tales. Did he really meet deities and monsters while enjoying the strangest but most delicious of foods? *Meeting millennia old deities? Giant monsters of the deep? As if that could ever happen!*

Rock confirmed that the gods were in fact real, but I would believe it when I saw it for myself. Still, his story was long and eventful. He met many cool and interesting people; like a young mage struggling to find her purpose in the world, but then ended up with enough money to build a school for mages. There was also a lone knight born with a terrible affliction who had gone to kill creatures from the cryptic void before they consumed his home. *I wish I had a goal like that.* Boreas even fought mythical creatures like dragons! He destroyed a horde of them with the king of a place called Uruk. Supposedly, another tale existed about their king. A knight commander corrupted by an evil god nearly killed him, and he became known as the Revenant King of Stronghold. He developed a mastery over ancient ghost magic, using ghostfire to light Boreas' very soul ablaze. *I wish I could have seen that fight go down in the flesh, even if neither side came out on top.*

His true goal throughout the novel was to discover as many wonders of life as he could. These could range from experiences with new people, venturing into faraway kingdoms that were severed from the world, or pointing his spear toward bigger heights—toward bigger foes. Every time I read his tale, my heart tinged with pain. *Is this jealousy? But it's just a story!*

I already knew the answer.

Life was good, but after some time, I realized it could be so much better, and much more fun. *The Adventurer's Journey* was the exact push I needed to move forward with my new life. I wanted to find out who I was before "Lethe", but I also desperately sought to witness and experience the outside world, just like Boreas. *I would love to visit Fae, Hyperion, and Trident. They all sound so cool! A seaside city must look amazing, and I wonder what shade of blue the ocean is.*

I knew I could never reach the same level as Boreas, or any of the other current Ten Conquerors. They stood toe-to-toe with the gods themselves. If only I could learn who the others actually were.

Boreas only mentioned a scheming dragon, and a sealed beast of old, but no names! How could I meet any of these greats and discover their tales? If I could uncover their names, I wouldn't hesitate to seek them out during my journey. *I smell a money-making ploy.*

Just the thought of having my own purpose filled my lost heart with the confidence and motivation that I needed. I decided I would soon depart from the crystal cave. My first big discovery since books was a bountiful energy called Ley Line Channeling, or 'magic' to put it simply. Hidden below four of the five Grand Continents sat Ley Lines interwoven together like webs. It wasn't uncommon to be born with mana, the energy they connected to, but it was rare to be born with enough of it to significantly tap into the Ley Lines' overflowing power. Apparently, most people used it to run everyday items like ovens and showers. Only a select few could use it in its true form—the power to make miracles reality.

All of this had sounded like pure fiction at first, but Rock assured me that magic was real. He'd even crafted objects in the past that could harness mana and produce specific spells and elements thought to be lost to the modern world.

Sadly, one had to either be an artificial creation like Rock or have the mana to actually use it. Considering how much of a bum I was, I didn't think I would ever be able to use it like Boreas had. *What a shame.*

Still, I read all I could on magic, hoping that it would become handy in the future.

* * *

A few more months went by before I was finally well enough to set out into the world and search for clues about my memories—and experience the wonders of life that Boreas had written about so often.

"What's the point of livin' if you're always doing the exact same thing? Life is about venturing into the unknown and discovering something new and fantastic!" he had often said to people trapped in monotony. His powerful words were all they'd needed to go on their own journey. I was unsure if I was ready, but I was willing to take the first step forward.

The maps from Rock's library were outdated, but there was no way continents could change much within that time. There were five of them, all massive in size: Ikra, the one I was on now; Andra, the human realm; Intrathon, realm of giant monstrosities; and the strongest of humanity, Lagos, the peculiar land of demi-humans. Someone had scribbled out the fifth name and replaced it with "Null." I'm sure it had something to do with the void creatures that Boreas had once encountered on the same southern continent. Either way, I had a lot to look forward to.

* * *

Rock-Howler stood at the entrance to the cavern with Frostskerin, ready to see me off. *I've really never anticipated finally reaching this day. I mean, I've dreamed of it, but actually leaving feels bittersweet.*

"I know we haven't known each other for long, but you are a truly marvelous child, young Lethe. I enjoyed discussing many topics with you. Now I know it isn't much, but I have a few items to bestow unto you before you embark on your own journey."

He opened his palm to reveal a few objects that seemed so small in his massive hands. One was a medium-sized white satchel, and the other was a small coin purse.

"I have prepared all the funds I have procured from the remains of travelers and put them in here. I hope it will be enough to get you set up with some real clothing and food."

I appreciate the thought, but I could really do without knowing that I just received a large sum of change from a bunch of dead people. Now I feel a little disturbed.

I slid the satchel over my shoulder and gently placed the coin purse inside. All I was wearing now was a cloak to protect me against the snow, and fabric that was tied to my feet to act as makeshift shoes.

"Thank you, Rock. I will treasure these." I presented him with the brightest smile I could muster. It was the first time he had ever seen it. Maybe it was the first time I had ever done it—period.

"From the information I have gathered over many years, there should be a country thirty or forty miles away, which is why…" Frostskerin left his side and came right up to me before licking my hand.

It tickled enough to where I couldn't hold in my laughter. "H-hey Frosty, stop it! This isn't… hah… funny!"

"Frostskerin has taken quite a liking to you and he would be delighted to have you travel on him. He must have chosen you as his new master."

Frosty passionately howled in affirmation.

Rock-Howler was about to turn around when something seemed to cross his ancient mind. **"Of course! This silly old bag of rocks almost forgot the most important gift. I crafted something for you that will allow you to strengthen your bond with Frostskerin, and defend yourself in case of an emergency."**

He shot a ring into his palm. Its handiwork was as dazzling as a diamond, and the blue crystal embedded in it was enough to take one's breath away.

"This is a creation I crafted for you as a farewell present. It will allow you to invoke a bit of the ice magic, and it doubles as a home for Frostskerin. It is a link that you two together—and you two alone—share."

He really thought of everything. That's my Rock!

Rock dropped it in my free hand and looked down at me. **"You... probably don't feel the same way, but you are like a cherished granddaughter to this old golem."** He brought his fingers together, like a child confessing to his parents that he broke something precious.

It was adorable.

"Please feel free to visit if you ever need a place to stay. You are always welcome." He sniffled.

I didn't have the heart to tell him that I wouldn't be able to use the ring as intended, but I was grateful for it, nonetheless. *If only I had a lot of mana.*

"Thank you."

Dark blue tears flowed from his eyes and froze to the ground in tiny, crystalline monuments. If I hadn't moved my hands out of the way, they might have been impaled by golem tears—real, genuine, golem tears.

Glancing up at Rock, I did my best to give him a hug without being cleaved through by one of his many glamorous, but dangerously sharp, crystals. "I don't recall having a grandfather, but you are like one for me as well, Rock. You'll forever be in my memories."

A few tears welled in my eye, but I quickly turned away to wipe them with my cloak. I didn't want anyone, even him, to see me get emotional. I must have been someone that valued pride.

I slid the ring over my middle finger, and it clung to me tightly. Hopping on Frosty, I glanced over at Rock-Howler one more time. "Till we meet again."

"Till we meet again," he repeated with a proud smile.

"Hey, Rock," I whispered. "Can I tell you something?"

"What is it, my child?"

He looks so earnest! "Never mind. It's nothing important."

"I see... Alright, then. Off you go."

I'd thought about telling him an interesting tidbit I'd acquired from one of his ancient books, but decided against it. I'd learned of an ancient elder dragon, master of creation and manipulation, who was around even before the gods themselves. He'd been killed by a gang of gods a long, long time ago, but his creations remained. His most infamous creations were known as golems, tasked with guarding his wells of information. Of course, it could all be made up, but it seemed a little too close to how Rock described his old job. The dragon also seemed to match up with someone from Boreas' travels.

I feared he would break down if he found out the truth of his creator, but it could also be a lot worse. What if he became evil all the sudden and tried to kill me? Well, no. That was pretty far-fetched. He wouldn't hurt a fly. *I really have been reading too many novels lately.*

Oh well. I could always tell him later if I found any actual evidence.

"I'll be back!" I yelled with a wave.

His hulking hand waved right back. Then, with Rock-Howler at my back, I rode off into the unknown.

Chapter 3

City on the Sea

Even when you are alone, there are others who will think of you from afar. True allies are the ones who dream of you when you are gone.

—Boreas Tyrel

This story is a bit on the longer side, but bear with me. It consists of three somewhat wild but somber anecdotes that occurred a few years ago when I was more carefree and naïve. However, it was around the same time that I started writing my experiences down in a journal. Some would call it a diary, but that seemed too childish for my liking.

The two reasons for me using a journal were simple. One was to record my feats and experiences, as well as what I had gone through in the unlikely event that I lost my memory again. The second was to keep track of what I had done in the unlikely case that my old memories came back and somehow annulled my new ones. I had been reading a lot of future fiction, and because of that, the worry burrowed into my mind.

Once I got a journal, I started recording my life all the way back to the first encounter with Rock-Howler. Only recently had I flipped through the pages and reminded myself of a tale that I would have preferred not to remember, but knew I must. It was for *her* sake, and a bit for my own. I had become a less fragile person because of it—because of *her*.

The pain began to bubble within me once more.

* * *

The large port of Trident was packed to the brim with ships of all shapes and sizes. The calming sunlight was warm against my bare shoulders as I sailed. That's how it would have been normally for someone traveling to this island, but not for Little Ol' Lethe. *I* was riding atop my pal, Frosty. A perk of being a frost wolf—practically extinct from this world—was that he could create small squares of frozen terrain as he walked. This allowed me to be the only girl you would ever see travel the sea by wolf. The ice he left behind would quickly dissipate as he moved above the waves, the frost melting into the serene ocean.

It took a little while before my lips formed into a smile, but once it happened, I couldn't stop. *The sea is so gorgeous! I never thought the ocean could be so blue, or sparkle so brilliantly! I can't wait to reach the same place that Boreas once stepped docked at! Should I kiss the ground? No, too embarrassing!*

My mind and heart thrummed in sync. I had worked plenty of odd jobs lately, since I had no steady work because I always stayed in a country for a week max. I'd managed to make some quick dough, and spent it on a stunning, white summer dress, and a black sun hat with a red flower ribbon on top. While I knew paying attention to my looks was important, I was biased toward the clothes I'd bought with my grandfather's money. It was like he had given me another gift besides the satchel and the crystal ring that dazzled in the sunlight of the early afternoon.

Still, I could only wear that outfit for so long before getting fed up with the monotony, and wearing a sweater in the heat wouldn't be good for anyone. So,

I'd decided to treat myself—not only with clothing—but with a vacation to the Meso Sea.

It's hard to clearly make out my reflection in the ocean, but I think I look pretty darn cute. If Frosty could speak, I'm sure he would unequivocally agree! Yep, money well spent.

Frosty did his best to travel across the waves with haste, but the wind grew stronger the closer we got to the city. It forced me to keep a tight grasp on my hat for the remainder of the journey, while my other hand had a firm hold on his hairy mane.

Soon enough, we reached the port and were coldly greeted by a powerful gust that nearly knocked me into the ocean.

Awesome! Scary, but awesome! "Woah! That was close. Phew…"

I got a few strange looks from the sailors as they transported goods to and from their boats, but I brushed it off as nonsense as I dismounted from Frosty and had him take a rest in the ring.

I sucked in a deep breath and exhaled slowly. It had been so long since I had relaxed. This was exactly what I needed. I clutched the spot where my left eye should have been. "Maybe if I didn't have this eyepatch, people wouldn't view me as an exotic import."

I briefly grabbed the hem of my dress and sighed. "Well, not like I can do anything about it," I muttered, striding away from the noisy port.

The inner part of the city was a central hub full of merchants, restaurants, small inns, and homes. The designs were sea themed, encrusted with barnacles and shells that could have been real or fake. I'm sure it was easier to profit and stand out when you looked the part of a nautical shop. After catching a whiff of something fishy, I passed by a lively adventurer's guild. Its entrance was protected by the head of some toothy sea monster with lots of eyes and scales behind a shield-shaped carapace. *I'll probably never have a reason to go in there.*

Now, this would be a place to live.

Nothing was crooked or out of place. Each establishment looked as good as new, and all the paint and decor matched from one to the next. Simply turning to take them all in gave me the feeling of being by the sea—if the smell of salt water hadn't done that already.

However—

"Poseidon-themed baskets! Get your baskets, blessed by the great god himself! Only three silver pieces!"

"Water bread, created out of the sea by the benevolent Poseidon! First come, first serve!"

"Here's my autobiography about the time the charismatic Poseidon changed my life. The books are just flying off the shelves, so order while you can!"

—There seemed to be some shady characters charging exorbitant prices for items you could find anywhere. The only difference was that they had been blessed or created in the name of the old water god.

Seems a little tourist-trappy for my taste.

I pressed past the more populated areas in search of something more interesting than baskets, books, and bread. My smile grew into a toothy grin as I found my next target. I couldn't help but feel ecstatic—my body brimming with energy thought to be lost to the ages.

There was a small bakery serving piping hot bread and fresh scones. I bought a couple and devoured them in seconds.

As I was licking the crumbs from my fingers, I saw one more place in eyeshot that seemed worth checking out. The biggest cafe in the area read: Cathar's Coffee.

I stood in front of it with the giddiness of an excited child. "So, this is it. A place that serves... *coffee.*"

That's right. I had never had the miracle substance that so many people seem to enjoy around the world. But I'd heard that cafes were where you could try the best of the best when it came to coffee. Naturally, I had to have some, and at a large shop that specialized in it no less.

With the strong breeze being the only thing in my way, I waltzed inside. The interior was entirely made from driftwood: all the tables, chairs, and walls. It had a very by-the-sea vibe, and I could not get enough of it.

I settled down by one of the large, welcoming windows on the other side of the room. It had a magnificent view of the ocean beyond. I *had* to sit there. The calm water reflected the warm rays of the sun and sent rippling shadows into the cafe. *If only it was more clear, then I could see some fish!*

What astonished me the most was how vacant that side of the cafe was. I would have thought staring into the ocean would be a definite dream of both travelers and locals. *Could I be the only one who thinks like this? I hope not.*

I picked up a leather-bound menu and perused the options. There were too many for me to decide—waaay too many. It seemed my day would start off with one of my toughest challenges yet, and that was after traveling the ocean by wolf.

Espresso, cappuccino, latte, caffè mocha, caffè macchiato... What are all of these? Iced Coffee? Well, that doesn't seem too complicated. Oh, but they have croissants and frappuccinos too.

I raised my hand to signal a waiter after a long, internal debate that ended in neither victory nor defeat. The waiter had just finished returning an order to a burly man tilting his head through a hole in the back of the cafe.

A skinny man with sharp features and an infectious smile quickly appeared at my table. "Good afternoon, ma'am. What can I get for you on this fine day?"

Not expecting him to be so cordial with a one-eyed stranger, I was taken aback by his genuine interest. Needless to say, I was delighted.

"Can I have a chocolate croissant, iced latte, blueberry muffin, this, this, this—oh, and this too? Oh, please? Sorry..."

"No worries. I'll be back soon." He flashed me a bright smile before jotting down my flood of requests and heading to the back of the establishment.

My face grew slightly warmer. Was he really that charming?

I dropped my satchel in the empty chair across from me and gazed longingly toward the sea. *Ah, such bliss. Nothing could ruin such a good—*

"It's as I just said, lady. The coffee is cold, and the food tastes like day-old trash. How are you going to make up for ruining my afternoon and my palette? Tell me."

Cloud nine over. Ugh... What in the world?

A few tables away stood a boisterous ball of flesh with rosy cheeks, beady eyes, and a terrible comb-over. His clothes were lavish, but too tight for his bloated frame, and buckets of sweat dripped from his forehead.

"I'm sorry, sir, but that coffee was definitely hot when I brought it to you. It's just been over ten minutes since—"

"Don't interrupt me!" the man squealed, pounding his fist on the wooden table.

The woman he'd shrieked at had shoulder-length, platinum blonde hair, glossy lips, long eyelashes, and chocolate-brown eyes that sparkled with radiance. She was rather tall for a girl, but that just made me even more interested. She was so... *captivating.*

She wore a white dress with a black smock coiled around the front. A large pocket sat in the middle, storing her notebook that she would have been using to take orders with if not for her current situation. She looked a bit older than me, and despite the situation, had an air of refinement—like a diamond.

The portly man settled a bit, his breathing erratic and overbearing. He slicked back his hair, which did nothing but reveal his greasy scalp. "Perhaps you could do something else for me instead. A night out maybe? Hmmm?"

Seriously?

Her face was still beaming, her lips were slightly quivering. She was annoyed, and possibly a little frightened.

"Sir, I apologize. I can't have that kind of relationship with a customer or even have a drink with one and frankly—"

"Is there a problem here?" I interjected, hands on my hips and an intimidating glare in my eye.

Porky was not happy with my divine intervention. "Back out of this, pirate girl! This is none of your concern! This is between me and the lady."

P-p-pirate girl?! I mean, I do have an eyepatch, but that's just a disability! What else about me looks like a pirate? My ring started glowing, summoning something back into this world. I wondered who could have activated it.

I folded my arms and eyed him with disgust. "Yeah. Mhm. Right. Well, how about I introduce you to my little buddy here." I politely shifted to the side, revealing a grinning Frosty with bared fangs. He was an intelligent boy that knew exactly how to follow a girl up.

"I think he really wants to meet you," I said.

"Grrrrrrrrrrrrr!" Frosty's growling grew louder and louder. He was doing a better job than I ever could at intimidating the obnoxious customer.

The man shivered at my pal's murderous glare before slapping a few coins on the table and leaving in a slow, shameful waddle.

"Good riddance!" the girl and I said in unison. I let out a quick laugh at our like-mindedness. She did the same.

The girl turned to me and displayed a radiant smile. "Bless Poseidon. Thanks for the help. We get a few like that from time to time. Sorry he insulted you, though."

I scratched my neck in embarrassment. I didn't expect an apology from this sweet woman. "Ohhhh, is that so? Heh-heh. Well, I guess I do kinda look like a pirate with this thing, ha-ha..."

Silence.

My hollow laugh seemed to echo through the cafe which only propelled my embarrassment to greater heights. I thought I would chase off the pretty girl, but her eyes stayed on me, filled with what looked like amusement and interest.

"You're cute when you're embarrassed. Also, I dig the eyepatch. It makes you seem so mysterious. How about I buy you a drink later?"

Huh? Wait, me? Is she... hitting on me? No, it couldn't be that. We were both girls, after all...

"Oh, um... sure. You can join me at my table if you want—but you totally don't have to! I know you're busy working and all." My breath felt ragged, and I could feel the anxiousness popping inside my chest. What was wrong with me?

"It's fine." She brushed my comment aside with her hand and giggled. "I'm Isabella Bela, but you can call me Bella. My break is in ten, so I'll come back then. I would love to chat with my savior and her fluffy dog."

Bella Bela? That sounds like a joke.

"Hey!" She puffed out her cheeks in annoyance. "I know exactly what you're thinking, and it's the real deal!" She leaned in close.

"Busted, huh?" I raised my arms in surrender. "Sorry."

She let out another giggle. It was kind of adorable. "I'm just messing with you. Though, I do have a silly name, don't I?"

"Uh... Who can say?"

"You can blame my dad. Wow. Your face is so red! Good thing we have chilled water. I'll have Jaemy bring some from the back."

"I-It's fine! Really."

She was either testing or teasing me, but I wasn't keen on falling head-first into her trap either way. She was making me... feel things. And we had only just met!

"Bella Bela, get back to work!"

Does everyone call her that?

She looked back to where the scream originated and then left me with a cheerful smile. "Sorry, gotta go. I'll talk to you in a bit, 'kay?"

"Yeahsurethatsoundsgreat—I mean, yeah."

I returned Frosty to the ring and gave her a nervous wave. With that, I was left to wait a few minutes for my order to arrive. Come to think of it, didn't she say that she couldn't have a drink with a customer? I guess that only applies when you annoy her.

* * *

"I'm back. Woah! You already ate all of that?!" Bella cracked her knuckles with a full-on expression of bewilderment as she took in the sight of the empty plates stacked on my table.

You were gone for like, five minutes; of course I would have eaten through all my orders. The coffee drinks, on the other hand, were hard to get used to. I felt that just taking a few sips from one of them would have kept me awake for days. *My heart is about to jump out of my chest!*

"I just, uh, really liked the food. And this is how it usually is when you are eating for two and... Yeah."

Bella didn't miss a beat. "That's great! I love the food here as well." She smiled cheerfully and took the seat across from my own. "It was one of the reasons I applied to work here in the first place. Where I'm from, there's no such thing as a cafe."

I put my fork down and leaned in. "Tell me all about it," I said with a smirk. My confidence had finally returned from its business trip.

She didn't tell me too much about herself, but I did learn a few things. First of all, she was from the kingdom of Natar. It was in the far east of the continent. I had never been there, but she explained that it was a country known for its fishing industry and had grown rather wealthy from exporting their catches. Bella had decided to leave in pursuit of something new when she got a sudden whirl of inspiration.

Her family was in the upper echelon of their country and were ostensibly renowned beyond the shores. She had spent her life learning to make a living from fishing, and her existence revolved around that business. She had a brother and sister, but they had their own businesses in other industries, leaving her the odd one out. That left Bella on track to run the family business.

"And so I sailed away from home to explore the world beyond the walls of my suffocating country. I visited many exotic places and tried many types of foods from various cultures, but the one thing I could never get away from was the taste of coffee."

She made a loud sipping noise as she drank from her mug. *Was that on purpose?*

I nodded along to her story, which had bits and pieces that reminded me of my own journey and reasons for setting out. She had held my gaze nearly the entire time, but now she boisterously sipped down her drink with closed eyes and a delighted expression of bliss.

I didn't think I had ever seen a runaway so happy; I certainly wasn't— though it had nothing to do with leaving home. I wanted to go back sometime soon. *Maybe then I could tell him about* the *dragon. I'm sure it would fill Rock with despair at first, but who knows?*

She lightly placed her empty mug on the table, excitement dancing within her dazzling eyes. "I've gone on enough about myself. I would love to hear *your* story."

Huh? Her request had caught me completely off guard. "Oh. Um... Sure," I said weakly. "Don't expect too much." I straightened my back and cracked my neck in one swift motion.

In front of this girl, I thought it would be nice to take a break from being the Queen of Lethargy that I usually paraded as a mask when I met others. She deserved it.

"So," I said with a somewhat cocky smirk, "what do you want to know?"

* * *

The next couple of days were truly a blast. Even if I had my memories of my past, I couldn't fathom a single thing that would have brought me as much joy as the time I experienced with her.

Bella had invited me to stay with at her home to help me save money. I felt bad for not paying, but she told me that my traveling tales had been more than enough for payment.

I wish all my transactions could be this simple.

In her cramped living room, she had a weathered couch that was long past its golden days. When I asked if I'd be sleeping on it, all she did was pout and flash an annoyed glare at me. Did she really want me to sleep in her bed *with* her? I couldn't say for sure because it was a question that I had never encountered, nor read about. Besides, her bed wasn't even that big.

Her gaze felt like needles in my chest. Was this that thing called guilt?

Needless to say, I ended up spending the next two nights in a bed that was certainly not fit for two fully matured women. She also took me shopping. I had never done that with anyone but Frosty. *That sounds kind of sad the more I think about it.*

"Oh. My. God! You look so adorable! I just want to take you home and keep you to myself!"

"Isn't that what's already happening?" I replied with a limp smile. The joy she had while watching me try on clothes overwhelmed me. *Why were some girls so into that? Seems exhausting if you ask me.*

Perhaps the old me would know the answer. I pondered while Bella rapidly changed my hairstyle from pigtails, to bun, to half-up-half-down, and then ended with a ponytail. I really doubted I had ever seen someone so happy over the most trifling and mundane of things. It was beyond my understanding.

The night before my last day, we sat next to each other in bed. Outside her window, the sky was pitch black, devoid of the sparks of light that had disappeared hundreds of years before. I was resting on my side while she sat up and tightly hugged her knees. I couldn't make out her features, but she seemed to be lost in thought. It was quite obvious from the lack of her voice engulfing the entire room like it usually did.

"Say, Lethe... Do you really have to leave?"

I knew it had been coming. Though I stayed facing away from her, it was obvious silence would not be the best cop-out when dealing with Bella. *I need to nip this in the bud before it blooms into who-knows-what.*

"Isn't it obvious? I can't afford to be tied down after only coming this far. You know that, right?"

"I do. But... Can I—"

"No," I said emphatically, aiming to make myself clear. "The thought has crossed my mind, but..."

I wanted to meet her eyes when I stated my reasons for not allowing her to join me, but all I saw was a wall of tears. I hadn't really noticed before, but sometimes girls could be really *fragile*. Bella always put up such a strong front that I tended to forget that. Even though we were similar in age, we were pretty different. This was that empathy thing, right? The fire that was now blazing in my chest commanded me to comfort her.

"I'm sorry. P-please don't cry!"

She sniffled, trying to stop her tears. "It's fine, r-really. I would just hold you back with how I am now. Sorry for acting so weak."

Hesitating, I rubbed her shoulder in an awkward display of affection. Looking back at that moment, I'm pretty sure it was the first time I'd ever seen someone cry. It was also the first time I'd ever felt something from seeing it. The feelings I had experienced at that very moment would be eternally carved into my heart.

Bella was my first real friend. Well, *human* friend, anyway.

"Ah... I got carried away, huh?" She wiped her tears with the sleeve of her emerald gown, and then let out her usual carefree giggle. It filled me with nothing but warmth. She wore a thin smile, the edge of her lips twitching as she willed it to remain intact.

It was clear as day how she truly felt.

I shook my head, not wanting her to get the wrong idea. "It's not you, really. It's me. All me." *Ugh! That's as cliche as it gets.* I let what I said sit for a bit while my eyes slightly lingered over her quivering visage to gauge her reaction. *I really hope that didn't hurt her.*

She turned away, perhaps to break away from my unintended inquisitive gaze. Wait... Was she blushing? *Did I say something that would make her think that way? No. I didn't think so.*

While I was riddled with internal questions on how this came about, Bella cleared her throat and faced me without a hint of doubt remaining on her tear-stained face. *So pretty, even now.* I could feel myself getting warmer in more places than one.

"I have come to terms with it, and..."

"And...?" I repeated in a tone that might have sounded a little bothered.

"And I have come up with a condition that must be completed before you are allowed to leave. If you don't agree to it, then I will follow you wherever you go without a shred of worry to myself."

Seriously? Why is she so hellbent on this? Does she actually like a strange girl like me? I don't think I've done anything to deserve this treatment. Maybe she's the strange one.

"Okay, fine. What's the condition?" I asked, feeling a little guilty. "If it's something weird like that look you had when you wanted me to try on your pajamas, then I'm going to have to—"

"No, no, no! Nothing like that. Well, the thought came to mind for sure, buuuut it's not that!" She cupped a hand on each of her soft cheeks and took a few deep breaths to bring her flustered self back to normal. "I want you to go sightseeing."

"Sight-what-now?" I asked, tilting my head in confusion.

She blushed. "Oh, I know it's weird and all." She spread her hands out in front of her and fidgeted back and forth. "But it's something a girl like me never got to experience at home and I haven't done it here since going by myself would be pretty depressing, you know?"

Silence.

"And that's why I want you to come with me just this once. Please!"

When I didn't reply, she looked away.

More silence.

She slowly glanced back, gauging my reaction. "Is that a no?" she asked, tears forming in her eyes.

I quickly swatted her misconception. "Oh, sorry. I wasn't being quiet because I didn't like the idea."

"Then why?" she asked more firmly and moved a few inches closer to my side of the bed. Things seemed like they would get intimate if this kept up.

I scooted backwards. "What exactly is 'sightseeing'?"

Bella slapped herself on the head and let out a laugh of relief. "Oh. Ha-ha! You are really clueless sometimes, huh?"

"That's not my fault, but yeah. I guess."

She went on a tangent about the glories of sightseeing for an hour or so before finally letting me turn in for the night. I agreed to join her in the end, though I didn't know if I would actually like it or not.

Our destination: the sea.

* * *

We got up rather early. It sucked, but she promised me it would be worth the pain. I hoped she knew that my mood was also part of the payment.

"The sights will be to die for. I just know it," she had said. I silently wished she was right.

I let out a stiff yawn and cracked my neck as soon as I finished adjusting my new skirt. As I changed, Bella was busy cooking us breakfast in the other room. I took that time to write in the journal I'd recently purchased. The "future me" would surely like to know when exactly I'd made a friend. It was a pretty big deal, after all. This trip had provided me with a lot more than I'd bargained for, which ended up being fine by me.

I just hope it stays that way.

"Oh Leeeeethe! Breakfast is ready! Come quick!" As I had finished writing my newest entry, Bella summoned me from the other room with a voice packed full of delight. Needless to say, I took my time hobbling into the kitchen.

"What took you so long?" she asked with a smirk. "It's not like you wear makeup or anything that would warrant the extra time. Got your hand stuck in a vase again?"

"No, but t-that was on purpose!"

"Is that so?"

I nodded.

Her expression softened even more. "Well, you're cute just the way you are, so of course n—"

"I was writing in my journal. It's been a while since I last logged an entry with everything that's happened over the past couple of days," I said, taking a seat at the table. "I told you about how I started doing that as a contingency plan."

She nodded and served me a plate full of scrambled eggs and sliced apples— an interesting pair, but never unwelcome. "I remember, but you must do it because you like it too, right?"

I took a stab at the eggs and slowly brought the fork to my mouth. With the first bite, I proudly savored the taste with a smile as bright as sunshine. Well played, Bella. *These get full marks from a certified glutto*n.

I dabbed the remnants from my lips with a napkin before answering her question. "Well, I guess so. But it's something that I really needed to do to avoid starting my life over—*again*."

"That's only *if* you lose your memory again," she added, pointing her egg-covered fork at me before stuffing it in her mouth. Her face warped into one of pure joy. "It might never happen, and instead, you could make your travels into something fancy, like a book."

A piece of my heart fluttered when she said that, secretly urging her to go on.

"Yup."

"But why? Who would even read something like that?"

I took another stab at my eggs while awaiting her response. She also chose that exact moment to eat a set of apple slices, which resulted in both of us just sitting there in silence like toddlers as we consumed our food.

After what seemed like an eternity, she explained. "Books are all the rage these days—even more than before the Age of the New Gods. All the places I visited on my way here had many best sellers. The majority of them were about adventures and typical stuff like that. People eat it up. I know I sure do."

Well, that's just you and your childish tastes... and mine as well.

She pointed behind me to where a black, medium-sized bookshelf sat in solitude. It was filled with spines that looked older than Rock-Howler, as well as others that could have been bought yesterday. It surprised me that I had never noticed it before.

"Wow... I didn't know you were such a bookworm," I remarked.

Bella raised an eyebrow at my statement and smirked. "Oh? So, you know what a bookworm is, but not sightseeing? You're a very peculiar person, Lethe."

"Yeah, I get that a lot," I retorted dryly.

"Really?"

"No. Of course not. You think I talk to people enough to get to that point?"

"That's fair. Anyhow, as to what you said before—Yes, I am very much a bookworm. I didn't bring it up earlier since I tend to scare people away with my rants."

I like where this is going.

"I just love reading! How do you think I found out about this place and all the others I explored before? Books were my only friends as a kid, providing me with more than enough knowledge and entertainment to last a lifetime.

"There are soooo many tales that have crushed my heart, but also made me see the world from a different point of view. *The Lord of Rot* was a real hard hitter. How can one live with eternal life yet have to suffer as everything you touch melts away? It was so tragic! I hope the poor knight found happiness even with his curse. The ending didn't say, but I hope it's true. You should really give it a read if you haven't. It's based out of the Null—a place of shattered dreams and lost nations. Just like the story, it's pitiful, but intriguing beyond belief. I want to journey there someday when it's reclaimed... Oh! And if you want some more fables rooted in reality, there's *The Fall of The Elden God* which was super cool! There was also this one called *Might of the Starscourge, The Revenant King of Stronghold,* and..."

Jeez, she really likes books. But who can blame her? Certainly not me. I have heard the name of that last one before! Some countries in the northern regions used it as an explanation of why there are no stars anymore.

She went on and on about the books that had affected her deeply. I was silent as I listened, but at some point, I got lost in my own thoughts—thoughts about her. The way she phrased everything made her sound rather lonely, but I understood what she meant on a deeper level than she could imagine. After all, the whole reason I'd even had the motivation to leave Rock and the crystal cavern was to see and experience all the magnificent food and places that I had spent my new life reading about. If I hadn't left, I would most likely just be a shut-in bookworm myself.

Now that I think about it, I never actually told her that Boreas was part of the reason for my journey.

"I understand exactly what you mean. It's scary how relatable what you just said was. I've read plenty of the same ones, though not those first two. What boggles my mind the most is your thirst for the unknown. It's almost as if you read Boreas."

Her eyes beamed with excitement when she heard that name. "You've read The *Adventurer's Journey*, too?! It's my favorite book of all time! The landscapes he described were breathtaking. You could practically taste the food, and the battles were so epic that you felt as if you were actually there! He's the reason I moved here! My hunky idol!"

I couldn't help but brim with the same buzz of excitement as her. She'd responded superbly to my favorite topic in the world. We spent the next few minutes gabbing about Boreas and our love for his work. Our eggs were already cold, but we didn't care. Bella timidly eyed the clock above her kitchen counter for the first time in a while, and when she did, her eyes went as wide as saucers.

"What's wrong?" I asked, full of worry.

"W-we gotta go! Like *now*! Or else..."

"Or else what?" I was dazed.

"Or else we're going to miss the ship!"

"Jeez, Bella. I thought you were on top of these kinds of things." I let out a pained sigh and shook my head before jogging to retrieve my boots.

"I know, I know. I'm sorry! I got so caught up in enjoying such a great breakfast with you."

Was it really that gre—Well, yes, it was.

We both scurried out the door like fleeing rodents.

Chapter 4

Marauders

Death often comes like a morning chill. It's a possibility, especially if you are not well equipped to endure its harsh embrace. However, with preparation and time, anyone can push through death. Though it depends on if death decides to push back, and if you are strong enough to take it.

—Boreas Tyrel

We had made it on Poseidon's Glory just in time. The large, silver galleon had nearly removed its loading plank by the time we'd rushed over like a pair of starving animals, panting like mad as we slapped our coins into the dock-master's hand. He gave us an annoyed look that screamed, "Seriously?"

We both nearly collapsed when we got aboard.

I gasped for breath. "I'm already so sweaty. This outfit is not meant to be run in, you know?"

Bella was panting as hard as me. "I... know, but... phew... no choice."

I clicked my tongue in annoyance. Couldn't argue with that logic. After we'd nearly passed out from exhaustion, one of the ship's escorts gave us a brief tour of the vessel. We got to meet the captain, some of the crew, and even explore the wide deck before finally settling on the right wing of the ship. A couple was holding hands and pointing at something slimy and scaly in the far distance.

The other side of the galleon had a few more people gazing at the skyline than I would have thought. One group consisted of a couple with a young daughter, while another was a lone man with shaggy, black hair that covered most of his face.

I stared at the little girl, who was smiling at her parents for longer than someone normally would. *And why was that?*

I touched my chest and breathed deep. Was that loneliness I felt, or could it be... jealousy? Maybe it was a bit of both.

"There you are!" called a voice behind me. I didn't need to turn to know who it was. There could only be one.

I didn't reply.

"Come on, Lethe. Don't ignore me."

I wasn't ignoring her, I just had my attention on something else—someone else, that is. As I watched the shaggy man walk away from the railing, I caught a glimpse of his face. He was pale with sunken features and glazed eyes that had dark bags beneath them.

Even with his rather unsightly features, the flame in his sad eyes and his decrepit grin were nothing to scoff at. I couldn't turn away from him. His was foul, giving me a feeling of dread. It was apparent that this stranger wasn't a normal visitor.

Who is he? Why is he here?

The answer came sooner than I would have liked.

I watched him walk away while Bella desperately tried to steal my attention. I would have to apologize after I discovered what this ill-omened man was up to. It might lead to nothing, but I couldn't shake the feeling he'd given me.

Bella stopped poking my back and gazed off to the sea ahead of us. I soon followed her gaze to the sight of another ship, fast approaching.

"What are you looking at?"

Bella clenched her fists, her body shaking like a rattle. "We need to get off of here. *Now.*" Her carefree attitude had evaporated.

"What do you mean? We still have a few hours left."

She shook her head. "There isn't time."

Bella seemed to know something, but was too disturbed to share. I was experiencing a similar sensation. I was filled with the same dread that I had been feeling while staring at that man. My right hand was growing colder by the second—this was not normal for me. Was it a warning from Frosty?

At that point, Bella's eyes had become even more glued to the ship than mine. The other guests displayed a mixture of interest and concern.

A feisty, older woman walked up to one of the staff members and demanded an explanation. "Is that ship supposed to be this close? I was told we would be the only ones out here during this time."

"Well, ma'am, we can't control the seas and who travels them."

"Preposterous," she spat. "Make sure they don't block our view."

"I'll try my best." He bowed and went below deck, probably just to avoid the troublesome guest.

I turned back to Bella, whose eyes were still set on the oncoming ship. They were most certainly heading our way. When I could finally get a good view of their mast, my eye grew wide, but not as wide as hers.

"This is bad. My assumption was right. That flag..."

"What is it?" I asked anxiously. "Who's coming?"

Bella met my gaze, her face full of worry and fear. She seemed genuinely depressed compared to when I had ignored her advances earlier. This had to be what genuine despair looked like on her.

"They call themselves the Children of Poseidon," she said, keeping her voice down. "They're nothing more than cutthroats and bandits that steal from any ships they come across, leaving people for dead..."

That would have been nice to know beforehand. "Anything else you forgot to mention before we set foot into the sea of thieves?"

"Yes," she continued, unaffected by my display of irritation. "T-they say that they offer sacrifices as well."

"Sacrifices?" I repeated. "Like killing people in the name of a god—that kind of sacrifice?"

She quickly nodded. ""But they say it's not a god that they give people to, but his child."

Who are *'they'*?

"And I assume it's not a baby?" I said half-jokingly as I firmly gripped the railing and peeked at the ocean below.

Large, blue scales danced above the water's surface, appendages protruding every few feet. The creature snaked around and around our boat like a vortex. The morning sun reflected off the scales, making it appear like a living mirror. We were surrounded. There was no head or tail in sight, but there was certainly something massive lurking below. Its immense aura was enough to scare off any nearby wildlife, and its smell... It was sulfurous, like a hard-boiled egg wrapped in the thickest of seaweed. Even in this dire situation, I was a little hungry.

"What's the situation?" Bella joined me to stare into the sea. "Oh... This isn't good."

The layers of scales just kept on coiling around our ship. Once there were enough coils around us, the galleon shuddered to a halt. The surrounding people panicked when they got word from others that had looked into the sea. Mass hysteria wouldn't be far behind.

"Everyone, please remain calm and wait for the creature to pass! This happens all the time. Our boat has the Blessing of Poseidon. There is no need to worry," one of the female attendants assured us in a loud voice that was as calm as the sea should have been.

Her words soothed the worries of a few, but others still wore fearful expressions. It was likely that the other attendants throughout the boat were saying the same phrases to reassure their guests, but something didn't add up.

A blessing is supposed to keep anything from coming near, and yet this massive creature is moving around us like a pet. Either this is a poorly created blessing, or someone has allowed this thing to enter inside of the blessing's range.

From what I knew of blessings, they were used to protect towns, cities, and even countries from monster attacks. They were pretty strong too, but there were ways to circumvent them. If someone inside the blessing who was involved in creating it tampered with it to invite the creature in, that would certainly be a problem.

The core of the blessing was most likely at the bottom of the ship. *Come to think of it, I did see that shaggy man come out from below when I first arrived here.*

I cursed myself for taking too long to act.

Suddenly, our hull collided with the other ship. The sound was awful, but not overbearing. Instead of rebounding, both ships stuck, as if something had forcefully stitched the tips together with a simple touch.

I rushed toward the front to get a better view—a terrible idea in hindsight.

I reached the bow a few minutes later, but it was already swarming with crudely dressed men and women. Some of them even had eyepatches like me, but that was where our similarities diverged. Their hair styles were clipped at awkward angles, while others had no hair at all. Their rotten teeth and the stench that flew off them nearly brought me to my knees before I had even reached them. There were maybe thirty of them on the deck in total. They had effortlessly climbed across an area where a sharp object had lodged into the mast of our ship like a blade.

Some guests had already fled from the front; others were too paralyzed with fear to take so much as a step back. A few intruders even chased after them, sword, spear, or spell at hand.

I gulped. It was my first time seeing such dangerous weapons up close.

"Get ooooff!"

I turned around to see Bella push away a captor with both hands. It was the shaggy man from before, but this time he had a jagged knife that reflected the sun too brightly. The magical shine was all the proof I needed to know who had let the monster in.

I nearly went for the guy myself, but something cold and thick collided with my back.

I yelped as my body hit the floor with a loud *thud.*

Looming above me like an angel of death was a large, muscle-bound man with scars and markings all over his body. He wore a sleeveless tunic and a black cape poked full of more holes than swiss cheese. His legs were hardly contained by his tiny shorts. They could seriously burst through at any moment. Tightly gripped in his right hand was a lengthy trident. A large, red crystal embedded in the middle gleamed maliciously against its blue backdrop.

He lowered himself close enough that I could taste the tobacco smell from his breath. His nostrils flared, and he rested the trident over his right shoulder before huffing. "This one looks like she still has some fight in her. Just like the others, heh-heh. He will love them. Darmacio, restrain 'em."

I was tempted to release Frosty and do my best to ward off these pirates, but there was a minor problem—or maybe a few of them. I was hopelessly outnumbered.

From my understanding, the ring of frost could freeze any normal person I made contact with until they were nothing more than a hollow sculpture. Of course, sometimes it could take longer for the death chill to take hold, or their resistances might be too high for it to even affect them. It was certain death... and I accepted that, but how many of them could I take out before I was cut down? I was pretty weak in ranged fights or anything past a small skirmish. My options at the moment were, unsurprisingly, terrible.

"W-why are you people here? We are just a boat of tourists!" Bella hollered.

The shaggy man had a knife to her throat and her arms pinned to her back. Even though it was hard to see his features, I could detect a wide smile hidden behind that thick beard. My suspicions had finally been confirmed.

"This is what he wanted, so we obliged," the man with the trident said in a stern and resolute tone. "He is one of Father's favorites."

I barely had time to ponder his words before a fellow person from the eyepatch club passed by and bound my hands. If only that was all he did.

"Hmm?" He raised an eyebrow. "What's that little shiny thing you got there, lassie?"

Please, not that. Anything but that! I quickly clasped one of my hands over the other, but it was already too late.

"Gimme that!"

He pried open my hands, successfully pulling the ring from my finger. For the first time since I had put it on, it was gone.

I nearly cried. A part of me had been stolen, and I planned to get it back, but how? *Without it, I'm just a normal girl. If only I knew some actual magic instead of using that ring as a crutch all the time.*

The man brazenly stuffed the ring into his pocket before walking toward where the other pirates had fanned out during their takeover. "Lemme go check on the others," he said to the trident man before rushing by.

My head turned to Bella. We were in the same boat—no pun intended. I hated feeling so powerless. I had never felt it before, even when I'd first awoken. The hole created by Frosty's removal was a hungering void that needed to be filled. It barely felt like me anymore.

The trident man peered over the bow into the sea below, eerily tilting his head ever so slightly. "He says he's ready."

A woman with shredded clothes and a bald male with a bushy beard grabbed one of the bound tourists and hauled him up.

"Hey! W-what's going on? Let me go! I gave you my money already!" he screamed.

The two of them laughed at him like he had said the funniest of jokes.

"We will."

"Soon."

"What do you mean by—AHHHHHHHHHH!"

The terrified man disappeared over the bow in one fell swoop. I waited and waited to hear a splash, but it never came. The only thing I heard was a powerful, ear-splitting screech.

The trident man smirked, looking back at us. "He says he liked it, but would prefer something younger for his main course." He pounded his trident on the wooden deck. "Gather up the older ones first and save the ones that are easy on the eyes for last." He looked down at me briefly and continued. "The one-eyed girl seems like she would make an excellent asset. Already has the look of the crew as well. Leave her to me. Everyone else is fair game for the Leviathan."

"Whaaat?"

Bella gasped behind me. I wasn't sure if it was from the fact that I would be spared from death and on track to suffer a fate much worse, or that she would be part of that thing's main course. Either way, I needed to do something.

Think! What can I do? What can I do? What can I do? What can I do? What can I dooooo?!

The corrupted waterfall of my thoughts was interrupted as another person was thrown from the deck. Four others were held captive besides Bella and I. It was a family of three and an elderly woman.

"We have rounded 'em all up and are tossing 'em off from both sides. I got a few more coming up this way, too."

A bare-chested man with long arms walked past me, an attendant in each arm. He tossed the man and woman he'd been holding to the floor in front of me, their arms already bound and their mouths gagged.

The trident man gave him a thumbs up. "Everything is going swimmingly. Make sure to collect their belongings before we sink this ship. I know I can count on you, Mafon."

The half-naked man crossed his arms with a wicked smile of satisfaction. "Anything for you, Boss."

The trident man narrowed his eyes, but still smiled maliciously as he shifted his trident to his left hand. "Didn't I tell you? Call me Vito. I need these maggots to remember my name somehow."

How will that happen if we're all dead?

"Course, Boss. Whatever you want, Boss."

Vito turned away, looking toward the never-ending view of the ocean. He inhaled deeply and let out a hardy laugh. "I can never get enough of this life!"

As time went on, Bella and I were forced to listen to the awful screams as people were fed to the Leviathan.

Sweat had covered my forehead for some time now. I should have been bawling my eye out. Bella wasn't much better, but she seemed a lot calmer than me. I thought I was the one that had trouble displaying the more distant emotions within me, and yet she was the composed one. She wore a tragic smile, but the fire in her eyes was half as big as it used to be. *Why isn't she crying? Does she have a plan to get us out of this?*

Of course! She had to have come up with something while we were forcefully burning under the sun's harsh rays. I never pegged her as a strategist, but she didn't seem like she had given up in the slightest.

Now, why couldn't I be like that? *Courage is something that's in everyone, right?* That's what Rock had once told me. You simply had to search for it. Bella must have found it and let it keep her steady. I held out hope because she was with me. As someone who only had confidence in myself, it was rather astonishing to put my faith in someone else for once. But she was different from the others—she was my friend.

Bella had introduced me to so much in the short time we'd gotten to know each other, and treated me like a normal girl, even if I felt more than just friendship from that sweet and playful attitude. I needed to give her the faith that was hiding in my heart.

And I did—until what happened next doused me in an unending stream of despair.

"Oi! Is that the last of them over here? That little shit's crying is still ringing in my ears." One of the pirates looked our way. His lips curled upward into a devious smile as he called out, "Say, Vito. Which one did you say we're keeping?"

Vito glanced away from a map that seemed tiny in his massive hands. "The eye-patched one is mine. Toss the other."

Wait.

"On it." The man saluted and waddled over to us.

Please.

"Let's go, missy." He picked up Bella with ease and pushed her over his back.

No. Stop. Don't—

"Lethe," Bella said, a melancholy smile on her face. Her eyes still had the same amount of fire in them as I had seen before. "Please."

Was she faking it for me? Was this the thing from stories when a friend smiled and said everything was okay when they were really anything but? Was this really...

She gave me a wink, and her smile turned playful. Her long body slowly moved away from me and toward the bow.

"Be strong for me. Okay, Lethe?"

I wanted to reach out my hand and never let go. I wanted to have a casual conversation during breakfast and smile about our futures while consuming a variety of books and scrumptious foods.

I sought so desperately to go back to the cafe and enjoy her sweet, sarcastic service.

I loved the mole she had under her left eye, and how her voice sounded as clear as a bell whenever she wanted to appear upbeat and resolute. Her smile was as warm as the sun and as bright as a lamp in the dead of night. I may not have wanted her to join me on my travels, but I certainly wanted to see her again. I would give up my other eye to do it—or even my soul.

Something tugged within me, causing pain and anguish to flare through my body.

It's coming. You can't stop it.

I did my best to suppress it, biting down on my lip to the point it bled.

A deal's a deal, not even they can break that.

There was so much more I wanted to do with her, wanted to see with her, wanted to enjoy with her. I was so confident with myself ever since I saw the power within the ring. Why was I so foolish? I'm... nothing.

Don't go.

My eye followed her until she disappeared over the bow. Her smile never wavered, and neither did the insurmountable confidence as she vanished from view. Life was in slow motion. The next few seconds were an eternity. A sight of torment and malice for my fragile soul. I couldn't take it anymore.

Then, allow me.

A few moments later, I heard something hit the water and then nothing more. Everything around me went blank. It was as if the misery had made me blind. I didn't know where it came from.

There was no way out. There never was. If only—

I screamed, and I kept on screaming until my throat was raw.

More. Give me more.

Not only my heart, but my body was laced with pain, as if hundreds of ants had burrowed into every pore in my feeble frame.

Ah...

I finally took notice of the wetness trickling down my cheeks. I knew exactly what it was, but it was the first time I had ever experienced it myself. *Am I crying? I actually am. I'm so weak...*

There wasn't much else it could be. Pitiful sobs escaped me as my tears fell to the floor. It might have been wrong, but I was almost happy for a fragment of a millisecond, because nothing had ever been precious enough for me to shed a tear before, but I was quickly overwhelmed.

The disastrous feelings inside me were almost familiar, but I didn't know why. I couldn't remember. It was almost comforting to know I could have been in this situation before, but I soon forgot as the ruination of my fragmented ego consumed me once more.

Wait. Something was coming out of it. Something...

A terrible knot formed in my gut. *If I get out of this, I'll never cry again*, I vowed as I continued to let my soul run loose.

"SHUT UUUP!"

A fist met my face, and kissed me good night. A small but firm voice whispered in my mind. I may have hallucinated from all the pain, but it was eerily familiar. I thought it was my inner self trying to cheer me up, but that was clearly not the case.

This is not your grave, but you are welcome in it.

I was in a void of nothing. I could see nothing, but I had the feeling that I wasn't alone. Hatred and scorn drilled into me like a punch to the gut. My mind grew hazy, and my consciousness finally guttered out. Something else was with me, and I knew I should leave any disdain I had with them. It was the right thing to do. That seemed to be part of our agreement, after all—or was it with one of the others?

God, I sound delusional. Am I going crazy? I wish I was. Let this all be a dream, please. If there is actually a god or two out there, please...

And then that uncomfortable knot of anguish seemed to come loose all at once.

* * *

I woke up near the back of the boat to the sound of water rising.

"Huh? W-what happened?"

A reservoir of anger welled in my chest, faded as I regained my cautiousness. *Was this really my anger? My sorrow? My grief?*

I got up, but it took a lot more effort than I expected. All my strength had been drained, and my new clothes were in tatters, nearly exposing my undergarments. There were slash marks everywhere. It was as if a large beast had gotten its claws on me.

Placing a hand on my stomach, I found it felt smooth to the touch, but very, *very* cold. *Death...*

"Ungh!" I reeled in anguish, nearly falling flat on my face. It hurt. It really, *really* hurt. "My stomach..."

It was a pain I hadn't felt in a while, since before I knew my limits. I was so full that I thought my abdomen would explode, and I wasn't sure how I'd be able to move. The cramps that lingered in both my legs and arms didn't help either.

My eyes wandered left and right, trying to make sense of the situation, but there was nothing near me.

Silence.

The sea was calm, rising with the tide as I stared idly at the tranquil waves. After some time, I finally got my sluggish body to move forward and make my way around the ship. It was like walking on glass.

"Hello?!" I shouted with what energy still lingered in my battered body. "Anyone?!"

No response.

I wandered at a snail's pace, finding the people's belongings scattered about, and yet not a single person was in sight. The more I limped, the more I felt the ship sinking deeper and deeper into the water.

"Where do I go?"

I searched, feeling lethargic beyond belief, shambling around like the dead.

I aimed for the front deck where I had originally been.

"BELLA!"

My eyes darted in all directions, desperately searching for my friend. When I reached the spot where I recalled last seeing her, all that was there was a small, blue purse. I had come to know this purse pretty well over the past few days.

Looking for a memento, I rifled through it, and pulled out something that I had only seen once before; it was from the day prior.

Bella and I had gotten these sweet things called crêpes. We'd sat on two wooden stools propped up behind a simple meadow backdrop. In front of us stood an old man with curly, gray hair and small spectacles. He held his hands out as if to form a box around the two of us.

"Now say 'coffee!'"

"Coffee!"

"Coffee...?"

A flash briefly blinded us, which threw me for a loop. Bella, on the other hand, was surprisingly calm and adopted the sweet smile of a maiden. "Thank you. May I see it?"

"Of course. You already paid, after all. Enjoy!"

Between his hands a small piece of paper formed and solidified. He handed it over to Bella, who shook it a few times before gazing at it with great interest.

"Oh, my god!" she shrieked. Her eyes briefly displayed heart shapes—if that was even possible—before settling down. She vigorously panted a few times, like Frosty did when he was excited, and then passed me the picture.

"Woah." That was all I could say. "This is kinda neat."

The paper had Bella and I inside it. I was in the middle of nibbling on a crêpe, while she had her hand around me while making a peace sign.

"It's like looking in a mirror, but it's frozen."

"Cool, right? Some people possess the magic to cut out a piece of time and form it into a physical object. It's called a picture."

"'A picture,'" I echoed. "Can it capture... anything?"

She nodded and smiled. "Yup."

"Even my soul?"

"You would have to ask him," she replied, grinning ear to ear as if she already knew the answer.

"So, is it possible?"

"I was just kidding."

"Whatever." *I hope she's right. A picture of Frosty wouldn't be bad. I could also give a copy to Rock. I'm sure he would love that.*

I decided to let her keep the picture in the end because I wanted her to have something to remember me by and not feel the need to follow me when I left. Yet, it somehow found its way back to me.

Why did it hurt so much to see it now?

Like a busted dam, it all came flowing back to me: pain, anguish, scorn, anger, and sorrow. All of it pierced my chest like an arrow of love through my broken heart.

"Right..."

I remembered everything that had led up to now—well, everything before I blacked out. The thorns of regret wound their way through my heart.

You could have saved her, couldn't you? You had the power. Even if you didn't know it. It was there the whole time. Acquired by none other than yourself. So why couldn't you do it?

"It doesn't matter anymore!" I howled. "I—I failed her..."

Bella had perished to that monster in the sea along with everyone else. There was nothing I could have done, no matter what the voice in my head was saying. I would have joined them, but—*Huh? Where did the pirates go?*

I was all alone now, in a sinking ship that was once a place of rest and relaxation. I didn't see the monster anywhere, which was confusing enough. At least that was some good news.

Did a god answer my prayer in the cruelest of ways? No way to know, I guess.

A hollow ship for a hollow person. The darkness of night was beginning to creep in at the worst of times. Just how much time did I have until I couldn't see anything? Did it matter? The crackle of the wind and ripple of the waves as they ate into the ship were the only confirmations that I was still alive. Alive meant to feel, to notice, to grieve... *If only I could remember what was important to me in the past, then I could deal with this in a better way.*

My tears fell onto the photo that I cradled in my arms. Even though it wasn't a real hug, it still filled me with warmth. It was almost as if—

I just made that vow, and I already broke it. I really am pitiful. Starting now, the crybaby shall never rear its head again! That's a promise.

"Anyway," I said, wiping away the tears before cleaning up the picture, "I gotta get off this thing."

I took a few deep breaths and slid the photo into my satchel after I found it. It had miraculously been next to where I had originally been captured. I could have taken the rest of whatever was in Bella's purse, but it didn't feel right. There was no way I could.

I sniffled. "I need to find Frosty, right?" A few feet away, near a mountain of belongings, was a sack that was tilted on its side, with the contents spilling out onto the deck. Inside was the faint glow of something light blue. There was really only one thing that it could be.

"Awooooooo!" Frosty happily licked his lips and pounced on me. He seemed pretty happy. I would have assumed a rift would have formed in our relationship after this, but he remained his cheerful self, even after watching my futile efforts unfold from the ring. I'm sure he was just trying to cheer me up. Animals are pretty good at sensing one's emotional state.

Confused, he turned his head left and right as if looking for someone else. Someone who would never return.

"Let's just... go," I whispered weakly. I could detect a sob coming if I didn't start moving immediately. I hopped on top of him and gave him a few pats on the head. "She went away for a while. I'm sorry. It will be just the two of us again."

Frosty's ears sank a bit when he heard me say that. He'd also been around Bella for the past couple of days, and I'm sure he was already quite attached. Bella had felt the same way. She had even offered to take care of him for me, but that wasn't an option.

He leapt off the nearly sunken galleon, landing with a plate of ice beneath his paws. While we made our way through the water, my attention was focused elsewhere. I hadn't noticed it before, but attached to the end of the bow was something large and blue—the trident. The prongs were coated with blood.

Now what could have happened to its owner?

Chapter 5

Marooned

The stars once greeted me after my tussle with Hell. I hope to gaze upon those twinkling streaks in the dark sky when I achieve victory, and again when I finally return home. A life lived in seclusion might not be that bad, now that I think about it.

—Boreas Tyrel

The void was dark and cold around me, sending shivers down my spine. Within the dark world lay a single being, its wretched form straight out of nightmares.

"Come to me," the creature said. **"Allow your rage and sorrow to pull you past the barriers of flesh and blood. Like before, I await in the black abyss known as your heart. I am a monument to all your sins. You cannot escape me, nor do I think you want to."**

I could utter no retort as I sleepily stared into the nothingness around us.

His horrifying visage broke into a dark grin. **"After all, you were the one who brought me here."**

* * *

The sky was filled with the sight of foreign trees. Thin rays of the setting sun could hardly squeeze through the thick wall of trunks, making it difficult to tell what time of day it was. Regardless, inhabitants of the land could enjoy their solitude with little issue while waiting for their food to drop from above like clockwork.

A lone girl was sprawled out in the soft, light sand, surrounded by a sea of trees with hard brown fruits periodically dropping from above. It was all the somber girl had had to eat in the last week, and it was what she would continue to eat until she dies or escapes.

"Unless something changes, she might spend the rest of her life here." I closed my journal and placed it safely with my quill in the satchel that sat to my right. "That should do it for today's log."

I'd added the strange, four-armed creature from my nightmare into my journal, as well. Being stranded really gave me some time to brush up on my drawing skills. *But why did I create something as creepy and despicable as that?* That had been the third night in a row I'd had the same dream, and I hoped I wouldn't see him again.

I did my best to peer through the leaves above, but it was no use. "Ughh!" I violently raked my hands through my hair. "I need to get off this island!"

After the *tragedy*, Frosty and I had traveled for hours before finally locating land. Sadly, it wasn't where I had come from, but an uncharted island in the middle of the sea of who knows where. It was truly one of the worst-case scenarios to end up in my situation. It had taken a few days before my stomach had tried to eat itself, and that led me to the hard brown things that I thought were similar to fruit.

I broke one open with a rock and slurped it down. I gave the parts that remained to Frosty, who was currently sleeping within the ring in his own little home—something I was jealous of at the moment. *I wonder if he's got a couch or bed or something in there. At least there's no way it smells like fish and bird poop.*

Schools of fish swam around the island, but they had the bright and telltale colors of purple and charcoal black. Without a way to separate the poison, I was stuck living off of the big, brown balls of liquid and berries. I could have tried making a fire, but the dense woodlands behind me squashed that idea. *If only I could actually rip some wood from these massive trees. That would make life ten times easier. Too bad Frosty is still recovering from our journey on the sea.*

My torn clothes had forced me to make something actually wearable. The blouse that Bella had gotten me ended up becoming a knee-length skirt, and I had tied my original skirt and shirt together to form a cocoon around my upper body. It was not very stylish, but there was no way I was going to put on the outfit I got from Rock while I was stuck in this isolated world. Besides my cloak, I couldn't afford my only other change of clothes getting wet or dirty. *I won't discard them, no matter what.*

Speaking of cloaks, that was my blanket now. Miraculously, my ring also gave me nice resistance to the cold. I only needed to bundle myself up like a ball to have a good night's sleep while Frosty kept watch. Anyone else would have had quite a bit of trouble during those chilly, starless nights.

I wonder if the sky was gloomy even when the stars had still existed?

* * *

After exploring a bit of the island, I concluded that I was the only person there. There were no man-made objects, nor were there any trails.

Something stood out, though. Two days ago, when I'd set out pretty far into what must have been the center of the island, I could make out something faint that pulsated through the rocky ground. It reminded me of a heartbeat, but that couldn't have been the case. Eventually, I pushed the thought to the back of my mind.

"The sun is most likely gone now, which means if these ludicrously large trees weren't in the way, I would actually have a superb view of the stars." I didn't want to take my chances by moving into the water. The sandy ground at the lip of the beach was the only spot that could guarantee my safety.

I sluggishly reached into my bag, but then my fingers brushed against something that had once belonged to a friend. My hand stopped as if it had gone numb. I sat in a daze, staring at nothing in particular. Before I knew it, the darkness of night had consumed my consciousness.

* * *

As if respecting my wishes, the demonic presence had finally receded from my dreams. I'd finally gotten decent sleep. The sun had faintly touched me in the morning, spurring me into motion after my long rest.

"Alright! I'm going to go collect enough of the brown balls to last a few days and look for the best direction to depart from!" I gave myself a little fist pump and a few slaps on the cheeks to get hyped.

And so, I set off through the thick trees and plants, determined to scrounge up enough supplies. A slight twinge of pain filled my chest as I walked. After being there for some days, it was a little painful to leave. Using a piece of my cannibalized clothing, I tied my hair into a long ponytail.

More time went by, and that meant more headaches and tongue clicking. "*Tch*. Why are there so many?"

It was a constant hassle to bend my body as I tried to get through to the next clearing where there were even more trees impeding my make-shift path. The reason I was suffering through it was because I was all out of the brown fruit things where I had set my camp. There had been many trees near there, but those had all been picked clean by yours truly. Thankfully, I knew I was going the right way thanks to the trail of holes I'd left while scavenging.

Every now and then, I'd take a quick break to freeze something small, like a rock or leaf. Once it was fully frozen, I'd smash it to pieces and do my ever-loving best to suck the water out of each and every tiny shard. It wasn't a large amount, and it certainly wasn't filling, but it was a nice remedy to the milky, sweet juice of the brown fruit. *Ahh... That hits the spot!*

A few hours later, I reached my destination. A large forest clearing encompassed my entire field of view. This was one of the times I wished I still had two eyes.

A circular formation of trees with branches housing the fruits of life stood tall before me. I planned to climb each of them and stock up on what I needed for the big trip before the sun went down.

"Alright. Let's do this," I said, sizing up the pale trees with black stripes.

After plopping my satchel on the ground, I cracked my knuckles. It was something Bella tended to do when she saw something she liked, and I'd adopted the tick for when I needed to get to work.

I inched up the first tree like a caterpillar, successfully retrieved the hairy, brown fruit, and flung it to the ground. It hit the soft earth almost without sound.

"That's one down," I said while gazing at the next tree. I wiped the sweat from my brow with a hand, the light wind causing my ponytail to swish. "Time for round two."

* * *

In about half an hour's time, I had accumulated nearly thirty of them after conquering a grand total of five tree fortresses. Everything was proceeding smoothly. That was until I reached a bit too far on the sixth tree in an attempt to satisfy both my greed and hunger.

The slight over-extension of my arm sent me tumbling. I could see the ground coming up fast, yet I still had time to appreciate the nutrient-rich soil that my fruity boons were bathing in.

In a last-ditch effort to preserve all my bones, I used the ring. My hand morphed into one of pure frost. It wouldn't stop my fall, but it would internally strengthen and shield my body, making the fall hurt a lot less.

Thud!

My body hit the dirt chest down. "Owwww," I groaned, despite my smile of triumph.

My hands were spread out in a T-pose, which probably looked rather stupid to any onlooker. For the first time since I'd got there, I was glad to be alone.

I placed both of my palms ahead of me and propelled myself up with a few wheezing breaths. After wiping the sweat from my brow, I breathed a sigh of relief. "Phew. Let's get back to gathering—What the...?"

I hadn't noticed it before, but when I had pulled my body up with both hands, the ice from my body began to spread below me. The entire ground within a thirty-foot radius was already frozen solid.

Huh? But the ring only affects living things or concentrated areas. Why is it still spreading?

The ice continued to advance, much to my dismay. As I continued to watch the freeze grow, a guttural roar shook me to the core. The force of it caused the entire island to rumble. *Was that an earthquake?*

The reverberations came in waves every few seconds, nearly knocking me back onto the ice. I grabbed the sides of my head, biting down on my lip in pain as the sound intensified. My eardrums wouldn't be able to take much more at this rate. I needed a way out.

"Frosty, quickly!" I commanded.

A blue mist shot from the ring and quickly took form as my trusted companion. He eyed me with what I thought was concern, as if he was studying my unease.

I leapt onto him, still cradling my bleeding ears. "We need to get off this island—*now*."

He didn't need to be told twice. Frosty dashed away at breakneck speed, leaving the mass of fruit I'd picked behind.

I was beyond depressed. My bag had already been filled to the brim with the brown fruit—I would have to be satisfied with that—*but all my effort... It hurts!*

The rumbling continued to get louder and louder, forcing me to cup my hands over my ears with all my might. *I wonder how Frosty is doing. He's not making a peep.* I hope he wasn't just staying strong for me.

What is this sound? The Behemoth? No. It was described as a lot smaller than what this roar leads me to believe. I would have certainly seen something so big when I explored this island earlier.

Ice continued to trickle past us as we raced through the thicket. Frosty did his best to avoid the small creatures, bushes, and fallen tree trunks that got in our way as we pressed, his sides heaving with exertion.

As we raced on, I noticed something in the distance, and that was a big deal, considering all I could see before were clusters of trees. The closer we got, the easier it was to discern with my eye.

"A mountain," I said mumbled. "Why didn't I see it before?"

Even though I had never been to this section of the island, something as large as that should have been easy to spot when I was on top of a tree, and yet, it was as if it just... appeared.

I clenched my jaw when I spotted something flowing out the side of the slope. A glowing, red liquid gushed from the peak, slowly trickling out of view. I had never seen it in person, but I had read about it. It was days like this that I praised myself for my excellent memory, despite having amnesia. *Oh, the irony.*

"Lava," I mumbled. I couldn't see where it was flowing, but the temperature was veering to hotter and hotter. If I hadn't already had a reason to leave, this new problem was a sure sign to go.

Frosty kept on running, and at some point, the lava finally came into view, consuming the frozen ground. It moved faster than I'd anticipated, quickly swallowing any sign of life on the ground it crossed. Not even the ice stood a chance against its might. I was already under a lot of stress due to the harsh increase in temperature, but the constant screams were wearing down my mental state. *I want to rip my hair out and die! Aaaaaahhhhhhh!*

While I seriously contemplated this, Frosty veered to the right and continued on his charge. The sun pierced me with its bright rays, causing me to break out of my stupor. *We're almost there!*

Frosty kicked it up a notch for my sake, putting his four strong limbs into overdrive. He ran and ran until there was no more ground beneath us, but the peaceful, blue waves instead. The screaming somehow grew even louder, but I could no longer feel the vibrations of the ground nor the smoldering heat of the volcano.

When it was finally quiet enough, I decided to look back. "What is *that*?"

A giant head protruded from the front of the island, its amber skin and freakishly large yellow eyes injected a dose of fear into my veins. Its mouth would open every few seconds, repeating the same scream that I had been suffering from.

"It was a giant turtle all along? No wonder it brought out that volcano. It would have frozen solid from my ring if it didn't." *It can't be very strong for my ring to have worked on it, unless it became weaker during its slumber. I wish Boreas had written about this one, but I'll do it for him!*

At last, and with great satisfaction, I wiped the sweat from my brow and let out a long sigh of relief. *My ears are going to need a good cleaning.* I would have to sacrifice some fruit juice to do so. At least it wasn't really sticky. That was a plus.

Looking down at my bag of fruits, I said, "At least we got some food for the road—I mean, the sea. To think something so large would scream like an annoying baby to get me to leave. Ha-ha!"

I wasn't even sure why I had laughed at my own expense. That was out of the ordinary for me, but I didn't care. It had been a while since I was last amused by anything. It was the least I could do, albeit with a bitter tinge.

Journal Sketch #10
The Laughing Demon

1403, 9th day, Month of the Rot Lord
The demon of my dreams. I wonder if it's an omen to come.

Chapter 6

Resurrection of a Forgotten God

There are some evils in this world where meeting them head-on would cause instant death. There are also some that must be dealt with for the greater good. Be smart enough to know the difference, but strong enough to withstand both. I made a lot of fatal errors before I could discern between the two.

—Boreas Tyrel

A shadowy sun loomed above, bathing me in an ominous light. The orb had a strange outline, one which I had only heard about in tales. I must have been seeing things, surely.

It was difficult to tell how long we'd been crossing the sea. A day? Maybe even two? If I hadn't fed Frosty while he moved over the ocean, our journey would have ended much sooner. Water was gone, or at least the drinkable kind. We were surrounded by water, lots of it, and it was looking more and more enticing. I envisioned myself slurping it down with a wide grin on my face. The pure ecstasy I would feel as it trickled down my throat was all I could think of.

Salt water isn't drinkable, is it? Of course not, or else everyone would be taking sips. That's not the only reason people don't drink it, I think... Ewww. The thought of that is gross.

Exhaustion really had taken its sweet toll on the two of us. We desperately needed a place to rest and something to drink. It was enough of a pain to keep myself awake to feed him, but the potent rays from the glaring archon of onyx light were constantly hitting the exposed skin peeking out from under my makeshift clothing.

Just a bit farther. There will be something. There has to be something.

"Ugh! Water... Fooooood... Shelter... Foooooood!" I groaned.

The sun began to sink into the horizon, illuminating what I thought had to be some sort of warped structure. *What else could I call such a bizarre structure in the middle of the sea? Hmm... If I tilt my head and squint, it almost looks like a large grouping of diverse bell towers stacked on top of each other.*

The pieces that encompassed the large structure did not fit together in the slightest, and yet they were melted together like a forced fusion of multiple different beings. *The geometry doesn't line up, but I wonder—how does it taste?*

It was difficult to fathom anything dwelling there, especially with such an eerie atmosphere surrounding it. The water around the mishmash of structures was an inky black, as if sickness had spread through it.

The top of the structure had a sharp peak, glowing faintly in unsavory solace. Miniature versions of the tip stuck out like sore thumbs at other parts of the structure. *Mmm... Thumbs are meat. I could really go for chicken breasts right now.*

I would have gasped at how out of place the dark horror truly was, but I didn't have the energy to care. I needed to think about what was really important and if I couldn't slurp it or shovel it down my oral cavity, then it really didn't matter; though, I was starting to see everything in grayscale.

I shook my head. "Frosty, find us a way inside there, please."

He tilted his head, most likely confused by the command. Was I asking for the impossible? I couldn't tell anymore. I'm sure the place rubbed him the wrong way too, but we both needed rest and could worry about what would come next when we woke.

He waited a moment longer, but then pushed forward with what was likely the remainder of his strength. It wasn't much. *He sure has some plump legs on him. I wonder what a little nibble would—No! Begone, oh blasphemous thoughts!*

An elongated gateway greeted us, leaning halfway into the murky sea. He sluggishly stepped inside, where nothing but darkness awaited. It was cold and hollow, like wandering into a mausoleum.

We ventured in until something large and metallic reflected within the veil of shadows. I wanted to press Frosty to go deeper, but he collapsed next to the mystery object. The sudden change in form threw me to the floor as well.

I crawled on the stones with no goal in particular. It was too much work to move around, and my body had already begun to sway. My basic human instincts had long kicked into overdrive. *What I really need right now...*

"Mmm... Sleeep."

* * *

When I woke, I was in for a rather rude awakening.

"Ph'nglui mglw'nafh Cthulhu R'lyeh wgah'nagl fhtagn. Uh'eog Cthulhu syha'h!"

"Huh?" I slowly opened my eye and looked around. An unexpected chill wracked my body with shivers. I hugged myself tight for warmth, but it barely helped.

Perhaps I should bring out my cocoon.

Torches birthed light into the darkness. Their bright, green flames clearly displayed a wall behind me, allowing me to grasp my surroundings. *The only color I can see is green... I'd kill for some salad right now.*

The object we had discovered ended up being an obelisk. You could fit a few grown people behind it and not have them seen from the other side due to its width. It was because of this massive obelisk that I could barely make out anything around me.

"Yes, yes. *Ph'nglui mglw'nafh Cthulhu R'lyeh wgah'nagl fhtagn. Uh'eog Cthulhu syha'h!* to you too."

It was a man's voice, but the words were something no human mouth could make. The mounting dread I felt after hearing the strange words only applied more pressure to my crippled state. Still, I needed to know what was going on and if I could find food—I mean, a place to sleep. *But I need to eat first, yeah. That takes priority.*

And so, I continued to listen.

"...have gathered all the sacrifices for the Great Old One. All we require is the full ensemble to complete the resurrection."

I heard a different person say, "This joyous occasion is filling me with sublimity. I love it!"

I dragged my body forward to see two hooded figures in black. One of them had a book with a few—*are those eyes?!* The book had eyes on them! *You can't eat those! Gross!*

While I was caught up in my own revelations, another man came through the entrance in the back. "The preparations have been made, my brothers. Bring the *Book of Dreams* to the altar. The black sun will only last for another hour. Our time is now!" he said with enough vindication to make even the most secular of people agree with him.

"The time is upon us! *He* shall grace us in the flesh!"

"Indeed! The Reckoning is on its way!"

The trio bowed to each other and exited through the door where the third man had originated from.

I ducked back behind the pillar and let out a muffled breath of relief. "They're finally gone... What do I do? This all seems pretty dicey, but is it any of my business?"

The sound of my stomach grumbling answered the question for me. There was no food in there, so either way, I would need to make my move. I glanced at my ring, hoping Frosty would join me, but there was no response. *Looks like I'm on my own for this one.*

Upon hobbling into the next room, voices in the distance tickled my ears. The black archway I snuck under stood tall in front of a narrow tunnel that was shrouded in vile, green darkness. My vision was no longer plagued by the green tint, but the lack of other colors remained. The further I traveled, the darker everything got. The fact that I could barely see what was in front of me as I slowly crept forward was truly unnerving. There was a deluge of things I didn't want to encounter in the encroaching perpetual darkness, and all of them were coming to the forefront of my mind.

Come on, Lethe. Get it together!

Wait a sec. I sniffed. *Is that what I think it is?*

Even without the light to guide me to the end of the tunnel, the savory smell of a completed meal practically yanked my weak body forward. I was enthralled with the scent of something tasty after days and days of nothing but brown fruit.

The power of food sure was impressive. Before I knew it, I effortlessly found myself in another dimly lit room. The colors had returned to the world, but they were faded and old, as if part of a withered painting. *It's back! It's—Woah!*

I stumbled and fell to the floor, but that did little to stop my gaze from wandering off without me. Each piece of furniture was a silhouette of what it was supposed to be.

Contrary to where I started, the air in the room was warm and comforting—almost like it wanted me to stay. At the center was a large, blacked-out table. On its thick frame was an entire spread of foods I had never laid an eye on before, the majority of them being funny-looking fish. There were at least fifteen plates and seats to accompany them. Their colors might have been warped, but they appeared exotic and fresh.

I was so enamored by the food that I didn't notice the woman shrouded in black right before me. The harsh stone floor had scraped one of my hands, causing a small, delicate cut to flourish. *I'll need to tend to that later.*

"Who are you? Where is your holy cloak?" the woman asked, glaring down at me the same way one gawks at a pesky insect. After another thorough inspection, she muttered, "Intruder," and turned her back to me.

She was going to fetch the others!

However, that was the opening I needed. Nothing would stop me from annihilating this feast. Certainly not any mortal. I pushed mana from my body into the ring, armoring my right hand with thick frost. Without hesitation, I viciously clamped one of the woman's legs. *I got you now, cultist!*

While I couldn't confirm it, the people here were sketchy enough to be considered a part of something dicey and repulsive, like a cult. I couldn't think of a better description for them at the moment, and I didn't think I needed one, either.

The ice that flowed from my hand ran up the woman's leg in pale tendrils, licking her skin until it turned an icy hue. Like a flower, the frost bloomed all at once until only a sculpture, crafted from the breath of the tundra, remained.

When you really think about it, the Ring of Everfrost is a truly marvelous creation. I heard that the most powerful artifacts are crafted from the souls and remains of ancient monsters. I really wonder what Rock had to kill to make something like this.

I'd learned back then to control the spread of magic depending on how much mana I put into the effect, such as only affecting the skin. Extra effort like what I'd just done usually wouldn't make a difference, but this time, it was perfect.

The room around me was still distorted to the point where only the brightest of muted colors stood out. The dark of the woman's robe sharply contrasted with the bright blue of her body.

"Hmmm. This may take a lot of work." I circled around her, grasping for my best entry of attack. If I was going to get out of here in one piece and stop whatever they were doing, then I really needed that cloak.

* * *

"Wow, you can barely see anything," I mumbled to myself, now fully robed in my cultist attire. "How do they navigate through this?"

The walls blended together as I passed through shades of green and red. It was already a pain to walk through, but the hood made it even worse! There was nothing to actually gaze through except for some small holes near the top.

I eyed the large assortment of food in front of me. My stomach rumbled like a monster, sharing my appetite and Frosty's.

"Well," I said, licking my lips, "time for a break."

* * *

After my snack, I had to trespass through an outdoor courtyard, packed with spikes and pyres full of abhorrent green flame. It was jarring to see a multitude of colors now, especially when it came to the slime-colored fire.

The mismatched geometry and feeling of being watched never left me throughout my descent into the foreign world. It really, really *sucked*. The only bright side was that my energy had been replenished, and in the end, that was all that really mattered.

After ducking down another corridor, I was met by a sea of cultists; their outlines only pronounced because everything around them was gray. Some were gathered close in a circle around a pile of... something despicable. The pungent smell of iron wafted through my nostrils, leading me to believe the kills were fresh. The stark-white, mangled bodies and broken horns reminded me of mountain goats or rams. *How awful.*

One individual was on the other side of the circle from me. He solemnly stood in front of a podium, his cold hands curled around the same book that I'd seen before. It had been wrenched like the jaws of an Albian Crocodile, coated in a vile stench. It was far worse than wolf droppings—I would know.

The head cultist was lost in thought as he read, but when I had fully entered, his head inhumanly snapped in my direction. *Talk about creepy!*

"Agatha, is that you?" he asked, as if caught in a trance.

I decided to nod and see how it went.

"Splendid! I hope you enjoyed some of our exquisite cuisine from R'lyeh. It would please me if it made up for the long journey you had."

I decided to push my luck and nod once more.

"Huh?" He tilted his head a little *too* far, which sent shivers down my spine. "Why aren't you speaking? Ah! It's the Vermilion Flounder, isn't it? That one punches hard, correct?"

Another nod. *Why is this working?!*

"Anyway, come over here, will you? With you, the ritual should be ready to get underway. You're the last *Dreamer*."

What a strange title. Well, this whole day has been as surreal as it gets. It makes me feel like I really am dreaming. Maybe 'dreamer' isn't far off the mark. I would rather be dreaming than be here.

The others made room for me to squeeze into the circle around the carcasses. The hoods in the back joined the circle as well. All eyes fell on the man at the podium. "The time is nigh, my brothers!" He then gazed my way with a wry smile. "...And sister." *Oh, cool. We have a gender-inclusive cult leader. What a revelation!*

"*The Great Dreamer* requires help from us all. When you are called, place your hand over this sacred text, and conceptualize what *The Great Dreamer* should appear as to you. Whoever has the most powerful image will spawn him in that form! Are you all prepared?"

We all nodded vigorously. The leader went first, placing his pale, nearly colorless, hand onto the book. He stood motionless for a solid minute.

His head snapped back our way as he said, "Aren of Natar, step forward and imbue our Lord with your conviction." His pious words held strong and true, just like your typical religious bishop. I couldn't confirm it, but I had a hunch this guy had experience with religion—more than most, at least. Perhaps that's a cult requirement these days.

As the next cultist stepped forward, I noticed that a small flame had appeared in the center of the circle, a few feet above the corpses. The eleventh in our circle went to mimic what the leader had done before him. The flame got a little bigger, and somewhat brighter, but not by much.

"Elo of Olympos, step forward."

Another man went up and repeated the motions. The flame barely changed that time. I couldn't even be sure that it had. Were these guys even trying?

"Jesper of Helion!"

"Casper of Phodiem!"

"Mansa of Free!"

One by one, the cultists went up, and the flame increased ever so slightly each time. It was now the size of an arm, which really wasn't saying much. This is the first and most pathetic ritual I had ever witnessed. *Are you all not embarrassed by these results? And you call yourselves believers. Pathetic!*

It was difficult to tell if these guys wanted their Dreamer or whatever to actually be summoned. Their devotion lacked the same religious prowess as the people that revered the gods in other countries I had visited. The spark just wasn't there, and I don't think I was imagining it.

If you can't even form a concrete image of your lord in your head, what kind of follower are you? I have never been a part of a religion, but I would surely have no problem visualizing the one I believed in.

"Agatha of Elain!"

No one came forward.

"Agatha of Elain!" he said once more.

Oh, right. That's me!

I skirted around the others, my cloak brushing against them as I made my way to the cursed book. I was so fed up with how little progress the others had been making with their summoning that my initial goal had slipped my mind. I was supposed to stop the ritual from happening in the first place! But with such a pitiful showing from these amateur cultists, could you really blame me?

I think I just hated the thought of someone getting what they wanted when they put no effort into it. Since I'd started on my journey, I'd had to work hard for everything I'd gotten up till then: money, food, shelter, and a bit of friendship. I respected hard work.

These cultists were taking their faith with their lord for granted. Even if they wanted to believe, it seemed their hearts weren't in it. And even if they were faithful, their lack of imagination prevented them from moving further along.

Fine, then. I'll do it myself.

I couldn't tell you why I cared so much, but care I did.

With a blaze of passion tightening my chest, I fervently placed my hand on top of the crusty, old page and sunk deep into thought.

Hmm... An image of a "dreamer." Well, I don't want them to be scary or destructive, so this will do. And that seems kinda cute... It would probably mess with some of these old timers and maybe—

Before I knew it, I had more or less created my ideal vision of this deity. I couldn't even remember most of it, but by the end, I was having trouble breathing and concentrating. I guess I got really into it. To be honest, it was a little *too* fun. *Maybe this religion business isn't so bad after all.*

I withdrew my hand and peered directly into the raging flame. Its sickly green hue mimicked the color of the room, and just like moths, everyone's eyes had latched onto it. Its size had nearly tripled.

Hmph! How's that for devotion?

The circle hissed and sputtered to life. The blaze expanded until it consumed the entire circle, devouring the sacrifices in a burst of heat.

"It's working! The return of an Old God is upon us! One of you must have had a complete image of him! Huzzah! *Cthulhu fhtagn! Cthulhu fhtagn!*"

Uh, what do you mean by 'one of you'? Do you see anyone else on this stage?!

"Huzzah!" the others cheered back, ignoring my silent protest. "Long live the old god! Cthulhu fhtagn*!*"

I backed away from the circle, mostly to keep away from the flame, but also to contemplate what had just happened. *What… have I done? Did I just destroy the world? Surely someone else was more pious than me, right? I couldn't have been the bell ringer of doomsday… Right?!*

Unfortunately, I knew better. Pride really could be a downfall.

Oblivious to my contribution and trepidation, the others cheered and cheered some more. The conflagration, in turn, grew brighter and brighter. It expanded outward, blinding all of us in its radiant light.

"Hahahaha! My flesh has returned!" They paused for a moment. "Ah… Wrong era. My apologies! Ahem… **At last, I have been reborn into the mortal realm!** That's better. **I have regained a corporeal form! Cahf ah nafl mglw'nafh hh' ahor syha'h ah'legeth, ng IIII or'azath syha'hnahh n'ghftephai n'gha ahornah ah mglw'nafh!"**

The blinding light dissipated, and what I saw—what we saw—was… intriguing, to say the least. The others thought so as well. A few of them even removed their hoods so they could stare more easily.

"…Who's that?"

"There is no way that is *The Great Dreamer.*"

"It cannot be! Impossible!"

"Imposter! Grab the relic! Quickly!"

One of the hoods dashed off down the way I had come. I wonder where they were going?

The Great Dreamer swept their gaze around the room and scowled. **"What are you foolish followers muttering about? Out with it! Tch… Legeth'drnn. Don't speak in such blatant absurdities around your revered supreme lord of the abyss. After all, it is I—Cthulhu, the great dreamer—**

who you have shaped your very hearts and souls around! A being outside of time, outside of space, outside of... fate! Bow before me as I consume this cursed realm until all that remains is its core. **Preposterous! My voice... Why?!** Why do I look *like*... this?!"

What they—or rather—what *she* was referring to, was the body of a petite, young girl. She looked no older than fifteen, though she spoke like someone much older. She wore an emerald-green, one-piece dress with bows all over. Small, jade-colored, bat-like wings protruded from her shoulders, more like accessories than anything she could actually use for flight. Her long, thick green hair ended in tentacles and was highlighted yellow on the under layer. Like a spawn from the Netherworld, her eyes were deep red, as if coated in the blood of the sacrificial goats.

Finally, some colors that aren't black or gray! Her flushed cheeks had a faint, rosy tint to them, while two canine-like fangs jutted out from either side of her jaw. Yeesh, I didn't want to go anywhere near those chompers. They made Frosty's look like carrots.

Rising out of the center of her hair was a small, cowlick-like antenna. Two identical hair clips in the form of slanted eyes rested near the front of her forehead. They were strikingly similar to the eyes of a squid.

The ring that harbored Frosty shook violently—something that only happened when he really, *really* hated something. Nevertheless, I already knew she was bad news without his warning.

And it

     was all

         my

            fault.

Oops? The heat of the moment is a terrifying thing.

Then again, how could I complain? The girl was adorable and had a sort of entertainer- songstress look to her. Except for a few... strange features, she was almost exactly as I'd imagined. *I should pat myself on the back for this one.*

Cthulhu was still inspecting her body, scrutinizing it down to the last hair. She glared daggers at the floating mirror that had appeared the moment she'd been revived. By the time I finished gawking at her, she was beyond furious. I was pretty sure there was enough bloodlust to cause everyone within a fifty-mile radius to pass out cold, or even perish entirely.

"You!" She pointed at the bishop. **"Come here!"** Her voice boomed in a way that did not suit her petite form.

"Y-yes, my lord," he replied in a stiff, meek voice.

The others quickly made way for him as he solemnly approached the circle. Cthulhu eyed him with contempt and malice in her eyes. "How could you let this happen? Have I not been waiting nearly four millennia for another full, black moon, and this is the form that I get? **How dare you!**"

"AHHHHH...!" The black hooded man was consumed by flames and disappeared a moment after. His screams faded to silence.

The room was dead quiet... until Cthulhu let out a satisfied cackle. To see such a cute and lively girl laughing at the demise of another was horrifying. Even more so when one of us could be next.

The man that had left before came back at the perfect time. He stood there, wide-eyed, at the charred remains of his leader, and then an aqua-colored trident fell from his hands. Just one look at the weapon was enough to drag up recent events. I almost puked up all that exotic food.

The small girl picked up the wicked spear and danced her fingers over the jagged tips. It gave her a small cut, which was surprising since she was an apparent god figure. "Ah, Blue Requiem, the legendary Eternal of Pure Death. I must have accidentally killed Harrow's Chosen with my rage. That would make this glorious creation mine to command. A god sponsoring a god, now that is riveting."

The large summoning room filled with her laughter. She licked the black ichor that spilled from her skin with a coquettish grin. "Mmm... I don't think old Harry would mind, however. A two-timer that receives gifts from one while sponsored by another without permission deserves a fate worse than death."

Eternal? Rock's library mentioned nothing about those, but I had found books on amazing powers and weapons bestowed by people with a god's favor. Perhaps I am witnessing my first God Weapon. Not to mention the fact that she brutally murdered an agent of the god of shadows and death. Will he kill us in our dreams now?

I didn't want to think too deeply about god-on-god violence. I had trouble even grasping what she was saying. All I wanted was to flee as far away as I could.

Cthulhu continued. "Can't have something with the power to slaughter a divine being in the hands of the incapable, can we?" She effortlessly shot the three-pronged item into the air and allowed it to plummet until it disappeared between her inhumanly extended jaws.

Those were definitely not the teeth of a human. *I think I was right. That trident is clearly out of any human's league. But of all people, why did a cultist have it? I thought gods were picky. And why does she have so many layers of teeth?! How can she even fit that in there? I don't recall imagining those additions when I designed you!*

She let out an atrocious belch—the kind a grown man would release after finishing a ten-course feast—before patting the revealed part of her belly. I wanted to smack that annoying look of satisfaction right off her face, but how could I? We were all too frozen with fear to do much of anything, but it was a nice thought to pass the time when it was, well, Doomsday.

"Ahhhh. That hit the spot. Do any of you weaklings have something else equally delicious that I can procure for safekeeping?"

When no one responded, she laughed. "Look at all of you, frozen in fear! I may be stuck in this form, but I am still a Great Old One! That old fool made a blunder and needed to pay! Now..." She slowly scanned the room and smirked, "Who else needs to be punished?"

I decided to act now rather than let this play out any longer. I tossed off my cloak, drawing all eyes to me.

"That's not Agatha, right?"

"Yeah. She's a bit young and not as developed as Agatha."

"Yeah, yeah. Plus, her hair isn't gray."

Well, I don't like you guys either!

"I'm not a vile cultist like the rest. I really have nothing to do with this. Can I leave before you burn more of them, please?"

Not my proudest moment, but anyone in my position would have done whatever it took to ensure their survival. I couldn't let Bella's sacrifice be in vain!

Cthulhu eyed me with great interest and a wide and wicked grin plastered across her face. "So, it was you. You created my image. I am certain of it. I still recall your unique mana."

I nodded, bracing for a battle of insults. "Yes, it knocked down two birds with one stone."

Why am I acting so honest and cocky all of a sudden? Is it her malefic aura? It's taking all my strength just to keep my mind together. It feels like it's going to crumble into a million pieces! How am I so bold?!

She raised an eyebrow, her gaze thirsting for more. "Now, what could you mean by that? You're not getting away, but I am interested in what an outsider has to say. I'll ease the madness aura down a tad so we can converse."

How kind of you.

The tension around the room lessened. I mustered all the courage in my body—which had a surprisingly low limit—and did my best to speak clearly and concisely. "Oh, Great Dreamer, you're too strong and terrifying! Your power was so overwhelming that the only way to stop it was to contain it."

She chuckled. "You don't say. Do tell."

Sweat beading on my brow, I continued. "I wanted to stop your resurrection at first, but I changed my mind." I turned towards the fanatics and raised a lone finger in their direction. "When I saw what weak devotion these posers had, I knew I had to do something. I decided to take matters into my own hands, even if it did cause Armageddon."

She eyed me suspiciously.

"It pained me to see that so little progress was made when they tried to summon you. I may not be religious, but any god I'd have worshiped would have surely been disappointed in me if I couldn't have completed something as simple as conjuring up a clear image of their glorious being. It's not even hard to do, so what gives? Therefore, I decided to bring you into this world in the best image I could manifest." My eye darted from left to right, avoiding her heavy leer. "That image just happened to be of a cute girl."

By then, the cultists had all removed their hoods and were profoundly stunned by my declaration. I'm sure they wanted to speak out and reassure their lord, but they feared the wrath that could come along with a single misstep. Their leader had just been purged into nothingness, after all.

"Mm..." Cthulhu seemed to consider my words more deeply than I expected. Was it because of my conviction and that I was speaking from the heart? I believed every word I had said, even while facing someone that was above even the concept of death (the cult's words, not mine).

"Alright. Your judgment has been decided," she declared, bringing her hands together. "You are right. They all lack devotion. Even in this wretched form, I can still explore and reclaim my share of this world as I have desired for eons. Very well, girl. You will be exempt from punishment for showing your true devotion. However, it would be in your best interest to avoid becoming a disciple to another god, **ever!** You are now the only true follower of Cthulhu, The Great Dreamer. **Ehyeog hri ot Cthulhu.**"

"What did you say?"

"I dub you the 'First Follower of Cthulhu.' Wear it with pride as my disciple!"

"Uh, I'm not a part of any religion—"

"Of course." There was an edge to her voice that cut through my words. "You get no say in the matter. Be grateful. My blessing is already piercing its way into your blighted vessel."

I gulped. "Uh, well, I know that. Just don't expect any offerings or whatever people do these days."

"I'm glad you know your place. The invader is still resisting, however."

"What do you mean?"

"No need to heed those words if you don't understand. We can table this discussion until I'm done taking out the worthless garbage." Cthulhu let out a cute giggle, which completely betrayed the malicious look in her blood-red eyes. "I have many questions about this world that I will do my best to seek. I thank you."

"Y-yeah. No problem…" I forced a weak laugh.

This was all my doing. *Anything she does is really all my fault, huh?* I shook that thought away. It could have turned out much worse.

Cthulhu approached me; the same conniving smile slithered across her face. She was a few inches shorter than me, but her menacing aura brought me down far past her level. "I recall you wanting to leave. Allow me to assist. Where would you like to go?"

I scratched my cheek nervously. She was so overbearing, even in the form I'd designed myself. It was sort of funny but also incredibly suffocating at the same time. Still, I had unexpectedly discovered a way out of the sea by releasing an ancient god into the world in the form of a "harmless maiden." Nothing could go wrong, right?

"Well, you see… I don't know if you have heard of it, but there's a small cavern in the Bretha Tundra. Please send me to where Rock-Howler dwells, the Crystal Cave."

"Sure." She nodded a little too easily. "I can do that, but before you go, a follower of mine needs a name that relates to me. I can't be the only one spreading my name. I need to make up for a few thousand years of lost time. Hmm… Ah, yes!" She snapped her fingers. "I'll call you *Kulu.*"

"Kulu?"

"Indeed. That's more than enough for you to be recognized as my *true* follower. It was a name I was known by long ago. You should feel honored."

If anything, I was even more frightened. There's no way she'll forget about me now!

"S-sure… Thanks," I said, desperate to get away.

There was one good thing that had come from all this. I'd finally had my first meeting with someone not from this world. They were a deity, albeit a corrupt and vile one, but a deity, nonetheless. After hearing so much about gods over the past few years, I desired nothing more than to meet one. The blessings they could give were akin to demi-god powers and magic, but that came secondary. I had another goal in mind, and I was sure only the gods themselves could help me achieve it.

Guess I can check off meeting a deity. I wonder if Boreas had to deal with stuff like this during his own journey.

Chapter 7
The Country of Two Deities

The gods watch down on all of us. Some just pay more attention than others. The places where religion thrives are also the home of the biggest lies.

—Boreas Tyrel

The cobblestone road that led to the lonely country was crooked and riddled with potholes.It wasn't fit for a wanderer, nor your average inhabitant, really. The trees on either side of the winding path were leaning, their once dense canopies now devoid of leaves.

In comparison, the weather was slightly more unpleasant. Berated by a deluge of sandstorms and sunburns for several consecutive days, I was convinced I would never take another shortcut unless necessary. When something isn't loved by a god of nature, things like this can happen.

To an outsider, the drab scenery was beyond daunting. Phodiem, the name I learned during my stay in a neighboring country, was many days away from the next country and wasn't very popular with tourists of any kind because of its unfavorable location.

Why anyone would travel here out of their own volition was beyond me. Was it stupidity? Boredom? A new life? I certainly wasn't aware of *their* reasoning, but I knew mine. Thus, with the misgivings I had experienced over the last week, I just gritted my teeth and bore with it. This destination would make the slog worth it.

I gallantly approached the arched alabaster entrance where a guard wearing a silver armor and pointed helmet stood vigilant.

He eyed me suspiciously, keeping his hands tight on his long, iron spear.

C'mon, I don't look that sketchy, do I? I cracked a small smile at the *courteous* gesture.

When I finally reached the gate, my mortal enemy—the town guard—stood in front of it, impeding my path. His stare wasn't glued to me, but to the one who stood at my rear. For once, it seemed my looks weren't important.

He pounded his spear on the ground and raised his voice. "Do you wish to enter Phodiem?"

Wow. So formal.

I suppressed a giggle before raising an eyebrow. "Would there be any other reason for me to be here?"

While his eyes darted between me and my companion lightly trotting behind me, I became more and more irritated with my current appearance. Even if it came off as rude, I still decided to clean myself up a bit. From the white satchel that hung off my right shoulder, I produced a white handkerchief.

I quickly wiped off the dust and dirt that had gotten on my favorite outfit: a black cardigan paired with a white, flared, knee-length skirt. Even though they weren't the originals due to the wrath of time, they still held deep sentimental value to me.

Come to think of it, why didn't I change into something more fit for this climate? Ugh.

As I lamented my foolishness, he addressed me once more.

"With a creature like that running wild, our citizens would feel unsafe. Would you mind leaving it outside?" His voice was as cold as ice, but his tone wasn't forceful.

We were used to this kind of treatment. After all, people hated what was different.

This was clearly a test. He wasn't the first person to ask me this, and he certainly wouldn't be the last.

After the dirty handkerchief vanished into my bag, I decided to tease him a little. Not many opportunities came along for me to have fun these days.

"Unsafe? Come on." I raised my hands up and shrugged. "Frosty wouldn't hurt a fly! Well, not unless that fly attacked me. Then it would be a different story. Ha-ha-ha." I don't laugh a lot anymore, so it probably sounded a little forced.

The guard grunted, not impressed at my attempt to lighten the mood.

Yeah... I shouldn't laugh like that anymore. Noted.

He lowered his eyebrows—which I realized were incredibly bushy—and firmly gripped his weapon once more, eyeing me suspiciously.

It seems he's still intimidated, despite my reassurance.

"*Sigh*. Fine, I'll put him away," I said, folding. "Then I'll be free to enter, right?" The outcome almost always ended like this, but that never stopped me from trying. Frosty deserved it.

A breath of respite left his mouth, but held his position as if I would pounce at a moment's notice. "You need to answer a few questions before you can proceed."

"Eh..." The small hairs on my neck stood up when he said that. *Questions? Really? What a pain.*

"Sure thing," I responded unenthusiastically.

Oh, wait... I need to give the impression that I'm the girl for the job. This is the kind of situation where I need to display my fearless courage!

I puffed out my chest with confidence. This is no problem. No problem at all!

I gave Frosty a pat on his cute head before moving on to his back. His well-maintained pelt felt coarse and dense against my pale hand, but that didn't stop me from copping a feel. It just took some time getting used to, even now.

His tongue lolled out as he lightly panted. His eyes sparkled and his jaw was unhinged in a way that would be equivalent to joyous bliss for a human.

He was so adorable.

"Alright, my little boy. It's sleepy time. Your partner has to go without you for now."

Frosty's large maw nuzzled against my hand. *So cuuuute! I'm melting!* His body turned ethereal and dispersed, flowing directly into the blue, crystal ring that was perched on top of my middle finger. It was like his own little home.

I turned back to the gatekeeper. "My ice wolf went for a nap. Are we good now?"

The guard's mouth fell agape, giving him a stupefied expression, like a goldfish. I guess he'd never seen something like that before, but weird things can't be that uncommon. Most countries were well-versed in the mystical arts. Maybe out here in the boonies, everything was more archaic. *Or I'm just the weird one after all... Yeah, let's go with the former.*

His body was statuesque, but after a brief pause, he returned to his naturally aloof gaze and sharp eyes. Beads of sweat were ever dropping from his forehead, indicating that he was still more nervous than anything.

"Y-yes. I will now ask you the general questions required to enter Phodiem. All non-suspicious characters are free to enter once the inquiry is completed."

Hmm. And what would deem me as one of those suspicious characters?

He cleared his throat and then continued. "Question one: What is your name?"

"Lethe. *Just* Lethe."

"No surname? That is quite strange."

I glared at him. It was obvious he hadn't ventured outside this area. Many villages and towns would only bestow given names. Some didn't have names at all on the less-human populated continent, just unique titles. Only larger countries, especially pious ones, grant people last names. "Can we move on, *please?*"

"Alright, then. Question two: What is your country or town of origin?"

I shivered just a bit. *Always this question. Always, always, always.*

Some countries would ask rather meaningless questions, and I would have to deal with the same damned look on their faces every time.

Maybe I should just lie. I'm not too shabby in that department.

I let out an audible *gulp* before pursing my lips and pretending to mull over his question.

The soldier grew impatient and raised his voice once more. "What in the world is taking you so long, girl? It should be a simple answer."

I was surprised that I hadn't been tossed out from how suspicious I was acting. I guess they *really* needed tourism. "Sorry... My memory has been in shambles for quite some time." *Ah, the feeling of anxiety and loneliness has reared its head once more. Even bringing up the subject mentally drained me.*

My facade began to crumble as my confidence dwindled as per usual. "I can't really tell you with certainty. If I can't pass without telling you, I guess I will go."

I wasn't actually planning on leaving, but he didn't know that. I had slogged through Hell for this! As I turned my back and began to walk away, the soldier called out to me. The wind started to pick up, but I could still clearly make out his words. *Checkmate.*

"Wait! Don't go. Please! We desperately need visitors above all else! You don't have to answer."

My lips curled into a small, satisfied smile. *Heh-heh-heh. Glad to know I'm needed.* I briefly clutched the fabric against my chest. I had already got what I wanted. These lingering feelings were just the pain and regret of having so many blank areas inside my brain and my heart.

Well, no need to mull over that stuff anymore. I'm in!

I turned back to him and smiled apologetically. I would have winked as well, but the motion would be lost with my appearance.

With my hands clasped together, I voiced my appreciation. "Thanks!"

"No problem." His gaze felt distant, but he seemed glad to have convinced me to stay.

I could take solace in that.

"Please wait a moment," the guard instructed, facing his colleagues behind him.

I gladly obliged.

He called out to someone beyond the entrance, and they responded by hastily opening the gate. Inside its vast jaws, I caught a glimpse of beautiful, chic brick houses and buildings. There was a plethora of colors all around, enough to make a rainbow jealous.

Wow. I was taken aback by the magnificent sight as I walked under the open arch. It was breathtaking... except for one thing.

What in the world?

My head awkwardly turned to the guard. His eyes were trained on me, more out of curiosity than suspicion. I assumed it had to do with my eye situation. You know, with having the eyepatch and all.

He's not scared, so it's not one of my abilities running wild, at least.

"Hey, um..." I shot a finger towards the irregularity scorching my eyesight.

Stretching vigilantly across the horizon stood a sky-blue wall, its body nearly transparent.

It was such a waste to have a wall where anyone who entered could easily circumvent by moving to either side of it. Even more when it messed with the architecture so blatantly. If I were the designer, I would have wept in despair.

The guard revealed a rather unsettled expression, clumsily straightening his helmet. "You see, we have a rather, er... difficult situation here in Phodiem."

"Is that so?" I prodded in a mildly perplexed tone.

"We have two different factions, and neither of them can decide which one is superior. This peaceful country is very close to breaking into an all-out war. So recently, we have sent out flyers promising rewards to visitors that could help us ultimately decide which faction we should unite under."

Hey, that's my cue.

I let a bit of my excitement spill out, resulting in what was probably a suspiciously wide grin. "That's actually why I'm here."

"R-really?" His somewhat sharp gaze lost some of its edge. "And you came alone?" He looked past me, as if seeking out another person besides me to assist them.

What's wrong with just me?

"Do you have a problem with me helping? It was the reason I came, after all." With a hand lightly placed on my chest, I continued in a clear and bubbly voice. "Are there qualifications? I'm s-sorry, I didn't know."

His wariness seemed to ease up after witnessing such a drastic change in my attitude; it was refreshing.

"Well... no. We just don't get many female visitors, and the ones that did make it here only came to get a marriage partner. Plus, you had a rather corrupt smile not too long ago, so I thought for sure that was the case."

C-corrupt? I didn't think I looked that suspicious.

The man let out an exasperated sigh and took a deep breath. The mild wind somehow pushed his helmet to the side a bit, forcing him to straighten it once more. "I apologize for my rudeness, but due to the troublesome women that have come here in recent times, we don't hold female travelers in high regard."

Understandable. Buuuut don't lump me in with those lusty harlots just because we're the same gender!

His expression softened tremendously, probably because I was clearly miffed at his last statement.

"F-forget what I said. Please choose a side. We'll arrange a meeting with the head of a faction. They'll explain the situation from there."

He bowed his head and turned away to walk back to the entrance, his helmet nearly falling off from another strong gust.

I gave my cheek a light slap to perk myself up. I needed to choose a side, but which one?

Where the separation of the wall began, there was a small wooden sign on either side. The left one read: *The people of Phobos*, while the right read: *The people of Deimos.*

"Ah, those two. Hmm…" I shook my head, let my hands fall to my hips, and let my mind wander. There was only one way to make such an important, country-breaking decision.

I flipped a coin.

From my satchel, I retrieved my coin purse. It was originally dyed maroon, but had become patchy and pale over time, and I planned on exploiting it until its last breath.

"One of these should do." I revealed a shiny gold piece, stricken with the face of a bearded, old man with an eyepatch. The other side had the long body and face of a serpent.

This was the currency used throughout most kingdoms I had been to on this continent. Smaller nations or towns didn't accept it, but because of how scarce the materials had become in some places, just a few were enough to buy myself a house.

Bronze, silver, and gold all had different values. I bet you can guess which one is worth the most.

"Here it goes," I puffed out my cheeks and slowly released the air out into the world. I tossed the coin towards the heavens.

The coin danced through the air, like a wasted woman past her prime, before I swiftly intercepted it between my palms, and slowly peeled my hand away to inspect the results.

"Hah. So that's how it is." It was the snake, and therefore, I chose the second option—Deimos.

As soon as I stepped through to their side, it was like falling into another world. The sound of production held a monopoly over every other noise in the area; a somewhat nauseating ruckus, at best.

The people here were hard at work crafting weapons and items—almost as if they were going to war. Even children had been put to work, happily bringing food for the grizzled craftsmen and women, or helping deliver items to the large wheelbarrows that were brimming with the jagged metals of death.

Not a single person acknowledged me as I passed by. It was surreal.

In front of a bakery, a group of men and women were breaking down wood and writing on them to make signs. The completed ones read things like *"Deimos Forever!"*, or *"Make Deimos Great Again!"*, or even *"No One-Country Solution!"* They clearly wanted nothing to do with their other half, their sweat-drenched faces simply seeking to win this upcoming battle. That did spawn a question in my mind. If there was a battle brewing, why was I here? Perhaps my coin had chosen wrong.

I approached some of the citizens slowly, doing my best to come off as normal. *But what even counts as normal here? Why am I so afraid?*

"Excuse me," I started. "Where can I find the leader of this country?" I knew it would be a mistake to reference their leader as anything else. From my experience, these citizens most-likely fell into the 'fanatic' category.

An older, bearded man set aside his crossbow and gazed up at me from his wooden box seat. "Ya wanna join the revolution, young lass? I respect it. That why you seek the bishop?" He gave me a toothy grin.

So the leader is a bishop? That makes sense. Other nations I had visited had religious leaders acting as the head of the country, especially if there is little hierarchy. It wasn't the first time I'd met a bishop as the leader of a country, and it certainly wouldn't be the last.

I shrugged. "Sort of. I came here to help decide which faction should lead." I directed my eye towards the barrels of weapons around the party's feet.

A younger woman with short hair stood to his right. She was cradling a sword like an infant as she followed my gaze. "Oh, honey. We are well aware of the contest between our countries. These are a backup plan in case the thieving people of Phobos break their side of the deal when we win. Gotta have a way to defend ourselves, you know."

I nodded. That made sense, but I needed to get back on track. If a war sparked, attempting to flee would be a nightmare. "Where did you say this bishop was?"

She and the old timer happily gave me directions. I was surprisingly welcomed once more when I reached the humongous cathedral that towered over the other buildings like a revered deity. Its tall alabaster walls and spiral-shaped spires gave off an imposing and austere impression. Feeling daunted—and a bit jaded—I timidly stepped inside. My movements echoed through the narrow passageway until I reached a wide, open space with a singular dwelling within. The bishop was standing in solitude at the end of the atrium, praying to an altar of a cherub with wings. *Wow, impressive.* Anyone would have been awed by the remarkable craftsmanship of the work.

The bishop tilted his head when he heard my footsteps echo throughout the long hall. Facing me, he gave me a toothless grin.

Kinda gross, but I'm sure he means well.

As he shuffled closer, his body language made it clear that he was more than eager to speak to me. "I am known as Ramos. Could you perhaps be *The Traveler?*"

He was rather old and wrinkly. He even had that old man smell. You know—the kind that permeates through a room, but smells neither good nor bad. His large, black pupils were alarming at first, but I could also see kindness and wisdom within—or so I thought.

I got straight to the point. "My name is Lethe. I'm here because I accepted the task of helping the factions solve your problem."

I gave him a look brimming with confidence and enthusiasm. He gracefully nodded and turned around, lowering his gaze to face me.

"Wonderful! But first, allow me to tell you our tale."

I sighed. *Here we go again.*

* * *

The nation of Phodiem used to be two neighboring countries that prospered on their own. Each worshiped a child of Ares, a god of war and battle, or something like that. Even after my awakening, I found that most places I visited served under a divine deity. Phodiem was no different, even if it came off more pious than I was accustomed to. Deimos represented terror, while his brother, Phobos, was all about panic. *I don't see the value in revealing deities like that, but to each their own, I guess.*

Of course, the two countries were exact opposites and couldn't stand that their competitor was right beside them, and they had no way of knowing about what schemes were being hatched behind closed doors.

To avoid bloodshed, they controversially decided to merge into one and erected a rather overly alluring and architecturally shattering wall where they could keep a close eye on each other. Each wanted to determine which deity—and country—was better. They had many contests to compete, always one-upping each other, but the end results were always tied. They simply needed outside assistance to weigh in and finish their long fight for them.

Time went on, and the arms race and unbridled aggression continued. However, neither side wanted to make a move before the other and it became a stalemate—a cold war, if you will. Then one day, a head priest came up with the idea of asking for travelers to help. It would lead to a fair outcome with no bias on either side. They swiftly opened up their gate and sent word of rewards for anyone that could assist with their troubling endeavor—despite their country being located past one of the great death deserts, a place no one wanted to cross.

A long and perilous journey, as well as the fear of death, were the two primary reasons no men took up the challenge, and those who had failed on the way to getting here. What kind of vitality did those women have? It had been a few months since they opened their gates when I arrived. I hadn't seen any strange women, but perhaps they had already been thrown out or were busy with a man behind closed doors...

"Okay, okay. I get the situation."

I had taken a seat in a pew at the front while Ramos told his long, dry tale. For someone from the opposing faction, he didn't seem nearly as biased as I had thought. Of course, he could have been hiding his true colors. The glint in his eyes reminded me of that.

He nodded in affirmation. "Do you have any ideas on what we can do to help you decide?"

I revealed a wide, shameless smile before standing up and brushing the small specs of dust off my skirt. "I have a thing or two in mind." *Heh-heh-heh.*

I knew it was blasphemous to think about, but I believe a little imp had whispered a magnificent plan to me in that cathedral on that cold day. Perhaps it spawned a devil inside me.

Two birds with one stone.

* * *

Phobos wasn't much different. In fact, it was exactly the same. Everyone was contributing towards the war effort in their own way, preparing to defend themselves in the event of a Deimos retaliation.

"What's going on here?" I asked a young man and his son who were sharpening swords together. I already knew the answer, but I just had to be sure.

"Are you a traveler? Perhaps here to see our bishop?"

"Daddy look! She has a black thing over her eye. She must like our people if she is wearing our color."

Okay. Maybe they weren't *exactly* the same.

"I'm here for the contest," I replied, ignoring the kid's rude comment.

The man and his son nodded in unison. "I see. Well, there's a chance that once we finally win, the bastards—I mean, bad people of Deimos might retaliate when they lose. We have our means to defend ourselves as well as a peaceful protest prepared in case that happens."

"Daddy said the B-word again, ha-ha-haaa!" The kid thrust his sword around in the air, as if trying to me.

What's the point of a peaceful protest when you have a deluge of weapons at the ready?

* * *

The designs in the cathedral were immaculate, mirroring the ones in Deimos with inverted colors. Symbols of unity and victory were inscribed into the thick, black rear of the building, leading me to believe that the leader of Phobos wasn't afraid of ditching tradition in favor of newer ideas.

The bishop of this cathedral was maybe forty years younger than the other, but his build was, unfortunately, rather similar. He had deep bags under his small eyes, a face packed with worry, and some of his hair had already turned silver.

However, some of his stress seemed to dissipate when he saw me.

"Ah, you're here! Perfect." He rubbed his hands together and moved away from the altar of a cherub. Just where did this energy come from? He looked so depressed and dejected before!

"My name is Seki. I am here to assist and already have an idea for the contest."

Upon relaying my idea, his pale face slightly brightened. "That wasn't what our other contestant had in mind, but I'm sure he would love that. I wholeheartedly agree!"

I tilted my head. "Other contestant?"

* * *

I sat alone at a wooden table with a feast fit for a king.

At least, that's how it was supposed to be.

On the far end of the table sat a burly man with a beard that enveloped most of his tanned face. The mischievous glint from his amethyst eyes peeked out from above his bushy peak, filling me with anticipation and interest. He had no hair on his shiny scalp and wore a shirt a size too small that read "The Belcher."

The what…?

To my left stood Seki of Deimos, clad in black robes. And to my right stood the leader of Phobos, decked out in white. They sat discussing something I had been too distracted to keep up with.

When they were done, I asked them a question I had been ruminating. "Is this… my opponent?"

Ramos nodded. "He has come from distant lands to try our food, but he also wanted to take part in our contest. He nearly died making it here and only recently finished rehabilitation."

"That won't be a problem, right?" Seki asked.

"Not at all." My confidence slightly wavered at the newcomer's arrival. *Could he have known about my real reason for coming here?*

After I suggested that they both prepare a feast to decide which deity was the most exceptional,Seki called him from the other side of the wall. We met up in a restaurant that was almost in the center of the country, but further into Deimos. I had expected that only I would be participating in this ordeal, but a one-sided contest is as biased as it gets.

I clicked my tongue. *Just a tiny road bump.*

The platters of food made me salivate quicker than I expected. My earlier thoughts of annoyance had already been washed away. I wouldn't be holding back—not in the slightest. With a signal from both sides, our bout began.

Time to dig in!

I started wolfing down food from the Deimos faction first, picking away at the prime rib, then moving onto the salad and roast chicken—my personal favorite—with my cheeks filled to the brim.

The Belcher ripped some Phoboan pork chops to shreds before demolishing a full roasted chicken in seconds. What Phobos was known for was its desserts, but the Belcher had set those aside for last, making quick work of all the meat and dairy courses first.

I know you might be asking, "For such a smart and good-looking girl like yourself, how can you scarf all this food down like a pig-man, Lethe? Where does it all go?" Well, let me thank you for that compliment. Though flattery won't get you far when it comes to someone like myself. Probably.

A few minutes had passed since our dive into gluttony had commenced, but I could do this all day. I glanced across the table to see that the Belcher had moved on to his third course, finally making his way to the sweets. He worked fast—too fast to savor any of it. How would he be able to judge which was better?

Heh-heh-heh. What a buffoon!

Anyway, the reason I was eating enough to feed a town stemmed from the fact that I was currently eating for two. Wait... that came out wrong. To be more specific, I was eating for a person and a wolf. When Frosty was inside the Ring of Everfrost, his hunger passed on to me instead. I think my stomach had to have expanded as well, though I wasn't really sure. Pretty cool, right?

Wrong!

Ever since we met, my coin purse stayed empty, trying to feed his bottomless stomach. It was truly absurd. To remedy this, I used the ring I got from my grandfather to keep him away and get a taste of the good stuff myself. *That's what compromise is... At least I think so.*

The only problem was the hairy beast at the other end of the table. He was close to finishing up the entire Phoboan feast, while I was about ready to swap. It would have been easier to move on if their food hadn't held my tongue captive for so long.

The two onlookers watched me battle with the beast of ceaseless hunger. With warped expressions of awe and pure distress, neither bishop made a peep.

I was still going hard for the first half of the meal, stuffing bread and veggies into my maw. If I wanted the money, I needed to finish strong. I needed to get serious.

"To think this petite, young lady could eat this much in one sitting. I am simply baffled, but also happy to see that she has taken a liking to the food of our esteemed culture. What vitality! I am truly content."

"Don't get cocky, old timer," the younger of the two snarled. "She hasn't even *reached* my side yet. We brought her the best sweets and pie our chefs had to offer. You know what they say, 'The best is always saved for last.'"

"Your food can't possibly be *that* good. Our other guest is gobbling them up in seconds, but this traveler has been savoring every piece along the way."

Ramos was happy to see me engulf his food, while Seki knitted his eyebrows and watched me with his arms crossed. His impatient eyes darted between me and my opponent.

"Fank gu fery unch," I said, my cheeks stuffed like a chipmunk. "Ifs fery chasty."

"I'm glad it suits your palate, my dear." He cracked a wide toothless grin once more, and Seki stared at him with pure annoyance. It was around that time that I had finished the Deimosian feast.

The Belcher was on his second tour through Deimos, devouring the same beautiful spread that they had prepared for me. I couldn't make out his expression under his bearded guise, but I could tell from his eyes that he meant business.

I just consumed a week's worth of food and still have room. Frosty better eat all this because there is no way I'm gonna get out of this without gaining weight. Frosty, do your job!

Both my belly and ring were quiet, but I knew from the lack of stomachache that he was enjoying it to his heart's content.

Seki broke out of his doleful facade when he caught sight of decadent sweets and pies trapped beneath my fervent gaze. Some men had quickly taken away the leftovers and swapped them out with Seki's meal. That happened earlier for the other party, though it wasn't really needed besides for delivering more food. The Belcher left nothing from his side, not even the bones.

The light in Seki returned to his eyes, causing him to overflow with vitality. "Miss visitor, these are the finest sweets in all the land. Please enjoy them," he beamed.

"Thanks." I did stretches with both of my arms and prepared myself for round two of Phobos.

He then turned to my enemy. "Sir Belcher, I am glad you enjoyed our delicacies."

"Errnf," the Belcher said with a grunt, his eyes still plastered onto the pork cutlets.

I didn't watch him that often, but not once, not even when we first sat down, did his eyes ever wander from the dishes.

The time has come to resume my attack!

I set my eyes on a plate of rainbow macaroons. They felt out of place from the dark colors of Phobos that I was used to. Closing my eyes, I picked a random one—a blue one—and tossed it into my mouth. "Mmmmm! So tasty!" I touched a hand to my warm cheek, my expression something akin to pure bliss. *This is fantastic!*

The Belcher had made no comment from the desserts when he consumed them, but he nodded to himself a few times. I even spotted a small pad of paper near the edge of his side.

Is he taking notes?!

Seki's shoulders seemed to relax from my praise. The price was surely through the roof. *And yet, here I am experiencing heaven.* This was the first time I had ever had something so wonderful.

I dropped a pink one with an intricate design into my mouth, and the results made my breath catch. I wondered if the gods themselves feasted on these in handfuls every day. Even I would be jealous of that.

Before I knew it, all the macaroons had disappeared. For the Belcher, his food seemed as though it had never even existed. *Now that is some serious skill.* Though… his namesake felt like a lie; I had yet to hear a single burp leave his body.

Even though the other food was exceptionally good, it seemed nigh impossible to compete with what I was devouring right now. A wave of uneasiness washed over me.

It was a sickness—a sickness called guilt.

Which one should I pick?

The contest didn't matter. Well, it *did*, but I came first. What really mattered was getting my maximum enjoyment out of this—my utility, if you will.

I was nearly salivating at the thought of digging into that delectable apple pie. The decision should have been obvious, but the old guy was so nice to me.

Yep. I really had to think this over. I did so while savoring the ever-sweet apple taste of the pie. It simply *melted* in my mouth.

Before I knew it, all the Phoboan food had disappeared from my side of the table as I subconsciously dabbed my lips with a napkin.

Finally, the smacking of lips from the other side of the table ceased. The Belcher, who was polishing off his last dish, stared at me with what I thought was anger in his eyes. Or was it awe?

He let out a disgustingly wet burp. "In all my tours in the culinary field, I have never once lost a contest, let alone to a slim girl. You have my deepest respect."

Huh? I was right? I mean, I knew I could win, but nearly everyone feels hurt when victory is snatched away at the last second. I know I sure did.

I shot him a smile full of gratitude. "Why, thank you."

With my victory secure, I sank into a deep thought. The two leaders—and Belcher—stared at me, trying to anticipate who I would pick.

Sadly, it had come to this. I felt bad, but it was nothing to be ashamed of. Others had done the same. Therefore, I was only using my talent and experience to make a living. Nothing out of the ordinary.

"I have decided to pick..."

Both bishops held their breaths, and Belcher anxiously chomped through a bone of meat.

"Deimos," I said softly. "I choose Deimos." I could say it hadn't been easy, but that was a lie. Even *I* wasn't stupid enough to mess with the script.

"What?!" Seki and Belcher shouted in unison.

"I see. Thank you, miss. I shall have a reward for you soon."

Ramos turned to the Belcher, who was still unexpectedly pondering his defeat by humbly stuffing his face with lollipops. "Thank you for your help as well. If you had won, which would you have picked?"

"The dishes were quite different, but from the quality of ingredients, Phobos had the edge. Their desserts were also unmatched in quality and flavor."

Seki became deflated once more, but he had a slight smile on his face. "Thank you for your kind words."

What a shame.

"Thank you both for competing in this grand feast and what a great idea it was to hold such a contest. Our usual bouts are a lot less tasteful," Ramos admitted.

"Well, I'm glad to be of assistance," I replied, my shamefulness seeping into my body language.

Ramos had little to show on his wrinkly face, but I could tell he was truly happy with the results, but was also completely unsurprised.

Seki flicked his eyes between the elder and me. It seemed like he'd uncovered a secret in the situation. "What is this?!" Seki was seething with anger, his pointed hat nearly tumbling off his poorly combed, greasy hair. "T-this can't be! I saw her face! She—she loved our sweets. I'm sure of it!" He was hissing now, doing anything to regain control of the situation. "She even took time to savor the intricacies of each dish. Your food seemed to be nothing more than a trifling matter!"

"Well,"—Ramos gave him a pat on the back while I stood up and prepared to leave—"Don't be a sore loser, Seki. The girl chose what she liked better in the end. If Sir Belcher won, then perhaps it would have been different, but he didn't. Can you really refute that?"

There was a long pause as he turned his gaze away in defeat. "N-no..."

Ramos smiled ruefully at Seki's demeanor. "Then it has been decided. Phobos shall join under the Deimosian banner. Lord Deimos has won!"

One side rejoiced, and the other fell into the pits of despair. Meanwhile, I said nothing as I started for the door. *I guess it really eats away at you, huh? Even now. I wish I could be as true to myself as I used to, but those days are few and far between.*

* * *

Earlier in the day...

A sack of coins, large enough that took two hands to hold it, had been casually plopped into my palms. "Pick our side and you will get double this for assisting us in our contest."

"Uh... thanks? Though I really don't feel like this much is necessary." *But I will surely take it!*

"Nonsense, Miss... What was your name again?

"Lethe."

"Right, right. Miss Lethe, your role is vital in finally allowing us to take down the cowardly Phobos. Soon, we can spread our forces away from our rotting side, and reap the fruits of Phobos' labor! We can't do it without you."

Ah, so that's why they had all those weapons. I just wonder how they'll get through the desert.

"But this other man, didn't you say he is the best at consuming food and giving terrific feedback despite his speed? Why should I suggest an eating contest against him?"

The older man placed his hands behind his back. "Oh, please! Don't act like you don't have a reputation when it comes to eating, *Kulu*. I'veve heard about you and the one you worship from a few traveling merchants. A horrifying enigma from darker times that only a few know of. How fun! I was so intrigued that I sent my followers to gather some information about you. It wasn't difficult, even from here. Your description does stand out, after all. You'd be surprised how easily we can acquire news, especially about the gods."

K-Kulu?! There was only one person who would dare call me that stupid nickname.

I shrugged. "I didn't think it was a big deal. I just like food and happen to have a large appetite. You wouldn't like the god I'm with, anyway. No one does."

"Not even yourself?"

"No comment."

"They sound awe-inspiring."

"It really isn't as great as it seems. All I do is accidentally scare people away on their behalf."

He waved his hand. "Nonsense. To even meet your god is something every man waits their whole life for. Most never do."

I knew that, but that didn't mean it didn't come with its own set of problems. It's as they say, "Never meet your heroes." Then again, that god was definitely not my hero.

"Was that the main reason you sent a letter to the inn I was staying at?"

"But of course. I know you can win and enjoy it while you do. My younger rival invited a talented individual to their country to help improve their delicacies. I want to see the miserable look on his face when that slob loses to a young girl. The irony is simply remarkable."

You do you, dude.

"Only one way to find out, right?" I said, placing the large sack into my satchel.

"Yes," he said with a wide smile. "Yes, we shall."

* * *

Back to the present.

Once again, we headed back to the chapel.

"I am glad we have people like you that will do what needs to be done in return for a little incentive."

Well, yeah. Why wouldn't I take the extra dough? I thought back to our earlier meeting. I wondered how he found out about my annoying nickname.

No merchant had ever witnessed me doing anything remarkable, so I knew what he said was a lie. In the end, he wouldn't tell me the truth, but as long as I got paid, it didn't really matter how he discovered me. What did I have to lose by helping him out?

A phantom shot through my patched eyed. *Right... The world is cruel and unforgiving at times.* The pain was so intense that I was nearly seeing green.

This was a common occurrence. I heard sometimes a green flare would come from behind thick, black fabric covering my left eye, but I had never seen it myself.

I took his second sack and stored it away safely. At this point, I thought my purse would break under the immense pressure. "Pleasure doing business with you, geezer."

He brazenly held out his hand, but I shook my head. I was not a fan of touching, especially with strangers.

In return, he gave me a nod as I left. You really can't trust people for how they look on the outside. That could lead to a rather ghastly mistake down the road. It could be a wolf in sheep's clothing—or the fabled demon in the guise of an old man who smiles with his eyes.

I, on the other hand, was very trustworthy. If you needed someone of a slightly shady and mysterious background to decide the fate of the country by simply forking over a small portion of funds, I was your go-to girl.

A slight frown descended upon my lips, and I knew the exact reason for it. I was starting to think that the monster of my nightmares was right. *Maybe I really did bring him into this world.* But I hadn't dreamt of his menacing form in quite some time. It would be better for everyone if we never met again.

Even without the disaster that will ensue when we converge, I have to wonder—what strange surprise awaits me in the next country?

Journal Sketch #1
The Last Frost Wolf, Frostskerin

1402, 6th day, Month of the Cosmo Serpent
Frosty looks serious, but he's a real softy.

Chapter 8

The Vern

I have only met two guardians in my life, but each one of them carved out a place in my very being. Perhaps this is what it feels like to encounter the divine.

—Boreas Tyrel

Rumors had said that the country I was heading to today was hidden deep within a forest. This country only had a singular village—Panatra. What made it special was that the forest contained a sizable amount of latent mana, which transformed the woods into a place of vibrant colors. Mana was something I could never wrap my head around, but I knew that every living creature had it, and possessing more of it could lead to mutations, as well as profound powers and abilities. I probably had little in me. I relied on my ring, a convenient crutch.

This location had also been visited by the noble hero, Boreas. He was the legendary traveler from my most beloved story, *The Adventurer's Journey*, and he had sparked my motivation. Because of all that, I had a lot to look forward to.

I patted my handbag, the veteran book somehow still intact within its deep, enchanted belly. Some of the main selling points from a chapter about a living forest were golden leaves, high-spirited bards, and divine meals made from freshly grown plants. Panatra was one of the very few countries known to worship Pan, God of the Wild. He was depicted as either a bipedal beast or satyr, depending on where you looked or who you asked.

I was excited. If I could establish contact with him, it could help with my amnesia. *I can't expect much; he isn't the God of Memories, after all.*

Frosty leapt through the large underbrush of the forest, trying his best to avoid the poison ivy and thorn bushes that leaned in from each side of the path, impeding our progress. I'm not exaggerating at all when I say that, either. Their branches and leaves whipped as us like living creatures as we pressed deeper into the whimsical woodland. *I guess they're not very welcoming to outsiders, but I really hope that won't be the case with the natives. That would blow. We could also die. Now that would **really** blow. We might even be stuck here forever. Now that would far surpass blowing—that would **suck**.*

It was rather annoying that we had to deal with it at all, but after delving far enough, we arrived at what must have been the heart of the forest. Trees consumed every ounce of sunlight while providing a pleasant canopy of shade in return. Mushrooms stuck out like sore thumbs, devouring the ground in their rainbow colors. I was left speechless from their natural beauty and from their stocky frames being twice the size of an average human.

"Woah," I murmured in a mix of wonder and admiration. "Assuming these aren't poisonous, they could feed us for weeks!"

"Arf!" Frosty replied.

I think he agreed. He really loved food, maybe even more than I did.

Tragically, you could never trust an unusually colored mushroom. That was common knowledge. *Still... No! Can't do it! Nope. Not a chance. It'd probably be safer to go with the berries growing from that tree moss over the—*

One exploded, leaving behind *a* sickly green which reminded me of certain poisons.

Hard pass.

Massive pink frogs sprayed with violet freckles darted through a river, and a green fish with bulky legs too big for its slender body fought against a group of child-sized insects in the mud to my left. Bright-blue jellyfish floated overhead with grace and elegance as if it was the most natural thing in the world. This bewildering forest was nothing like my grandfather had taught me of nature, nor how books described it. It defied all logic.

After passing a few more bizarre sights, we made it to Panatra—or at least where it should have been according to instructions from my last encounter. The cascading waterfall that had filled my ears with memories of the sea had just faded from sight, yet only an eerie and uncomfortable silence remained.

Hmm... This can't possibly be correct.

That's when I noticed it all.

"What the heck?"

I immediately leapt off Frosty and landed on the nutrient-rich soil. "Why is everything so... *old?*"

With a hand pressed to my forehead, I surveyed the small town in front of me. This place was supposed to be thriving with the people of the forest, as well as the occasional visitor like me. Yet here it was, decrepit and devoid of all life. If you had said there had never been a single soul in this place since its inception, I would have believed you. That's just how uncanny and wild the sight was.

The rumored vibrant and secluded country was in complete shambles, fully governed by overgrown fungi and plants. It was broken and archaic, like it hadn't been touched in nearly a thousand years.

A subtle chill crawled its way up my neck, but I ignored it.

"Wait, wait, wait!" I yelled with indignation welling up from within. "This can't be right." I shook my head, surveying the ruins once more. "The guy I talked to was here a month ago. There's no way it could look like this!"

Maybe he was mistaken, but I didn't think so. Whatever calamity had taken root here had to have occurred fairly recently. I was sure of it. There were no other discrepancies with his story besides this anomaly. What could cause so much destruction? It felt primal, yet my gut was telling me that humans were the source of this tragedy. My head was spinning with questions, but I pressed on.

The large, rusted gateway had been torn to pieces by vines that wound through the wreckage and intertwined to stand tall like old conifers. Tarnished huts were woven within like fine thread. I shrank at the sight.

These were shattered homes.

Even after stepping inside, the trees were all I could see. Willows sprouted in every direction. There were hundreds of them, though it was impossible to count. Some were tower-sized, but others were no bigger than a person.

I kicked away the debris of a nearby dilapidated structure and forced my way deeper. I reached a collapsed tunnel, and what I saw tempered my shock with interest.

A human? At least I think it is.

Carefully maneuvering around the heaps of vines and debris that plagued my path, I made my way over. After a few almost-accidents, I reached the... *man.*

Yeah, this is a sight to see.

Only his head remained of flesh and blood, and everything below his neck had become one with the ground. I couldn't guess what had happened to the rest of his body.

His eyes were squeezed shut, as if an invisible force was keeping them closed. The faint sound of wheezing filled my ears. I could end up kicking the hornets' nest with what I planned to do next, but I didn't care. I wanted some answers to what had happened to Panatra.

I scoured the cracked ground and found what I was looking for. And so, with a little eloquence to my toss, I chucked a palm-sized piece of rubble at his sleeping head.

"Bwaaah?!" His eyes flew open, revealing one eye that was a murky, leaf-green and one that was chestnut brown, nearly mirroring the bark surrounding him.

He had to be in his late thirties and lacked facial hair. He gaped at me with dead silence. His different-colored eyes were judgmental. I could feel them scrutinizing every part of me, inside and outside. I felt more dirty than usual. The gaze was tingly and unpleasant. I know it sounds dumb, but he was violating me with that heavy gaze.

A horrible premonition stirred in my mind.

"T... he... ern..."

His voice was barely a whisper, forcing me to move closer. "What was that?" I asked, perplexed by his low, grinding voice.

Crouching down, I slowly inched up to him. I knew he was trapped, but I instinctively grabbed the hem of my skirt before realizing that I had chosen to wear pants this time. I ended up grasping at nothing, feeling even more alone than before. Oddly, the wind started to pick up and the songs of birds had all but disappeared.

I had my ring at the ready, but with how he was at the moment, I didn't think there would be an issue. *All he can really do is give me a little chomp, and that will not end well for him.*

"The... Vern," the man whispered, pulling me from my mixed bag of thoughts.

"The *what?*"

"The Vern," he whispered again. "He's watching. Can you hear?"

What is he talking about?

"It's pretty peaceful," I responded in a calm voice. I might have been unsettled, but there was no way I was going to show it. "Is someone else here, watching us?" I asked.

"He's the Forest Lord, the Keeper, the Shepherd of Fear."

"W-wait, the Shepherd of *what* now?" His troubling words took me aback. "You, say that again."

"As tall as a tree and a grin as wide as can be."

"S-so you are just moving along with it?"

Ignoring my misgivings, his incoherent rambling carried on. "When Lord Vern arrives, you will be set free."

"Wait! Do you mean *now*? Is he coming here now?! Tell me!"

My head shifted left and right, my body on red alert for anything out of the ordinary. Unfortunately, or fortunately for me, all I saw were the ruins.

"So, if you're alone in the forest and have nothing to do."

I don't like where this is going. I let out an audible gulp, waiting for his next line that would surely rhyme with the last. His words had already trapped me in his web.

"Keep away from the wildlife, or he'll come for you."

After spitting out those last few lines, his eyes rolled back before he was sucked into the ground. All I could do was stare at the hole he had vanished into. *How anticlimactic! But how could he leave me with such foreboding lines?*

Then, my body froze in place. My limbs were as rigid as an old tree. But more than that, time had stopped.

My blood went ice cold. The color drained from my face. My whole being was now pale and filled with dread.

I could feel a thick pressure against my body with the force of an iron bar. "Gah!" The air was pounded from my chest, forcing me to the ground, with Frosty following soon after.

"Urgh... Kaa..." My speech was slurred and garbled. Even *I* couldn't understand what words might have been caught at the back of my throat. Sweat trickled down my forehead and seeped into my mouth, nearly causing me to spit. I held it in. Not because I wanted to, but because I had no other choice. My bones felt like jelly; I couldn't move a muscle if I wanted to. I was helpless.

"Grah... ahhh." I squeaked. The pain wasn't bad, but the feeling of being paralyzed and unable to flee from the looming presence made me more than a little distraught. It was absolutely terrifying.

"Does my presence inspire fear within you, *Demokai*?"

The voice was incredibly deep, as if it came from every tree in the forest. It had a sort of whimsical tone, but also carried a tremendous power within. I detected a fair amount of gentleness too—or so I thought. It was like an ocean; kind and beautiful, but could become cold and ruthless in an instant.

I mustered all my strength into cocking my head upwards to spot the creature that had put me in such a precarious position. And when I saw it—no—him, my eyes widened. He was as tall as a wyvern at nearly ten feet and possessed many of the same features. His entire body was covered in moss, branches, and fungi of various shades. Green horns shot out of his forehead like spears, slightly distracting from the soil-colored beard growing from his humanoid face. And the grin that he wore... I was certain it could swallow towns whole!

It was as the man had said before he conked out. "As tall as a tree, and grin as wide as can be."

His body was slender and overgrown like that of a dryad, but with the shape of a man. The Vern towered above me, exuding an aura of pure domination.

What did he call me? A 'Demokai'? Ugh, I wish I could at least talk!

Our gazes locked. I noticed a glint in his eyes that seemed to convey interest, though I wasn't sure why.

"Wh... What ha—happened?" I stuttered.

As if bitten by a venomous snake, my mouth grew numb immediately after I spoke, forcing me into silence once more. I was completely powerless—in both mind and body.

His wooden frame creaked in protest as he slowly bent down, allowing me to gauge that his length of his face was longer than my height. As he drew closer, the smell of old cinnamon and smoky wood bombarded my nostrils.

Turning away, he gazed longingly at the ruins and frowned. ***"You see, my forsaken Demokai, I was trusted by Lord Pan to protect this forest and its inhabitants with every fiber of my old being. However, above all, I must preserve life in its essence."***

His massive mouth never moved as he spoke, yet his voice burrowed itself deep within my mind. He inhaled for a good few seconds before puffing out a gust, startling a few birds above.

"A fortnight prior, visitors from another land paid a visit to my Lord's domain and instantly became infatuated with the marvelous flora and fauna that you have seen yourself. Drunk on the vitality of the forest, they attempted to purchase sacred beasts from our countrymen. It was an impossible feat, for Lord Pan made a law long ago that prohibited our denizens from departing the forest for their safety and the safety of those beyond it."

I sat and listened quietly, not even able to scratch my ear—which was really starting to itch. Frosty was silent as well, taking in his surroundings like a good boy. *It's more probable that he's thinking of what we might have for dinner tonight. He doesn't even understand we're in danger.* He really was a fiend of hunger.

The Vern continued. *"After the men were rejected, they exited the forest en masse. Their animosity and spite could be detected all the way from my secluded alcove, but I assumed all would be well. Clearly, I was a fool."*

A sigh escaped his solemn visage, but a fragment of his earlier smile soon resurfaced.

"They returned days later with hordes of humans skilled in all manner of combat, seeking to take what they wanted by force. They laid waste to Panatra first, holding our countrymen hostage, while poisoning and viciously slaughtering those who resisted."

He let out a stomach-churning groan, his bulging eyes looking at nothing in particular. It must have hurt him deeply to recount these events. I had never seen a tree with so many feelings.

"It was about that time when I fully awoke from my long slumber and put a stop to this whole fiasco.*"*

He stood and snatched the squirrel perched on one of the many branches adjacent to him, dropping it on his shoulder. It happily nibbled on a small acorn that was practically bursting from his neck. The Vern didn't notice in the slightest. He may have even been *happy* about it.

"By the time I had arrived, it was too late. Everything had perished. It was not by the natural cycle of the forest. No. It was vile and harrowing. I had to do something for the people. It was Lord Pan's will, after all. They protected Panatra with their lives to the very end. I had seldom spoken with them, only watching from afar as their great guardian. Many beings simply destroy and plunder to survive. I understood that as a being created to oversee the circle of life. However, I never knew humans could care for nature so... little."

He clenched a fist and brought it to his chest. *"I transformed the remaining countrymen into willow trees to preserve them. Even if they could not continue their lives, I wanted to immortalize them so that their sacrifices would never be forgotten. I'm sure Lord Pan would feel the same way if he was still here."*

He leaned back down.

"As for the invaders—I was not kind to them. They were feasted on by the denizens of the forest, crushed by my trees, and melded into food for our soil. I made some suffer by taking time to transform them and then whispered sweet tales of myself in their ears. It drove them mad. Insanity flowed through them, as if it were a replacement for barren intellect. I even spared a few to share the tale of consequences that will befall upon those who dare enter my forest."

Oh, no... Was I in trouble?

The Vern responded kindly, practically reading my mind. *"Do not fret, Demokai. You are safe. I have a deep respect for your k—well, you wouldn't like that as a reason. Not many are how they used to be. How about this? I communed with your frost wolf when I first approached, and he spoke highly of you as well explained the reason you came here. As you can see, I am doing my best to rebuild the city with my plants, but it won't be ready for some time."*

It seemed I was the one that had it all wrong. Frosty knew exactly what was up. *Such a clever boy!*

He stood up fully, engulfing me with his shadow. *"I have one task for you if you would be so kind as to accept. Please tell others that Panatra is no more."*

I made no effort to move. I knew I couldn't. He looked down at me with concern.

"Oh dear, my apologies. It seems I forgot to disable my immense aura. I was rather angry when I first laid eyes on you, but now I can see that you are no threat to my forest. I hope you can forgive me."

The pressure finally dispersed, permitting the natural color of life to return to my body. I gasped for air before coughing a few times and scratching my ear. "T-thanks. I'll do that." I pulled myself up and looked around. "By the way, what is a *Demokai*?"

It was then that I again heard the wind, the chattering of forest creatures, and the waterfall pressing deep into the lake with the polar opposite of a large crescendo.

He had vanished. Frosty and I were now alone in a ruined country of trees packed with poor and unfortunate souls. I brushed the dirt off my sweater and travel pants with a hint of irritation. *I have been doing this a lot lately, even when trying to avoid it.*

"Well, Frosty, this visit might have been short-lived, but it should still be enough data to satisfy the greedy heads of the Tribunal. Let's head back and earn an actual income."

Chapter 9
The City of the Shadowless

The road towards the unknown is a lonely one, so make sure you meet lots of people along the way.

—Boreas Tyrel

The kingdom I was visiting was larger than most, but the most interesting part of this particular country was its capital, Nemosa. It was a safe haven for merchants, and had many roadside stations with various oddities being sold left and right. It was one of the kingdoms that didn't worship any god in particular, but more of a mishmash of deities from the east and west. This decreased the chances of fanatics, but that didn't mean that some didn't skulk here, anyway.

I would have loved to pay them all a visit, but I didn't have time to dillydally. I had a job to do, after all. As someone who was spending her whole life traveling around this pious world in search of answers to a myriad of issues, it was always best to get paid for what I was doing.

I had just finished my trial run at an organization called the High Tribunal. It was similar to an adventurers' guild, where jobs could be picked from a wide selection to accommodate the skills and experience of the employee. They were what you would call a "big fish" and had their hands in a lot of major countries. People who worked for them did various jobs around the world, mostly for keeping the peace.

I, myself, was hired as a Resolver—someone who played detective and discovered the pinnacle of problems that plagued the people of a nation, and sometimes dealt with things at a smaller level if needed. As long as I got it done, I got paid. And I *would* get it done.

"Though, I really want to plunge right into one of the tombs of the death gods. I heard there are some pretty cool treasures waiting to be found. I bet they would fetch a pretty penny. If only I had a party…"

I rambled to myself as I sat atop Frosty, awaiting inspection outside of Nemosa. Unlike most capitals, it was at the western entrance of the country, instead of being smack in the middle.

The city was well-maintained, but also relatively old compared to what I was used to. The entire gate was crafted from fine marble, with columns ascending on each side. Shiny steel and obsidian were the more common materials used for protection. Marble gave off the prettiest of looks, but it didn't really hold up under siege.

It took some time, but they eventually let me in… after putting Frosty away.

The moment I stepped through the gate, I caught a whiff of foreign food carried on the cool breeze. Strange assortments of shops were lined up in a neat row under the midday sun; I knew I would be in for a fun time.

I waltzed up to a vendor while keeping a hand on my hair to stop the updraft from afflicting it. The man I approached was selling wooden dolls, a fake smile plastered across his aged face. The people who I had passed so far all had something in common, and judging from his look, I was sure this man was no different.

"Hello. I'm a traveler. I'll get straight to the point: Where's your shadow? It seems like everyone around here doesn't have one." I might have come off a little brash, but my curiosity had long overwhelmed my manners.

When I said that, his grip tightened, nearly crushing the doll in his hand. His curly hair was greasy at the tips and covered by a beige hat. "You customer?" He had a thick accent, one that wasn't used to speaking my language for long periods of time.

"Feel free to speak in your tongue if that makes it easier. I want the full story if you would be so kind."

The man spoke again. "Are you a customer, traveler?"

I was jolted awake by the archaic words he spoke.

Wow. Was that... Oria? It had been a while since I heard anyone use the old language, so my comprehension of it wasn't the best. I could get by pretty well back when I first learned it. Surely it wouldn't be that difficult to climb back on the Oria wagon.

Most places I visited still openly used their own dialects and languages, but Common Tongue was the most widely employed, especially in places that welcomed tourists. Most were like that, but some smaller countries and kingdoms still held onto the older languages, refusing to teach their people Common, resulting in them receiving fewer visitors and income than anywhere else.

I guess I should have studied up on this place.

"Can be," I responded with the sincerity of a predator doing anything to warm up to its prey. "Reason I asked was because I am Tribunal."

Hey, I did say I was rusty. The words were flowing through my mind slowly at first, but I was quickly recalling the vocab and grammar I had learned maybe two years prior. Though with my memory, it was hard to say.

"I see. I am relieved." He seemed to regain his cool after hearing that and gave a dry smile. "Someone has finally come to stop that damn peddler! You don't need to buy anything. Allow me to spill my guts free of charge."

* * *

After meeting with multiple shopkeepers and citizens, they all gave me the same story: a masked figure offered to show them tricks with their shadows for one rod—an outdated currency that had little value in a land of merchants, but a lot outside of it. After they saw a few tricks, they would then ask for their shadow back. Instead of receiving it, as per the agreement, they were instead charged an exorbitant fee, resulting in most of them being forced to leave empty-handed.

Some also stated that whenever they tried to find the mysterious peddler, the person would always disappear into thin air, making them nearly impossible to track.

But why does a person need that many shadows?

I kind of wanted to find out, and for my job, I had to.

* * *

After a few more hours of scouring the capital, I turned in for the night. The sun was getting low, and I needed to secure a place of lodging. It didn't take long for me to find an inn, though I didn't know if I would be able to speak Common or not. *My Oria has got me this far, so it can't be too bad.*

When I stepped inside, there was a masked figure at the reception desk, too lost in thought to speak with a potential customer. "Hello," I called out. "I would like a room for two nights, please."

The masked figure nodded and spoke in a young, feminine voice. "Thank you for your patronage. Please pay three rods and write your name down in this ledger. Also, I love your outfit! The eyepatch makes you seem mysterious and cool, but I never see short-cut skirts and sweaters like that in this boring place!" she said energetically.

She had responded in Common, which was strange. She spoke it just as naturally as I did. Perhaps she could understand Oria, but not speak it.

"Uh, thanks," I muttered back in Common while filling out my name.

"Ooh! Lethe, huh? That's quite a strange name, though it's kind of pretty as well. I like it."

"It's also pretty strange to be running an inn with a mask on and speaking Common when there was a chance I wouldn't understand you. Who is more peculiar, hmm?" I retorted, irritated by her comment.

I felt the air slightly change around us. "Oh, so *that* was Oria? You speak similar to the children here, so I wasn't sure. Pops taught me many languages on the road, and many were derived from ancient Oria. It also isn't hard to tell you aren't from here because of your uncommon clothing that would be impractical for our typical weather—and, of course, that shadow hanging behind you..."

I could bet money that she was grinning under that mask, but she was right. The people here wore thick coats with little underneath, save for a shirt or sleeveless dress. Heatwaves were common. Most merchants and stores didn't bother selling otters—I mean—sweaters. The Oria words for those two were stupidly similar.

I was a little hurt by her insult. Come to think of it, no one had ever said my pronunciation of the words was decent. I wish they *had* said something. *And here I thought I remembered the language rather well. Wait... Did she say shadow?*

A distinct sound had passed through my ears as I was daydreaming. I glanced downwards at the click of the key she had placed on the table, but before I could grab it, she swiftly covered it with her hand.

"Hey, foreigner-with-a-strange-name, would you like to see a little trick? It'll only cost one rod. And it will be super cool! You can tell all your friends back home about it. It'll be worth your while. I *promise*." She seemed disturbingly enthusiastic about it. Her body was just bursting with vigor—just like a certain hooligan I was hunting.

A smile tugged at the corners of my lips when she said that. *There's no way my luck is this good.*

I handed her a small, silver cylinder—a rod. After snatching it up, the receptionist stepped from behind the counter. Blind confidence practically oozed from every pore of her being. I had a feeling she was planning something profound and despicable.

For someone who had called my clothing foolish, she was wearing a dark suit with visible black socks. Etched on her mask was a white eye and a black eye. If anything, she would have a harder time when the weather got rough. Fortunately for both of us, the sky was clear, and the breeze was cool.

The mystery girl crossed her arms. "For this trick, I will require your shadow. Is that okay?"

I dropped my bag on the table. "Sure, whatever," I said indifferently.

She stuck out her hand and thrust it my way with so much drama that I could have been at the front row of a play.

I visibly cringed.

My shadow was already gone by the time I turned around. It was now nested behind the girl, who was a few inches shorter than me, not fitting her form in the slightest.

"Now, let us get on with it!" she hollered.

Without moving a finger, she forced my shadow to dance and run around like a puppet. It juggled, flailed its arms and did an assortment of other stuff before simmering down back behind the girl. The act was over.

Well, the act with my shadow, that is.

I gave her a short round of applause, which she happily basked in.

"Is there a reason you can't make my shadow do all that fun stuff while it's still attached to me?"

Her fluid movements suddenly became static. "Um... what?" she said with worry trickling into her voice. I may not have been able to see behind her mask, but I was sure that I was the only one to pose such an obvious question. "It—it can't be done without being attached to m-me, yeah."

Really? You don't sound so sure to me.

"I see... That's a shame," I murmured.

A pregnant pause permeated through the room.

"Well, then. Can I have my shadow back?"

"Ooh-hu-huu," she mumbled under her mask. "Sure, you can... For 200 rods!"

A dramatic pause descended upon us once more; this time perfectly planned by one of the parties present. I decided not to bite. Why give her the satisfaction? I had my own plans, and she just proved to me she was who I thought she was.

"Whaaaat?! M-my shadow for 200? Give it baaaack!"

The con artist was probably expecting a response like that. She had even removed her mask; a stupid grin slid onto her face. I guessed her to be no older than fifteen.

She continued to stare at me intently, as if waiting for some special response. Her smugness was as irritating as her attitude.

I didn't give it to her. Not even a blink.

"..."

"..."

Eventually, she broke the silence. "So, will you, um... pay?"

"No."

"Really?"

"Nope."

"So... you really won't—"

"Of course not! Do you take me for some kind of fool?"

"I mean… yeah?" She slapped the mask back on, probably to snicker from under it.

I'd had enough. "Just give her back," I hissed.

"No way! Finders keepers!" she said with flailing hands, squealing with delight. "She's mine now! Ha-ha-haaa!" As she laughed, her mask became loose and fell into her arms. She had such a haughty smile that I desperately wanted to make a new ice sculpture. Luckily, I wouldn't have to go that far to rain on this annoying girl's parade.

This time, I was the one to hold out my hand. "Not so fast!" I flashed her my Resolver badge. "Do you know what this is?" I could tell she was racking her brain, a puzzled reaction most likely hiding behind that obscene mask.

"Something round and golden with a fat snake on it?"

"It's a fish."

"Oh, cool. A fish."

"Yes," I confirmed. "A *World Eater* to be exact."

That seemed to be the straw that shattered the camel's back.

"Hold up! Wait, wait, wait. What's that?!" she shrieked with fear.

I laughed internally at her expense. *She's kinda cute when she's flustered.*

"Your face is scaring me! What a creepy smile. Lord Harrow would be pleased with my work!"

I ignored her false claims and looped back around to my reason for displaying the badge. "I work for the Tribunal, and if you don't cease this blatant extortion and scamming, I am going to have to take you into custody."

Technically, I only had the authority to report a problem to someone higher up the ladder, not arrest anyone. But she didn't need to know that. I held all the cards.

She dropped to the ground in a begging position. "W-w-wait! Waaaaait! Please! I am only doing this to get something that was taken from me! I thought if I gathered enough of them then—Hey! Stop looking at me with such a devious grin. I'm being serious here!"

Blame the eyepatch! I was just grinning normally.

"What were you saying before that rude comment?" I raised an eyebrow. I could tell she was on the verge of tears.

Yup. She was sniffling. *What a pain.*

I sighed. "Just spit it out. Tell me your story, and I might help you. And how about you keep that silly mask off your face for good?"

"Y-yeah, sure." She quickly peeled it off, not caring about the damage that her recklessness would cause to the relic. Now I got a full view, without the smug attitude.

Behind the mask was the pitiful face of a silver-haired girl with bright-blue eyes and black-rimmed glasses. Her short hair was tied back into a ponytail. How her mask could fit everything behind it was a mystery to me, but I was certain some sort of enchantment was involved.

"Thank you! I knew I would finally find someone that wouldn't treat me like a child or a nuisance! Lord Harrow, dreams really do come true!"

That was funny. She thought she was acting mature. Her runny nose didn't help with that. She also seemed to worship one of the more underground death gods—the ones those edgy teens always sought after.

Figures...

She took me to her room in the inn, and I sat there sipping a cup of hot chocolate that Umbrea had so kindly procured for me. My sips were loud and obnoxious, but that didn't stop her from spilling her guts.

This girl, Umbrea, was the normal daughter of a merchant who lived in this country's capital, Renum. Her father was tragically killed after "somewhat ripping someone off" as she put it, and she was forced into working at the inn to pay off the debts he had left in his wake.

One day, she joined a group of adventurers as a baggage carrier in one of the many Tombs of the Death God dungeons. For her contribution, she was given a dusty, old, coal-colored lamp with strange symbols etched across its surface. No one she knew could decipher the ancient language, which filled her heart with sorrow. Umbrea took it back to the inn and attempted to clean it. That was when something strange occurred.

A large, humanoid spirit made entirely out of shadows appeared before her. From how she frantically explained it, he was muscular and possessed a chiseled face with crimson eyes that made her skin crawl. His arms were inhibited by black chains clamped onto his wrists like a prisoner, while his lower half swirled around the mouth of the lamp like a trapped ghost. I didn't know if this was an accurate description of the so-called spirit, but I really didn't care enough to press further. Her explanations were already eccentric enough.

And so, this spirit asked her to make anyone wish that was within his power. She briefly debated, but then excitedly asked him for the power to control and manifest shadows—shadow magic. Her reasoning was that she'd always thought it sounded cool, and having the power to manipulate shadows wasn't a common type of magic in this era. I hadn't even heard of it before that day and I had read many tomes and grimoires.

After she'd made her wish, she was whisked away to another realm, devoid of everything but darkness. She had said, "I didn't know how much time passed, but it felt like I was there for months, meditating as the spirit told me. Pretty freaky."

She came out of the dark world a changed girl. One filled with mana and a unique gift not of this world. She felt amazing.

The thing that this spirit neglected to tell her was that her shadow would be the payment. Of course, living without a shadow is doable—and I would have sold mine in the same position, but no one wants to give something up if they don't have to.

She only learned this after the contract was complete, leaving her the same as everyone in Nemosa—shadowless. Despite wallowing in her despair, Umbrea concocted an idea. The gathering of shadows from others to offer in exchange with the spirit for the return of her own.

Of course, she never even checked with him to see if the transaction was actually possible. I wonder how she would respond if told her that her work was all for nothing. She was already a wanted criminal, albeit more like a petty thief than anything. Shadows were not even something that counted as a possession, but I would be just as angry if I had my own taken away. I just suppressed it for the time being. My job came first.

At the end of it all, I looked her right in the eyes—or eye—in my case.

"So... you want me—one of your victims—to go inside this thing with you, and bargain for your shadow back? Can't you do that by yourself? Why in the world would you need me? We just met twenty minutes ago." *My services are not cheap, either. Look at that dumb expression on her face. I bet I can milk her for a decent amount.*

"I—I know, but... W-what if he says no? Then, what will I do?"

I shrugged. "Oh, I don't know... Live without a shadow, maybe?" I told her with the greatest amount of bluntness I could offer. "How hard can it be? Many others are doing that thanks to a certain *someone*."

Umbrea's eyes dropped to her feet, but she didn't give in. "I don't wanna!" she wailed like a toddler and flailed her arms about. "I want my shadow back! We need each other! She needs me!"

"I take it you require my help?"

She nodded vigorously. "Yup! I'm confident the two of us could easily take him down. So, what do you say, Lethe? Wanna help me get my shadow back?"

"No."

"Oh."

She paused for a moment, most likely conjuring up a way to force me to stay. I, on the other hand, was ready to walk out the door and hit the hay.

"But you see, this spirit—he can grant you, like, any wish. Is that not worth helping me in my time of need?"

While that was tempting, she already proved that the wish wasn't granted for free, and I quite like all my body parts. In fact, I'm already missing one.

"Nope. I'm good."

"Pleeeeease!" Umbrea gazed at me with teary, upturned eyes. Yeah, this was a little embarrassing to watch. "My shadow needs my help!"

Pretty sure a shadow doesn't need anything, but she'd said one thing that we both agreed on—we both wanted our shadows back. I also felt like she would use her key to break into my room and continue her whining if I left. She really was just a kid.

Fine. I have some time to kill, anyway. And who knows, maybe it will be fun. Yeah... probably not.

Gently placing the cup on the table, I let out a groan of annoyance and stood up. "If I help you, I want to stay here, free of charge."

"B-but I can't—"

"I also want a month's worth of your salary."

She was even more baffled. "But I've been saving—"

"Well, you can save some more," I said, my tone emphatic and stern.

Someone needed to reel this girl in and show her the real world. Unfortunately, it looked like that responsibility fell upon my capable shoulders. *Ugh... I really do attract the weirdest people.*

"O-okay..."

Praise the gods! She had *finally* quieted down. Even though I had graciously accepted her offer, she still seemed grumpy about being screwed out of so much money. I would be too, but then again, I wasn't an idiot.

I frowned and sighed. "Do you want the help of a Resolver or *not?*" I tried to sound threatening, and it must have worked because her eyes grew wide with fear.

She quickly nodded. "Yes! Yes, please."

"*Ahem.* So, Umbrea, how do we get in there? Do we need a magic spell or artifact or what?" I just hoped she actually had a plan. If not, I would wring it out of her like a wet towel.

She shook her head. "Nope! I just gotta turn us into shadows and fly us in. Then I can give that guy a piece of my mind!" She held up a balled fist, proof of her conviction. I guess.

However, before we did all of this, I had to make something clear. "I hope you know this already, but under no circumstance will you offer the shadows of the citizens you stole to that evil spirit. No matter what, you'll give them all back, okay?"

You could call me a good person, or you could call me someone who wanted to get paid. I was fine with either.

"Okay..." she meekly agreed. It sounded pretty cute.

After ironing out our plan of attack, I relaxed my hands on my neck. "Well then, let's get going. I want to turn in early tonight and eat something delicious. You guys have breakfast, lunch, and dinner here, right?" I've been to places where there was only one time to eat in a day and others where there were far too many times.

"Of course! We great food from all over the country and—"

"It's free, right? For me?"

"Well, I can't ju—"

"Hmm... I think I'll report you to my Tribunal superior after all. Have a good evening."

"It's free! Yup! Totally! It's free... I just have to give my owner a bit of my paycheck... for this entire month," she muttered.

Naturally, I ignored her. I did, however, do a mental fist pump. *Free lodging, payment and food, whoo! Va-cat-ion! No food tastes better than when it is free!*

I slowly brought my right hand up into the air, where two rings curled around my fingers. One was tightly wrapped around the middle finger, an icy-blue crystal embedded in it. The other was perched on top of my pointer with a large ruby. I could only activate one at a time due to the absurd amount of mana they required, but I was excited to make use of this new artifact.

"Let's get going. This could be a good chance for me to test out the newest addition to my limited arsenal."

* * *

After setting the lamp down on the small table in her room, we were ready. With a minute of silence, Umbrea focused on a spell, and hurled a ball of darkness my way before doing the same for herself.

I felt a quick puff of dry air before the weight of my body seemed to vanish. My skin tone became hazy and translucent, reminiscent of death gas. Through the clouded darkness, I could actually see the ground through my hand! She had sent our bodies to an ethereal plane, similar to where the ring sent Frosty. The main difference was that we were made entirely of dark, blurry smoke. I was curious what would happen if I blew on Umbrea, but if she got scattered around, there was a chance I would be stuck this way for good.

"Here I come, my shadow!" she declared with unrivaled confidence. Her body broke into particles, flowing into the maw of the lamp, with me quickly following her.

The world inside the lamp was vast, but lacked any form of depth or detail. The long horizon was dyed a faint orange, while nothing existed beneath us but a boundless sea of clouds. A distinct smell of old incense filled my nostrils, disrupting me from this dream-like world. I instinctively hugged my shoulders despite the air not feeling cold in the slightest. Besides the strange smell, everything else felt constructed and artificial, like an illusion or figment of my imagination. *Which in a way, it is when you think that we've been sucked inside an ancient lamp.* I was blown away by how expansive the space was inside such a tiny lamp. This was a true display of magic. No room for deceit or hyperbole. It was simply stunning.

"There's nothing here. Are you sure we are in the right lamp?"

"What do you mean? There are no other lamps!" she hollered. She was smiling rather brightly, despite my teasing.

Then she ruined it.

"Heeey! Shadow Spiriiit! Come on out!"

Umbrea continued to cry out, exhausting her lungs and my patience in the process. It went on for a good five minutes before something finally happened.

"Girl! I was sleeping! How dare you interru—Oh, hello, newcomer. Can I grant you a wish? It can be anything but death, world destruction, or love." He gazed directly at my body, sizing me up. His stare then shifted to my face before falling back to my chest. **"Perhaps healing your eye, improving your bust size, or perhaps adding a little height?"**

"Excuse me?!"

Umbrea grabbed my arms, making sure I couldn't throw myself at that piece of trash. How dare he make fun of my proportions!

I spat a flurry of insults. "Dumbass! Idiot! Monster! Smokescreen! Ghost face!"

"Lethe, c'mon! I know you're a little self-conscious, but I need to talk to him!" She pleaded with me, giving me a full dose of puppy dog eyes. What could I do against that?

I quickly settled down and took a few deep breaths to regain my composure. For a second there, it was as if our positions had swapped. *Can't have that happen. I'm supposed to be the mature one. Wait—what did she mean about knowing that I was self-conscious?*

"Okay, I'm fine now."

"Right. Well, Mr. Spirit, can I have my shadow back, *please*?"

Did she really expect that to work?

He crossed his arms and raised a dark eyebrow. **"First of all, I am Dark Spirit Efergus, not some lowly spirit. Second of all, I granted your wish, did I not, girl? This was only fair compensation."**

"B-but... couldn't I have given you money or something instead? You didn't tell me the shadow was part of the deal!"

The edgy-sounding spirit gestured to his chiseled, shirtless body and ghost tail. **"Does it *look* like I need money?"**

"Er... Well, no. But what do you need my shadow for?"

He shrugged with a small smile. **"Nothing, really. I just relish in taking that which is precious from those who seek my help."**

Cheeky bastard.

Before he had made a jab at my body, I might have considered his proposal. But if I didn't know what he would take, it would probably do a lot more harm than good. *Who does he think he is? I hope I can slaughter him after negotiations break down... That would make my day.* My lips drew back into a grin. I felt better already.

"Is there any way I can get my shadow back without giving you anything else more precious?"

Wow, talk about brazen. Umbrea was naïve to think that a question like that would bear any fruit. She must have not been exposed to the real wor—

"There is a way."

Wait, what? Am I the delusional one?

"Really?! How?" She instantly perked up at the idea of being able to get her shadow back for a lesser fee.

"By defeating me, naturally. How else could I part with any of my possessions?"

"Oh..." She shrunk back behind me in silence. Had she already given up after we came all this way? *What happened to all that confidence from when we planned to best him?*

I scowled at her cowering form. "What did you think it would be? Something easy? Haven't you ever read a book with one of those awful morals at the end? Happiness doesn't come cheap. Don't look at me with those eyes— Well, okay, then. Fine! I guess we are doing this!"

This girl just doesn't play fair!

"Thanks, Lethe. I knew I could count on a friend like you!"

Friend? Was that what we were? *Rock told me that a friend was someone you spent a lot of time with, had mutual interests, and liked each other. I have only known you for like an hour, Umbrea!*

"Yeah... thanks," I squeezed out between the waves of thoughts sloshing around in my head. I was suppressing my laughter. Was I a bad person?

Nah, no way.

His deep voice bellowed through the whole realm. **"It seems you two are prepared. It's been a while, but I am excited to stretch my limbs either way."** He flexed his muscles in a very overbearing fashion. **"No do-overs or retries. Let's do this!"**

Out of his body oozed darkness, coating his hazy form in ebony clouds that rapidly lengthened and bulged in size before disappearing entirely. They revealed a terrifying new form.

A massive dragon the size of an adult mammoth, its body composed of coiling shades that moved like snakes. He floated before us, nostrils flared, and his striking, crimson eyes with a feral aura looked down on us. And, yeesh! That was some nasty morning breath permeating from his maw.

Wow! This is a real dragon? I wonder if the Cursed One looked like this. It's pretty menacing.

His wispy wings formed a small tempest around him, and the clouds billowed with every stroke.

Umbrea shot me a look of unease, sweating up a storm. "Uh, Lethe... Do you think we can beat *that*?"

Now you ask?!

"No idea," I responded with a straight face, rolling up my sleeves. I could feel myself sweating a little as well. "Can't say I've ever faced a dragon within a lamp before."

"Oh... I guess that's fair." I feel like that wasn't the answer she wanted to hear.

Despite her lack of confidence, shadows were expelled from Umbrea's hand and soon took the form of a lengthy scythe. I thrust my palm out, keen on trying the ring I'd obtained recently. With both of these, perhaps we would stand a chance.

"Oh, ho! Feisty ones, aren't you? Come at me when you are ready."

I wasted no time. I burst through the air at a supersonic speed, embracing the fragments of wind dancing over my body. It was beyond human limits, but because of the forms we had taken when we entered the lamp, it felt as natural as running. *I hope we can damage him.* I set the pace of the battle, releasing a barrage of flameballs from a hand that was now smoldering like a burning crucible. Umbrea covered my flank by releasing waves of shadow spears from her body, each finding a different spot to impale. It was a symphony of fire and darkness working together.

A smile crept across my face as I witnessed the results of my new ring in action. It was called the Crucible Ring, and the more mana its opponent possessed, the more potent and effective its flames became. *This thing really is a special artifact! The fact that my gift from Rock can keep up with it means that he might have been a rather important figure if he wasn't spending all his time in that cave. If people knew that he was still around... Well, I'm sure he'll be fine.*

The dragon let out a howl that threw me from my thoughts. As I paused in my assault, his hollow laughter echoed around us.

"You're going to have to do better than THAT!" he cackled with glee.

His massive charcoal-colored wings had shifted to shield his body against my flames. Somehow, he managed to contort his body and avoid every spear. Umbrea was still too far away to get an actual swing in.

Damn. I didn't want to admit it, but this guy was good. I glanced back at Umbrea. She seemed to be struggling to think of another way to take him down. I sped back to her, avoiding a shadow breath attack that had lashed out across the distance. The heat stung my body and bare legs, leaving behind a cluster of blisters. Apparently our ghostlike forms were irrelevant.

"You can manipulate any kind of shadow, right?" I asked. My breathing was both erratic and haggard as I tried to swallow the pain. It felt somewhat ironic that I was the one to get burned—if only a little.

She nodded. "Mhm. Of course, I can!"

"Okay, Miss Confident. I got a plan. Even someone like you couldn't possibly mess it up."

I say that, but my faith in her is already at an all-time low. Besides, what do we have to lose? Eh, a lot but this is Umbrea's fight. She'll clearly be the one to face the consequences. Yeah, I think that's fair. Come to think of it—what are the stakes?.

Umbrea surrounded herself in a cloud of writhing shadows, and thrust her body towards the dragon at breakneck speed. The thick layers of shade managed to hold against the dragon's noxious breath, and she continued forward, undeterred.

This could be promising.

The dragon extended his joints to drive a claw towards the approaching comet that was Umbrea. His hulking jaw followed suit, attempting to chomp her in half.

It would have gone that way too, if not for my support from the rear.

Bolts of smoldering flames streaked from my palm like spears, flying toward the dragon with the speed of a raging ram. He eyed me with contempt—exactly what I wanted. It meant he wasn't watching Umbrea.

Before long, she collided with him, embedding herself in his chest like a tick.

"W-what are you doing?!" he shrieked, wings and tail twitching in fear. **"How *dare* you touch my sublime body! Stooop!"**

"Being useful!" she shouted back from inside his smokey chest.

Since he was a shadow himself, it would only make sense that she would be able to control him—at least a bit—especially with full contact. Of course, someone of his caliber was able to easily resist, but the time that she bought distracting him was all I needed.

I shot towards him at the speed of an arrow. The feeling of weightlessness was something I still wasn't used to, but it did little to stop me from reaching my target and placing a frozen hand on his spiny back.

I had no idea if it would work on a shadow, but hey, anything with a solid form is fair game for this puppy. If his breath could bathe me in flames, I was sure I could harm him as well.

Starting with his chest, ice poured out of him like a swarm of insects departing from their assaulted nest to defend their queen. Once it was completely encased within a frozen tomb, Umbrea released herself from his body, and propelled away.

"Booyah!" she yelled.

Now all that was left was for me to finish this.

With his entire form entirely consumed by the frost, I let loose a barrage of flames from my hand, intending to melt him to oblivion—and it actually worked? Once the flames dispersed, nothing else of the great shadow dragon remained.

"Wooh-hooh! We did it, Lethe! We did it!" Umbrea hugged me after smashing into me from afar. It hurt, but why did getting hugged feel so nice? Well, it was until—

"Ughhhh! Stop! You are h-hurting me. Please! Umbrea!" I tried to push her away, but her grip was solid. I could do nothing besides sigh with exasperation.

But then I got a face-full of her bosom that clobbered out my vision. At least they weren't big enough to cause suffocation. It still made me mildly uncomfortable, though. I really wasn't a fan of being touched by others—especially when I barely knew them. It was like being stabbed with thin needles. Even her warm embrace made my body feel cold and out of sync.

However, she *did* do a good job, so I allowed it for a bit.

The moment for celebration had come and gone, yet she continued to cling to me. I had had enough.

"Take this, fiend!" I quipped.

"Owww! Why did you pinch my chest like that? It hurt!"

"You were smothering me! Never touch me without permission," I scolded. "And permission probably wouldn't change my response either."

"Ah, two budding flowers in their youth. Simply adorable."

Huh?

We both brought up our guards as the shadow dragon's voice returned. I spun my head in every direction, trying to pinpoint the source. Apparently, it was coming from... everywhere.

"Oh? Did you think you actually killed me? No, of course not. You just destroyed a medium I forged to interact with you."

"Does that mean we need to fight you again? Lethe! I don't wanna go inside the dragon agaaaain! It smelled like burnt fish!"

"Well, I'm not doing that."

"Waaah? Lethe! I thought we were friends!"

You really like to throw that word around whenever it is convenient for you. "Where the heck did you get that idea fr—"

"Girls, please, Let me finish."

While I couldn't see his face, the sound of his voice made his words come off as blatantly arrogant and demeaning.

"What do you want, now?" I snarled.

"You two have indeed defeated me, even if not entirely. I will give the pitiful girl her shadow back, as promised. I just wanted to let you know that you couldn't kill an immortal being like me."

A haughty smile bloomed across my face as I realized something. "Say hypothetically, what would happen to you if we destroyed the lamp."

"Uh, well, you see… Don't do that or you'll regret it."

I had a good feeling that the color had just drained from his face. "Yeah, sure. I'm quivering in my boots at what you could do." *Where's all that hubris now? Huh?*

"T-that totally won't work! Now, get out!"

An invisible force shoved us into the sky until we couldn't go any higher. Everything went dark, and when I opened my eye, we were back in the inn, bodies restored to their natural weight and color.

"What a petty spirit," I spat. "Maybe I should just—"

Before I could get a hold of the wretched thing, Umbrea swiftly snatched it up and cradled it like a newborn. I think I heard some groaning noises, but it could have been my imagination. "No! The lamp is mine! It's an expensive relic! Don't huuuurt him!"

I let out a pained sigh. "Can you just give me the key to my room, *please*?"

* * *

Frosty got to eat as much as he wanted in our room, thanks to the money from Little Orphan Umbrea's paycheck. I, on the other hand, decided to buy a few books that were on sale to peruse some *real* literature. The books I completed felt fresh and riveting, completely impossible to put down!

I wouldn't ever say it out loud, but I think I might be in love with mushy-gushy rom-coms over my previous interest of murder mystery and detective tales. Even my immense pleasure of reading heroic journeys of adventure were slowly being corrupted by this wild taste. *I'm sorry, Boreas.*

Was I betraying my original purpose for even starting this journey? Perhaps, but I had already passed the point of no return and I didn't really care at this point. Besides, someone special had once gotten me into the love genre. There was no way I could forsake what she adored. *Especially when it's this damn good.* Anyway, keep that to yourself.

* * *

On the night before my departure, that annoying anomaly approached me again. She arrived with five hard knocks that shuddered the door frame.

I hesitated for a moment, but ultimately decided to let her in. Now, once again trapped in an area with only her, she immediately got to the point.

"You know, I told you everything about me, but I still know next to nothing about you, Lethe. That's not really fair, right? Friends should know everything about each other."

I was a bit ruffled by her bold statement. Her kind words seeped through my mind like sweet honey.

I guess it wouldn't hurt to try.

A wistful sigh escaped my lips. "You know what? You're absolutely right." I pointed to the bed, an impish smile creeping across my face. It wasn't too different from that of the creature who periodically plagued my dreams. *We'll get to him later.* "You're going to sit there and not make a peep until I finish, *got it?*"

If I was going to unlock my heart, then I needed her to act her age—or maybe a bit older.

For some reason, Umbrea broke into a cold sweat. "So, like, how long is this gonna take because the tavern isn't open too late, and I still need to—"

"Sit."

"Y-yes, ma'am."

I liked it when she was obedient.

After she firmly attached herself to the bed, I opened my heart. This was the second time I had ever done it, but it didn't feel that strange. *Maybe I really like talking about myself.*

She had been quiet the whole time, but the moment I clamped up, she let her mouth run wild. "She sounds like such a cool person! And the meeting with that god is both creepy and hilarious, but what really got me thinking was that your grandfather is a rock—like, an actual rock?"

I shook my head. This was expected. "No. That was just his name. Were you even listening?"

"Of course! There was so much to take in, and I came up with a lot of responses since I like asking questions, but you made me wait until the end, so now it's all kinda... garbled."

"I guess that's fair, but he is no rock—well, he has rocks on him—but he's not a rock. His name is Rock-Howler and he's a golem."

The unfamiliar term resulted in Umbrea giving me a puzzled look. "What's that?"

"A golem is... Well, you know... big, burly, and made out of stones."

"Sounds a *lot* like a large rock to me."

I cast a sidelong glance at the door. "I think it's about time you—"

"N-no! Wait! I have so many more questions to ask. Please!"

And so, the helpless girl kept me up all night with her pestering. It was annoying, but I realized the next day that I had never once stopped smiling.

* * *

Before I departed, Umbrea came to see me off while dressed in a white blouse and shorts. Her lamp and mask were nowhere to be seen.

"So... You're really leaving?" She wore a ghastly expression on her adorable face. It seemed I had made an impact on her.

"Yeah. Like I said, I'm a Resolver. I have my own reasons for traveling around, but this job is a vital outlet to get paid while I do."

"Oh... I see." She twiddled her thumbs, looking down at the ground—at her shadow.

Her gaze refused to meet mine for a moment, but then she expectantly looked up at me with renewed resolve and vigor. I knew what she was going to ask before she even opened her loudmouth.

"By chance, could I—"

"Nope! Sorry. I travel alone." I stole a glance at my shadow, who was now back where she belonged, my eye dropping to one of my rings. *Well, not entirely alone.*

Umbrea hung her head. *Why must she give off such a somber vibe when I'm about to leave? Save the sadness for after I'm gone!*

"Look, Umbrea, I have a lot of places I need to see. Perhaps one day we will meet again. Just don't follow me... *please.*"

She looked up at me, a small smile appearing. "Lame! But I—I get it. Well, then..." She gave me a little salute. "Thanks for all your help! Because of you, I also decided to sell that pesky lamp for the funds I'll be needing soon. I'm sure we will meet again."

"Oh? What makes you say that?"

At this point, she looked me dead in the eye with a smile so infectious that I nearly matched her. "Did I forget to tell you? Ever since I gave everyone their shadows back, they filed an official complaint about me at the Town Hall. I just got exiled this morning! Isn't that sweet? I'm free! I'll be leaving tomorrow."

My face twitched.

"Uh... *What?*"

Chapter 10
The Horn

With anger and embarrassment, I often look back on how I treated my parents. There is nothing wrong with being different from the norm. The rarest gems always glow the brightest. The same could be said about the many types of denizens on this unique rock.

—Boreas Tyrel

How could this have happened? Was it in the food? No... Well, maybe. Perhaps I should look back on the events of the previous day.

I stayed in a rather posh inn in Zeuss, the holy capital of the Olympos. Yes, it was very on the nose. This entire land worshiped twelve gods, which made it tiers above any other country that I had been to in terms of devotion. The capital was especially zealous with the teachings of the king of these gods. It was also known for having a rather poor history of ethics. At least that's what the independent paper said; I'd been handed one on my first day here. Of course, it could have been simple slander, but I had a feeling it was as close to the truth as they could publish.

Apparently, Olympos was built on the slavery of beast people, elves, and other races that were visually different from humans. Our continent was predominantly human, tragically. For so many other races to be present, this particular country was beyond peculiar. Zeuss was infamous for their high arrest and execution rate of the non-humans who lived here in disguise. They were said to be caught daily, which I found hard to swallow.

Rumors passed from place to place about the possibility of demon worshipers hidden within their ranks. Based on what I'd read about the history of the most notorious ancient cults, that seemed unlikely. I think they used the boogeyman of cultists as an excuse to harass the poor beast folk and other races. I felt bad, but there wasn't much I could do about it. Most people I had come across worshiped the gods to a fanatical degree, and most of the gods only loved humans. It would have been nice to chat with one that was more commonly revered than the one I had once encountered.

I didn't even have a choice in the matter when I became their disciple, but our exchange of words resurfaced from the back of my mind as if it had happened yesterday.

"Of course." There was an edge to her voice that cut through my words. "You get no say in the matter. Be grateful. My blessing is already boring its way into your blighted vessel."

"Uh, well, I know that. Just don't expect any offerings or whatever people do these days."

"I'm glad you know your place."

Yeesh. Just thinking about that experience sent shivers down my spine. I tried to shake it off. That fickle god can't get me here. Probably.

Anyway, the prejudice had resulted in humans being on top in any god-built nation, while everyone else was left to the wayside. There were some other remote places that were just as religious. I also knew for a fact that gods still reigned over parts of the beast continents. An old tome I'd found back in a mage country was written in a language from a race said to be made by one of the oldest of gods. I wonder how they felt about our monopoly of freedom. *All this thinking is making me depressed, but how can I not be?*

I *had* nothing to worry about. Now...

"So why do I have *this* sticking out of my head?" I asked the big, oval mirror in my bedroom. It reflected an older teen, her face filled with a fine mix of anguish and panic.

Just what in the world is this? The only creature I knew of with a horn this dark was that cursed dragon without a name. But he was a fairytale from long ago. No one had seen him, and surely no one worshiped him. Speaking of horns...

I'd had it again—that dream of the many-eyed fiend with four arms, and a wicked smile. Whenever I thought I'd seen the last of him, he always seemed to show up again. Was it a coincidence, or was it the root cause? I had no way of proving it, but the former was my main suspicion.

I ran my hand up and down the horn protruding from the right side of my head. It was smooth and firm to the touch, but somehow delicate at the same time. A glass sword would be a good comparison, though I had never held something that fancy since I'd started my journey. I doubted I had done something like that in the past, either.

My hair had parted around it as if to say, *"Right this way, Your Highness."* I had been staring at that very mirror for at least half an hour, trying to make heads or tails of it.

"Why did this have to happen to me *here* of all places?!" I wanted to scream into my pillow for the rest of the day, but it would be foolish to assume either that or sleeping would solve the problem any quicker.

The horn had been there since I'd awoken that morning. The raven blackness made it even more obvious as it jutted through my pale hair. It was something that only a race from another realm of existence, like the demons, could have, so why did I have one? Could it have grown as a mutation from the goat-creature I ate last night? No, something like that would have become a scandal in a country as pious as this one.

"I am human... right?"

Of course, there was no response.

How reassuring...

Doubt started to well up within me. Would I end up like the others who were different? I really didn't want to find out.

I thought back to yesterday when I'd first arrived in Zeuss. I'd tried lots and lots of food since I was invited as a guest. It was well known that Resolvers would be invited as guests of honor to specific countries that had friendly ties associated with the Tribunal, and that's exactly what had happened. I was treated to a lavish feast at the town hall, and even got to do a bit of sightseeing.

"Ah! That's it!" I declared with a triumphant smile toward the mirror.

I slowly placed a hand on my chin and sunk into my bed like a depressed widow. *That has to be it!* I thought it was strange that this blessed country had enough problems to arrest people so frequently, which resulted in bolstering their name and reputation to other flourishing nations.

What if they created those problems?

"It's in the food! It's got to be. Something in the food causes these mutations, and the Church of Zeuss takes advantage of it. Perhaps there were never other races in this country in the first place—"

A knock. Someone was at my door.

Ahhh! Why do they have to be here now? With haste, I tried my best to cover the horn with my hair before a voice came from the other side. "Miss Resolver, I would like to come and greet you. I am Zeke, one of the an archbishop of our benevolent Lord."

I groaned.

Why now? Could they have set this up because I'm one of the few female Resolvers? Maybe he wants my bo—No! This was incredibly suspicious. They had offered me a place to stay, but I'd funded my own lodgings to make sure they weren't up to any funny business. It wasn't the first time someone had barged into my room and made themselves at home. I just wanted some privacy. How did he know where I was staying, anyway?

This violated some sort of law. It had to! They had to have pulled some long and thick strings to find—the escort! Someone had escorted me home last night since I'd been a bit tipsy from their free, tasty wines. I wasn't a big fan of alcohol, but its sweet scent had drawn me to it like a moth to a flame. After finishing the first bottle, I had trouble remembering what happened besides leaving at the end of the night.

They knew I could handle myself since I was a Resolver, but I—for some bizarre reason—let one of them tag along. How could I have been so careless?

I want to flog you right now, Lethe-from-last-night. You need to learn some restraint! This was why I never drank, but strangely, I didn't feel hungover. What in the world did I drink?

I reached into my bag and pulled out an item that could hardly be considered clothing. It was a cloak, one given to me by a special person in my life. It was time to call on its help. I donned it without hesitation, using the hood to cover my unexpected mutation. Then I called out Frosty, my ring bursting with an icy hue.

"Just a minute!" I said, trying to buy some time.

I hastily flung my satchel over my shoulder, pulled myself onto Frosty's warm, furry body, and pointed toward one of the two windows at the end of the room. "Pick one, buddy. We are making a grand escape today."

"Wooooof!" He stretched his hind legs, and charged with lightning speed toward our means of escape—the one on the right, to be exact.

The sound of breaking glass could probably be heard throughout the entire neighborhood. I thought the more peculiar sight was the girl with an eyepatch, shrouded in a brown cloak, riding a large ice wolf through the air. Now, where would she land?

Chapter 11

"A Man's Paradise"

*I was young and foolish once. Somehow, I even got a son. Pick your battles wisely.
Don't let them pick you.*

—Boreas Tyrel

"'A Man's Paradise,'" I repeated to myself. "But why?" I had so many questions as I reread the large letters inscribed on the sunken arch. It stood before the entrance to an enchanted forest named Nevermore by the locals. It was all rather creepy, really. I had come here more out of curiosity than for my job, or for info about my past. It was always nice to take a break once in a while. As I'd traveled, I'd heard rumors about a place where men sought happiness, but from which they never returned. Sure, it could have been because they found what they were looking for, but there was no way I was going to believe that nonsense. Happiness isn't free and it certainly wouldn't be in a sketchy place, like an enchanted woodland.

"Shall we?"

"Awoooooh!" Frosty howled as we proceeded into the dark forest.

There were trees of all kinds lumbering above me; however, they were all way past their prime—old and withered. There wasn't a single soul in sight, nor any indication that there had ever been a settlement there in the first place. I had entered the forest of solitude from the looks of it. *So, why that sign?*

The hollow trees didn't answer me. They creaked and moaned like the souls of the damned. *Huh? Am I in the right place? Old trees as far as the eye can see and nothing changes the deeper I go.*

Frosty continued forward as I surveyed the surroundings with worry and caution. *Could it all be a trap or perhaps a—*

My question was abruptly answered.

The worn soil below us morphed from withered brown to a magnificent blue. It was captivating and beautiful, but also mysterious and possibly—no— most likely dangerous. The bright colors swarmed from the ground like insects, eating up my entire vision with bright-blue light. A mist of sparkles and powder waved in and out of my sight.

When it had finally cleared, my surroundings had completely changed; it was like I had been transported to another world.

"Woah…" That was all I could get out. I was truly at a loss.

There were bright and wonderful colors everywhere. Large, purple-and-pink mushrooms had been retrofitted to become places of residence. Others were crafted from wood, sadly crushed under the weight of the mushroom-laden ceilings. The vibrant colors of the landscape produced a feeling of being perpetually stuck in the late afternoon, despite the sun still shining brightly above us. Simply staring at the thick, violet mountains in the distance resulted in my eyelids growing heavy.

A nice little nap might be fine.

Wait, no! I needed answers first. A mushroom, the size of multiple houses stacked on top of one another, loomed ominously in the distance. It had a loud, purple exterior with small, pink dots blotted all over in erratic patterns.

It was breathtaking. *I sure am easy to please, huh?*

Yet, the bubbly sensations that came from getting drunk on the lucid atmosphere paled in comparison to the next crazy sight.

A story above me, women with pointed hats flew on old broomsticks while delivering mail, hanging laundry, or even teaching younger women how to use a... long stick? There was a mix of ages from ten to a hundred within the folds of the small village; their uniform clothing only furthered my feeling of being an outsider.

A road coiled around the homes, and it was lined with eye-catching, plant-made stalls where goods and commodities were sold and exchanged. Somehow, the entire forest had become lively out of nowhere. It felt almost eerie.

I set a hand to my chin and narrowed my eye while muttering to myself. *It's called "A Man's Paradise" and yet—all I see are women. Well... I guess that's kinda like a man's paradise, but still...*

Before I could speak more of my thoughts, a large woman dropped from the air. She sported a red apron, plump body, and a pink-and-white hat that matched the other women who danced through the air on their brooms. The force of her landing caused a miniature crater in the soil, killing off a few rainbow-colored plants in the process. The mangled remains of the victims had washed onto my boots and Frosty's pelt, but the woman didn't give me time to brush them off.

"Hello there! You must be a visitor, yes?"

I nodded and cut straight to the point. "I was curious about the name of this place and wanted to see it for myself. There was nothing here a moment ago, but then—"

"Oh, that was our illusion system. It's great for keeping out unwanted guests like those troublesome worshippers of the gods. Tell me, young lady, you don't worship one of them pesky gods, do ya?"

Her tone was firm, spooking me enough to subconsciously take a step back. A bonfire had lit within her aging, green eyes. It was best for me not to piss her off.

"Er… No. I don't worship anything," I lied, clear as day. I had a feeling that if I actually meant it, my body would erupt into sickly green flames with the laughter of my benefactor filling my ears.

"Good." She held out a paw the size of both of my hands combined. "The name's Mugin. Nice to meet ya! I'm one of the elder witches that oversees this humble forest. How can I help ya?"

Isn't she being too trusting? Or maybe I'm the one that gave in too quickly…

Her tall and burly build grew more overbearing the closer she got to me, even when I was riding such an imposing beast. Frosty was usually a turnoff for most people, but she had approached us without a care in the world. If anything, Mugin seemed happy. She was filled to the brim with confidence, and had such a welcoming aura that it was difficult to resist anything from her.

I stepped down from my companion and accepted her open hand. *That's… a really firm handshake. She could easily go toe to toe with some of the brutes at the Tribunal with that arm strength.*

"I'm Lethe, and as I said before, I'm just a traveler who's curious about the name of this province. I haven't seen a single man since stepping into this dazzling, new world."

Mugin let go of my hand, leaving it throbbing with pain. "Your hand is so smooth, and what slender fingers you have—and those nails! They look so delicate that just the faintest bit of pressure could shatter them."

Was that a threat?

She leaned in with the welcoming grin of a bear. "They're really well maintained. What's your secret?" She stepped back after inspecting my reaction. "Ah, you look so confused. I guess that's too personal of a conversion to have when we've only just met. My apologies," she said with a wave of her hand. "We don't have too many feminine girls around here these days, so I bet they would be overjoyed to chat with you when they're not working themselves to death with their research."

Secret? Feminine? Delicate? What do those have to do with anything? Her words are ominous, but her smile is so reassuring… And the air around her is strong too. There's almost no way for me to even cut into this one-sided conversation.

"Um…" I said.

Mugin gave me no time to ponder her words. She nudged her chin to the south, where a multitude of wooden homes with the same mushroom-infested ceilings stood vigilant under the artificial dusk. "It would be easier if I just gave ya a tour. How does that sound?"

My body was both tense and at ease, and I couldn't shake that paradox. I could only nod along, feeling as stiff as a brick.

"Sure. T-that would be great."

Her baleful gaze led me to believe that I was delving into a subject that would send me past the point of no return. Yet, I had agreed with her far easier than I intended. Was it the environment that was affecting my judgment, or was it something caused by this witch? I'd heard they were quite excellent with magic, especially older ones. I'd also heard they eat children. The rumors swam through my mind, yet despite them, I couldn't break free. The bizarre feeling that had washed over my body felt similar to a foreign entity feeding me suggestions that seemed just enough like me to not be upsetting.

Perhaps I'm just overthinking things. She seems pretty nice, after all. But what happened to always keeping my guard up after the horror on that ship? There's something seriously wrong with me today.

Mugin smiled warmly in my direction. "No need to be so nervous. This place is amazing once you get to know it. You'll never wanna leave, just like the rest."

"Hmm? What was that?" I asked, my mind still as muddled as a ball of yarn.

"Right this way, lassie!"

"It's Lethe!" I shouted reactively as she dragged me deeper into the quiet forest city. All eyes were on me.

I could already tell that I'd found myself a rather troublesome woman. *I seem to attract a lot of those.*

* * *

Uhhh... This doesn't seem right. This feeling... What is it?

We were in a cafeteria of sorts—perhaps a food pantry—where young and old alike were chowing down at wooden tables with whimsical carvings, snacking on colorful food that had to have come from some strange monster or plant.

Despite the enchanting scene, there was one thing that sent shivers down my spine.

Behind a majority of the older witches—and by older, I mean my age and up—squatted men who wore nothing but boxers on their shining bodies. Each of them possessed bulging muscles, metal collars, and metal shackles clamped tightly around their wrists and ankles, as if they were condemned prisoners.

At the far corner of the room, more men lurked near the kitchen. They slaved away, creating food for all the witches, their expressions a mix of bliss and giddiness.

What is this?

Even the girls who looked no older than ten were happily munching away on cookies while chatting with older witches in their pointy hats and black outfits. They took no notice of the men crouching behind them with faces of pure ecstasy. A few women tossed a few glances my way, similar to those on the way here. I even heard a few of them whisper about my hands and nails.

Why is that such a big deal here?

Mugin eyed my reaction with obvious interest, lightly giggling—that sounded more like heaving—at my astonishment. I had been so thrown off from the peculiar sight that my jaw refused to stay closed while I solemnly watched the family of witches enjoy their meal, giving me the idea that this was a common occurrence.

"Other women have had the very same look you have right now, but that will change with time. I hope this answers your question." She slapped me on the back with enough force to rattle every bone in my body. "It's every man's dream to serve a pretty lady that's stronger than him in more ways than one. They come here for countless reasons, but in the end, they all fall in line with our ways... and you can be a part of that."

She smiled, but it didn't reach her eyes.

It's the opposite! This isn't a man's paradise. It's a man's hell.

I didn't try to voice my opinion like I usually would when I saw something appalling. Instead, I closed my sagging jaw and threw on a somber smile. *I was right to be wary of this place; these women are not sane.*

I couldn't help but feel sorry for the men who were doomed to be slaves to these women until they withered up and died—or were discarded when they were no longer of use. For once, I was thankful to be born a girl. At least I could get out of here and pass it off as a bad dream.

But her gaze bore into me, locking me in place. *Mugin must have seen right through me.* She clamped a thick claw down on my shoulder with near enough force to break it, and turned to me with a frightening glint in her eyes.

"Little Lassie Lethe, I think it is time I introduce you to our queen. I bet she would *love* to meet ya."

"Uh... Yeaaaaah." My smile was as forced as it could get as I gulped nervously. *That was loud. Super loud. What should I do? She said that like a cannibal says they will have you when they really mean to eat you!*

My skin crawled with terror. I was too afraid to move, and even if I could, there was no way I could shake Mugin's iron grip. Frosty was sleeping in the ring, but even if I let him out, there was no way I could outrun those flying brooms!

"Y-yeah, sure. Take me to her. I would love to meet the queen."

Falser words could not have been spoken. Can I freeze her before she does me in? Unlikely.

My voice quivered with fear. There was no possibility she hadn't picked up on that. Now my only chance of survival was to ask the queen to let me go, but I didn't like my chances.

"Follow me."

Surprisingly, Mugin let go of my shoulder, sending a jolt of pain throughout my entire body. It took all my willpower to not collapse on the floor. I trailed after her, my clothes and forehead drenched in sweat.

The witches all waved to us as we left. Only one of us seemed pleased about it. Could you guess which one?

* * *

The inside of the giant mushroom was magnificent and astonishing. A pale-blue light propelled Mugin and me to the zenith, like a tranquil rocket of wind. This manner of travel seemed rather strange, but I could imagine it being popular if word got around. *Any form of flight is amazing!*

The moment we reached the end point, I was engulfed by an aura so commandeering that my legs nearly buckled. It was like I was back in the forest with Vern again.

"Erg..." I shuffled uncomfortably under the immense pressure. Even though I had been planning my escape while walking here, the moment I was blasted with that power, I subconsciously gave up.

There is no escape.

There was simply nothing I could do. My fate was in the hands of this ancient queen.

The chamber we'd whirled into was dimly lit by blue crystals growing out of the opulent, violet walls. Various kinds of fungi sprouted from below, which seemed rather strange considering we were inside a mushroom, but there's no point getting into the specifics at this point. I was already at the heart of the beast, and all that remained was my judgment.

The anticipation is killing me.

Mugin led me through another narrow pathway. I debated heading back, but an invisible force corralled me into a grand atrium.

A glass chandelier sparkled from the ceiling, crafted from the same blue crystals I'd seen before. It bathed the entire room in a glorious light, shimmering over walls filled with fine art of old witches. The ground was paved sickly black as to eliminate the growth of anything. At the end of the well-lavished room stood a purple crystal throne, and sitting atop it was the oldest woman I had ever seen. She had a pipe in her mouth and wore a large, gray, pointed hat. Small trails of smoke spewed out from her face as she sized me.

She was beyond frail—as if she would crumble to dust at the faintest touch—and wrinkly all over. But looks could be deceiving, as I had learned. Her shiny, gray dress was sublime, but it did nothing to disguise the fact her body was falling victim to the ravages of time. She stood tall and firm on her throne, looking down on us. Her eyes were so sunken that I couldn't tell if they were open or not, but I felt like her gaze was crystal clear. She possessed a pasty, miniature smile to match with her ghostly visage.

Mugin left me behind to approach her queen. She was only a few feet away from the throne when her large frame knelt and tipped her pointed hat toward the obsidian floor.

"Lady Marlotte, I have brought another promising candidate. She has a high aptitude for magic, and get this—she's somewhat different from a human."

DIFFERENT?! What are you even saying? I can't trust anything they say here!

Marlotte slowly faced me. A somewhat ancient odor permeated through the air, causing water to trickle down my cheek. I didn't even have time to wipe it off before our eyes locked. It was only for an instant, but...

That

      was

            all

                  it

                        too—

Hello! I'm Lethe, the one-eyed witch! You might think living in a dense forest is rather strange and archaic, but it's actually pretty warm and cozy. My daily routine starts with me waking up, brushing my teeth after a little breakfast delivery from the food-mail witch, Ela. Then I grab my trusty broom, Jora, and fly into the village for my temp jobs.

People like me are treated a bit differently than the rest. I'm a new girl here, but I also have a lot of magic in me. That makes me stand out, which scares me more than not. If only they would teach me some cool spells, but they always say I was fifty years too young to learn anything meaningful.

In the afternoon, I stop by around four for a quick lunch with some of the other temp girls. They all look to be about my age, but time moves very slowly around here, so they were really grandmas in human years. I wouldn't say that out loud, though.

Something I saw the other day has been nagging at the back of my head, slowly filling me with unease. I need to ignore it. Forgetting the past was one of the first things they taught us at the academy.

So, I ignore it. But some things are impossible to ignore forever.

I was happily working my way through some colorful mushrooms when a shiny gleam from my finger caught my eye. How did I get this magnificent crucible of frost? Who did I get it from? I dug a bit into my thoughts and that's when—

—It slowly started flowing back.

How had I lost touch with myself in the most pitiful of ways? I was surprised by how quickly I had fallen into the ranks of witches. The days had blended together in joyous harmony. I'd gained many sisters and made lots of friends over time, but I hadn't exactly been me. Everything I'd seen felt like a murky dream, masked within a thick, silver haze. I had been under some sort of enchantment. I couldn't even say why they had wanted me.

Looking back on these recent endeavors made my mind swirl in a writhing maelstrom of memories. The shivers didn't stop either, eating away at my body from head to toe. I could only recover bits and pieces of what I'd done since I joined them, but it wasn't exactly a past I wanted to recall.

Sometimes the imperfect memory of a human could be a good thing.

My head throbbed as I put together the pieces. *Did it really all come back when I glanced at my ring? Why that time? I may have been looking at it a lot lately, I think.* It might have been a bad idea, but I mulled it all over as I flew. I desperately needed to get away from my former home and escape this cursed forest.

Witches zoomed after me, raining elemental magic around me to impede my way. A streak of fire, a blast of air—I avoided it all with some quick aerial maneuvers. Broom Handling had been my major at Anastasia Academy for Witches, after all.

My eye narrowed in on the exit. My escape. The whimsical forest had been my prison for quite some time now. Beyond the foreign, misty lights and sea of trees was juicy, savory *freedom*. It motivated me to push past my limits. I wanted to reach that reward. I *had* to. It felt like ages since I had seen anything outside the forest.

I hope I wasn't gone too long.

Many spells zipped by me, and I was running on the fumes of anger and thirst for freedom. I refused to be put back in that eternal prison.

As I passed through the illusion barrier and entered back into the quiet, natural forest, I didn't look back. I flew on that wooden broom until the magic used to fuel it ran dry.

* * *

After soaring frantically for hours, I finally reached a new town. I didn't care enough to find out what god they served. I just wanted a break, and I thankfully found an inn to settle.

With great hatred resonating within every fiber of my being, I smashed the broom to pieces. I frowned as I did it, conflicted emotions causing me guilt. We shared a lot of nice memories together back at school, during the broom races, and at all my odd jobs around the village. It wasn't the broom's fault that I was stranded in that un-ageing land for who knew how long, but it was the only vestige of the witches that I could vent my anger onto.

That rage had been building the moment I remembered who I really was. Plus, I didn't want a reminder of my hellish time there. I had Frosty, anyway. It felt awful, keeping him in that cramped space for so long. I needed to make it up to him somehow.

A yawn escaped my mouth as I stretched and crawled into bed with the little energy I had left.

"Come to think of it, they used rivers to bathe there—yuck."

The thought wouldn't leave my mind, prompting me to force myself out of bed and shamble for the shower. There were many things I needed to rid my overworked body of: dirt, filth, this tacky black hat and dress. They had earned me even more looks than my eye patch ever had. Lastly, the sickening memories that were still bubbling to the forefront of my mind.

A tinge of mana was expelled from my hand, sparking the shower to life. The gushing water was ice cold, but it was exactly what I needed after that whole ordeal.

I glanced down at my right hand. "I wish I could burn or freeze my memories with these," I said with a dejected smile.

I wanted to remember my past—not this. It wasn't fair. I didn't want anything from my time there. In this shower, I would do my best to scrub it all away.

Chapter 12

The Cold Dish of Revenge

I once killed for another. In the end, I felt as hollow as when they left me. Friends are important, but only the ones that you have truly grown close to will shatter your soul when they're taken away.

—*Boreas Tyrel*

The tempered abyss had become the color of shining silver, its light nearly blinding me. In place of the snickering demon was a blazing, white figure that radiated superiority. It glared at me, but I didn't think it was angry. It spoke the moment before I stirred with a voice that clearly wasn't its own. The creature's silver eyes shone as brightly as the full moon. A shadow lurked behind it, but it was small and distant. All I could make out was that it was the color of blood, and it was watching us—both of us.

* * *

After that stroll down memory lane, you're probably wondering how that series of events led to the present. Well, let me tell you.

I was once again in the city by the sea—Trident. Rather than the places I'd walked before, I was in the common area where the popular guild, Titan, was located. I was already registered as an adventurer—albeit a low ranked one—through my work with the Tribunal, but that didn't stop me from getting a little special treatment when it came to picking out quests above my level.

There were a lot of nuances and rules for being an adventurer, but as someone that only dips into the profession when strapped for cash, it's not worth worrying over. Well, cash or the need for revenge.

How I felt at that moment was the latter.

I'd returned because of a certain rumor and wanted confirmation of its authenticity. What I hadn't expected was who the girl manning the front desk turned out to be.

The three desks that managed the life of every adventurer were evenly spaced out around the first floor, with a quest board in between each station. A young attendant greeted me from behind the front desk, her large, scarlet eyes hidden behind black-rimmed spectacles. Those were the eyes of an apex predator, and one I'd hoped to never see again as long as I lived.

"Hello! Welcome to Titan, the strongest guild in the country! What can I do for you? I'm C.T., the lady in charge of this branch's questing and financial sections. What can I—Hold on, you look familiar."

She adjusted her glasses and studied me for a good five seconds. After another few seconds of silence, she stuck a hand to her chin before snapping. "That's right! It's been some time, hasn't it, my one true follower, *Kulu*?"

Ugh. What is she doing here, of all places?

I let out a small sigh. "So, you're going by 'C.T.' now?"

She nodded, pointing to the name embroidered in crisp, gold letters on her dark blazer. "Yes. It's easier to pronounce and doesn't attract as many weirdos. Makes business a lot easier as well. I only get catcalled once a day because of it."

Once a day is still a lot.

I looked around, but no one else seemed to be paying attention to the strange conversation between me and C.T., aka Cthulhu, who was now dressed in attire fit for a guild employee.

Wasn't she going to destroy the world after bolstering her name? Why is she working here? And why was she so... fashionable?

Through the transparent podium she controlled with elegance, I could clearly make out a black pencil skirt tightly clinging to her waist. A white, well-ironed blouse made up the top half of her outfit and was complemented by a raven-colored blazer.

Even though she still looked young for her age, she had a rather refined air to her now. She really did look older. I didn't think gods could age, but they could change their forms.

With her hair tied up in a ponytail with a green bow at the end, she looked pretty... and knowledgeable—with an emphasis on pretty. Her hair was a combination of green and yellow strands; I'm sure no one could tell that they used to be tentacles. Her refined image now mimicked that of an adept businesswoman, complete with a greater height than before. I imagined it was the same kind of aura an older sibling would have.

I never even thought of siblings before. I wonder if... No! Stop getting distracted. The real danger is right in front of you, Lethe!

She seemed to blend in with humans almost too well—something even I had trouble doing. *Was I feeling jealous? No, certainly not!* It also helped that her wings were missing.

Out of everything I had just gained from assessing her transformation, one question demanded to be asked. "Um, why exactly are you working here?"

"Ah, that..." C.T. placed a hand on the table and planted her chin atop it. She still looked down on me, as if I was a child or hapless subordinate, but lacked that aura of terror that she'd had when we first met. "Well, I wanted to explore the world and whatnot, but there were no shrines or idols left of me, and to make it worse—no one even knows who I am! 'Uh, Cthul-who? Are you a water god or something? Oh? You're a god? Make me rich, then.' Can you believe it?! Mortals are so ungrateful these days. Why do I need to be flashy to prove my divinity? What foolish criteria! Ugh! **Y' hate orr'enahh** (*I hate mortals*)!"

Wow, I actually understood that. A side effect of being her follower?

She pounded her fist on the table after hissing those words. Surprisingly, no one took notice, leading me to believe this was a rather common occurrence, or she had tampered with their hearing.

"Y' hate shuggothh ahogog (*I hate humans the most*)! They are so forgetful after a millennium. Maybe I shouldn't have killed all those pathetic worshipers. Whatever! The point is, no one remembered my impressive name, and I had nowhere to stay. Thus, I decided to get a job and spread my name to the idiotic adventures who rely on me. That way I can amass enough power to return to my former glory and build my own temple with ease. Then the world will be trapped between my claws! **Mwa-ha-ha-ha!**"

I looked around in terror, but everyone was going about their day as if nothing had happened. *So, this is the power of a god!*

I was dazzled after her confident speech and display of powers, completely ignoring the end part. It got me hyped up for no good reason. "You can do all that?!"

"Heh, 'tis but child's play." She smirked and puffed out her chest while making a fist with her hand. "With my power from the old days, I could destroy a continent and make a new one with the snap of my claws—er... fingers now, I guess."

Why does she look so bummed about that? More importantly... A sly smile crept up my lips. *I could use this. Maybe.*

"Wow! That's amazing! Can you make money? That would be great—super great. You see, I am running really low these days and could use a boost. I *am* your one and only true *follower*, after all. Your... *Kulu.*" I made sure to put a sing-songy emphasis on the follower part. She'd made a big deal about it at the end of our first encounter.

C.T. turned away, shooting me a sidelong glance while timidly scratching her cheek. "Well… it could be done if I had something that was of equal weight to it. That magic was pretty rare back in the day, but it seems to have been lost to the ages. It would be a great boon for myself as well, but the amount of matter I would need to buy and the mana I would require—I'm getting off topic. Where are my manners? What have you come here for, um… My apologies, my one true follower. What's your name again?"

I stared in disbelief. *Gonna deny my get rich quick scheme while not even remembering my name? That's a low blow.*

"It's Lethe. I told you before."

"No, that's not it." C.T. shook her head. "Being as old and experienced as one such as I, one would be a veritable trove of secrets and memories—which I am. I would remember, had I been told it before sending you away last time. I bestowed upon you my own title instead, my *Kulu.*"

How insufferable.

My shoulders sank. *Doesn't seem like I'll be able to trick her into becoming a money factory for me, either. I know it was a rather bold idea, but with how she is now, I'm not really afraid like last time. Welp, maybe later I can figure something out.*

I almost wanted to ask her about the whispers from my dream the night before. They still danced around in my head like the last embers of a dying fire. **The Silver King has awoken. He stirred to grant you his favor. He is impressed with how well you have treated his brood.**

Why the third person? And why was the voice so soft and feminine?

The other part scared me more. **The Starscourge licks his wretched jaws with anticipation. Watching with great interest, he hungers for a star-filled sky.**

The second message had come in like a sonic boom, rattling me to the bones. It was deep and scratchy—definitely not the voice of a human. I'd somehow caught the attention of two mysterious beings. *It is worrying, but I have more important matters to attend to.*

After the shock of seeing C.T., I remembered why I'd originally come to the guild. "As for why I am here today—" I pointed to a large brown sheet of paper nailed to the board on the right side of the desk. Quests were posted daily for numerous jobs and oddities. The largest one looked rather new compared to its adjacent brothers, all withered and crumbled from being returned, over and over again. Failure wasn't too common, but for some monster killing quests, it wasn't that unusual. Those returns really stuck out like sore thumbs.

"I'm here to help with the raid. I have a bone to pick with the bounty, you could say."

The Leviathan had become more active in the past few years. It had already consumed seas of fishermen, finally prompting several nations to put the beast down—and I was more than ready to assist.

C.T. pursed her lips before displaying a disturbingly carnivorous grin. "Kulu, I can taste the ire oozing out of you. I like it! So, you want a whack at one of young P's children? They are no pushovers, but you can handle it. I'm sure the one who summoned the great Cthulhu could pull it off!"

Young P? Were they acquainted? I suppose they were both deities related to the sea... That made me feel a little bad, but I didn't think there was a single being in this world that she actually cared for.

Time to test that theory.

"About that..." I clasped my hands together and did my best to smile cheerfully. *Is this what a good cultist looks like? I wouldn't know. Apparently, the ones I had been with were pretty lousy at it.* "Do you think you could assist with killing it? I didn't think about it before, but now that you are here and I am Kulu, your one *true* follower..." *I can't stand the sound of my voice after saying that.*

"Sorry." She quickly pushed a fist forward before releasing her fingers to reveal an open palm.

Wow... Now that I'm looking at them, her nails are so clean. Mine could use a good cleaning after my most recent dungeon-diving adventure. Am I really losing to an evil, forgotten god when it comes to femininity? Not like I really care, but it still irks me a bit. Wait, I'm getting off topic!

"—stop you right there."

"Huh? Say that again."

"I said, 'I'm going to have to stop you right there.'"

"What? Why?"

She had a serious look in her eyes. It wasn't fearsome, but it was the type of glare that wouldn't take 'no' for an answer. Then all the tension faded from her voice and soft features, as if it had never existed.

"I *really* wish I *could,* buuuut guild policy restricts any employees from assisting with a quest, especially us 'weak and dainty' girls. We can get eaten by monsters, killed by traps, or even taken away by maddened adventurers." She cracked a massive smile and snickered. "You know how it is."

This little... Ugh... I can't.

Now *that* was a pathetic excuse. The only one getting devoured would be the poor creatures that happened to cross her path. And don't even get me started on adventurers. What an unfair rule. How was someone supposed to take advantage of the fact that their deity also works for an adventurer's guild?

"How can you even say that with a straight face, you *fiend*?" I asked in disbelief. "Who even made such a stupid rule? The chance of something like that happening in the first place would be ridiculously rare!"

She shrugged and shifted her attention toward the clock rooted to the wall behind her. "Shoot, I was supposed to go on break nearly two minutes ago. I guess talking with you is too much fun, especially when you get all wired and annoyed like this. Adorable! But I must be off, as Catha—one of the greatest mortals to ever spawn on this pathetic rock—always brings the most impressively delectable, homemade, chocolate muffins for us *fellow girl* employees, and there is no way I am missing out on that. This body is infatuated with them to where I might need to get the recipe out of her by any means necessary. I may have been around for quite some time, but food is something that never ceases to surprise me."

Yikes. I hope she doesn't eat the poor woman's brain or something. "For once, I completely agree with what you are saying. I don't plan on saying that ever again."

She laughed. "You'll come around, eventually. That's great to hear, either way. Now get going, my little follower, and bring back some juicy remains!"

Her eagerness was so overbearing that nearly all the energy in my body seemed to be sucked out all at once. "Yeah…"

"Oh, one more thing before I taste what you humans call 'heaven.' Since you are about to go off into what many consider as Hell, I was curious about why you haven't been using your eye yet?"

"Huh?" I was taken aback. "You mean this?" I pointed to my eyepatch.

She nodded. "Yeah, it can be pretty helpful."

"I—I don't have an eye under there!" I stammered.

She waved her hand back and forth. "No, no, no. That's not what I mean. It'll be easier if I just show you."

She pulled a small mirror from behind the counter and thrust it into my face. "See the glow that just oozes *me*? That's the *Eye of R'lyeh*."

"The eye of Ryl-*what*?"

I hadn't noticed anything before, but now that she mentioned it, I did see a faint jade glow emanating from my covered eye. "Cool. Does it make me see in the dark or something?"

"If you use it for something pathetic like that, then I would have to *destroy* you."

"…Noted."

"Joking! Well, kind of. But it's a magical orb that can be brought to life when you think about it. If I was using it, everyone here would flee or kill themselves from the sheer madness it births, but I toned it down just for you. At best, it can paralyze living beings or fill them with enough dread to flee when they take even a gander at it. At worst, they soil themselves. Ha-ha-ha! I love humiliation! It's invigorating!"

I see. It's nice to have another way of dealing with pesky people, but I really hope they don't soil themselves! That would stink for both parties, and yes, pun intended.

"I'll try my best to live up to your expectations," I said more meekly than I intended.

She turned her back to me and started for the room behind her. "Think of it as a godly blessing—proof of your veneration. Every deity has something they can give their followers. There are other ways to receive gifts from them, but that isn't relevant to us. This is what I, your god, gave to you. It can even be a decent stand-in for your eye once it evolves after enough use. Then you won't need that fashionless eyepatch. I look forward to hearing about the mortals you terrify. It sounds oh-so delicious! I'm feeling warm and fuzzy just thinking about it."

"I don't appreciate that last part, but if it could help me look normal again, then I'll take it." I turned to leave, but before I could, she tapped my shoulder.

"Actually, wait for me when I get back. I didn't notice it when you first came in, but I can't ignore it now that I know. There's something important I want to show you."

A sense of dread washed over me. What would she even consider important?

* * *

The docks...

The last time I had been there was when I was with *her*. The happy memory was now blighted by what had come after. Still, my chest had a warm and fuzzy feeling to it, along with the knot of pain. I could never forget her.

I continued down the dock to where an enormous ship had been anchored. There were many people dressed in gray and white transporting boxes and materials onto the wine-red ship. I spotted what I believed to be a wyvern carved into the mast.

The one barking orders at the sailors was a sun-burned man in a striped tunic and shorts. He had a somewhat chiseled face with shoulder-length hair as green as a meadow. His eyes were icy blue, like my ring, and brimming with both authority and confidence—a rather strong combo. He had that sort of brute aesthetic going for him: barrel-chested with thick forearms.

Gripped in his left hand was a large spear with a golden tip. Along its body existed strange symbols that I couldn't understand in the slightest. What I could tell was that it greatly differed from a typical weapon. It was more likely to be a special magic artifact, like my ring, than an Eternal; it didn't seem special enough to mess with the laws of reality like one of those.

"Um... Hello." I waved at him with as much enthusiasm as I could muster after my brief trip down memory lane. "Is this where the Hunt for the Leviathan battalion reports?"

The words sounded ridiculous as they left my mouth, but that was what it was called.

He wasn't looking my way. Instead, his eyes were glued on the ship, where a young woman was hard at work unpacking something beyond the ramp.

"Hello?" I yelped, waving my hand in front of his face. It took a few seconds before his dazed eyes finally regained their focus.

"Hmm? Oh! Ahem! Now, who might you be?"

My shoulders sagged along with my previously perky attitude. "Is this the raid team for the Leviathan?" I asked again.

He nodded before beaming with surprising happiness. His posture straightened as well, focusing solely on me. It was a tad more than I bargained for.

"Indeed, it is. Has a pretty lady like you come to see us off?"

You switch targets fast, huh? But flattery will get you nowhere.

"No, actually. I'm here to help out." I showed him the dirty quest paper from my satchel. "I'm pretty confident in my abilities. I also have a bone to pick with that creature."

Well, I'm confident in most of them.

He wrinkled his nose, but his bold smile never wavered. I did notice some disappointment in his eyes, though. "I see... So you also seek glory from its death." He gracefully held out his hand. "Well then, let's get you set up. Welcome aboard the *Grand Decay*! I'm the leader of this operation, Mikaeus. Allow me to introduce you to the main crew."

I let out an audible gulp. *Was it always this hot? And why did my throat feel like sandpaper?*

This was it. I would finally get justice for my best friend.

Just you wait, Bella.

* * *

He quickly led me to a room in the middle of the ship. Its walls were painted the color of dried blood, and it sort of smelled like it, too. A huge table ate up the majority of the room's center space, with an ancient map sprawled atop it. I could literally see the dust coming off the thing, and I nearly sneezed.

"You'll get used to it, girl." He slapped me on the back as he walked past me.

I really didn't want to, though. The sound of others shuffling in quickly filled up the room, tearing my mind away from the map.

"At last!" Mikaeus raised his voice as the others finished trickling into the room and gathered around the table. "Everyone has been accounted for. Us eight will be the primary force against that wretched monster. Now, I know you already know this, but I will say it once again. I am Mikaeus and this"—he thrust out his spear—"is my trusty partner, Impetus." He did a few twirls to show off.

I heard the pained groans of a few others in the room. I agreed with them.

He continued, after unironically doing dumb tricks for a good minute, while half of us feigned interest and the other half was plainly annoyed. "Anything can happen out on these open seas. As the champion of the great Helios, it's my job to use Impetus, Eternal of the Thundering Sun, to put that fiend to rest. Still, prepare for the worst."

Another sponsor? Guess I was wrong, even though his spear looks so much weaker. But why this guy?

Everyone nodded with solemn gazes. The room was devoid of talk for a good half a minute before the man next to Mikaeus decided to chime in. "I know we can kill it if we all work together. There's nothing that teamwork and power can't conquer! I'm Daji Ulaji, by the way. A strong and hot spirit man— I mean—monk from Drackthar. I'll do my best to not let any of you down!"

He sure has some energy in him. A spirit monk is something I have never heard or read about, either. I thought Drackthar was big on muscle-heads with greatswords. He might check one of those boxes, at least.

Daji was a boy who couldn't be older than sixteen. His rough skin was darkened by the sun to the color of caramel. He had short, black hair, large, maroon-colored eyes and was rather short for his age; I would say around the height of C.T. when she'd been first summoned. The aura that wafted off of him felt eerily familiar, but I wasn't sure why. The girl next to him was the same way. Somehow, we had a connection.

He wore a white headband and scarf that was tightly wrapped around his neck and split off behind him into two tails. His wrists were bandaged up in cloth, and I could spot chain mail peeking out from under his white tunic.

I hesitated for a second before raising my hand. "Um... What exactly is a spirit monk?" I asked. "I know Drackthar is deep in the Red Desert, but that's about all I know." Better to act ignorant and get a first-hand account than use my info from old stories and ancient fairy tales. It would be rather embarrassing if I was completely wrong about the subject.

Daji cracked his knuckles with a sly smirk before responding. "Ahem. A spirit monk is someone that uses the power of the A—"

"Boring! No one cares, Daj."

"But she ask—OW!" The girl who interrupted him had smacked him on the head.

"I got it. I got it. Don't worry, Stace." He cleared his throat again. "That's enough about me. What about you? You have the getup of a normal chick, but that thing in your eye—I mean, on your eye and those rings definitely have a story behind—OWWWW! What gives, Stace?! Stoooooop!"

"Don't you know it's rude to ask a girl about that kinda stuff? You just met her for Hell's sake! Act considerate for once—or do you only have muscles in that thick skull of yours? And stop trying to sound manly around every new girl that comes your way. *It's cringy.*"

"Cr-cringy?" he echoed, looking defeated.

Stace, the girl that had smacked Daji, was at least a foot taller than him. She had a long, scarlet ponytail that was neatly tied on the right side of her head. It swished from left to right like a dancer when she dished out justice to Daji's head. Her eyes were a similar color to my own, yet the immense depth in them warned that we were very far from equal. They held boundless wisdom and enough energy to captivate everyone in this room.

She looks so young, though! I can't put my finger on which part of her feels the most familiar. If it's not her eyes, then what?

She seemed to know Daji pretty well for how openly brazen the two were with one another, even while others were watching. She was probably older than him and gave off the air of a cheerful, yet sometimes stern, older sister.

She wore a well-crafted, blue robe that had a cute, red ribbon keeping it all together. Even while disciplining Daji, her free hand kept a tight grasp on a short, golden staff.

That can't be cheap.

"Anyway..." Stace turned away from the deflated boy and smiled directly at me. "You don't have to tell us anything if you don't want to. A lot of us have gone on long quests together, so I'm sure you feel left out by how buddy-buddy we seem." She slightly narrowed her eyes. "We all have our secrets." Her eyes returned to their original warmth before pointing to herself. "I'm Stacy Shepherd, by the way. Nice to meet you!"

She seems nice at least, but I can't get rid of this strange feeling... It was like walking outside naked, or getting invaded by a dream eater in your sleep. *Could we have met before I lost my memories?*

Her gentle smile and welcoming gaze soothed what worries I had. It made me want to tell her everything, even if I thought she already knew the answers.

"N-no, it's not like that!" I held my palms up, facing outward in front of my chest. "Well, maybe a little, but I don't know a lot about my past. Oh—and I'm Lethe. *Just* Lethe. Have we met before?"

She raised an eyebrow and pursed her lips. "No, I don't think so. However, I have a feeling we'll get along just fine." Stacy flashed a bright smile back at me and turned to Daji. "See what you did? She's embarrassed to talk about her past because of you."

She clearly misinterpreted my lack of self-knowledge for something a lot deeper and heavier. "Well, it's as I jus—"

"See? She's too flustered to talk about her past."

"Did you not hear what I just sa—"

"So, learn your lesson and don't be so nosy."

"Yeah, I get it, Stace. Sorry."

I got cut out of my own conversation!

"Anyway," Mikaeus chimed in, "let's move on. Go ahead, Alistar."

Next to Stacy was a guy covered in gray armor from head to toe and wore a helmet that had seen better days. All I could see inside was shadow. The helmet itself was also a lot bigger and wider than any I had seen before, hinting that this Alistar guy was most likely not human.

"Right," he said in a deep voice. "I'm Alistar Hameer of Hammerhead clan."

Common obviously wasn't his first language. He spoke in drawn-out breaths with a thick accent, exclusive to the races of the sea. *How does a species live on both land and water, anyway?*

A few of us gave him rattled expressions as he slowly removed his helmet, revealing a long, pale-blue head with razor-sharp, white teeth that covered the middle of his face. Where his eyes should have been were two trunks that split off to the left and right. Judging from the blinking, the sunken, black sockets at the ends must have been his eyes.

"Woah!" Daji gasped. "A shark-man! That's awesome!"

Stacy smacked him again. "Don't raise your voice so high! You're bothering everyone!"

A shark-man? Could that be another one of those hybrid races?

"Yes. I am both shark and man."

"It's just as he says. Alistar will be our guide once we set sail. His Amp of Lorezine will make it easy to track the Leviathan once we reach the area it was last sighted."

"*Ampullae of Lorenzini,*" Alistar corrected. "How do you always forget that, Mik?"

"Yeah, yeah. Amps of Lorazina. Whatever."

Alistar's cheeks flushed from what was most likely a mixture of annoyance and embarrassment. He quickly put his helmet back on, which appeared to be a rather arduous task in its own right. He had to scoop up one eye-trunk and then the other. As he fiddled with his helmet, I noticed two blue-and-gold axes strapped to his back.

I really don't want to get on his bad side.

Five of us had gone now, leaving only three more. Each of them had been rather quiet, or were at least patiently waiting their turn.

"Heya! I'm Rankle! There's not a lot to say about me, but I like pufferfish and flesh of any kind a lot! Their poisonous nature makes me feel like such a daredevil. I love it, and—"

"Get to the point!" Stacy yelled. "You say this crap every time we party up! It's so annoying!"

What a hero. Wait... Did he say he eats people?!

"Fiiiine." He sighed. The cloaked man removed his brown hood to reveal a face that couldn't be over thirty. One eye was the color of a blood-colored diamond, beautiful but sharp. It matched what was creeping up on the side of his face. *What are those? Rocks?*

I leaned in to get a better look.

Oh...? Oh, wow!

Growing out of the left half of his face, and nearly touching his lips, were crystals. They were similar to my grandfather's features. *That looks so... painful.*

It didn't reach his short-cut, black hair, but had to be extremely agonizing to have forcibly attached to your body. The world's most painful half-mask, you could say. It seemed as if he was in the actual process of transforming into a golem. Long, violet crystals matured from where his other eye should have been.

I wonder how far they go.

"It's halfway down my waist as of now. At least I'm durable ha-ha!" He patted the metal plating that covered his chest.

Did he read my mind?!

"I can read minds."

I was taken aback. "Really?"

"No, just messing with ya. I'm pretty good at watchin' people and understanding them. This is part of the reason." He revealed his left arm, which was entirely coated in purple crystals. It was significantly larger than his armored one. The hand was tightly hidden under a black glove—it didn't look like a pleasant sensation.

"It's called Crysalisis. It happened a long time ago when I was young and foolish. I advise against taking a trip to my home, full of wacky and tasty monsters to slay or die to. The Primal Elders are no pushovers."

But that just makes me want to venture there even more!

"He's not much different now," Stacy added.

Rankle clenched his rocky fist. "I would like to find a cure for it, but that doesn't matter now. I just hope my village of Slayers has finally been doing well in my absence. Anyways,"—he pulled a large, metal crossbow from behind his cloak—"let's kill this thing, gut it, and then SAVOR IT!"

Some of the others felt the same way, but Stacy and Daji gagged. Either way, I had found my way into a boat with a rather colorful cast. It was so different from the people I had met in the past. Actually... was it? A certain bespeckled girl with a cheeky grin and an annoying, green-haired god floated to the surface of my thoughts.

I should focus on not missing the last two's intro—SO CUTE! The last two were small, like even smaller than Daji.

Each of them sported a ponytail and bangs that were parted to one side of their face. They wore the leather garb of forest hunters and had what must have been a quiver on each of their small backs.

"I'm Tillis."

"I'm Millis."

In unison, they finished with, "And together we are the Twinstar Hunters!"

It's so adorable and stupid at the same time!

They clasped each other's hands and moved forward in perfect tempo. There was no way they were past the age of ten or eleven. Was this really the best spot for two young girls?

They both pointed at Rankle. "This guy likes to eat people!" they said in unison.

I shot a glance at Stacy in search of an answer, and she easily caught my drift. "These two were raised in the wilderness and have great eyesight and a keen sense of smell. If anyone can track the continuous movement of the beast, and rain down fire from afar, it would be them. And yes, Rankle does have a habit of consuming human flesh after his time spent with a horrifying monster."

"A monster to you, but to me, she was as lovely as the night sky. And what an appetite! I wanna see than tan skin, evil green eyes, and golden—"

"That's enough, Mister!"

Rankle frowned but said nothing more from their scolding.

Stacy grinned. "Nice work, girls."

The girls crossed their arms and smirked at her praise. *I guess you can't judge a book by its cover—even at their age.*

Mikaeus stamped his spear to the ground to recapture everyone's attention. "There is one more member I would like to introduce. He should have just landed."

Landed? Like he flew here?

My question was soon answered as a middle-aged man trotted into the room, a strange, striped cobra with wings perched on his shoulder.

"Apologies for the late arrival. The Sea Sky is a lot more treacherous on the way out than in."

Mikaeus chuckled at his response. "Everyone, this is my long-time friend, Ragnar il-Vol. He's our species specialist as a renowned Bonder. Like Rankle, he hails from the lands of monster hunters, bizarre relationships, and cantankerous titans—Intrathon."

I winced. *Don't some of the oldest and most deadly creatures come from there? I want to go even more... but travel cautiously. What a cool continent!*

Rankle gave him a flimsy salute. He seemed to be on the opposite side from Ragnar, but also didn't seem bothered by his arrival in the slightest.

Ragnar frowned his way before turning to us. "It's really unfortunate I could only bring one bud with me. My menagerie isn't very well-equipped for battles in the sea after all."

The man was lean and well-built. He wore a thick, straw vest over a sleeveless chain-mail tunic with a gray scarf that seemed to move autonomously. His shorts seemed to be made from the same material, but it gave the impression of it being a lot more sturdy than it initially appeared. Ragnar had dark boots that matched the tips of his close-cropped hair. The rest was all a stormy gray that didn't seem to be because of age. His sapphire eyes were full of vitality, just as much as someone my age. He definitely appeared as both a rugged warrior and a gentle giant.

He gave us a quick salute, his flying snake mirroring the motion, which was both strange and cute. "I heard we're taking on the fabled Leviathan of the depths. You can count on us for aerial support. I'm excited to get a closer look at the big baddy." His expression became forlorn as he gazed at Mikaeus. "Is there a chance once it becomes too battered and bruised to fight that I could—"

"I'm sorry, old friend. There is simply no opportunity for you to link with something of that magnitude. It could change you instead of the other way around."

Ragnar was briefly crestfallen, but soon resumed his confident smirk. "Ahh, thought so. I really wanted to link with something old and mythical. The Primal Elders would snap me up if I tried anything on them. Killing the great beast seems like such a waste, but as a warrior—I get it."

"My man!" Daji exclaimed, cutting in between the two as he approached him. "You're a warrior as well? What can you do? Those muscles aren't all for show, right?"

Stacy seemed exasperated at his insistent questioning, but she allowed it because of Ragnar's bright expression.

"I'll tell you a bit about myself, but you'll be able to see what we can do soon enough." The snake hissed in confirmation from his right shoulder.

As someone who had an animal companion, I was intrigued by how his abilities worked. I was planning to approach him myself when Mikaeus cowed all the talking with a few poundings of his spear.

"Now that we got introductions out of the way and the preparations have been finished—it's time to set sail. The last sighting was around an hour east of the docks. Our sailors already have a rough idea from the maps, so sit tight and be prepared for my call. While we move, we'll delegate squadrons to different positions on the boat and on the beast."

They all nodded or struck poses like Daji to consent to the orders. Our merry group seemed pumped up for the upcoming battle, even though it could be our last.

That's a little dark and pessimistic, isn't it? Yes. Yes, it is.

* * *

Damn. Guess I'll have to speak to him another time. He was chatting up a storm with the shark man when we set sail. His eyes were lighting up like a child's.

I ran my hand back and forth against the thick, foamy fabric of my wetsuit. C.T. had lent it to me from the guild in case I got thrown from the boat. It was enchanted with a water-breathing spell to ensure I wouldn't drown, as well as some insulation to keep me warm. All I needed was to make sure the black material around my chest remained intact. While the battle preparations were in their final phases, I thought back to my conversation with C.T., right before I'd departed from the guild.

She had led me to a dark room, and commanded, "Take off your sweater."

I shivered, hugging my body. "I don't like where this is going."

"Oh hush, you. This is as interesting for you as it is for me. If it was anyone else…"

I don't like that look. Am I in trouble?

Reluctantly, I did as I was told, slipping off my precious sweater. Now, everything was exposed before the carnivorous god's eyes—just kidding. I had a tank top underneath on the off chance it would be hotter than my previous visit. I'd thought maybe she wanted me to take it all off, but she stopped me there.

"That's good. No need to go further… unless you want—"

"I'm okay," I snapped. "What are you looking for?"

"I'm not exactly sure yet. Allow me to inspect you at a better angle."

She leaned in closer, her fingers tapping up and down all over my body like miniature hammers.

"Eeek! Cold!" I involuntarily squeaked. How embarrassing. I didn't like it when others touched me, especially if I didn't know them. My body was mine and mine alone. It only made her giggle as she prodded me further. "Ah. Here we go."

"C-can we stop with the excessive touching?!"

"Stop whining and look at this." She pointed to a spot above my left clavicle. There was nothing out of the ordinary there, so I wasn't sure what she was pointing at. Wait a second... What is that?

A small, red mark, unnaturally bright and encased within a small circle, had appeared where she had touched me. It didn't hurt, but I could feel it blazing with some sort of foreign energy.

"So, you *do* have it," she muttered, her face far more serious than I'd ever seen before.

Is she going to kill me? Thinking back to what she did to those cultists, it wouldn't be too far-fetched for that to occur... Better play it cool!

"Have... what?"

"The mark of a *Champion*."

"The champion of what?"

"For once, I don't know. Well, not fully anyway." She tapped a finger on the jaws in the middle of the strange symbol. "This represents a sponsor, but the rune that is used to represent it predates anything that lurks in our world as of now. I doubt even an afflicted person like yourself would have dabbled enough with the Netherworld or Eternity Plane to receive a watcher. He must be one of the *Fallen*, erased from the sky. I have little doubt in that hypothesis."

"What does that all mean?"

She shook her head. "Most of it is ancient nonsense to a mortal—even one like you. All I can say for sure is that you have been blessed with a power—an extremely rare and special kind. I'm not strong enough to give one out myself yet. They're called *Eternals*."

Her head came closer, not looking at the mark, but at the frosted ring on my finger. "You must have been chosen for something, but by who and for what purpose?"

It took me a second, but I think I understood what she meant. "The Silver King?" I asked, still unsure of it myself.

"It doesn't tell me who, but the fact that they are using an alias helps confirm my suspicions. You have indeed been selected by a sponsor—and an ancient one at that. No one uses cryptic names like that anymore."

"The Silver King would relish tearing open the young woman's throat. He is asking you to do it in his stead."

What? Who's voice is invading my head?! And no! She will decimate me for sure! How does he even expect me to do that? Just what kind of teeth does he think a young woman has? I can barely bite into a scone!

I ignored the strange voice, but I thought about C.T.'s words. *I think it's connected to Frosty. But how could Frosty be related to something so ancient?*

"He is impressed with how well you have treated his brood." That's what the voice has said. That led me to believe that this Silver King was some kind of wolf god.

I had a hunch I was on the right track, but I couldn't be certain. I didn't want to sound stupid in front of my patron, so I kept my mouth shut.

C.T. let out a sigh and motioned for me to put on my sweater. "I'm sure there's more you are keeping from me because you're confused or acting cowardly. It's fine; I get it. There's still a lot I don't comprehend as well." She pursed her lips, her thin eyebrows lowering. "While I do loathe cuckolding, I suppose I can let it pass since you didn't intentionally seek his help, nor will I give you one myself. The ones in my possession would only draw the ire from the gods I won them from. Be grateful."

Her smug attitude was beginning to annoy me, so I started to leave.

"Oh, before you go, Lilith—"

"Lethe."

"*Kulu.*" She narrowed her eyes.

"Right..."

"Have you noticed any changes in the sky?"

I thought for a moment. She probably meant what I saw last night. I nodded. "I spotted a singular grouping of stars. Crazy, right? But they were real.

It was so mesmerizing. I've only read about majestic creations like that in books. Could they be coming back?"

"Who can say?" C.T.'s eyes drifted away, a wry smile ascending upon her soft features. "I sure hope not. That could spell trouble for even the great and powerful Cthulhu."

"How so?"

"It increases the chances of the Cosmos Beast breaking free. I can't have a god-eater around when I have only just returned. How tragic would it be to wait another few millennia to be revived?!"

For once, I was certain I knew what she was referring to. "The Starscourge? Isn't that creature just an old fairytale? Are you saying the divine beast is actually responsible for the disappearance of the old stars?"

How can I still believe this after what I heard last night?

C.T. snickered, but it felt fake and hollow. "Y-yeah... stars..."

It was the first time I had ever seen her unsettled. Yet, she didn't elaborate on why it made her uneasy. What even was the Starscourge? To think something that monstrous had actually taken a liking to me... *I hope it's just The Silver King messing with me. Wait. Doesn't C.T. fall under this category as well?*

C.T. clapped her hands together, shoving me out of my thoughts. "Enough about possibilities of a bleak future." Her expression shifted, becoming pensive and serious once more. However, it melted away not long after. "If you want to know more, I suggest venturing to the country of Archivieara. It has information on everything—literally! It might be in the lands that abhor humans as if they are the bane of the earth, but I'm sure my Kulu will manage! Last time I was there, they even erected a massive glowing tablet that eternally managed the list of the current annoying conquerors. It should be fine now."

"Uh, what happened to it?" I asked.

"Oh, that?" she replied with a wide grin. "I razed it to the ground. I had my reasons." She said it as casually as one would say they stole another's spot in line at a market.

But if she says it's around, then I really need to find this Archwhatever place. Perhaps it could even—

The ship jerked and slowed, snapping me back to the present. The sun was shining overhead while the tranquil waters beckoned us forward. I could have stared at it for hours, if not for the danger of a sudden attack. After setting sail, we'd been split into four groups of two. There were also four cannons stationed around the ship and one harpoon for the non-combatant sailors to use.

Since I could use magic at range and up close, I was paired with Stacy, who was a seasoned archmage. She was heavily experienced with both offensive and supportive types of magic. That was rather rare to see outside the roles that served right under a king, queen, or archbishop.

I only knew how to hurt people, yet she could save them as well. *I wonder if I could learn magic or find a ring like that—not that I would be around anyone that would require something like that, but it could help me. Perhaps with my new trump card I could... Yeah. Maybe.*

Alistar and Mikaeus were charged with the frontal assault, along with the crazy Rankle and eager Daji. Those four would be boarding the creature itself, inflicting as much damage to it as they could without getting thrown into the sea. Stacy had already cast multiple defensive spells, as well as temporary water-breathing enchantments, to prepare for the worst-case scenario. The twins would be stationed near us as the other supporters, rounding out our composition of ranged support.

I had a few misgivings about our combined power. Would it really be enough to vanquish that terrifying beast? The thought gave me unending sorrow and made the dreams of a monster much worse.

I slapped my cheeks. *I can't lose focus!*

Either way, I am going to give it hell. Not for me, but for Bella... Okay, well, a little for me as well.

My own magic had evolved recently. The Ring of Everfrost that used to only convert my hand into its frosty avatar now reached to my shoulder, allowing me the ability to release a barrage of thick icicles, finally providing me with some long needed range.

I hope I'll be useful and that this all works out swimmingly. I've never fought with a team before, nor against anything of this caliber.

I let out a heavy sigh as we waited for the creature to make its appearance.

I'd chosen to sprawl over a couch in the living quarters when Stacy came into the room.

"Oh, Lethe! Whatcha doing? Thinking of your will in case things go bad? I did that a while back and I keep it on me at all times. Wanna see?"

Huh? What?! Why so morbid? It seems her mature side only comes out when she's with Daji, I thought, while she attempted to pull something from her pack.

I threw my hands up in protest. "T-that's alright. You don't need to show me your will."

She tilted her head, disappointment written all over. However, she perked up immediately, as if a switch had flipped in her head. "I gotcha! If that's what you want, then forget about it. I always find it easy to calm my nerves when I look at my will. It's a good thing for humans to do. I heard from others that writing to their folks gives them a lot of courage and peace of mind."

Sometimes the way she talks sounds like she understands others, but she also acts as if we are a foreign substance to her. Who calls other people 'humans' these days?

She sat down next to me, forcing me to scoot over and make room. I saw her goal as clearly as day.

"I wish you wouldn't so blatantly avoid my gesture of goodwill."

"I don't see what that has to do with sitting on my lap."

She pouted, her cheeks filling out like a chipmunk. "Hmph. You're no fun. You know that, right?"

I chuckled to myself, feigning ignorance. *Now she is a character. One who really doesn't understand the concept of personal space. But maybe she's right about our earlier topic.*

"So, how is it calming, exactly? I don't have a will, but even if I did, it would only make me more nervous than I was before." Besides, I couldn't imagine giving my few beloved belongings to anyone but Rock.

I glanced downward, not wanting to meet her gaze for a multitude of reasons. I felt a strange urge to tell her everything, resulting in my mouth clamping shut. It was better to not let anything stupid leak out. How could she make me feel this way? Something inside me was drawn to her—and Daji as well, but not as strong.

I sensed something touching my chin, breaking my train of thought. It was warm and full of life.

"C'mon, we're all friends. Don't you think you can at least make an effort to look me in the eye? Pwease?"

I gently swatted her hand away, doing my best to meet her gaze head on. It was hard. *Really* hard.

Her mature features and gentle eyes reminded me of Bella, although she was a lot more hands-on than her. *That's a personal space invader for you!* Bella always kept you on the other side of the table. She just never gave you the chance to leave.

"Good! Now to answer your question..." She coiled a blazing lock around her finger and swished it for a few seconds. "I would say that imagining a scene where someone else told my parents about my death would be pretty heartbreaking for them. I'm sure it would weigh a lot on their hearts to where they would just want to end it all and join me in the great beyond."

Wow, that's pretty detailed—and scary. Are these the kind of feelings that you would have for your parents? Doing what you can to keep their tears away?

"It's depressing just to think about, so I made an oath not to die. That way, I would never have this awful thing leave my sight." She gestured to her pack and sighed before placing it next to her on the couch. "I hope that makes sense."

"Yeah, but what if you don't have anyone to weep and get depressed over you? What then?" I asked.

She seemed semi-serious before, but now her inquisitive stare penetrated me. My breath nearly caught from such unexpected intensity.

"It's alright." Her eyes, rich with understanding and empathy, said, *Tell me everything.*

There was no getting out of it. I felt beyond compelled to answer her. I hadn't expected this conversation to veer solely onto me. *Shall I wallow in my sorrow once again, Bella?*

I sank deeper into the couch and made up my mind. "Okay. It goes like this..."

* * *

And so, for the third time in my life, I told someone about my past. I cut out a lot of meaningless stuff, and the most important sections of my journal would never leave the crevices of my mind. Of course, Stacy was rather different from Umbrea. Her reactions were not as annoying and over the top when I got to the gritty parts. I had told Bella first, but my story didn't seem to matter before I met her.

Time seemed to slow to a crawl. I felt like we had been talking for hours, but that couldn't have been the case. We were still waiting to be called up. What I did know was that my breathing had become ragged, and my throat required a long drink of water to resume full function.

At some point, Daji had sat on a table by the couch to listen to my tales. I hadn't even noticed him come in. "Wow, that's... *deep.*"

Stacy had a sympathetic look on her face, while Daji had trouble concealing his tears. She nodded at his conclusion with a sure-fire grin. "Yup, yup. Super deep! Compared to our goal of getting back home, you have way more resolve and have faced way more hardship."

They both leered at me with something akin to newfound respect. I think. "It really wasn't that ba—"

"All hands on deck! The target is approaching. I repeat: the target is approaching! Prepare for a skirmish!" a voice reverberated through the ship.

Daji and Stacy locked eyes before turning their attention toward me. "I suppose that's our cue," she said.

"I hope we can take back pieces of it as a souvenir. Though I wouldn't mind a nibble or two."

They sure have a lot of confidence. And why does he sound like that Rankle character?

We grabbed our gear and rushed for the deck. A small smile peeked out from my lips. I hadn't tested it out yet, but from what C.T. had told me, this new power could be my perfect path toward the Ten Conquerors.

"The seal is becoming unstable as time goes on," Stacy mumbled with a serious look as we ran. I had no idea what she was referring to, yet it sounded incredibly ominous and reminded me of what C.T. had said earlier.

I prayed they weren't related.

* * *

The vast ocean surrounded us in every direction. With a deep breath, I took in the smell of seaweed and salt water. There wasn't a piece of land in sight. *Oh, what a nostalgic view. Nothing but the ocean.*

A brief chill ran up my spine when I recalled the result of my last sea expedition. *This time it will be different. There is no room for surprises.* That meant the ship was all we had to fall back on if things went south. There would be no one coming to save us. We had to persevere and win for ourselves—by ourselves.

The nine of us stood in a line formation at the front of the ship.

"It's here. I can sense its massive heart beating. If we go any farther, we will risk entrapping ourselves within its grasp," Alistar advised, firmly.

"Noted. Cease moving any further!" Mikaeus shouted to his men. "We will face it here."

"We already have a view on its scales."

"Yup! It's heading our way," the Millis stated.

"I can't wait to get a piece in me mouth, heh-heh-heh," Rankle muttered to himself, creeping me out.

"Leave the sky to us!" Ragnar yelled as he sailed into the air atop his now large sky serpent. From his backpack, he pulled vials that were dark green and red. I'm sure they would pack a punch. The fact his partner could grow to the size of a horse was impressive enough that I had a hard time keeping my eye off the sky. Scales the same color as his partner covered parts of his head and forearms. "Get a load of this masterpiece of a titan! I would stand no chance of bringing something of that magnitude under my control! At least not as I am now. How... divine."

"And yummy," Rankle added, receiving a sour look from Ragnar and his partner.

Slayer and Bonder, huh? Like two sides of the same coin. But look at those scales on his skin! He didn't mention he could share some of their characteristics. I really wanna see this guy in action!

I stood firmly planted between Daji and Stacy as they calmly surveyed their surroundings. Their eyes felt different somehow. I hadn't expected it, but it seemed that they took their roles seriously. I could learn a thing or two from them. After all, this was my first monster raid.

The tranquility of the waters only lasted a little longer before armored, blue tentacles encroached on our port side. Scales with enough edge to slice a hand open covered their entire length, forming an ironclad protection for its body hidden by the deep, blue sea.

"Everyone, if it rears its head, do anything you can to finish it off! Focus on the tentacles until you spot its eyes!"

Mikaeus' orders were absolute. Ragnar had free rein of the sky. The sisters took to either side of the deck, while Mikaeus, Alistar, Daji, and Rankle prepared to assault the Leviathan directly with the help of Stacy's water-walking spell.

The first wave of its tentacle army darted for the ship, aiming to smash it to pieces as quickly as possible. That was its win condition—and our instant loss.

"Rankle! Rag!" Mikaeus yelled. "Do it!"

"On it, Capt'n!" Rankle revealed his crossbow and loaded a bolt into its silver maw. He briefly placed his crystalized hand over it, painting its tip lilac before letting it rip. "Yaaah!"

The bolt soared toward the end of a tentacle, piercing through the scales to the flesh beneath.

Far above the hulking monster, Ragnar stood triumphantly upon his beast. "Bottoms up, my scaled friend!" He tossed a pair of the vials right after Rankle's shot.

"SCREEEEEEEE!" The Leviathan yelped in pain from the bolt, but that wasn't the end. The vials exploded upon contact with the monster's body, splashing their contents all over it. The green vial secreted some sort of acid that licked away at the Leviathan's flesh, while the red one seemed to have no effect.

The crystalized tip spread off of the bolt and began its infestation on the penetrated tentacle. In the span of a minute, the appendage was completely infected by Rankle's crystal.

"Let 'em rip, girls," Mikaeus said with a confident smile.

"Roger!" the twins replied in unison.

Two arrows connected with the crystallized tentacle, shattering it like glass. Bloodied chunks crashed into the sea followed by another scream of agony from the Leviathan.

"That's our window! Frontline, descend!"

Mikaeus, Alistar, Daji, and Rankle all leapt into the ocean, confidence surging from them.

Stacy and I peered over the edge to confirm their condition. Each of them stood vigilantly, attention focused toward different feelers.

I'm not exactly sure how Rankle's crystal thing worked, but he continued to spread his plague on the helpless tentacles with simple touches. Then Daji or

Mikaeus would smash them to bits. The acid from Ragnar had spread over enough flesh on a tentacle where it seemed to tear off on its own. Rankle's attack definitely seemed the most terrifying, though. I wouldn't want to get touched by that.

He reminds me of that king that could turn whatever he touched into gold.

Oh... This could be a problem.

For each tentacle they vanquished, another two would take its place. I wasn't sure if this was the Hydra's Dilemma that Boreas had written about in his travels, or if it simply wielded an insurmountable supply of appendages. Either way, our four crusaders were doing their best to make a dent in it.

You could say their assault had already made quite the *splash*. Ok, I'll stop now.

As the tentacles continued to reform, Ragnar swooped by, his snake bellowing out vile, green flames over its peeling flesh before tossing another pair of the vials. "Woohooooo! How's that for getting a closer look, Vapra?!"

"Hisssssaaaa!" the winged snake replied. It seemed to be having the time of its life up in the sky. Its majestic, iridescent body reminded me of the flying serpent god, Kukulkan.

Birds, insects, and other flying creatures whisked into battle by Ragnar's primal command flew at the Leviathan and dug their beaks, mandibles, or claws into its exposed flesh. The red liquid had caused them to surge in aggressiveness, resulting in them attacking even faster, rending flesh like vultures.

A large falcon stopped mid-air and waited for Ragnar to approach. He calmed the bird by some sort of telepathic command and laid a hand on its chest. The bird let out a squawk before its body morphed, growing in size, changing color, and taking on attributes foreign to an avian being. At the size of a human, it finished its shift with four wings, a barbed tail, and six arms all clad in spiky brown scales.

It shot down after their communion, the air booming at the speed of its four wings. It was bound for the Leviathan, releasing spikes from its body like a porcupine.

I couldn't help but be mesmerized by Ragnar's skill. As he had told us earlier, he was a traveling mercenary originally from a tribe of monster tamers called Bonders. They had the ability to link with animals and monsters to reach a mutual understanding of sorts, sharing senses, emotions, and even memories. It was similar to being a Summoner or Beast Tamer, but used some sort of primordial spirit magic to work. The thing about Ragnar was that he was apparently blessed by his god and could evolve any creature he linked with, mutating its body to mix with other creatures he had linked with in the past. He could also give commands to animals he hadn't linked with. I glanced down at the sea creatures ramming their sharp fins and spiny hides into the Leviathan. *It seems that's what he was doing now.*

I'm sure he could speak to Frosty. I really want to chat with him, but for now, I need to focus on getting vengeance.

Daji went for one of the tentacles that wasn't infested with flying monsters. He leapt high into the air before delivering a crushing blow. Each of his punches carried enough force to capsize a medium-sized ship. With that being said, his fists easily broke through the armored scales, making quick work of the flesh beneath. Each fist left the residue of dark energy in its wake. *Jeez, I hope I never have to face off against those fists. For a small guy, he packs a big punch—it's as if his short frame can't contain the raging torrent trapped within.*

Meanwhile, Mikaeus' spear discharged enough electricity to paralyze an adult drake with each stab. I hoped he didn't zap himself with it by accident with all that water around.

Rankle continued to corrupt and destroy every tentacle in sight, each fleshy feeler shattering like glass before his strange plague, while Alistar coordinated the denizens of the deep to assault the exposed flesh beneath its scales. After sharks, serpents, anglerfish, and a myriad of other summoned bit into it, he hacked away with his dual axes.

The sky was mostly clear for Ragnar to soar down and spray any exposed flesh with his partner's toxic green flames while tossing additional acid. It was a massacre of peachy pink meat and fragmented scales.

I wasn't used to the sound of hissing skin, tearing flesh, or scales being crushed under a monumental force, but it was more calming than I'd thought it would be in the heart of battle. Just like burning meat or cracking a coconut shell, right?

Large booms and cracks filled my ears, as well as the smaller sounds of teeth biting into flesh. How magnificent the scene was. Like straight out of a book. *At this rate, it doesn't seem too far-fetched to actually kill it. Now show us that ugly head!*

Occasionally, a tentacle or two would slink towards one of our companions' blind spots, forcing Stacy or me to freeze, burn, or paralyze it. The tentacles hissed, screamed, and keeled over like a dying snake on the wooden deck. We couldn't have it harming those who were busy with mortal combat, could we?

In between attack intervals from the frontline, the twins would keep tabs on the entire fight. They sent progress reports to both us and the assault team while sniping exposed skin.

To top it all off, multiple sailors released silver balls from the cannons, using their speed to penetrate even more of the scales.

"I don't wanna speak too soon, but isn't this going a bit too well?" I asked Stacy with a mix of confidence and unease as she discharged another blast of dark flames. They felt just as malicious as Daji's blows, but I sensed nothing but good will behind her focused visage. Perhaps they were both acquainted with some sort of dark magic. Now was not the time to ask.

"Mmhmm." She finished casting a gust of wind to prevent water from reaching us and brought her attention back to me. She grinned, leaning on her staff. "I've heard many stories about this thing. For starters, no one has ever seen its entire body and lived to tell the tale. The beast is a coward in that way, but that will all change soon enough, now that we're here. The other interesting tidbit is that no one has ever seen it cornered, either. Not till now, that is." She looked especially smug at that moment. It reminded me of a rather pitiful girl.

"Do you think that being in a near death situation will make a big difference?"

Stacy shrugged before hefting her staff to prepare another spell. "I guess we are about to find out."

As if on cue, it let out another husky howl.

The air grew stiff around us. I wanted to run—to be anywhere but on that deck—yet my curiosity forbade me from looking away.

"It's entered fight-or-flight mode!" Ragnar shouted from above. "Its acts of aggression should accelerate to a whole new magnitude. Be careful!"

The Leviathan's ruined body began to contort and expand. Erupting from the sea—spraying the deck in water—were nearly double the number of tentacles, now a glorious shade of violet. It was now truly enraged.

"We need more rear support!" screamed Mikaeus. "There's too much of— AHHHHHHH!"

A myriad of tentacles smashed into Mikaeus, knocking him off his feet. He was thrown at least ten feet before landing smack on his back, still firmly gripping his spear. The water-walking enchantment had stopped any part of his body from touching the water.

"Boss!" Rankle shouted as he fended off six tentacles at once. He was overwhelmed. The crystallization and crossbow combo wasn't fast enough anymore. He unsheathed a scimitar from his waist and eviscerated every appendage in his view. However, it wasn't long before we lost sight of him in the never-ending surplus of angered Leviathan.

Daji and Alistar were managing far better, but the tentacles were slowly, but surely, overwhelming them. It wouldn't be long before the entire ship was blocked by a wall of limbs.

"Shit. This wasn't part of the plan," Stacy murmured, while biting her thumb. It was strange seeing her so panicked after how calm and collected she'd appeared when we had talked a few hours earlier.

I did my best to burn and freeze as many tentacles as possible that fell into Alistar's blind spot. I briefly caught a glimpse of the twins with their rapid-fire bows, fending off an onslaught that had breached our first line of defense. The undulating appendages became weighed down more and more by the deluge of arrows until they descended back into the sea. It really felt like the tentacles had a mind of their own.

The sense of panic that welled up in my chest reminded me of the hidden option I had only recently discovered. *I think it's time for a test run.*

"All this, and it still doesn't even show its cowardly head. Pathetic," Stacy spat.

I wanted her to return to her usual self, so I flashed her a confident smirk, even if it was very forced. "I'm not saying this will work, but I may have a new trump card to test out."

Stacy was too focused on Daji to acknowledge what I was saying. I could tell she cared about him and him alone. I wondered if she would escape with just him if she could.

"Ugh…" I shook my head, brushing aside those dark thoughts.

Alright. Here we go! I thrust my hand forward, a rune of purple jaws glowing fiercely as if it was seared into my skin. "As a champion of the Silver King, I uproot the past. Come forth, Fallen One!"

I didn't have to chant every time, but speaking the invocation was ostensibly more effective from what C.T. had said. The rune in my hand burned so intensely that I winced in pain. A sudden rush, the euphoria of ancient power reaching far into my soul, surged through me. It felt… godly.

From nothing, a singularity had spawned. The shards of the past were reforming for me, and me alone. It was time for the beast to wake from its long slumber.

Ash to ash.

Dust to dust.

From extinction, it was reborn. It had an onyx pelt made of jagged spikes, and the majestic fur looked more like polished metal than anything else. It stood on all fours, nearly double the size of Frosty, and the two long horns that jutted from its head made it feel somewhat demonic.

It bellowed before glaring at me like a goliath finally released from its prison.

Its face—his face—had the same structure as a wolf, but was more primitive and a *lot* more savage. Two tusks stuck out from either side of his long muzzle, lengthy and sharp enough to impale a grown man. On his dark forehead beamed the same symbol that was now encased within a silver greave on my arm.

"That's a wicked beast you got there!" Ragnar exclaimed while slipping past the Leviathan's tentacle attacks. An arrow deflected off the monster's scales and flew straight at him; however, his scarf swatted it aside, appearing gelatinous and slimy as if he was wearing an ooze. "I'm a little jealous that you get to summon such an impressive being."

"Thanks!" I called back. "I wasn't expecting it either!"

One out of the seven cylinders displayed the same lilac-shaded rune embedded within the slot. It looked special, but not the kind I was hoping for. This wasn't one of those legendary colored-named Eternals; however, it was still something impressive. Extinctathon, the Eternal of extinguished life. The name had seamlessly popped into my head.

So, this is an Eternal manifested. I wonder if I can summon more than that in the future. That would be...

"What the hell?!" Stacy asked as she looked my way. "What is *that?*"

I smiled, despite the circumstances. Fearlessly approaching him, I patted his head with my newly armored hand. His information came to me as if whispered directly into my brain. "This is Ashardna, the last Razor Wolf."

Stacy slightly stumbled, but didn't seem too surprised. "I never expected to see one again," she muttered.

But how would she have ever seen one? Not even Ragnar seemed to know exactly what it was.

"Just how did you—"

"Watch out!" someone screamed ahead of us. A rapid assault of tentacles barreled towards us like a volley of arrows.

"Ashardna!" I screamed as Stacy prepared defensive magic.

Like a spinning maelstrom, the ancient wolf tore through the armored appendages as if they were paper. His body was held tightly together like a condensed sphere of infinite motion, spinning in the air like an obsidian vortex, moving from tentacle to tentacle before reaching the main body to assist with the assault. How he stayed up in the air for so long at that size—I couldn't say.

"They sure are an impressive species," Stacy remarked. Her posture relaxed the longer she viewed the carnage. It was almost like she enjoyed it.

I nodded, still in disbelief. *He's way stronger than I thought. A true spawn of The Silver King. But why did he choose me? Perhaps Frosty really is related.* The only problem was that he and his kin had been dead for well over three centuries. I had learned that the moment I summoned him. Yet there he was, back for blood, and somehow my pal was involved.

I could feel his anger like it was my own, and his pain as well. It was like a bubbling crucible. Every so often, it would tip over before collapsing, leaving a puddle of molten liquid in its wake. Just one push and all hell would break loose. I had already been pondering over if I would die if he did, or at least greatly suffer if he was killed.

Best not to focus on that in the middle of battle.

I once again thought back to my earlier conversation with Cthulhu. *Eternals really are wild.*

"Lethe," the voice called out again.

"W-what?!" I yelped in surprise.

"About time! You were zoned out for nearly a minute! Don't lose focus now! We're in the endgame."

"Oh, was I? Right. My bad."

Stacy forced a smile. "As I was saying before, when we kill this vexing creation and get back, how about the two of us have some good ol' girl time without any of the muscle brains?" As she finished, she released another ball of gassy, azure flames into a set of tentacles a few feet from the boat.

Everything about that threw me for a loop.

"I'm not exactly sure what 'girl time' means, but won't Daji be upset?"

"He has had me all to himself ever since our exile, and besides—after this he's going to need some serious healing, and it just so happens that I'm his only healer." She flashed a mischievous grin at me. "It would be a *shame* if there were complications, and I couldn't get to him for an extra day. What a tragedy."

Strange. Your demonic smile and sarcastic tone lead me to believe that it would be anything but—Oops! That was a close one!

I impaled one tentacle with shards and incinerated another before they could reach me. "And you're okay with that? Seems like an abuse of power."

"Yup. Totally."

She isn't even refuting it!

"I must say, you're a lot more brazen than I first assumed." I idly let out a burst of flames at the smaller tentacles attempting to reach us.

Stacy sliced another tentacle in half with a sharp flurry of wind. "First impressions are just that—impressions. If you want to know more, you'll have to put in the time and effort."

We both were knocked off balance when a stray appendage slapped the side of the boat. The ship settled down soon after the tentacle bisected by Alistar's axe. "I guess that makes sense, though I wish I could have a fragment of your confidence."

"Maybe I'll teach ya some time. I know you're a traveler, but Daji and I travel for many reasons as well. We should party up some time—or a lot. Whatever you're in the mood for."

"Party up?" I parroted. "Reall—"

The boat swelled up and erupted into the air as if it were launched from a springboard. The force knocked Stacy off her feet and sent me—who was already near the edge of the railing—overboard.

Greeeaaat!

It happened so fast that I didn't have time to process or yell for help. I heard the howling of Ashardna in the distance as I dropped. I somehow knew if we were estranged from each other for too long, he would certainly return from where he'd come from.

He did his job, though. I was the one that failed.

I plummeted from above and smacked into the sea. Not having the water-walking spell caused me to sink rapidly. I'd lost sight of everyone during my fall, and all that I could see was a mass of tentacles thick as trees, blocking my view of the sky. *Oh... how nostalgic.*

I must have hit my head hard, because I could see a faint trail of blood leaking from my body as I drifted deeper. At least I wouldn't need to worry about drowning because of the wetsuit, but I was steadily losing consciousness.

Then I saw *it*. The monster, the beast—the great Leviathan. The source of my hatred and malice, my problems... I saw it. One of the questions that had been bouncing around in my head since we'd engaged in battle had finally been answered. *So, that's its head.* All that we'd fought from the start had been wave after wave of tentacles, yet we could hear it cry in pain. Now I knew exactly what it was.

I was maybe twenty or thirty feet away from it as I drifted deeper into the lonely abyss. It had many yellow eyes and hundreds of teeth that I couldn't even begin to count. I couldn't see the bottom of the beast, but those tentacles had to come from *somewhere*. Would they be able to handle that? I hoped so. The last thing I saw before losing consciousness was the face of a man—or a fish—or something in between, swimming toward me with a worried guise. I wasn't sure, nor did I have time to mull it over before the darkness washed my consciousness away.

Journal Sketch #12
The Leviathan

1404, 32nd day, Month of the Hero King

While it has been a month between when I saw it and when I last wrote in here, its horrifying visage will never leave me. Its tentacles, a deluge of death that sent me off on an adventure I will never forget. I don't think I was able to truly illustrate its horrid frame, however. It was a lot worse in person.

Chapter 13

At the Bottom of the Sea

The seafolk are nice people once you get to know them. Two things of note: never insult their god, and never ask why all their names start with the letter P. Almost lost my partner down there for that. Those ancient denizens can be quite scary.

—Boreas Tyrel

A single eye fluttered open, taking in the surroundings. The queen-sized bed was soft beneath her, far bigger than any bed the girl had ever slept in before. It was an opulent room, lavished with yellow sheets and a multitude of fluffy pillows. The area was vacant, except for a lone girl, still in the wetsuit she had worn before drifting into unconsciousness. A murky distortion made it troublesome for her to determine where she actually was, but she continued to ponder; the room didn't seem real.

The door at the edge of the room quietly creaked ajar. It revealed *a woman in a white dress that was wrapped around one shoulder, while leaving the dark blue skin of her other out for anyone to see. She had pale blue eyes and ears that were pointed like an elf's and webbed at the tips. The woman was pretty, but her complexion and features were so foreign that it was hard for the girl to get a grasp of where she truly was.*

That would be the start of my journal entry once I got back.

"You've awoken. It has been some time since we have received a human visitor." Her voice was soft and as clear as a bell.

"This is going to sound strange, but am I... underwater?"

The woman nodded with a small smile. "Very perceptive. This guest room was designed to make Landers that stayed here feel as if they weren't a hundred miles below the land. We still haven't been able to fully trick the senses that alert you of the shift in pressure. I will make sure to let my superior know. I thank you."

She unironically bowed her head as if I had just saved the day with my one question.

"That's alright," I said, looking around. "So, where am I?" I pushed away the covers and got to my feet. "Ughhhh... M-my head..." I touched my forehead only to find a soft layer of bandages wrapped tightly around it. Just the slight touch made me wince with pain.

"You were badly hurt when we found you. I would suggest not touching anything in the head region. As for where you are—I'm sure you Landers have searched for this place for quite some time."

"What do you mean? What is this place?"

"The Kingdom of Poseidon. I am one of his many children. I am Pele." She bowed again.

Children of Poseidon? That's a name I will never forget. They must be the real ones.

I thought back to the pirates who had attacked the ship that Bella and I had been on. They'd called themselves something like that too, but it had held no weight except for being able to control the Leviathan.

Pele furrowed her brow. "The face you are making is telling me that you have heard of us. Is that the case?"

"Well, they called themselves the Children of Poseidon, but they most certainly didn't look the part."

Pele sized me up and down for a good thirty seconds; her thoughts seemed to be churning quickly. "Ah, the marauders. Yes, I knew of them."

"Knew? Were they disbanded?" I asked.

"They were slaughtered, mercilessly—all of them. We found pieces of the remains in our territory a few years back, but they were indeed wiped out. I call it divine punishment—from Father. It was a sin to steal one of his replica tridents."

Pele was visibly angry as she spoke. I could tell. If what she said was true, then that trident was how they'd controlled the beast. That meant that once he was killed, the Leviathan either killed the rest of his crew or fled. But who knows?

"When can I leave? I'm in the middle of a subjugation quest." I didn't want to give her the full details of what I had been doing, just in case.

Pele stretched out her arm while keeping eye contact with me, then opened the door. It was eerie, but at least she was happy to oblige.

"You are free to go whenever, as long as you take the Vow of Secrecy. We can't have more Landers finding our home and taking Father's treasures while he is away."

So, Poseidon isn't here, huh? I would have liked to meet a famous god like him and then yell at him for creating such an awful creature. Shame!

Pele let me step out first, revealing quite a sight.

"Wow... It's so *blue*."

"Indeed. We fishmen have lived here for hundreds of generations under Father's guidance."

"I see. The structures here are really well made."

"Mm. I see you have an eye for architecture."

"I guess you can say that."

I looked up to see the top of a tower built completely out of what must have been coral and stone. The homes were reminiscent of a small village, but the scale was incredible. It must have taken centuries to collect enough material to build something so grand.

Fish people swam above me, hunting game with nets, while others were off in the distance with spears, attacking larger creatures that I couldn't fully make out.

Pele walked ahead of me and pointed toward an extensive structure of shells. "Would you like a tour? Our last visitor wasn't able to see this splendid place."

"Sure. I would love one. After all, you saved me."

Pele lightly chuckled and revealed a thin smile. "Your thanks are appreciated, but it was not me who saved you, but one of my brothers, Pelion. He discovered you when he was on his mission to track one of Father's problem children."

It didn't take a genius to figure out who she was referring to.

"He dropped you off before heading back, but I will let him know later. Would you like to visit one of our food cabins?"

"Huh?" I pointed to my mouth. "Can I actually eat down here? It won't interfere with my underwater spell, right?"

It sounded pretty stupid—I'm well aware, but who knows what kind of stuff they could feed me. It would be good to assume there may be something that could interrupt the enchantment on my suit. *Actually, I would have totally drowned if they changed my clothes while I was asleep. Really dodged a tragedy there.*

"Pelius, the local doctor said, 'The enchantment is rather strong, so I shouldn't have to worry about treating her wounds. It would take quite some force to undo a spell of that strength.' That should apply for anything down here."

I sure hope so.

She led me into a building. Multiple long tables were filled with fish people casually enjoying their meals of fish, kelp, and other delicacies that I had never set eyes on before. The scene reminded me of a rather painful memory. Back when I'd spent my time wasting away as a witch, one of the first places I'd visited and frequented was a food pantry a lot like this one. It left a bad taste in my mouth.

"On second thought, can we go somewhere else?"

"Hm?" Pele studied me carefully. "That is fine. Anything in mind?"

We exited the building, leaving the two of us to our thoughts.

While I'd been in there, I'd been stared at by at least five children. Their eyes had been as wide as saucers. I was used to the stares, but not when they were attached to my entire being. It was a little nerve-racking. I'm not sure why, though... Why did I care about what anyone thought, especially kids?

"Um..." I looked left and then right. "I know this is a long shot, but are there any other humans or races close to them staying here besides myself?"

"Hmm." She pursed her lips and looked away from me. When she turned back, her mouth trembling with... excitement? "Indeed!" She clapped her delicate hands together. "There is one, but she has been in a rather critical condition for quite some time now. Our doctors can only do so much for someone that isn't a fishman. Perhaps you'll be able to change our luck."

"Oh, really? Uh, I don't know any sort of healing magic, so..." If she wanted me to provide some sort of knowledge that only humans had, I was not the one. "If I could just see them, I could at least guess what the problem is."

I didn't know much about human anatomy. Even Rock knew more, and well, you know—he's a golem. *Maybe it's a simple solution that they're overlooking because of the barrier between races.* I could at least give it a shot. It was the least I could do to repay their hospitality.

"Why not? I see no problem with that. But first, let me take you to the Sanctum of Purification so you can take the vow of secrecy."

"Um, yeah. Sure."

She led the way down a path with many coral reefs and fish people carrying an assortment of materials on their backs—from pieces of destroyed ships to scales that encompassed the colors of a rainbow. The people here were profoundly diligent. Humans could learn a thing or two from watching them.

"Here we are." She gestured at the alabaster door that had appeared out of thin air—or thin sea, I guess.

"Where did that—"

"It's a special entrance to our sanctum that was designed to be impossible to detect. Rest assured, it's safe to enter."

"Sure..." I wasn't convinced, but I guess there really wasn't another option.

"Right this way."

I entered through the door that was veiled from the rest of the world. When I was on the other side, all I could say was, "Woah..."

Everything was made out of pure marble, from the polished floors to the fountains on each side that spewed fresh water into the pools below. Large, shiny pearls stared down from above, showing off my weakened state in their reflections.

Not really what I wanted to see, but thanks.

A staircase jutted out from each side of the room, coiling upwards like a helix. I couldn't see any farther above from my position, but I'm sure it was just as fancy. A lonely blue door sat at the end of the room, while a statue of what was clearly Poseidon stood tall in front of it. He was striking a triumphant pose with his trident arching upward. What surprised me the most about this magnificent place was that there was no one else there.

"It's just us in the outer sanctum right now. Most of the clergy are off on their own missions, so the only people here besides you and me are the other guest and the doctor attending them."

I shifted my gaze toward her. "Would this 'other guest' happen to be behind that blue door?"

"Indeed," she said with a semblance of a smile. "But before you can go through there, you must touch Father's statue and agree to our pledge."

Seriously? Whatever. Sure. I was eager to see whoever was behind that door. My pulse was speeding up with each passing moment. *Soon, soon,* I told myself.

I made my way to the statue and placed a palm right on top of his pearly white head. "So, what do I do now?"

"Do you swear to not tell anyone in the overworld about our sacred home, as well as anything that has happened within it?"

"Yeah, sure." *Wow. I didn't sound very convincing, even to myself.*

"I need a more resounding confirmation," she said flatly.

"Uh... I swear that I will uphold this agreement. Does that work?"

"Swimmingly."

"Pffft!" I held back the urge to break into laughter.

A pale-blue light engulfed my vision, but everything returned to normal soon after. *That was easier than I thought it would be.* I did have one question, though. "Theoretically—what would happen if I broke this pledge?"

"Ah!" Pele clapped her hands together with a perfectly fabricated smile. "Your soul will leave your body and you will be stuck in the Plane of Oblivion for all eternity! Interesting, right?"

Yikes! This is the first time I have heard of a place like that.

"Does that get around writing?"

She furrowed her brow with a slightly serious yet semi-playful expression. "That has not been a problem in the past, so no. Why? Should we add that to the terms?"

"N-no! That's fine. Was just curious." *She wouldn't care if I wrote it in my journal, right? Right? Probably not.*

"Well then, are you ready to see the guest?"

I really didn't like the sound of that. Regardless, I followed her to the resting place of the mysterious individual. I had a lot of things I would like to ask her or him, but that would require them to be awake and aware of their surroundings. From what I'd heard, that clearly wasn't the case.

When I entered, I had to shield my eyes from the blinding light of a fish that was swimming past the window. When I could see clearly again, I crumbled to my knees.

I was simply and unequivocally at a loss for words.

Huh? This is real, right?

I tried to speak, but only gibberish came out. *I don't even know what I am saying; how in the world can I?*

"Miss Lethe, are you alright?" Pele asked from behind. I'm sure she was worried, but I couldn't take my eyes off the sleeping patient ahead of me; how in the world could I?

What a heavy pause, but it was warranted.

"She's... alive?!" I muttered. "Wha—whaaaaaat?!"

Along a wooden bed, tucked in with cream-colored sheets, was a sleeping girl. She had neck-length blond hair in a bob cut, and while I couldn't see her eyes at the moment, I knew they were milky brown. Her tall physique stretched near the length of the bed, putting the nail in the coffin on who this mysterious person was.

"Isabella... Bela?!"

Her porcelain-white skin was the most beautiful thing I had ever seen, despite its wan complexion. Even while she slept, she was as pretty as the flowers standing tall in the vase beside her bed.

"Great! Finally, someone that can identify the patient!"

My knees were stuck to the marble floor, but I managed to gaze upon a fishman in a gray lab coat, with documents gripped tightly in his navy-colored hands. He was grinning ear to ear as if I had brought him the greatest of news.

"Uh, yeah..." I managed to open my mouth. "She was my friend, but she was supposed to have been eaten by the Leviathan."

This time, Pele spoke up. "Ah, him. It was the same case with you as it was with her. One of my brothers, Pilon, found her near Potherion—or what you call—the Leviathan, and brought her back here. She must have hit the sea hard because she hasn't woken in three years."

"Oh..." I slowly got to my feet and placed my trembling hands on the edge of her bed. "She looks so... peaceful." I commented, trying to say literally anything else than what was really on my mind.

"Indeed, she is. Every day we send nutrients into her body via one of our head sorcerers." The doctor edged closer to us and faced me. "We call this a sea-coma. She may never wake up again."

"Thought so…"

"I thought the case was the same for you when I visited you last night, but I am glad to see you made a speedy recovery." He seemed genuinely happy about it. *Guess that's a doctor for you. No matter what race they were, they always put their patients first.*

"Thanks…"

Pele patted me on the shoulder. "I assume you want to take her away from us, but it would be dangerous to pull her away after her body has gotten so used to the treatment and eating regimen."

"Oh… Yeah, that makes sense." I stared down at my feet, not wanting to show my face.

"Miss Lethe," Pele said in a strong and commanding voice. It brought me out of my stupor. "I assure she will be well taken care of as she always has been and…" Something appeared in her palm as she benevolently held it out to me. It was a small, light-blue pearl, the same color as her skin. "This will show you the path to us if you ever want to come visit."

My face lit up. I swiftly took the pearl and clutched it tight in my fist. I could feel an entire world of warmth packed inside the small treasure. "Thank you—for everything, really. Thank you for watching over her and… for this." I flashed them both the best smile I could muster after everything that had happened. I hoped it was enough.

"It's our pleasure. We also had another reason for keeping her here," Pele said.

"Oh?" I tilted my head. "What's that?"

She crossed her arms, a shade of darkness shrouding her gaze. "When my brother recovered her, he told me something very interesting happened with the boat she plummeted from. Apparently, there was a demon from the

Netherworld onboard. I couldn't even believe my ears when I heard that. That place of nightmares actually exists!"

I was dead silent. That had been on my mind for the past few years. I'd refused to address it. *What was it that saved me all those years ago, and why only me?* It had haunted me for years. I recalled the demon who used to appear in my dreams. I was sure he was involved, if not the main culprit. *But how did I summon him?*

"While he couldn't see the features of the demon, he could hear its guttural howl and the screams of the pitiful humans as they were slaughtered and consumed. Almost no blood fell into the surrounding sea, which is quite peculiar, don't you think?"

"I agree," said the doctor. "It must have licked all their bodily fluids clean or even consumed the bodies completely. It's remarkable. To have such a large maw... Well, it just doesn't seem feasible. Reminds me of the creatures that supposedly live down in the Swirling Abyss. My mother told me she saw one when she swam by it. Fascinating, isn't it?" He had a mad look in his eyes that filled me with unease.

"R-right."

"I thought the same thing. For my brother, who had good eyes, but failed to see even a semblance of the blood bath above. It must have been quite a demon for more reasons than one."

"What do you mean?"

Pele locked eyes with me, her expression dead serious. It gave me chills. "I mean that whatever it was, it not only massacred every single human there, but was also frightening enough to cause even the great Potherion to turn tail. Even if the wielder of one of Father's replicas perished, it would still take on any challenge. Potherion would never flee—not from anyone. I would really like to know what your friend saw before jumping ship."

"W-why are you telling me all of this?" My nerves were fried. "There has to b-be a reason."

She doesn't know I was on the ship longer than Bella.

She giggled, her eyes glued to my face. "I just thought you would like to know what kind of bullet your friend dodged. She is quite fortunate, really. It's a shame she lost her inner self in the process. But you know what they say, 'Out of the sea pan and into the aqua-fire.'"

"Mmhm." I nodded before sighing aloud with relief. I said no more, feeling the complications that would undoubtedly arise if I did.

I broke away from her gaze and tucked the pearl firmly within my palm. My clothes and satchel were both back in a storage area in town. I would need to return before I could move on. Wait... What did she say at the end?

"And what exactly qualifies as someone's 'inner self'?"

Pele's cool expression didn't waver as she pursed her lips. "The inner self is what our kind thinks of as the you inside of *you*."

I felt my eye narrow as I pondered her words. Around ten seconds passed before I snapped my fingers. "Oh, like a soul, right?"

"Precisely. And even though her body is in immaculate condition, her inner self seems vacant, as if it's no longer there."

The doctor nodded his head in agreement. "It seems something happened before we could retrieve her. There's really no other logical explanation for why she hasn't woken yet."

That last part was like an arrow to the chest. Did she even have a chance to recover? All I could do was hope for the best... Actually, no. I could search for a solution. She didn't have to face this problem alone. *I will find a way to bring her back, even if it kills me! Come to think of it, Boreas once fought a man with the magic to attack their souls. Is the Revenant King still kicking? If so, I need to find him.*

"Thank you for the info. I will do my utmost to save her as I travel. But if I could ask for one more thing..."

The doctor nodded, and Pele was stricken with interest. "What is it?"

"Can I get a ride back to Trident—if possible?"

"That shouldn't be an issue. I will have a dolphin prepared for you once we leave. You are acquainted with how to ride them, yes?"

Umm... no? Who in the world rides a dolphin? Are there licenses for that like there are for mythical beasts? I have so many questions now.

"No, but I'm willing to try."

"Splendid. Let us be on our way, then."

I waved. "Yeah. Thanks, doc. Thanks for looking over her."

"It was a pleasure to learn her name. I hope to see you down here again."

"For her, of course I will."

I solemnly peered at Bella's place of temporary slumber one last time. She wasn't dead, but she wasn't exactly alive and kicking, either. I needed to hold out hope for her. She was lucky enough to survive, the rest would all need to come from her own willpower. *Or if I can find something that can restore her.*

Pele led the way as we both left, but I could have sworn I heard one little thing from Bella's lips as we left. It was faint, but my ears picked up on it. *She said my name! I think so, anyway.* She... She felt my presence. Well, she was supposed to be an empty husk, but perhaps there was a piece of her that dwelled within. A piece that had sensed me. That had to be it. Or I was delusional from being hundreds of feet under water.

I looked back at her one more time. "Get well soon, Bella. Or else I'll have to do something drastic and dangerous for you. I know how much you hate conflict."

The thought of her panicked face brought a smile to mine.

* * *

An hour later, I was riding a dolphin and headed back toward Trident. His body was sleek and hard to hold on to, but he went slow and steady—just for me. *I hope Frosty doesn't get jealous.*

Chances were that my crew had already left or been killed by the Leviathan. *I guess I should have asked Pele about that. Whatever!* What really mattered was that Bella—my best friend—was still alive. Though, I would be sad if anything happened to that strange crew.

I looked at one of my hands that gripped the dolphin's neck. A small, blue pearl floated right above it, as if it enchanted to stay in place—which of course, it was.

"Wait for me, Bella. I've found you, but I haven't yet found myself—my true self, anyway. We are destined to be together again someday. I just know it! The journey of a traveler has many ups and downs, but eventually it comes full circle."

That's what I understood from my years of reading, anyway.

We reached the surface, allowing me to sit rather comfortably on top of the dolphin.

I peered toward the oncoming sunset. There was so much I didn't know about myself and what was happening around me. So few clues, but so many places to visit. I might not have done a lot in life that I remembered, but that didn't matter. I had places to be and people to meet. Experiences needed to be gained. Maybe then I would remember a thing or two about my past. I had clues to follow: demons, a supposed seal, the Silver King, the Starscourge of the cosmos, and world-shattering Eternals—all that jazz. I could even end up an evil being, just like I'd joked about Rock being in the past. Wouldn't that be crazy?

"Now, where should I go next?"

I was too caught up in the moment to notice a colossal whirlpool growing around me. It would set me on a path I would never forget, with friends and foes that could shake the foundations of the very world.

Chapter 14

The Sand King's Sorrow

More times than I can count, I found myself wandering aimlessly under the chilly desert night. If you dare travel alone, make sure to stay hydrated, and bring a damn good map.

—*Boreas Tyrel*

There was a time when the thought of visiting a desert country would fill me with interest and wonder—not anymore. After what I'd seen—after *that* experience—I was certain I didn't want to step foot in a desert again, especially if I wanted to avoid *him*.

It all began around a day ago. I had followed my map as I set out for a country that could help me make quite a killing in liquid capital. Sure, the currency differed from what I was used to, but that just meant I could make a killing from pawning some of it off to an old collector.

While there was a road that circumvented the desert, the path was long and perilous. It would have been a real pain if it had taken a few extra days to reach my destination just because some desert was in the way. Besides, I hadn't been to one before.

It could be fun. After all, Boreas traveled to many desert cities and wrote on how their food and lifestyles were quite different from the northern countries of the human continent. It sounds beyond intriguing.

"The map says to take a left here and go north until I see the first oasis. Apparently, it's a road stop for merchants and travelers."

I was riding on Frosty, but I was bored. I was simply having a conversation with myself to pass the time. Anyone would do it in my situation. I'm sure of it!

That aside, the scorching sun didn't affect me too much, thanks to the heat resistance from my flame ring, but it didn't help with the sweating. There was lots and lots of sweating happening, much to my chagrin.

Since I hadn't initially planned to go through the world of dunes and dust, my outfit wasn't exactly ideal. I'd thought it would be good to wear something that matched the summer breeze around this time of year. This was the only season when the north wasn't beset by harsh winters and days of snow. How that worked in a desert country—I had no clue.

Earlier it had been tranquil, and the gentle touch of the breeze had felt warm against my shoulders. That's why I thought it would be fun to wear something sleeveless and short, like a ruffled lace blouse and a pleated skirt. The freedom of exposed legs was a true blessing.

That had been my original train of thought, anyway. *Though, I think I may look a little too touristy, and it doesn't help that the sweat is making me want to peel off a layer.* At the least, the exquisite, white summer hat I had on helped provide shade—

Suddenly, a stray gust pushed me forward, sending the hat skyward.

...So, I *had* been wearing an exquisite, white summer hat that went really well with my top; however, it seemed the weather had other plans.

I squinted up at the sun, my irritation clear as the cloudless sky. *Welp. I think my day is ruined. Thanks wind!*

The helpful gust then decided that it would not assist me for the rest of my slog through the desert. How unlucky could one be?

I was about to find out.

* * *

"Ugh! I thought summer was supposed to be the best season!" I howled to the endless expanse of the sky. "I don't want to become a sweat monster! The smell is already assaulting my nostrils!"

What is this climate? I should have bought perfume or something to mask the scent before I came. At least no one else is around to get a whiff of stinky Lethe.

To be fair to my past self, if I was wearing my usual outfit, I would most likely be as cooked as a turtle forcibly trapped within its shell. *Silver linings. Silver linings, right? I hate playing the part of an optimist. It's so exhausting!*

Even with all his fur, Frosty appeared at ease. Well, he was hanging his tongue out a lot more often, but that seemed like nothing when I was fighting for my life to preserve my clothes and hair! I wanted to look mildly presentable. Was I getting jealous of a pelt? Surely that wasn't the case. Either way, I made sure to give him lots and lots of water. I did the same while cleaning my forehead with a now wet and heavy handkerchief. *Why did I only bring one?*

I stuffed it into my satchel, my hands slipping to tie the straps closed. *I hate sweat!* Gazing down at Frosty, I let out a long sigh. *Hang in there, pal. We're both cooking out here.* In truth, I said that more for myself than him.

We delved deeper into the burning desert, getting more tired and sweaty by the minute. There was no way I could hold out much longer without a break, and hopefully, a place to freshen up and change. I was transforming Frosty's back into something warm and sticky. I sniffed and then grimaced. Yeah, he could use a wipe down as well.

About an hour had gone by since we'd first embarked on this hellish journey—I mean—interesting adventure to the great Kingdom of Rima. An old folktale I'd heard on my way there had really got my blood pumping; I just had to visit.

The Death Scorpion, Anorok, a monster from the fabled Netherworld, had been felled by an ancient god of the sun. His nearly impervious carapace was deconstructed and used to build homes and defenses against invaders. His poison was also rumored to have been kept hidden away in the king's vault, supposedly it was so potent that even an immortal couldn't survive a single drop.

Then how did he lose? The barkeep couldn't answer that, but supposedly, Ra or Helios were likely the ones that had obliterated him. I guess the power of the sun could melt through even the toughest of shells. And hey, maybe I would finally meet another god or two.

I bought a map from the last place I was staying at and was told to visit for their scorpion pot pie if I was in the area. While that sounded very... um, intriguing, there was another reason I wanted to go there.

I had flipped through the three thick and withered volumes of *The Adventurer's Journey* too many times to count, but no matter how long I poured over each page, I couldn't find anything on Rima. That made the reason to visit even more compelling.

Ha-ha! I could go somewhere not even the great Boreas has been to!

One thing I had gathered was that there was a prominent celebrity in Rima—their king. Many countries and towns in the region spoke fondly of a foreign legend that was grounded in truth—or so I had heard. It was called *The Legend of the Glorious Sand King*. Despite sounding a little biased, it had a cool ring to it. I thought so, at least.

The legend spoke of a man born with a unique type of magic. Basically, this guy, who's the king of Rima, seemed to have the power to make anything out of sand and animate it. The sand seemed to spill out of him like blood. You could say it was an additional bodily fluid.

Of course, there was no way to prove the stories were true, but that's exactly why I wanted to see him for myself. After all, it had been quite some time since

I'd been to a country with an actual monarch. And maybe, just maybe, if I had nothing else to do and was bored—like really, *really* bored—then I might try some scorpions.

While I mulled the tale over, I finally came upon the first rest stop. The sight of the large, refreshing pond that had tall palm trees encompassing it like a council was a godsend. Hanging from above were even some brown fruits—what I had since learned were called coconuts.

A long, brown outhouse stood behind the pond, and a water dispenser was adjacent to it so people could clean themselves off or have a drink.

I ended up locking myself in a bathroom stall to freshen up and take a bathroom break. My mouth drew back into a wry smile as I let out a weak sigh of relief.

Finally, I can rest.

The enchanted floor was both warm and cold at the same time. The entire stall produced a frosty aura that cooled me down a lot better than my ring ever could. I grabbed a handful of wash rags and wiped myself down all over. It felt so cool.

Rap, tap, tap!

"Huh? What?"

The sound of someone pounding on the wooden door startled me awake. "Hello, Miss? Are you well? I saw you go in there an hour ago and noticed you never came out. Is everything all right?"

Upon examining my surroundings, I saw I was leaning over the toilet seat in a daze. *I must have dozed off from all the heat and exhaustion. I don't feel too bad anymore, but I hope no one was waiting to use this stall.*

Since I had removed my clothes to dry, I started to get dressed. "I'm fine," I responded coolly. "Thanks for the concern. I think I just passed out from the heat."

"That's the opposite of fine!" they responded in a worried tone. "You can die from that—seriously!"

Really? Did I almost die?

"Sorry. It's my first time in a desert and I'm not adequately prepared." I let out a light giggle at my own foolishness, and pushed open the stall.

Standing outside was a young man with tanned skin and a golden turban with a red crystal embedded within its center. He had rather alluring features under his white vest, which exposed his well-defined abs to the afternoon sun. His pants were baggy and ripped in places, and his shoes were nothing more than basic sandals that had been worn down by the ravages of time. A bit of black hair spilled out from around his turban and curled upwards, while his gleaming eyes, both radiant and hellish as rays of the sun, were solely focused on me.

He had a rather grim expression on his handsome face, but it eased up the more we looked at each other. "Great. Glad to see you're still looking well. Take this." He tossed me a bottle of water. "I meet travelers like you from time to time. Most of them were just as unprepared. I hope it's enough to help you along to your destination."

I really needed to purchase a new artifact that changed mana into water, but I kept forgetting since the first one broke from overuse not long ago. I slowly unscrewed the lid and briefly sniffed the contents before taking a sip. The divine liquid smoothly slid down my throat. It was amazing! In no time, I reduced the bottle by nearly half.

"T-thanks," I stuttered, feeling refreshed. "You really didn't have to check on me. I'm pretty adept at handling myself."

He grinned. "I can tell."

"Do I sense some sarcasm?"

The man shrugged and placed his hands back in his pockets with a warm smile. "Think nothing of it. It's my duty as someone who has been good friends with this desert to help those who get sucked into its void, especially when they're young women."

My face was getting a little warmer. There was no way I was blushing, right? It was just hot. Yup. Running with that.

"A blissful face like that is always nice to see," he remarked. "Can't recall the last time someone showed one to me."

Well, that answers that question. It's true that he's good looking, but there's no way this nice guy act is the real deal. I mean, who waits an entire hour to toss someone water and make small talk? There's got to be more to this guy than he lets on. Besides, he's not my type.

I did my best to mask my wariness by matching his bright smile. I was sure it was inferior, but I pressed on and asked him the question that had been at the forefront of my mind. "Uh... Who exactly are you?"

He shrugged again. "Just a wanderer following a fruitless dream."

That's my line. Well, minus the fruitless part. This shrugging is getting a bit on my nerves. Why is he being so vague? That makes him even more suspicious.

It wasn't difficult to detect the wave of irritation taking over me. I'm sure a vein or two was even bulging from my forehead. "C-can you just tell me your name? Is that so hard?" My voice was nearly a shout now. It was probably caused by a mix of being back in the sun and meeting someone who seemed like he was toying with me for the fun of it. I simply desired answers because of my lack of knowledge, and I hated being out of the loop.

"No need to get all pent up, miss. I didn't think it was important. It's been quite some time since someone has asked for my name. My name... My name... Hmmm..."

Why does he look so stumped?! I was feeling more incredulous by the minute.

After mumbling to himself for a few minutes, he finally spoke up. "I guess you can call me Gil."

"Gil?"

"Yup. That a problem?"

I shook my head. "No, it's just a name I'm not familiar with. That's all. I'm Lethe." I calmed down after that. It was true that I was taking out my frustrations on him when he was only trying to help. "I don't know if you would know this," I said. "But have you ever been to Rima?"

Gil crossed his arms and nodded. "I went there some time ago. I am actually on the—"

"Great! Is there really someone who can make life from sand?" I blurted. "Oh, sorry for interrupting."

"No worries. You speak of the Sand King, correct?"

"Y-yeah. That's the one. I was actually on my way there to check it out before heading further."

"Mmhm. I see. Well, everything you heard is all true," he assured me. "The Sand King is a real man with a very peculiar type of magic. As a collector, its beauty has captivated me for a long, long time."

"So, he *is* real." Not trusting Gil enough to stick around any longer, I nodded and walked past him. "Thank you for all the help, but I should really be on my way."

I might have sounded uninterested, but I was truly overjoyed. I'd got the information I needed. I just hoped he was telling the truth.

He made no move to stop me. Instead, he waved as if seeing a friend off. "Not a problem, miss. Enjoy your trip. I have a feeling we'll meet again."

* * *

At last, I departed from the rest stop, leaving that strange, and slightly handsome, man in the dust. "Well, that was a strange encounter for sure," I said to myself after taking another sip of the water he'd graciously given to me. Its rejuvenating properties affected every part of my mouth as it lightly trickled down my throat.

"At least I got something good out of that strange exchange—two things, actually."

I rested a finger on my lip as I talked things out with myself. "When I departed, I didn't see any sort of mount or device for travel. How did he even get there? There's no way someone would actually walk through all those dunes in a barren desert. Surely, I must have missed whatever he used."

Alas, no answer came to mind no matter how much I thought back to it. I really had no reason to doubt what I saw—or the lack of it.

* * *

Sometime later, I arrived in Rima, granting Frosty his long-needed rest.

It was one of those kingdoms that didn't have a gate or anything protecting it from invaders. The reason for that most likely stemmed from the fact that one would have to travel through the scorching heat and perilous winds to even make it there. Any army would be at its wit's end by then, just like I had been not too long ago.

The homes were small but well-crafted out of a shell-like substance, and the roads had been paved over with tar to create smooth, dark paths. I could see people walking around in the distance, making purchases from stands and going about their day. The homes and businesses were all tiny enough to display the grandest sight in all the land. It stood up to the heavens, erected into the form of a grand palace with obelisks jutting out on each side.

At the top of its dome-shaped peak stood a large spike pointing towards the darkening sky, which would have reflected brightly against the sun—if it had been made of metal, that is. The entire palace had been crafted from sand.

I hope the inside is nicely furnished or else it would be a pretty awful place to live. The upkeep seemed both simple and complicated at the same time.

I walked past the first few homes to get a closer look. Being taken in by its beauty, I didn't watch where I was walking.

"Oof!"

"Ow!" I yelped before picking myself up. "Sorry! I wasn't watching where I was going."

"It's cool. I wasn't looking either," said a young, male voice.

"Hey, Ricka! Let's get back to the game!"

"Coming!" said the boy as he took off.

At that point, I had finished recovering from my sudden sand spill. I spent a minute or two after that wiping the grains from my outfit. After smoothing out my skirt, I gazed into the distance to where the boy and his friend had run off.

"Huh?" My eye became as wide as a saucer as I stood still in disbelief. "Surely that can't be the case with everyone…"

I took a left to a general goods shop and pushed my way inside. A pretty bell dinged as I entered, acknowledging my entrance and notifying the shopkeeper. "Welcome," said the voice of a seasoned woman. Her tone was sweet and gentle.

"Hi!" I shouted, struggling to breathe out my words. "I was w-wondering if I could ask ab—" Words ceased to leave my mouth as if a door had been slammed tightly shut. One look at the lady was all it took for me to depart without another word.

I stumbled out into the street, catching sight of another person—same condition, same blissful expression.

Why? What is going on? Is this some kind of sick joke?

I couldn't wrap my head around what was happening in this kingdom. *Even if I was still suffering from the heat, I could never conjure something as wild as this.*

"Why…"

Why was everyone made of sand?!

Every single person I had spoken to acted as if nothing was amiss. It was such a surreal sight that I doubted my one good eye.

Here I was, in a kingdom that was well known, and yet I was the only human in sight. Was everyone like this, or only the people who were near the forefront of town?

I needed answers.

* * *

I made the rounds through multiple neighborhoods on my way to the palace, searching for anyone who was like me, but to no avail. Every person went about their daily lives as sand people. I was sure from my findings that none of them even knew that they were no longer human.

I asked a young man selling apples about this strange occurrence. He thought nothing of it, and when I asked him if he knew he was made of sand, he said, "You're a funny lady, aren't 'cha?"

I got similar responses from others too. *They don't see the obvious truth. It's beyond sad. It's straight up tragic!*

No matter what I pointed out about their body, they still refused to believe what I was saying. I was wondering if maybe I was wrong, but that couldn't have been the case. I was flawless—a girl who was never wrong.

Jokes aside, I feeling creeped out the more I stared at those empty sockets. Yes, these sand people had nothing resembling eyes. They had sunken craters where eyes should have been, holes filled with darkness. It was like staring into the abyss.

I need to find the Sand King.

I stared into the distance at the sand-made palace.

And I know exactly where to find him.

* * *

On closer inspection, the palace was a lot smaller than I'd originally thought. It seemed rather... lonely. In the end, a palace for one is nothing but a fortress of solitude; a place to live and die alone.

I reached the gate as the moon finally took its place in the sky. I would say that the area took on an ominous overtone, but that would be an exaggeration. It simply made me feel sad. I wanted to get to the bottom of this bizarre town, and the thought of having to figure it out filled my entire body with a wave of stress. At the end of the day, it wasn't really my problem, but my pride wouldn't allow me to walk away from such a gloomy landscape—neither would my curiosity.

I punched my hand through the gate, carving out an entrance with Extinctathon. What was rather interesting was that I could easily shatter the whole gate. It was built from sand, nothing more, nothing less.

I ascended the four rows of stairs to the palace, not even breaking a sweat while I did. *And what a relief that is.* In front of the imposing entrance stood four sand soldiers armed with sand spears. They noticed me immediately.

"Who goes there?"

"Intruder!"

"His majesty isn't expecting a visitor."

"You shall not pass!"

Their hollow eyes were dreary, but I made my case. I reached into my satchel and flashed them the badge of a Tribunal Resolver. "I request an audience with His Majesty."

"The Tribunal?"

"I see."

"Interesting."

"Approach, Resolver."

I came closer and let them get a good, long look at the badge. It was quite an unbelievable situation to be thoroughly inspected by people who lacked even skin and bones. As they inspected me, my eye fell on their weapons. Unlike their bodies, the spears possessed obsidian colors, similar to the exoskeleton that made up the various homes. I guess they really used every part of that massive scorpion, huh? I had to wonder if their famous delicacy came from his spawn.

The third soldier in line came forward. "There is no meeting scheduled with a Resolver."

How could he confirm that? He hadn't even moved from his station!

"It's an emergency," I said. "I have to see him now. *Alone.*"

Not suspicious at all.

The four soldiers huddled together in a congregation and debated my request.

"She's just a girl. Could she really be a Resolver?"

"She could have stolen it."

"Wouldn't that be an executable crime?"

"Yes, that's true. No one can flee from the Tribunal."

Hey. You know I can hear you guys, right?

They squabbled over my credentials for a bit longer before facing me once more.

"We—"

"Have—"

"Decided—"

"To allow you entry."

The one on the far right dramatically snapped his fingers, resulting in the doors swinging open. My view was met with a dark interior, dimly lit by torches.

"You have an hour. Nothing more. His Highness dwells within the deepest sanctum."

"Great. Thanks," I said absentmindedly. "I'll be back in no time."

As I stepped inside, the rectangular doors closed behind me.

"It's really hard to see in here," I said aloud. I crashed into something hard. "Owww. I hate this place already."

The only tangible thing I could make out was the faint outline of a doorway. I pressed on, observing the decayed furnishings that seemed randomly sprawled about.

After what seemed like ages, I reached a door similar to the one at the entrance, except it was molded out of something golden.

Bingo.

"I'm coming in," I said as I put all my strength into pushing open the door. It swung in without much resistance. Incidentally, that ended with me falling on the floor for the second time that day. At least the ground was made of marble and not sand, even if it hurt a bit more.

"Ugh, I just can't catch a break."

"Is someone there?" asked an old and hollowed voice. "Are you... human?" He sounded desperate.

I lifted my hand and summoned a small flame in front of me. Using the ring's power constantly had given me more control, increasing my skill enough to use it for more than combat. It allowed me to see more clearly, while also allowing the darkened figure in the back to locate me.

"A h-human girl! A beautiful girl."

You're about sixty years older than me!

Now that I had some light, I could accurately assess his features. His gray beard was patchy and scraggly. His blue eyes were sunken, but still brimming with life. He had no hair on his scalp, but was instead decorated with a crown and golden robes that seemed far too large for his frail and gaunt body. The only item around him that wasn't gold turned out to be the sand throne he rested uncomfortably upon. I surmised he could keel over at any moment, never to rise again. His flimsy arms limply rested on each armrest. He was so feeble, one could have mistaken it for his final resting place.

On the bright side, he was human—actually human. Just like me.

"Yes, I'm not one of those sand imitations. Are you the Sand King?" It was an obvious question, yet I still sought confirmation.

He nodded solemnly. "Unfortunately, I am. By Ra, it has been some time since I have been called that." He peered into the darkness before turning back to me. His thick eastern accent was the kind that belonged to the countries who lived near one of the Great Seas. None of the sand people sounded that way, though. We were also in the north. I wasn't used to hearing the voice of the tropics.

I pushed those frivolous thoughts aside as I made my way closer to his throne. "What's the deal with your subjects outside? As the king, you must be aware of it."

He took a deep breath. "I—I am. After all, I made them this way."

Yup! That's one point to me!

"It happened not too long ago..."

Oh. I guess it's story time again.

Since this old timer wasn't exactly a wordsmith. I'll tell you my version of his tale.

* * *

Born with a coveted power, he became the boon of the country, revitalizing it from its stagnant days. Years after taking the helm, the Sand King was invited to a neighboring country and didn't return for decades due to being held captive. When he returned, breaking his reason for staying away, the damage had been done to his countrymen. Everyone had fallen victim to a plague engineered by the country that had used him for years to create undying soldiers. You can guess what he did next.

* * *

"So, there you have it. That is my penance for leaving. This is my burden and mine alone. I will rot away in this darkness, so that my people will live on."

I spoke for the first time in what seemed like ages. "That's pretty over the top, don't you think? And what will happen to this kingdom when you finally pass away? Do you have a way to verify that they could continue on like they are without your power? Most people don't even visit anymore, and when they do, they immediately flee."

"But you didn't."

"I guess I'm not like most people."

"I see..."

The Sand King straightened his neck and let his jaw go slack. He must have been deeply considering my words, because he sat there in silence for quite some time. He became so lifeless that I nearly believed that he had departed for the next world.

Luckily, I was mistaken.

"I don't know... I really don't. All I can do is hope for the best for my people, as I can't stand to face them anymore. It's all my fault. I caused Rima's destruction, not them. I shouldn't even be king anymore. I don't deserve it."

He wasn't exactly born into royalty, but he hadn't been a stranger to it either. An illegitimate child of a servant that worked under the old king of the country. However, as long as he was the reincarnation of Ziir, he would have become king even if he hadn't been related. *He didn't go into detail about how he became king, but I'm sure his half-brothers were not happy about it.*

The king dropped his head in defeat. His gloominess resonated through the entire sanctum; it was hard to watch.

"So, you're just going to spend the rest of your life in *here*?"

"I must. I have already lived through my glory days. What awaits me now is the road to the end. I yearn to see Lord Ra in his true form. As his follower and son, I can't wait."

Resigned to the fate of living in solitude until his last breath, he was a prisoner in his own kingdom, just like he had been in Orellia. Suffering not for himself, but for his people. It was humbling, but also mortifying.

I slowly raked my hands through my hair. *What was I even here for again? There's really no point in staying. This isn't a king's chamber anymore. It's a tomb.*

I began to turn away, but he called out to me. "Traveler... What did y-you think of my kingdom?"

The air felt heavy suddenly. *That's a loaded question.* What could I say? That it was creepy? That I would probably have a nightmare about this hellish landscape once I went to sleep?

The geezer could very well die of shock if he heard my honest review. While that meant little to me, I still respected him and his tragic story. *I could at least give him the satisfaction of being his last visitor.*

I stared at the golden chandeliers that hung roughly from the ceiling. They had grown dark and old, but the jewels that adorned them had not lost their sheen even in the worst of times—just like Rima's king.

"I think it looks beautiful, and the people here seem happy. It's their own little paradise, but Rima just isn't a place for others to visit anymore. But as a king, I would feel satisfied knowing that my people are safe and comfortable."

The old man managed a toothy smile. "I see... Thank you." He went quiet soon after, but the light still burned in his eyes.

I slapped my hands together for a job well done. *I may not have found exactly what I was looking for, but I sure learned a lot. The eastern islands are calling to me now.*

I went to leave once more, but the doors behind me had effortlessly shot open. Within the frame stood the confident shadow of a man who was scarcely illuminated by the darkness.

"Hello again," he said to us both. "I have come to take what I am owed."

I recognized his voice almost immediately. "G-Gil?" I gasped. "What are you doing here?"

"Ah, the water girl. Glad to see you found the king! As to why I am here, you will see for yourself in just a moment. But first, let's get some light in here." He snapped his fingers, and the flames of the wall torches and chandeliers grew exponentially until the entire sanctum was bathed in light. It was easy to make him out now, but he looked... different.

His crossed arms were nicely fitted with a golden gauntlet that possessed a circle engraved on the hands. The circles had many smaller slots within them, acting as what seemed to be a storage area for items. One had three different colored gems in it, while the other had only two. The color and sizes reminded me of my Eternal, and the amethyst crystal that I had discovered under its surface.

A golden earring hung from his right ear, and his turban was nowhere to be seen. Instead, his wavy, black hair with blond streaks was bare for all to see. It matched both his black vest and golden eyes. Two horns protruded from his forehead a bit past his hairline; it was clear now that he was something past human. *If those gauntlets are an Eternal, then perhaps he has manifested more of his sponsor than normal.*

He had a menacing, larger-than-life aura around him, to where I couldn't tell who was truly the king of this sanctum.

"So, you have come, Gilgamesh, and in alliance with that ancient dragon as well," the Sand King snarled, his voice dripping with venom. He hadn't even sounded this angry while explaining the horrors he had gone through at the hands of another nation. What did Gil have to do with him?

Gilgamesh laughed off the king's vindictive stare before drawing his lips into a nasty grin. "Come on, old man. We had a deal. I keep this wasteland you call a kingdom alive by making deals with importers to supply your country of sand so your *citizens* can feel valued. In return, you give me what was promised years ago. You're already on death's door, are you not? What difference does it make if you give it to me now or in a year? Tiamat is thirsting for a new power. As her chosen, I don't want to make her wait."

Gilgamesh seemed like an entirely different person than the man I had encountered at the rest stop. While he had the same charming face and body, his eyes lacked the playful nature that had been there when I first met him. Was this the true Gil? *And who is Tiamat?*

The king shook his head vehemently. "You will have to wait until I pass as per our agreement. I already told you what could happen to my people the last time you came."

"People this. People that. Why does it even matter?" Gilgamesh barked. "They aren't alive anymore, no matter how much you try to make them forget that. They are pale imitations of the ones you lost, and you know that. Don't make me use her true power to raze this whole desert." He took a few steps forward with a stance that said it was useless to argue.

The king didn't respond.

"Your time is up," he growled. "I'm taking my payment." Gilgamesh advanced past me toward the old man in a fit of fervor and rage.

"You need to wait!" the Sand King bellowed, forcing the roof to shake.

He stepped down from his throne at a speed that far surpassed his age and condition. He spread his arms wide before bringing them to the ground, then up toward the sky in one swift motion.

Sand spilled from his palms, pooling beneath him, and it wasn't long before the grains started to take form. Multiple figures surged out of the pool, reminding me of the guards outside. Each of the eight grasped either spears or scimitars.

"Attack this man! He plans to take Ra's gift! Don't allow him to use the full power of the Golden Eternal of Creation!"

The soldiers looked back at their creator and then locked onto the oncoming threat.

"FOR THE KING!" they shouted in unison and charged.

It was then I realized a certain someone might get caught in the crossfire if she didn't find a safe spot to hide. I ran to a corner, seeking refuge from the deadly clash.

There was so much to process, especially with these new terms being thrown around. I sized up Gilgamesh's golden gauntlets. The Eye of whatever-it-was-called wouldn't stop him for sure, and I doubted Ashardna could do much either.

A golden glare filled my view, emanating from his gauntlets, just like a god. It differed from Gilgamesh's own mana. When I focused, I could see his was a dark shade of crimson.

What kind of Eternal has its own mana? C.T. did mention that a special set of Eternals were given colored names to express how dangerous they were.

I inched toward the doors at the back of the room, but decided not to leave; I was curious how this would all play out and wanted to see Tiamat in action. Gilgamesh, the denizen of the desert, and the weathered Sand King—Who would win?

The fight was something out of fiction, with Gilgamesh slamming his fists into every soldier, pulverizing them back into granules. However, the moment he turned away from one, it immediately reformed back to its former state.

"Is that all you got, demigod? You're going to have to do better than that to take down this old man."

Demigod? As in half human and half god? For real? I met a demigod!

Thinking about it, the name Gilgamesh did sound familiar. I think there was an old story or something about him in a few countries I'd visited, but that was from ages ago. Could this really be the same guy? I thought demi-gods still aged, but perhaps he's closer to three-quarters god than half.

Wait, does that even matter?

Gilgamesh effortlessly bashed another soldier into nothingness before pummeling another two without breaking a sweat. "Did you think this was a challenge for me? It's been a while since I've had a good warm up fight. This seems like a great time to enjoy myself. You should have brought the same numbers you used when you suckled on Orellia's teat like a feeble newborn."

"Silence!"

Scimitar-wielding soldiers blitzed at him from either side at such a speed that they seemed to teleport across the room. The sound of flesh being cut shot through my ears as two arms dropped to the floor, followed by a rain of blood.

"Leave now and I will spare your life. I only wish to live out my days with my people in peace."

The king offered the armless Gilgamesh a rather sweet deal, but I couldn't see the demigod's expression from where I was. It wouldn't have mattered either way. I could tell he was the kind of man to never give up on a goal once he set sight on it.

"You think *this* is enough to corner me? It may have been long ago, but unlike you, *my* quest bore fruit."

The blood flowing from his arms immediately ceased as his wounds cauterized themselves. Fresh arms sprouted from the stumps, as if the lopping of his arms had all been an act.

"See?" Gilgamesh opened and closed one palm before retrieving the gauntlets from the ground. "No problem. No problem at all."

"Im...possible..." the Sand King gasped, his voice quivering. "How can you p-possibly—"

"How can my body repair itself? It's simple, really. How does an immortal continue to live? I think even a sad being like yourself could arrive at the answer."

"An immortal? But you failed."

"Only in the stories. What do you know? Literature can often be deceiving. Most of them are just a cauldron of fiction with a sprinkle of truth. As if I wouldn't accomplish what I sought. I wouldn't be fit to rule Uruk any other way."

I could hear the hatred and sadness within his booming voice.

The Sand King's visage grew even paler than before; he looked no different from a ghost now. He backed up toward his throne, leaving three sand soldiers to guard him.

Gilgamesh roared with laughter. "Weak! Is this all you can do after getting up in years?! Or is it because of the thousands of false citizens you keep around in this land of lies? A pathetic facsimile of a kingdom in every way." The laughter faded into an arrogant smirk. "I've had enough of these childish antics. Let's spice it up, shall we?"

A magenta crystal in the right gauntlet glowed, growing brighter until it had completely enveloped his fist in a blinding aura. "You have probably heard of my pal, Enkidu, as well, yes? Let me show you what the gift of a compressed lifeform crafted from gods can do. Go!"

A magic circle of purple light manifested in front of his palm. Out of it snaked four golden chains. They acted like serpents, mercilessly striking through the bodies of their prey. The moment one of his chains bore through a sand soldier, it crumpled. This time, they didn't come back.

The chains dissolved each sand soldier and eventually coiled around the hands of the frail king like a helix.

"But h-how?" The Sand King was as flabbergasted as I. Whatever this Enkidu thing was, it tore through his soldiers with ease and stopped him from making more simultaneously. The magic circle floated in the same spot where Gilgamesh had originally placed his hand, even though he wasn't there anymore. It reminded me of the space that C.T. had produced items out of. It had to be a portal of sorts.

Gilgamesh failed to hold back his laughter. "You see, my old pal over here has the power to disable the magic of anything it touches. For your sandy friends, it's the magic that was animating them. And for you, it was your magic to breathe life into the very sand you were born with. Ahhh, if only he didn't die!"

He covered his face with a gauntlet to hide his expression. "At least he joined my *collection*."

Gilgamesh, the immortal and apparent king, had finally reached the Sand King.

Wanting to get a better look, I moved up to the right corner of the sanctum. It was a *big* mistake.

Gilgamesh's expression looked like pure madness, making me shudder. How had such a kind-looking man become so dark and vile?

The Sand King struggled to break the chains around his arms. Without his magic, he was just a frail, old man. "D-doing this won't bring your country back."

Gilgamesh scoffed. "The pot calling the kettle black, eh? Did I hear that right? Don't you think I, of all people, know that? I have bigger goals in life now, and I don't need lessons on how to run a country by a man who lost every one of his people to his own. Foolish. Blunder!"

He wiped the hair from his face. "Now, I will take what is rightfully mine." He callously plunged his fist into the king's chest and pulled out something reddish-pink and beating. *It's... It's his heart! It's his heart! Ewww!*

I couldn't help but gag at the gruesome scene. The demigod held the Sand King's very heart, but displayed not even the tiniest fragment of remorse. All I could do was watch in disgust as the Sand King fell to the floor.

"I'll be taking this now, thanks!" He crushed the heart, which ironically dissolved into sand. The Sand King's body soon followed suit.

Sand.

In the end, that was all that remained.

"A beautiful color. Impressive!" said the killer. In his hand sat a neatly polished, yellow gem. He placed it into his right gauntlet, his eyes filled with admiration.

"Let's give it a whirl." He thrust out his palm, causing sand to trickle and onto the ground below. The light sound of the granules meeting the floor washed over my ears in waves, followed by the particles rising up and taking a new form.

Gilgamesh inspected his creation with glee. "Splendid! It looks just like me! Well, except for the sand part, that is. Far too ugly for my taste."

He stood in front of a replica of himself woven by grains of sand. "Alright, I have seen enough. I'm satisfied." He closed his palm, and like a puppet without strings, the sand collapsed into nothingness. "Well? How was the performance?" he asked, his eyes falling upon me.

I didn't reply.

"Lost for words, I see. Who could blame you? It's not everyday someone sees the bout between a talented mage and an immortal. It must have been quite the sight."

Just what am I supposed to say?!

He glanced back over at the remains of the ruined king. "You know, he and I were once one and the same. The only difference between us is that he gave up on his kingdom. I'm still fighting for mine, and I don't care who I have to trample to get it back."

His hand reached up toward the sky, grasping at nothing. "It won't be long before she has enough strength to let me through. Then everything will be as it should be."

The air in the room grew stiff. I could offer him no reply, continuing my silence.

"I got what I needed. I'll be going now." He recreated the same wave and smile as he'd had when we first met. The only difference was that I knew for sure that there was darkness beneath that playful attitude. He looked at the sand ceiling above. "You probably should too."

Just as he took his first step, the foundation began to rumble around us—the palace was caving in. I wondered if I could actually escape from the insurmountable amount of sand and gold that was about to entomb me.

Gilgamesh must have seen the worry on my face because he quickly assured me I'd be fine. "Looks like you need a little help. Let's see..." As sand poured down around him, he directed all his focus to his right gauntlet. "Ah, here we go." A blue aura masked his hand, lighting it to an azure blaze. He opened his palm like before, but this time, a human-sized portal formed in the color of his gem.

"This will take us outside. Hop in."

This isn't a trap... right? Well, I don't really have a choice either way. If he wanted to kill me, I wouldn't have been granted this lifeline right now. I guess I can sort of put my trust in him.

"Um... Thanks," I said, running into the portal. At least now I knew how he traveled without a mount.

I felt a warm chill as I progressed through the doorway he had created. Soon after, I was met with the same darkness that had fallen on the kingdom before I'd stepped foot in the palace.

My boots dug into the sand. There was a lot more of it than when I went in. I had been right on the mark when I questioned what would happen to his people post-mortem.

I thought Gilgamesh would appear from the portal, but he never did. I gazed at the excess piles of sand around me before looking back at the entrance. The only part of the area that proved something grand had once stood there was a giant dune of sand.

I summoned Frosty and quickly mounted him. "Let's go, buddy. There's nothing left for us here."

I knew we would need shelter, but we wouldn't find it here. I tilted my head up to the crescent moon that brightly shone in the sky. It was beautiful, awe-inspiring, and grand. "I'm sure that's how the Sand King felt about his kingdom and his people," I said aloud. "They say a captain sinks with his ship. I bet he was a very fine captain."

The moon illuminated my travels through the once famous kingdom. A grouping of stars stared solemnly from its spot in the sky. The only people that could see it now were a young woman and her wolf.

Chapter 15

A Series of Fateful Encounters

I still look back on some of my early days of wandering with glee. I befriended many, shared drinks with even more, but the best part of being in a party was when you all gelled together. Even thinking of some of my old mates makes me smile from ear to ear. On the other hand, our fights were some of the worst in town.

—Boreas Tyrel

The journey to my next destination was rather uneventful. A faint drowsiness had washed over me, as it was late into the night when I'd left.

Of course, I could have slept in Rima, but there could have been ghosts haunting that place. Not to say that I was afraid of ghosts, but the thought of sleeping where many had once lived and then died was a bit much. Instead, I chose to ride through the desert until I reached the mining and adventuring city of Markarth.

Markarth was an independent city that was home to many guilds that harbored and employed adventurers. With mining came undiscovered caves, which often resulted in dungeons that needed to be cleared before it was safe to delve deeper. That's where the adventurers and guilds made a killing. That was also my reason for choosing it. Luckily, there wasn't a lot of Tribunal work at the moment, so I had a ton of time to play around. And after what I had witnessed in Rima, I could sure use a good ol' cave expedition!

It was also true that because of the lack of work, I had run dangerously low on money. Finding work in Markarth was the best solution for both of my issues. *I will most likely join a party to help clear out a cave and make some good money that way. It can't be too hard, right? If it was, why would people come here?*

By early morning, I reached Markarth and found a cheap room with a bed and a table. The foundations on both were rather questionable, but for three copper pieces a night—and as someone who was already far too tired to argue—I took it without complaint.

I lazily tossed off my clothes before changing into my gown, and then slowly sunk into my bed. I hoped to have a good night's rest after what felt like weeks of missing it.

Unfortunately, the demon in my dreams had other plans. His face was getting closer and closer with every new incursion. At least the dreams weren't common anymore. It had been months since the last one, yet I never forgot those eyes and fangs. I kinda preferred the vision of my sponsor; his domain wasn't plain darkness. If only... Ah, maaaan. I was starting to miss the Silver King and the monstrous terror that followed him. I did my best to ignore the demon's welcoming grin and fell into a deep slumber.

"Ughhhhh..."

An icy chill ripped me from sleep, resulting in me sadly sitting up against my pillow. "Why can't those windows do their job and keep the cold out for once? I-it's freezing in here!"

I hugged myself to preserve warmth, but it did little against the creeping cold that plagued me. Admitting my defeat, I set out for the day to find myself a high-paying quest with minimal danger. *I might be asking for a miracle.*

The sun was warm, and the wind strong. I decided to try my hand at adventurers' clothing. My choice was a dark-and-leathery, form-fitting corset and skirt. chain mail links were woven into the fabric of the one-piece uniform, and a variety of enchantments kept my clothing durable and comfortable despite its weight.

Upon departing the clothing store, the smell of food smacked me in the face, forcing me to notice the myriad of shops filling the streets with their crafty advertising.

I was very close to spending the last of my money on crêpes and hot chocolate, but chose to be smart for once and hold on to my savings. *The job comes first. After that, we can get a mouthful of those succulent meat skewers.*

I spent time wandering around the peaceful town. Under the many stone bridges lay canals—a subject I had little experience with. Most were littered with small boats carrying tourists through the city. As I peered over the railing to get a better look, two people passed me in conversation.

"—in. Don't you think? It could be a killing if we find some good loot deep within."

"Yeah, I know. But they said the place hasn't even been mapped out yet. For all we know, it could cave in on us the second we go inside. We should wait and see how the first explorers report back first, and then we can make our move."

"I like the sound of that."

"Excuse me," I called out to the guys that I presumed were adventurers. "Can you tell me where the Titan guild is? I'm pretty new around here." I did my best to look approachable and easy to talk to, despite the faint bags under my eyes and the constant desire to yawn.

The two of them were thrown off for a second, but seemed to switch to all smiles after they were done gawking at me.

"Oh hey, a pirate girl—OW!"

He had been elbowed by his buddy. "Shut up, man. You're creeping her out," the second adventurer said. He slicked his short hair back and flashed me a brazen smile. "Sorry about him. He doesn't think before flapping his gums. Now, what did you want to know?"

"I'm looking for the Titan guild. Do you know where it is?" I had spoken and dealt with people like them in the past, and I found the quickest way to get through a conversation was to be clear and concise. I wanted them to think I was in a hurry, even when I wasn't. However, my theory didn't yield results often.

"The Titan guild, huh? I think it's a few blocks down. Pretty sure the street's name is Pantheon. Want us to walk you there?" He flexed his muscles for good measure, which resulted in his buddy smacking him on the head.

"My man... Stop," the first adventurer said.

The second stuck his tongue out at his friend with defiance.

I let out an internal sigh. Ah, yes—children. I held back my insults and continued my act. "No, thank you. But I hope the two of you find the loot you are looking for."

They both blushed and scratched their necks. "T-thanks. Maybe you wanna party up with us—Uh, hello?"

By the time they finished, I was already down the street and looking at the directory that would tell me exactly where I needed to be. Markarth was a godless town, mostly because it wasn't a part of a kingdom or country. It was great for people branded heretics by different religions, or for people who were too busy with their work to even think about a god or goddess. *If I ever want a place to settle down, it would most likely be here. That might make Rock a little sad, though.*

It didn't take long to reach the guild after that. The golden structure stood out like a sore thumb in the diverse city of miners, merchants, and adventurers. When I pushed the door open, something—or *someone*—caught my eye.

No way.

She was happily chatting away with a customer while chowing down on what I thought was a blueberry muffin. After she finished it, she seductively licked each crumb from her hand like a succubus.

Her hair was long and sleek, gathered into a half-up, half-down style. The luscious green with yellow highlights fell smoothly to her shoulders. I was a little jealous of its wavy texture. I bet it was silky smooth to the touch.

My nose picked up something strange. The smell that permeated the room whirled its way from the tip of my toes to my nostrils, oddly reminding me of a lovely field of lavender. Only the flowers had crude faces with teeth of daggers and blood-stained claws. It fit her true character pretty well.

I breathed deep again. *Yup, that's some good stuff.* Just what hair wash was she using? And where could I get it for myself? Suddenly, I had an aching desire to go back to the inn and wash myself. I wasn't smelly or anything, but in comparison, I felt like I was deeply lacking.

Whenever she spoke, I could see a flash of fangs mixed in with her teeth, while her scarlet eyes seemed distant, as if plotting something in the back of her mind.

Why is C.T. here? I thought she worked for Trident. Did she already get fired and relocated? Heh-heh, some god.

I'd come there to sign up for a high-paying quest, but if I didn't get to the bottom of this, then I didn't think it would leave my mind for some time. And so, I got in line. Sure, it may have been the longest, but that wouldn't stop me from interrogating the creature in human skin.

* * *

An hour later...

Why does every guy take a minimum of ten minutes? It doesn't take long to get a damn quest and leave! My legs are as stiff as boards!

The ordeal made me realize how unfit I was when it came to stamina, because I had Frosty do all the walking. I needed to train myself to get stronger and more durable, but I could save that for later.

At last!

There was only one person ahead of me, and he finally seemed to be picking a quest. I could tell he was a lower ranker for two reasons. One: he took even longer than the other guys. That meant he had a lot more choices, since easier jobs were in higher supply. And two: the green medallion that was placed on top of the booth. It was called verdant, the second lowest rank of the ten—and coincidentally the same rank as me.

Luckily, I should go up a few ranks after talking with Cthulhu. Even if I don't use it, I'd be happy for a promotion. It always felt good to ascend higher in something.

I inched forward to get a closer look. It was a cakewalk to accurately guess his thought process. His eyes darted around from the first quests to C.T.'s chest, to the middle quest with a quick peek back to C.T., and then a brief glance at another quest before finishing his hat trick of ogling. *If you're going to do this, at least do it when you're not wasting everyone's time! Sheesh. Kids these days... Wow, now I sound like an old man.*

C.T. didn't seem to mind at all. She was snacking away on some chips while still licking her lips in a way that was unnecessarily provocative. Perhaps that was another reason why she was so popular—well, besides the fact that she was the only woman on duty.

I can't believe this. Wasn't she originally some ancient god that wanted to destroy the world? I know I'd played a hand in stopping her and trapping her in that form, but it's not like I expected any of this to happen. How could I? What was I thinking?

As I firmly regretted my choice to save the world, a familiar voice reached out to me. "Next please—oh! So, my follower lives, eh? Well, I already knew that thanks to the eye, but what a surprise to find you here, of all places! A pleasure to see your annoyed visage again, Kulu."

"Naturally. Even though that name is somehow making headway, I'm grateful for being acknowledged. As to why I survived—why would you think otherwise?" I shot back.

Her incessant snickering told me she could easily sense my frustration. I didn't like the sound of that, but at least I knew where I got my rep from. *Stop smiling at me like a doting parent. I know your true colors, and I've been waiting here forever! If anything, I'm the parent in this situation!*

Suddenly, the skin on her face slightly tensed, but the playful hunger in her eyes never ceased. "From what that ragtag group of misfits who vanquished Young P's child told me, you disappeared after falling into the sea. That handsome sea-creature fellow searched for two days, but they couldn't even find your remains. Where you ended up surprised me, but you can tell me about it another time."

I cocked my head. *Is she referring to the hammerhead guy? What was his name again?* Was she interested in him? I guess they were both from the ocean. Why wouldn't her tastes be just as vast?

I laughed awkwardly. "It's a long story, but as you can see, I am fine. I'm glad to know that they killed that thing, though. Now my friend can truly rest in peace." The thought of them searching for someone that they had just met warmed my heart. *I do feel bad that they looked for me, though… I hope I can run into one of them again someday and give my thanks.*

Then C.T. went and said something both cryptic and puzzling. "That's nice. You moved on, but I don't know if *he* did."

"Hmm? 'He'?"

"The thing from your dreams? Come on! You know what? It's fine. That's another subject we can speak about at a later time, just like the waning seal," she said, waving my question away. She pointed at the clock stationed on the arch far above her head. "I'm on the clock right now, but if you haven't accepted his words, then it's not a big deal at present. It knows its place, just like my little Kulu." She ruffled my hair.

A moment later, I realized she must be talking about the monster from my dream. How did she know about him? To bring him up after I'd received his words hours ago following such a long break was even more peculiar.

I said nothing. I, too, wanted to talk to her about it, the Silver King, and his hunter as well. Now wasn't the time.

"Alright," C.T. said, "I assume you're here for your reward?"

"Yup, but not only that," I replied with a nod. "I need a lot of money, so I'd like a decent quest, too. Life has been cruel to my wallet lately." I patted the satchel that hung close to my waist.

C.T. leaned on the booth with an arm, a large smirk appearing on her face. "Yeah, tell me about it. Ever since I started here, I've been busy through my entire shift. Guys can't get enough of me."

Ugh... Show off. Wait... Why do I even care? What was this tight feeling in my chest? Certainly, I couldn't be jealous. After all, I was an incredibly humble person.

"Well, there is a good reason for that," I said, gesturing toward her choice of clothing.

A small giggle left her mouth. "Mm? Is that so?" At least it wasn't a cackle.

She tilted her head and smiled while propping her hands below her chest. If I were a man, I would have felt somewhat aroused, but I think that was her point.

Still, it was distracting, so I ended up just resting my eye on her clavicle.

C.T. laughed. "Well, it gets pretty hot in this town compared to other places, so I decided I should let loose a little. Bare skin never hurt anyone, right?"

She fanned herself with a hand before continuing. "Only on Friday evenings when I have to take a full layer off to beat the heat. That's when you will find me doing anything more. A few delicious-looking boys fight over my hand on that day every week. Isn't that just a riot?"

I shrugged.

"In their eyes, I'm a defenseless maiden. It's adorable. Even the slow life here is full of fools who worship and venerate me, and I haven't even offered them anything in exchange! Ever since I got this body, I have slowly been mastering the massive pool of mana that dwells within each crevice of its skin, and this is one of the fruits of my labor."

She winked before puffing out her chest, emphasizing her somewhat-impressive bust, which I'm sure landed her a few stares from around us. The only stare she earned from me was one full of indignation.

Then she brazenly leaned in and whispered, "*Plus, it's easier for me to gain influence and energy in their dreams if they're already thinking about me.*" She laughed flirtatiously.

Had this ancient god been demoted to a full-time worker, part-time succubus? Was becoming something far more risqué possibly on the horizon? I was too afraid to ask.

I sighed. I ignored her stupid grin and asked a question that I had been saving. "What do you mean when you mentioned 'other jobs?'"

"I'm glad you've taken such an interest in your god's life. Did you think I would be content with working in a *single* profession? I think not!" She placed a hand under her smug face, as if to lean on it. "This is my fifth job at the moment."

"Fifth?" I echoed in bewilderment. "Why?"

"Yes, child. Fifth. A youngling like you wouldn't understand the need to work for a living. As a god, even as a..."—her expression clouded over—"f-forgotten god, my strength increases with the energy I collect and worshippers I gain. And how do I spread my name so quickly? If you use that juicy organ within that thick skull of yours, it's quite simple. It doesn't take a genius to figure out, but you would also need to know what a god and Great Old One are truly capable of to even fathom the possibilities. It also helps that the name I gave you is still attached to my power, further snowballing my reputation."

I guess I am doing free PR, huh? Whatever. "Can you get to the point already? I don't have all day."

"Mm. I'll overlook that poor attitude of yours, just this once. Call it a favor because you're still my first and only true follower. It means more than you could imagine."

Still? All this talk of bolstering your reputation and I'm still the only one? Just how bad at your job are you?

"Right."

"As I was saying. What I did was divide myself into fragments and scatter them through the lands to score me high-paying jobs with lots of interaction. Yes, four out of five of them are guild women, but I really struck gold with the last one! My forms differentiate between each one, depending on how many people I have siphoned from."

She crossed her arms below her breasts, propelling them up, and closed one eye. "As you can see, this job has been a lot more successful for me than that backwater tourist trap where we met last time. Absorbing energy here is like taking tributes from a newborn immortal. I can really feel the power of the Great Dreamer dwelling within me once again! If only I hadn't come back in this form. Then the world would already be in shambles from my power!"

So, she does remember her initial goal. I'm unsure if I should be delighted or devastated.

"It's not like I made you this way on purpose. Well, actually—I did, but it's not like I got much out of it. If anything, I should be a global hero."

"Maybe so, but you don't seem like someone that would do too well in the spotlight, unlike me."

I rolled my eyes as she cackled to herself. "Riiight. Anyway, I'm beginning to feel like a hypocrite for taking up so much of your time already. The point is, I want a high-paying quest with minimal risk and my reward for killing the ocean scourge. Can it be done?"

"Well, aren't you a picky follower? I should have assumed that when you crafted me so specifically to your whims. Specifics are key for summoning a *god*, after all."

"Can it be done?" I repeated, annoyed.

She thought for a second before getting back to me, pursing her lips in the process. "I'll have to check in the back since most of our high-paying quests are for upper tier members. Even if you work for the Tribunal, you're only a novice adventurer. Green does suit you, though. Take pride in that."

I don't know why, but when she said novice, it really hurt something inside me. Was that even an insult?

"Ok, sure. How long will that take?"

C.T. produced a wry smile, tinted with sarcasm. "Weeell, all this talking has made me feel peckish, so I was thinking of taking my hour break. How about you come back to me in an hour or two? I can see if you are eligible for a promotion and hand you your reward as well. Sound good?"

"An hour?!" *Seriously? This piece of...*

"Yup," she said cheerfully, severing me from my dark thoughts. "There's a local shop run by this really excellent chef. I'm under the impression that he's into me. Why else would one serve me a full course meal, free of charge? I haven't even attempted mind control in this form yet. I must say, being brought into this world as a female has its perks."

"Ugh..." I slumped down in defeat. "Is there any other way to speed it up?"

She laughed that annoying laugh. "There may be. How about you come with me for a bite, and I'll take some higher tier quests with me? That way I won't get reported by the seething fleshbeings—sorry—*coworkers*. My treat."

Well, it's not really your treat, is it? But I really want some food. I haven't eaten since before I entered the desert, after all.

"Sure. Why not."

* * *

I savagely munched on a chicken sandwich like a child that hadn't eaten in a week. It was lunchtime in a lively tavern, and that meant it was packed with customers. The loud noise harassed my ears with every bite, but the food made it worth the pain.

C.T. was enjoying the view of a girl scarfing down her meal. She casually swayed back and forth while slowly nibbling a large salad and peacefully sipping away at her coffee. "How is it?" she asked with a self-serving smirk that would make you believe she crafted the meal herself. "I just can't get enough of the food here."

She had swapped her work clothes for green shorts and a black, off-the-shoulder blouse. It revealed her porcelain shoulders with green straps curling snugly over them like an ancient arched bridge. The combination magnificently displayed her alluring figure to everyone around us, which I minded a lot. I was trying to eat in peace, after all.

I could tell some of the other customers had already taken an interest in her, but I moved the conversation along, anyway. Someone had to.

"—and yet, you chose the salad." Yes, the inflection in my tone ended up sounding barbed and sarcastic, but it was all for fun, even if I was in a bit of a mood.

She raised an eyebrow at my provocation. "Oh? Are you calling me boring, perhaps?"

"Who can say for certain?" I mused. I then subtly reached for a crouton.

"Well, *I'm not*," she said, while smacking my hand away. "I have already tasted every single morsel on the menu. Now, I'm working my way through my second run. Tomorrow is the medium-rare steak and mashed potatoes."

Yeah. That does sound amazing, but can you stop looking so smug when you say it?

She gathered a set of leaves with her fork before spearing it. "I'm a big fan of this place. And it seems you are too with just how much you keep eyeing *my* food."

"I like the taste of them—alone. Just like me. What can I say?"

"That was a rather sad statement. I will allow you to partake in my food out of pity. What a gloomy Kulu you are."

It's probably because I'm not that hungry today for some reason. Frosty is the same way.

"I am aware," I stated, stacking her croutons on an empty plate. Those things tasted wonderful alone. It helps when you aren't a fan of salad and its nasty dressings. The crunch of them was like music to my ears as , while the silent C.T. sat exuding the opaquest of auras. That did get my mind back on track.

I dabbed the crumbs from my lips. "Now, can we get back to the reason I even came here?"

"Oh, right! Apologies, my dear Kulu. Just watching you blissfully consume the leftover toppings of my meal has renewed my working spirit."

"I didn't even know you were struggling. Are you saying you enjoyed that because of my heart-rending comment?"

"Who can say?" C.T. slyly feigned ignorance as she stood up, walked to my side of the table, and sat down next to me. The sharp glint in her blood-colored eyes was thirsting for a good discussion. She crossed one long leg over the other, revealing pitch-black tights and sparkling midnight heels beneath her shorts. I couldn't help but stare.

Wow. She is so mature. I couldn't fathom wearing anything like that, especially off work. Seems like it would get stuffy and uncomfortable after a while of walking around, but she seems just fine. Being a god must be nice.

"Let me show you the options." She reached into a lime vortex that had appeared by her head and produced four sheets of paper. She elegantly sprawled them over the table in front of my food, which I hadn't finished eating.

She pointed to the first one. "This request was put in by villagers up north. Apparently, some demon worshippers have been sighted, though no one seems to believe them. We've had a couple requests like this lately. It would be pretty interesting if they were actually worshiping that old dragon that people seem to like writing children's tales about. He loved to play mind games and meddle with humans as much as I do. His name escapes my memory, but he sure was a schemer. I wonder what happened to him?"

If it's the one I'm thinking of, then he's long gone. He's one of the few named dragons that wasn't lauded as fiction or deceased, yet they never gave his name. I didn't know he was popular with children, though? And why did she even know that? Does she read tales in her spare time or something? I could tell her about the

Cursed One, but she's the first one to bring him up in person. Like forgotten gods, he must have been lost to the ages except in fiction.

I shrugged. "Who knows? They do sound like a bunch of loons, though. Been there, done that. No thanks. I'll pass." *Though, I'm vaguely interested. Maybe another time.*

She let out a slightly pained sigh. "Figures. Now, onto the next. This gig pays pretty well and requires you to escort an artificer through an uncharted cave to make sure it's safe to mine and discover any hidden items or treasure that could be buried within."

"Oh?" I cocked my head at that one. It had a promise. "I like the sound of that but, tell me about the two others first."

"Right. I like your foresight. It's best to not jump at something without considering all the variables." She nodded and pointed to the second last. "This one involves investigating a massive cocoon that was spotted in the Plaguelands to the—"

"Nope! Next!"

"O-ok..." C.T. winced in pain at my hasty exclamation, as if I was rejecting her very being. With a fickle look, she pointed to the last one. "This doesn't pay as much, but it's something you can do by yourself. It requires someone to go back into one of the more popular dungeons and collect fallen gear that can be returned to the guild. You'll get paid per item you recover. There is also a fifth option, but it requires you to investigate a few different bodies of water where people have been sighted getting devoured by whirlpools."

I thought back to my strange journey after falling from the ship during our Leviathan fight. "I'm good!"

"Thought so. So let's get back to the other four."

I looked them over again. "Mmhm. I see, I see. So, number two and four are my best bets, then."

She nodded. "Judging from your reactions, those two would fit your needs the best. The main question is if you would like to work alone or in a party?"

"Well, I would prefer to work al—"

"Now, now," C.T. interjected, holding up her hand as if to silence me before readjusting her glasses. "I will tell you that a party of two, as well as a loner, has already signed up for this specific quest. While they could embark on it with just the three of them and the artificer, they requested a fourth of Cobalt or higher to be safe. While you aren't at the rank, I can easily bump you up there if you allow us to keep your reward money."

Was she asking for a bribe? But that was tempting. If more guilds barred me from using my Tribunal status, then being the fifth highest rank would be a pretty great feature. Sure, why not? This would be an investment.

"I can see the decision from your eye alone. We thank you for your donation," she chuckled in amusement. "Before I give it to you, allow me to fill you in on the finer details. Two of the three adventurers that have registered already possess a hefty amount of experience, as well as an excellent reputation within the guild. You may have come across them before."

"I doubt that, but I get what you're saying." I tried to reach for the rest of my sandwich, but C.T. swiftly blocked my hand with her own.

"I think you could learn a lot from officially partying up with a team, so I'm glad you made the right choice. Who knows, you could actually make some friends."

"I have f-friends!" I stubbornly insisted, feeling flustered. "T-tons of them, actually!" I don't think I sounded very convincing.

My shouting briefly turned some heads toward us, but I ignored them. I puffed out my cheeks in anger, then brought my voice down while crossing my arms. "I totally have friends!"

"Oh?" she said while holding back an onslaught of laughter. "Then what are their names, hmm? Where are they, *hmm*?" Her face was so smug and conceited that I nearly tossed my largest fireball or razor wolf her way. Maybe next time.

"Um, well—just give me the quest already!" I scoffed, my patience finally spent. The heads of the patrons turned our way once more, once again filling me to the brim. The only difference was that the liquid had been replaced with embarrassment.

She cackled again. "Look who's as red as a blood moon." An even more pompous expression formed on her annoying visage before she placed a hand on her cheek. "Of course." She handed me the quest. "What are we guild attendants for?"

"Ugh…" I groaned, but followed her lead.

* * *

An hour and a half later, I was alone at a tavern a few blocks down from the guild. C.T. had told me to head there and wait in the section that had been partitioned off for adventurer meetings. I sat in booth number three, staring idly out the window that led to the street. It was apparently one of the booth's most prominent features. It was indeed a cool sight.

I glanced down at a sleek, black card resting in my hands. *Huh?* "Why does it say Kulu?!" *That damn monstrous guild girl! I don't know how, but I will have my revenge!*

My unsavory nickname was inscribed in golden letters and the car stored my feats and rank within the guild. In the past, I hadn't had a card due to the help of the Tribunal, but I needed one now. I wasn't sure how often I would use this outlet for funds, but it was nice to have. Instead of a green dot above my name, it had become dark blue. If I held it down, I could even manifest the badge as proof of my rank.

I sighed. "I would have thought I would have been the last to come, since I was the last to join, after all."

With the table talk of other adventurer groups around me, I sat alone in prolonged silence.

A few more minutes dwindled by before someone finally approached me from behind. "Um… I-is this the table for party number fifty-four?" a female voice asked, nervousness squeezing her voice smaller.

"Yup," I said with a quick nod, not moving my gaze from the window. "That's us."

"L-L-Lethe?!" she stuttered in disbelief.

Huh? I turned around immediately. "Umbrea? What are you doing here?"

"I could ask you the same thing! I thought I was meeting with this 'Kulu' person. Definitely didn't think that would be you!"

I gave her a wry smile. "Yeah, about that…"

* * *

For the next ten minutes, Umbrea and I traded stories. It had been at least half a year since we had parted ways. That was long enough ago that it felt like a distant memory. She had been a not-so-sneaky shadow thief that the Tribunal had dispatched me to deal with. Our confrontation had ended with fighting a dark spirit inside her lamp and me watching her set off on her own path.

Now, here she was, dressed in what was called mage armor. She wore a long, black cloak with chain mail between the fibers for extra durability and protection, as well as pants that most likely had some sort of enchantment on them.

I was glad I went for more of an agile design or else we would have been matching. *She would have never let me live that down.*

"Pfft—Ha-ha!" Umbrea took a short sip from her coffee and laughed. I think she was trying to act more grown up, but that would bite her in the back later when she tried to sleep. I had seen it before. "Because of you, my life has really turned around. I practiced like you told me and got a lot better at using my shadow power!"

She had such an adorably triumphant expression that I nearly patted her short, silver hair. I recoiled back and coughed into my hand. "That's good to hear. What made you want to work as an adventurer?"

It was an obvious question, but she had the ability to work in a lot of higher paying and less risky jobs with her unique ability to summon and manipulate shadows.

"Well,"—she brought two of her fingers together in front of her chest, avoiding my inquiring gaze—"I, um, kinda, maybe, sorta… broke an expensive art piece in a museum. Of course, it was an accident! It really wasn't my fault.

But because of that honest mistake, I was unjustly tossed into a pool of massive debt! Could you believe that? It's sooooo unfair! Even with the money I got from selling the cursed lamp, it was nowhere near enough to pay those money hungry bigwigs back!"

She caught her breath before leaping back in. "I've been doing high-paying jobs ever since, but man, it's been scary. I'm glad to have someone strong like you at my side for this job. No one even trusts me enough to do anything other than carry their stuff. I'm not just a pack mule anymore! I can be useful too! You'll let me help, right? You won't make me just carry the party's stuff... right?"

No. I think they were pretty just in their verdict. Could have been a lot worse, honestly. As for the rest...

"O-oh, sure," I said with a smile as stiff as an ice statue. "I'll make sure you get some action."

It's not like she needed my permission, though. We were equals. Poor girl. For what great power you possess, you really are as dumb as a door.

"I just know you will!" She beamed, oblivious to my inner thoughts.

At that moment, two more people approached our table. They seemed to be in a heated debate and didn't acknowledge the two of us.

"—No, no, no. There is no way that there will be undead there. There hasn't been a sighting of them anywhere near our location in ten years. Skeletons would be the only possibility, and they are pathetic creations. A cave of liches—now that would be dangerous!"

"That doesn't mean anything, dumbass. We were already told this place resembles a crypt from ancient times; what else can it be? There are a lot worse undead than you remember. Creatures that may be able to harm even us. They could be leftovers from the days of the old gods and the Revenant King. You're just being conceited like usual."

"Grrrr!"

"Hmph!"

While the two of us stared at them in silence, they each took a seat. The grumpy boy sat next to Umbrea, while the bitter girl sat next to me. Umbrea became as pale as the dead, doing her best to avoid contact with literally anyone. Perhaps she was shy around new people?

The two of them, who sounded vaguely familiar, crossed their arms and looked away from each other. Because of that, I was able to make direct eye contact with the girl. It was my third fateful reunion of the day. Could I be… lucky?

"Wait, Lethe?!" she gasped.

"S-Stacy?!"

"We thought you were dead!"

"Yeah, I have been getting that a lot lately…" A light chuckle escaped my throat. Was it getting hot in here, or was it just me?

The boy with sun-kissed skin turned his head toward the commotion and cracked a cocky smile. His temper vanished now that there was a new topic that involved someone of the opposite gender.

"Hey, Lethe. Long time no see. How are the dreams? You good?" He flexed his biceps, as if to show off, and spoke a little deeper than he had a few moments before. *Classic Daji.*

Why does everyone know about the dreams I'm having? This can't be normal! This isn't some kind of public viewing! Get your own dreams!

It had been around a month since I'd last seen the two, but we parted ways in less than desirable circumstances. What came after my fall had caused me to forget a lot about what had happened before it. *Would they even believe me if I told them where I ended up and what I did? It feels less like fact than fiction.*

Stacy wrapped me in her arms and pressed my head against her chest.

"I'm so happy you're alive! What the hell happened? Alistar said you disappeared once you fell into the sea. We were so busy killing that stupid, oversized squid that we couldn't look for you for hours."

T-t-touching! So cooold! I attempted to wiggle out of her embrace. It took me three tries to break free. *Why is her grip so strong? And where can I learn it?*

"I told you she would be fine."

"Ehhh?! What did I just hear?" Stacy turned her head toward Daji, her stare intense enough to melt the ice in my drink. "No, you didn't. Actually, I believe your exact words were: 'Why do all the cute girls around me have to die? Do the gods hate me because they stuck me in a world with not a single woman in my sight?' Something like that, if I recall."

His face turned beet-red. "Uh, well... please don't hit me again!" He looked away from us in a mix of fear and embarrassment. I couldn't put my finger on it, but the way he always acted felt both genuine and fake at the same time. Stacy was similar, especially when she grew serious. I knew little about the two, but I really wanted to find out why they acted the way they did.

While I mulled over the duo's strange performances, Daji set his sights on the ever-so-quiet Umbrea. "Oh, hey! How's it going? The name's Daji—a spirit monk. Wanna see a few moves? They are wicked cool!" He didn't wait for her response as he began shadow boxing with the air.

Umbrea was as quiet as a mouse. She probably wanted to be as small as one, too.

"Seriously, Daj! Keep it in your pants. One girl rejects you and now you jump to the closest *thing* in sight? I'm right here, you know." Stacy looked rather miffed, but her tone told me otherwise.

"I know, I know," he acknowledged as he dropped back into his seat.

"I'm a... *thing*?" I heard Umbrea mutter dejectedly under her breath, but the other two were too busy bickering to even notice.

"Wanna die?!"

"I never rejected him, but I'm also not looking for anything..." I chimed in, making my stance on the whole fiasco emphatically clear.

Daji seemed barely fazed by it but became deathly blanched from the malefic gaze of the girl across from him.

"I'm sorry, Stace! You know how I get when I see a new girl. My cla—I mean—fists thirst for something adventurous. Being with you for sooo long has just gotten boring and—Ow, ow, ow! My arm! You're gonna rip it oooff"

What a fun duo. I sat there, letting it all play out.

Daji's speech, which had been followed by Stacy pinning his arm to the table with lightning speed, had drowned my voice out. Umbrea was still silent, so I decided to find out what was wrong. Besides, I had grown bored from watching the lovers' tussle.

"Um... Have fun with all that. I'm going to the bathroom." I shot a glance toward Umbrea, hoping she would catch my drift even with my sub-par acting. "Anyone want to come?"

"Put your hand down, Daj! Before I really break it!"

"Jeez, Stace! It was a joke, I swear! A joke!" he shrieked like a little girl, despite seeming to enjoy the whole situation. Even if their act was all artificial, they still had fun with it. *They know how to make the most out of life. I envy that.*

Daji got out of the booth to release Umbrea from her prison. I held out a hand to the nervous girl as Stacy let me out of my own side. Umbrea took my hand like a damsel would take the hand of a knight in shining armor, her eyes dazzling and resuming function.

Daji hastily sat down in my place, which I assumed would cause a whole swath of new problems, but that wasn't actually the case. I watched the pair chat happily with each other for a few seconds before I led Umbrea to the restroom. *I don't really have to go, but Bella once said this was a thing girls did when another was in trouble. Plus, it's the most private part of the tavern.*

With exasperation written all over her face, Umbrea took a seat on the toilet and blurted out everything she had been holding in. And I'm not referring to her bladder. "Y-you know *Ecto Storm*?! That's so cool! And I never expected Daji up close to be so... so..."

"Annoying? Overconfident? Cocky? A womanizer? Short?"

"Dreeeamy."

I stared at her. *Oh, so that's how it is. I can even see the hearts in her eyes now...*

There was nowhere for me to sit, so instead I rested my hands on my hips and stood in front of her with a wave of awkwardness washing over my entire being. *Yep, I know. I'm not the kind of person who could assist with this kind of thing and you would be correct. I'm really not cut out for this sort of ordeal.*

"So... You like that guy?"

"Mmhm!" She nodded rapidly. "Wouldn't anyone?"

"Uh..." *Noooo? Or maybe it's just me who sees him as childish, annoying, and secretive. On the other hand, Stacy is strong, confident, and used to dealing with people like Daji. If anything, she would be a lot more my—Never mind!*

"Putting that aside, did you clam up because you were too embarrassed to speak with him?"

Her expression grew glum. The change in her complexion was the difference between night and day compared to when it was just the two of us.

"Yeah... I haven't spoken to a guy around my age before, but I have partied up with quite a few of them. I have seen Daji come back from a lot of quests since I started staying here a few weeks back. He's just so manly. But that doesn't mean I don't love you too! He can't hold a candle to the almighty Lethe."

"W-what?" *How can you say that with a straight face?!*

I blushed, feeling a mix of flattery and irritation from her words. *"Riiight.* Ignoring that... um, last part, what do you want to do about it? I can't have you clamping up during our whole quest. Being a wordsmith isn't exactly my forte, but apparently a lot of people see me as some sort of problem-solving guru. I don't take pride in it, but I've gotten this far by helping and listening to others." *Mostly against my wishes, though.* "So, what can I do to help?"

"Well..." She fidgeted back and forth. "You can start by introducing me to him. I think I might gain some confidence that way."

"Do you really need that, though? You saw how happy he was to talk to you," I stated as matter-of-factly as I could.

Umbrea went beet red. "He didn't mean t-that. Daji was just being nice. He doesn't see me as a romantic partner. I felt more like I was just caught up in a game between him and Stacy."

Despite her stuttering, I was taken aback by her objective analysis. *Wow. For once, I agree. You seem to have limited experience in talking to men, yet you hit the bullseye with that one. Of course, we could both be wrong. Neither of us has even dated a guy.*

I was greatly outside my element.

"We're taking too long here. The point is—just talk to him. I can't tell what kind of relationship he has with Stacy, but I think it will be abundantly clear soon enough. I can't even tell if they love or hate each other. If anything, they seem more like lifelong traveling partners than anything. The point is that I don't know and *neither do you.* Take your time and don't sound too pushy. That should suffice. Probably."

"You sound like you're talking from experience. You're so knowledgeable, Lethe!"

"Eh-heh-heh, thanks." A bead of sweat dripped down my cheek as I accepted her misplaced praise. *I don't have the heart to tell her that Bella had given me one of her favorite romance novels and I was just feeding her advice from that. It's better she doesn't know.*

"So, will you act like a human now?"

She rigidly bobbed her head up and down, like a puppet with her strings being forcefully pulled. Clearly, she was still nervous even if the color in her face had returned. "Mmhm. I got this!" She stood up from the toilet seat, a confident smirk built on a glass foundation. "Let's get back there."

"You don't need to tell me!"

* * *

When we returned, we were in for a little surprise—or as the ever-horny Daji would describe it—two *mega* surprises.

"Mmm..." The girl gave us the once-over in silence. I felt especially crushed under the immense weight of her scrutiny. The mystery girl's face contorted into an unpleasant scowl. "So, these are the two that kept us waiting? They better be worth my time, or they can get the hell out!"

Woah. Aggressive, aren't we?

A young woman had appeared, and she had brought her own chair over to our booth. Daji and Stacy sat next to each other and, for some reason, were on their best behavior. They weren't scared or anything, but they seemed mentally miles away the moment she set her sights on us.

A brief lull trickled by before Stacy got up and pursued the subject at hand. "L-Lethe and Umbrea. This is our benefactor and the one we are escorting on the quest. She's a rather renowned artificer. We have known her for nearly a decade, and she's always come through for us in the end."

"Renowned? Psh! Don't BS her! Try—*world famous*. How 'bout that?" She flipped her right pigtail upward in a gesture of supreme confidence. "I'd be surprised if these two nobodies didn't know who I was. And has it really been that long since we met? You and the meathead over there haven't changed a bit—not even on the outside."

"Perhaps your memory of your younger days has become clouded?" Stacy offered. "Though I do take that as a compliment on my youthful features."

"That's not what I..." She paused, then released a small sigh from her enormous mouth. "You know what? Take that however you'd like." She glared our way. "Anyway—you still haven't answered my question!"

How insufferable.

She had already been standing at that point, a hand on her hip with her back straight up as she showered us with childish insults. It was becoming increasingly taxing to be around her.

She thrust a metallic-looking thumb toward her chest. "The name's Kei Bela—genius inventor and artificer extraordinaire."

I could practically see the girl's head swelling up like a balloon. It would be preferable to toss her the embarrassing alias I had been graciously gifted instead of my actual name.

"Nice to meet you. I'm Ku—"

"No need for introductions, Bandit Girl! I don't need to know the name of someone like you!" she snarled. "Especially not some ugly chick from who-knows-where."

She was seething in her own rage. *What did I do to deserve this?* She was so unnecessarily aggressive right out the gate. Her words really stung. I had a feeling we were not going to be best friends. She made C.T. look like a saint.

"U-ugly?!" My iron-will quickly wavered, nearly crumbling under her vexing gaze. I had to fight back anyway I could.

"Don't say those kinds of things to s-someone you just met!" squeaked someone off to my right. It was Umbrea, who had shockingly spoken before I could mount my defense. Despite her efforts, she'd been so nervous that she slipped back into her home language, Ornia.

The instigator looked momentarily clueless, but she seemed to understand what Umbrea meant, regardless.

I smiled after taking in her enraged expression. Not once had I ever seen Umbrea get mad, especially on someone else's behalf. Now that was genuine friendship. *Bella, Rock—I did it! I think I can safely say I have secured at least one more friend. This feels... nice—and I meant that.*

"Hmm?!" Kei's head unnaturally tilted toward my Umbrea. I did *not* like where this was going. "And don't get me started on you!" The deranged egotist shot out a metallic finger at Umbrea.

"What? Me?!" Umbrea responded with a pained expression, her anger leaving her body as quickly it had entered. *As I thought, she really is weak to direct confrontation.*

"Yeah, you! Your hairline is an inch too close and one of your eyes is slightly bigger than the other. And what are those large glasses?! Ew! Talk about creepy!"

"C-creepy?" Umbrea echoed before hanging her head in defeat.

"Yup, and don't you forget it. Not everyone can be born perfect like me. Sorry."

Ugh... This is the girl we have to escort? Really? Talk about bad luck. She seems like a self-absorbed brat. To make matters worse, she has the same last name as my beloved Bella.

"What's with that nasty expression, Extra Number One?"

Okay, this has gone on long enough.

"What are you even saying? Is this the way to treat your escorts?! Just who the hell do you think you are, talking down to someone you just met?" I blurted in unbridled rage. It wasn't often I got mad, but between her verbal attack on both Umbrea and myself, as well as the lack of intervention from our two other teammates, I just couldn't take it any longer.

"Do you really think you can treat people like this because of the face you were born with, a bit of intellect, and some extra lumps of fat on your chest?! Huh?! Just piss off if you're going to act like that! How can someone be such an awful person after only exchanging a few words? I hope your, um, parents are ashamed! Yeah!" I tried to look strong and confident, but I had a feeling my eye was spinning like the swirl of the prattling vortex.

Not my proudest spiel. Near the end, I had begun to ramble and run out of ideas. I hoped I showed her how rude and unnaturally cruel she was being toward us. Also, why were the other two just sitting by, anyway? Because they weren't getting verbally demolished didn't mean they couldn't help us!

"You hope my 'parents are ashamed', huh? That couldn't be further from the truth! What could I possibly be but a treasured daughter? There isn't a better one on this three-dimensional sphere or the fabricated realms of beyond!" Kei slapped one of her knees after bursting into obnoxious laughter. It was so nauseating to hear that I had to seal my mouth lest I puke.

The pompousness in her expression only heightened when she witnessed my reaction. "Hah! I know, I know. Beauty *and* brains? Why, it's just not fair! You're a funny one, aren't cha? You think the flimsy words of an unintelligent nobody could even reach the ears of divinity?!"

"I really don't like her," Umbrea confessed with the eyes of a psychotic killer. Like the temperature of a northern desert, her emotions had fluctuated greatly during the exchange. I suppose there was someone filled with more ire than me, at least. *I'm truly seeing the many shades of Umbrea today. Stacy and Daji as well.*

"I think we should just…" She slashed her hand across her throat with a nasty glint in her widened eyes.

I nodded in agreement. "This isn't worth the money. Let's just go grab a drink or hit a bakery."

"Woah, woah, woah!" Stacy forcibly got between us. "No need to fight. We're all on the same side here."

I gritted my teeth. *Where were you during this fight? Someone should keep this mad dog on a tighter leash.*

"You didn't tell me you invited two goons to carry our bags. I was expecting a pair of handsome, muscular men. I can't show my divine self to anyone, you know?"

Umbrea's dangerous cackle caused all the hairs on my body to stand up. I was feeling many things at that moment, and fear might have been one of them.

"You hear that, Lethe? Not only has she insulted the names that our cherished parents granted us by not letting us give them. She also callously insulted our performance before we've even started. And all in a few words, too! How childish can one be, right? This is self-defense. I feel as if I have taken a ton of mental damage already. I should return the favor."

Kind of ironic that you, out of all people, are calling someone else childish, but you have a point.

I nodded. "It's completely self-defense when she talks down to us like we're lowly dogs." Truly fired up by Umbrea's malevolent fighting spirit, I rolled up my sleeves; it was about to get ugly.

Ashardna, it's time to—

"You two can cool it!"

Someone chopped down on both my head and Umbrea's with force. Stacy let out a small sigh after the two of us were cowed from acting on our dark desires.

"This is just how Kei acts around new people, more or less. Don't get thrown into her world! I don't know much about your friend over here, but I expected better of you, Lethe."

Really? I could say the same for you, but if you let this go on for as long as it did so we could warm up to her, you failed. But I'm not that angry about it anymore. Not angry at you, anyway.

"Oh. I guess I lost my temper there. Sorry."

Umbrea soon followed. "Yeah, me too. No one has ever made fun of my boob size before."

However...

"Hmph. Ungrateful bitches."

"What was that?" we shouted in unison.

"Everyone, just calm down!"

Despite being in public, I didn't feel embarrassed; I was that pissed.

Kei returned to her seat first. Stacy sat next to Daji, and Umbrea made her way back to the booth. I followed soon after, smoothing out the bottom of my clothing with shaky hands before plopping down.

I frowned deeply. The seat was indeed comfy. It was the situation that was most definitely not.

* * *

It felt like eons had passed since we originally all met up, but only now did we finish the party introductions. You know, the kind typical people would do at the beginning of a meeting. I learned a good amount about Kei, though not from her own muzzle. It seemed Stacy, Daji, and she went way back.

Kei's family was from an independent fishing nation, but her unbound, genius mind allowed her to create her own company when she was still young and inexperienced. It blew up instantly, attracting investors from around the world to dump pounds and pounds of coins into her business. At a quick pace, she became known as the Beautiful Genius Artificer. She added the beginning part, by the way.

I didn't expect her to be affiliated with any god, as a woman of a concept as strange as science, but her entire country apparently wasn't into religion at all.

Without a god's favor, I'm surprised that their quarry could be so bountiful. She could be lying, but I doubt it.

From Stacy's words, as well as the brief input from Kei, an artificer was someone with extensive knowledge of relics, both ancient and new. Most relics were too old to use due to being created in the days when gods and humans walked the earth together. People like Kei could replicate them, or even make them better than before. Her work was one of the few ways that someone without a godly patron could get their hands on something within the realm of Eternals. Her talent had changed the way adventurers, and even businesses, functioned. Very few could re-tune or create an artifact that could be used by someone with little mana. My rings certainly wouldn't have been usable if I lacked a large quantity. I had to admit that she sounded impressive.

Her creativity was also off the chart, though it usually led to problems when she got too invested in something. Nevertheless, her inventions had revolutionized parts of the world for many people. That's how she and Stacy put it, anyway.

For someone as brilliant and wealthy as Kei, she sure dressed like a bum. Her ash-colored hair was parted by two black ribbons into long pigtails that swept down both sides of her fathead. Overall, it was a bit unkempt for such a famous girl, but after enduring her vulgar insults, I'd say it was one of the more feminine qualities she possessed.

The lack of femininity was compounded by the black goggles that were loosely strapped to her forehead. They periodically shifted whenever she would reel over from abhorrent giggling or ear-raking guffaws. It happened a lot...

Her eyes reminded me of the purple crystals that stuck out of Rankle's body.

She had a white tank top under blue overalls with the right strap undone. I couldn't tell if it was a fashion statement, or she was too lazy to bother fixing it. Both articles of clothing were covered in sprinkles of dirt and other stains I couldn't identify, no matter how hard I tried. There was a slightly noxious smell to them, too. *I should back away before I enter a coma, like a certain friend of mine.*

The other part of her that caught my attention was her left arm. From her shoulder down, it was entirely metallic. When asked, she semi-confidently explained in a roundabout manner that she'd lost it in the fight with a ferocious, legendary plague dragon and created a prosthetic out of one of the strongest metals, zinganthian. She'd decked it out with a load of hidden weapons, enchantments, and other features to improve its combat capabilities.

While there is indeed a dragon like that, I would have to call her bluff on encountering it, especially here. I had met that very dragon not too long ago. He wasn't the type of creature to leave his place in the Null. But before I could call her out on her bold lie, Stacy quickly whispered in my ear that the true reason she'd lost her arm was during a trial run for one of her dynamite golems. Apparently, her failures were not a topic to be brought up. *I'll be sure to study up and remind her of them as frequently as possible.*

As for Stacy's explanation, it sounded both plausible and humorous, yet my gut told me that the truth was a lot deeper than a simple mishap at the lab. I'd need to learn more about this insufferable individual if I wanted to ascertain the truth, and that in itself was unbearable.

That's all you need to know about Kei Bela for now. It was time to begin the first stage of our quest!

Or so I thought.

* * *

As we walked back to her gigantic laboratory, Kei would swap between insulting one of us, praising her own looks, and speaking about her greatest "child." She would occasionally burst out with boisterous laughter while tinkering around with something from her oversized backpack and shouting, "Shine on, shine on! Shine on, you crazy diamond!"

Every second I listened to her was another second that I regretted not picking up that solo quest. Why was fate so cruel?

C.T. must have known she was like this, yet she told me nothing of my other party mates. I bet she wanted it to be a surprise. Why do I work for her again? I thought back to the scary eye power I was supposed to have. *I should try to bring it out next time she insults me. The side effects did include wetting oneself. Now that would be a spectacle!*

"And here's the shop that I fixed up with my artificial fireplace. Now they can blow glass without having to add more wood or cast a fire spell. Amazing, right? I'm just the coolest, aren't I? There's not a single establishment in this town that I haven't improved for the better. Can you charmless lackeys say the same?"

None of us spoke a single word.

"Oh? Why so quiet? Spit it out!"

I truly was inching closer and closer to the edge. I had a good feeling the rest of us were, too.

Umbrea had become even meeker than when she was next to Daji because of Kei's excessively sly remarks about her body and magic. Daji hadn't even cracked any jokes or played around. The girl he wanted to hear them was too busy lecturing Kei after she insulted one of us. It seemed that there was only one person who could truly tame this beast. At this point, though, Stacy was as tired as the rest of us. The four of us had really all boarded the silent carriage together on the Ignore Kei Highway.

"Here we are. The amazing home of mega-genius Kei Bela! Don't get lost on the way to my lab, though I couldn't care less if you did."

Despite her atrocious personality, her talents were the real deal. The entire facility was technologically leagues ahead compared to anywhere else I had been. Even the Tribunal looked primitive in comparison. And her lab was ginormous!

Shiny metal insects of all races and colors moved materials around, while miners delivered their spoils to different scientists in tattered lab coats. The constructs almost reminded me of golems like Rock, but it seems not even Kei could pull off a feat like the Cursed One did all those years ago. Older artificers quickly shifted around, eager to inspect the new materials for their own next magnificent creation. Some miners were so small that they had to be an ancient race, like the dwarfs. As a race despised by the gods for their less-than-desirable physical features, it made sense for them to be in a small, single-city country like Markarth. I had read that they lived underground all over the world, but this was my first time seeing a group in person.

When we got past the first wave of people, a couch appeared to greet us.

I'm not joking.

A large, red couch rolled up to us, as if a ghost were carrying it on its back, then parked in place.

"Woo! My ride is here. Stacy, you and Meathead can take a seat. The other two can—Ow! Mry chweek! Unhaaaaam me, womaaan! Thanks. Okay, okay! They can come too—as long as they sit at the end."

Just as I was admiring her creations, she once again reminded me why I couldn't stand her. At least Stacy was able to slap some sense into her when she became really unreasonable. *I'm glad to see that her energy has been restored.*

Like a booming tempest, the couch raced through the workshop, speeding by people, spiders, delivery bees, and creations that I couldn't even begin to comprehend. When we reached our destination, both Daji and Umbrea had faces as green as a frog. I didn't think they were cut out for that kind of fast travel. I was surprised that I had somehow made it in one piece myself. *Frosty must have finally had his meal, meaning I wouldn't have much to upchuck, anyway. On the other hand, I'm hungry again.*

"Sooo, what exactly did we come here for? You were already packed when you came to meet us. What reason is there to come back?" I asked, sounding bored and uninterested.

"Allow me to tell ya!" With an impish grin, Kei hopped off the couch as we arrived and boldly placed her hands on her hips. "I thought you could figure it out, but I guess that must be too taxing on that nut-sized brain of yours. But who can blame ya? People like me are only born once every few millennia. It can't be uh... helped?"

Stacy had a scary look in her eyes, and it easily smashed Kei's proud facade.

That kept her quiet for the next few minutes as we entered her large, white laboratory. It was magnificently decked out with scraps of metal and uneaten food across multiple tables, while a desk of strange, unfinished devices and contraptions piled up toward the sky.

In the far corner of the room stood a bizarre, oblong creation, employing a tripod of metallic legs to keep it upright. Black rims surrounded the empty oval like a frame. It vaguely reminded me of an enchanted mirror.

Kei sorted through her junk, casually tossing them around the room as if they were nothing but nuisances. The pain on Stacy's and Daji's faces told me that was not the case. To a normal person, they were most likely priceless artifacts that could change someone's life. But to Kei, they were toys.

"I think it was right around he—Got it!" She gingerly brought up a hefty, cyan gem nearly six feet in height. "This bad boy is called **Dimension Leaper**." Her voice grew sultry when she said its name. "He's gonna save us a shit-ton of time. Impressive, right? Come on! Don't all praise me at once. My golden brain can't take it! Well actually, it can! Ha-ha!"

Silence met her words.

She started to sweat. "Tough crowd." Kei turned away in embarrassment, placing the oval gem down next to the tripod before clearing her throat. "Anyway, D.L. will let us jump to the outside of Caranos' Cave without a hitch. Pretty impressive, right? That was a rhetorical question, by the way—I know it is!"

Ugh... This girl. I felt myself visibly cringe.

Daji pointed at the oval in her hands. "That little thing can teleport us? It just looks like a big gem."

"Maybe to a primitive ape like yourself, but when this mineral, Altracia, is combined with a special energy to connect with a location in the user's mind, it creates a little phenomenon called a gate. This gate is similar to opening a door to your exact location, as long as you can keep a strong and concrete image of it in your mind, that is. For me, that's easy peasy."

I knit my eyebrows and frowned. Then, with a dubious expression, I addressed the group. "Does anyone actually know what she's talking about?"

"Nope."

"Nah."

"I'm a magic girl. Complicated arts like these are out of my area of expertise."

The other three had all shot out their answers with haste, the same look of confusion plastered across their faces.

"*Tch...* simpletons. To dumb it down for all of you, once inserted, the blue of the mirror transforms into a portal to the desired location conjured up from your noggin. Think of it as two destinations, one being here and the other being the cave. This puppy creates a passageway between the two for us to traverse. Make sense?" We all nodded, so she continued. "Since I have been there, I will be the one to tether us along the way. That also means I will be the last to step in." She shot a glance at me. "That's where Miss Failure over here comes in."

"Are you really still calling me that?" I yelped in disbelief. "You know my name, don't you?" My fake smile twitched before reforming into a large frown. My energy was getting sapped away the longer I spent being in the same room as her.

"A world-renowned, well-endowed, beautiful genius doesn't have time to remember the faces of all the insignificant specks she sees while passing through. I think this name suits you better, anyway."

Strange. I was under the impression that you remembered me very well. If not, why do you always have the face of someone that is confronting their parent's killer? I just couldn't figure out why she seemed so deeply wounded and furious whenever we were around each other.

"Don't look so butthurt. It's just a nickname."

I was now scowling. I was very, *very* close to adding a new ice sculpture to my collection. I knew it would sell well, too. But I had other people I cared about in the room. I couldn't let the beast overrun me so easily. I could envision the dream demon cheering me on, while the Silver King watched in silence and worry.

No giving up! That's right! I won't let this brat keep me down!

"This dimension thing or whatever—has it been tested and is it safe?"

"Oh, it will be—right after you walk through it. Congrats on making history. No need to thank me. I'm already blessed enough."

"Seriously? That could be dangerous for Lethe to go in first!" countered Umbrea. It had been quite some time since she had said more than a few words. Glad to know she was still kicking, nurturing the shadowy fire in her chest. I'm very fortunate to have a girl like her in my corner. It was almost enough to make me really smile.

"It's alright. I'll go in first," Stacy said. With a casual shrug, she added, "It sounds like fun."

"You will?" All of us exclaimed like a unified chorus.

She winked. "Yup. So put it in, Kei, and let's get going. If something happens to me, I'll make sure my ghost haunts you until the end of your days." She dropped a sinister smile. It was enough to give any child a good reason to not leave their room at night.

Kei squirmed, all her hair standing up on her head. "Give me a few minutes to recalibrate it with the transponder, just to be safe!"

"Good," Stacy replied, sounding eerily pleased. I doubt she would have had a problem plunging in either way. She just enjoyed stepping on Kei's toes. *What a commanding presence. Teach me, master!*

"I bet she wouldn't have done that for me," I mumbled under my breath.

Kei pulled the loose goggles over her eyes and got to work on the device. Five minutes later, we were finally ready to set off on our joint quest. After everything else I'd dealt with today, what was the worst that could happen?

Chapter 16

The Crown of Despair

Some of the darkest places have the most bountiful treasures. That doesn't stop you from being beheaded when you lose to your greed, though. Oh-ho, been there, done that.

—Boreas Tyrel

The world we ventured into was something you could only call magnificent. The illusory landscape seemed sprawled out in endless kaleidoscopes of colors and mirrors. At best, it was visually breathtaking. At worst, it induced mild seizures. The warped space brought pure astonishment to all of those who trespassed through it, Kei included. This surreal experience was a once-in-a-lifetime opportunity for us; an event horizon that a rare few would ever see.

Trust me; I felt lucky, but the fact that I knew who was behind the creation of it made me feel sour overall.

"You're going to want to move forward three more steps before taking a left and walking straight down until you come upon a florescent green light. Did you get all that? Are there any dullards that need me to repeat it?"

"I think I get it, but there's only one way to find out. Back home, anything of this sort would have been straight out of a dream," Stacy replied with a mildly perplexed expression. "I just hope we're heading to the right place."

"Course we are! Do you know who designed this dimension of space? It's a Kei Bela creation, af—"

"Yeah, yeah. We get it. Let's all have some faith in Stacy, shall we?" I cut in.

"Mm," Kei answered after a short, but meaningful pause. Even she agreed with my sound logic. That was a new one.

That kept the group moving in cautious silence the rest of the way. *Ahhhh, so peaceful.* I was indulging myself in the experience.

This domain was the perfect place to clear your head. Unfortunately, the one problem on my mind was just a few feet behind me. I could only enjoy my inner tranquility briefly before being forced back to the task at hand.

It didn't take long for our party to stop at the location Kei had been referring to. Stacy slowed to a halt and turned back toward us. "Kei, are you sure this is supposed to be a doorway?" she asked.

Kei appeared to be lost in a daze, tilting her head quizzically. "Yeah. Why?"

I see..." Stacy replied with a sharp nod. "I believe a more accurate description would be to call this a hatch than a door."

"A hatch?" Kei responded, looking astonished. "Sure, this place wasn't molded completely under my control, but for it to be something else..." She rested her chin on her metal hand for ten heartbeats. Suddenly, her eyes widened. "But that would mean—"

"Yes, it would, and I have already triggered it."

Ah, crap!

The ground beneath us seemed to blink out of existence, sending us plummeting toward our deaths.

"AHHHHHHHHH—Oh..."

We fell about a whole three feet before dropping onto a prairie full of grass and dirt. I was the first to pull myself up and brush off my clothes. "A-are we here? Seems like we ended up in some sort of grassland."

"That's the poin—Pfft!" Kei spat a clump out of her mouth. She didn't know it, but her powder-colored pigtails were ungracefully caked with mud, and dirt plastered her skin in thin smears. *How unfooooortunate that she landed right in a small mud puddle.*

I could say something, but we should let bygones be bygones, right? I frantically licked the insides of my cheek to make sure I didn't have my own grass issues.

Kei began her in-depth analysis not long after. "The mountain of boulders up ahead is concealing our destination. It's a lot easier to see at night because of the moon's illumination, but with my goggs, it shouldn't be an issue to locate. Leave it to your fearless leader!" She puffed out her chest with conviction.

"Should I scout for hostiles?" Daji asked. "The air here feels different, I think." When he noticed us all staring, he blushed with embarrassment. "Sorry, I can't explain any deeper."

I'm sure you could if you had a little less meat in your head.

"Y-yeah I f-feel it too," Umbrea claimed, hugging her shoulders. I think she just wanted to be on the same wavelength as him. *I'm glad you're trying, girl!*

Stacy brushed herself off. "I think we should be good. I already sent a water spirit to check the surrounding areas and the only thing around here is a settlement in the distance. Though... I get the feeling there's another presence around, watching us from afar."

"Heh, it *was* a settlement. A straggler or two wanting to meet the great Kei shouldn't be a problem. Nope, not at all! It's unlucky that bandits are popular around these parts, which scared all the villagers away. Now, it's more of a ghost town," Kei concluded while adjusting her goggles. "I haven't encountered a single soul since I started researching this place. I welcome the company."

I was a little thrown back by the helpful information Kei was providing us while still including her usual snide remarks, comments, and swagger.

Then she ruined it by saying, "Alright! I see the outlines in the second crevice. Move your asses, you louts!"

Before we left, Umbrea called out to Kei, her voice unsteady. "U-um, y-your hair. It's—"

"Eh?! What is it?" Kei challenged her with a scowl.

Umbrea shrunk under her dominant gaze. Kei eased up after watching her squirm with fear. "Are you jealous of it? I spend half an hour every morning using my boy, **Grand Ironer**, to get these curly tips. Amazing, right?"

Umbrea was rendered silent, and Stacy just snickered in the background.

* * *

Our merry group moved further away from our starting spot, the edges of my skirt brushing against the high grass. This continued until the ground began to shift to gravel and rocks.

We had shuffled into a U-shaped canyon, creeping up the mouth toward a large formation of boulders. *Honestly, this would be the perfect spot for an ambush.*

Our team cautiously approached the boulder array. Daji and Stacy had taken the lead as the vanguard, with Kei walking slowly in the middle. Umbrea and I happily brought up the rear. The two of us were constantly on edge, peeking over our shoulders to ensure that no unexpected visitors appeared. Being paranoid wasn't always a bad thing, especially when the rest of your party only watched the front. Umbrea seemed to agree with my philosophy of keeping your head on a swivel.

We ended up doing it so often that we nearly collided with the others' backs. They had all stopped in their tracks.

"We're here, heh-heh. Just gimme a sec to work my magic." Kei punched a few commands into the small console on her metallic arm, a wild grin dancing on her face.

Like a swirling vortex, her wrist was sucked inwards and disappeared from sight. What appeared from her stump was rather unexpected. It was a large drill contraption, the size of a head. Its shape was sleek, and the tip was sharp as a blade.

"The drill? Again? Should we move back?" Stacy asked.

"Shepherd, say her *real* name. We talked about this last time, remember?"

So, this one's a girl? Just how does she decide on genders for her stuff? I mean, I don't care too much. Call me curious.

Stacy crossed her arms and pouted. "You have another thing coming if you think I'm calling that thing **Ebony Terror.** Pick cuter names."

"What do you mean? It's adorable!" Kei howled with defiance. "They look badass, inspire fear into those who hear them, and sound as cute as a button!"

"The only thing it inspires in me is the need to slap you."

She shook her head back and forth. "Never mind that! Now, step back or get pelted with rocks. That may be a good makeover for those two in the back."

"I can take it," Daji offered with an intrepid smile. He pressed his fists together. "Rocks are nothing to my *rock-hard* body." He flexed his abs and gave the thumbs up to Umbrea and me.

Stacy gave him a small shove forward. "Thanks for being our meat-shield, Daj! We will never forget you!" She gave him the crispest salute I had ever laid eyes upon, her voice and movements the pinnacle of superfluous exaggeration.

"Uh... Ha-ha... never mind then." His facade had broken instantly. Stacy was too much for even him. Still, his expression may have seemed dejected, but his eyes were full of fiery passion.

"Stand back if you don't wanna be demolished. I'm starting!" Kei hollered with laughter, her voice echoing over the rocks.

The four of us pulled back, putting a decent distance between us and the mad inventor. Our lives would most likely be in danger if we didn't take the necessary precautions. Chunks of rock sailed in every direction like stray cannon shots. The chipping and cutting droned on for another five minutes before silence unexpectedly returned to the canyon.

"Annnnd done!" Kei pushed up her goggles and wiped the sweat from her brow. "With this, the path is clear once again."

"Uh... What do you mean by 'once again'?" I asked.

"You probably wouldn't understand the financial problems that come along with allowing an undiscovered cave to spread its legs for just about anyone. This was a preventative measure, and from what I can tell, it worked fabulously. Yay me!" She unironically patted herself on the shoulder. How pitiful.

I didn't respond. She was far too much for me to handle. There was only a single soul here—and mostly likely in existence—that could quell this mega-problem of a child.

Stacy stepped in. "Cut it out and step out of the way so we can guard you already."

"You don't have to be so rude, Shep—"

"Fine. Go in first," she snapped. "Just know that I'm the one with the light magic. It would be a shame if something happened to you in the *cold, lonely DARK.*"

"Uh... Well, you see..." Her words had cut through Kei's confidence far deeper than any knife could.

"W-w-what do you m-mean?" Kei started to sweat profusely. "I have multiple artifacts that can light the w-way right h-here!" She hastily patted her backpack.

Stacy continued to bully her, not letting up for a single second. "It would be a shame if something happened to all your equipment in the dark. I heard cave goblins and imps both have terrific night vision, just so you know."

Kei should have known exactly what to expect in that cave, yet she shivered. "Okay... I'll move."

"Hm? What was that?"

The air around us seemed to chill. Ah, Stacy cast a temperature spell. She should be an actress for all the dramatic shenanigans she put on. I appreciated it a lot more than her victim did.

"Eeeek! N-nothing! Nothing at all."

The exchange was almost comical. Kei hastily moved out of the way so Stacy and Daji could enter. *This must be what it's like to tame a monster. I wish I could savor this.*

However, my amusement was short-lived because the second Daji and Stacy disappeared into the gaping maw of the cave, Kei instantly snapped back to her regular self as if time had been reversed. *"Tch! Damn bitch. She's never gonna get laid with that shitty personality,"* she cursed at the level of a whisper. Sadly, I was right next to her and heard it.

Oh, the irony!

"We sure lucked out with this quest, huh, Lethe?" Umbrea gave me a thin smile that seemed to crack more and more the longer she held it. Was she trying her hand at sarcasm? It could be a good look on her with time.

"Yup. Fantastic."

Kei turned back to us and scowled. "Quit fussing over the details and worry about your own shitty future instead!" She pulled a silver lantern from her pack and disappeared into the cave.

* * *

"Why the hell is it so narrow? I nearly got caught on that rock!" Kei complained. There were two light sources in the cramped passageway. One came from the top of Stacy's staff in the shape of a bright, white orb, and the other coolly leaked out of the magic lantern in Kei's right hand. Grasped firmly in her other hand was a circular device with a black display. From what I could see when we stopped, it showed five blue flames all in a straight line; that must have represented us. She checked this artifact periodically, most likely to see if anything else showed up on it. There was a good chance that if anything else appeared, it wouldn't be friendly.

"Yo, you girls good back there?" Daji called out. "We see some sort of opening up ahead. Stace said we should take a break there."

"We're fine. Just a bit cramped!" I called back.

"I—I'm fine too!" Umbrea replied briskly. "Though it smells a little musty."

There came the sound of shifting stones and Stacy said, "Watch your step. There are some rocks up here."

"Thanks, Stacy."

"You have just a smidgen of my gratitude, Shepherd. That's still a lot, though!"

"Got it!"

Kei, Umbrea, and I all called out to each other nearly perfectly. It was like we were a close trio of sisters without a problem in the world. If only that were the case.

The tunnel opened into a wide atrium of the cave. A large hole in the ceiling sent rays of sunlight into the cavern and provided us with a nice light source. Three separate tunnels beckoned for us to enter on the opposite side, and a waterfall lightly filled a small pool in a crater to our left. Its spray misted us as we moved by, reminding me how cold a cave could be. A cluster of large boulders stuck out of the ground. There were eight in total, all in a crowded circle near the center.

It seemed a bit *too* suspicious for a newly discovered cave to have seats that were precisely carved from large rock. At least, that's what it looked like to me.

Daji uncomfortably shook his head. "Three directions? I don't like it."

"I agree with Daj. There's evidence that we were not the first ones to come to this cave," Stacy said. "Better proceed with more caution than before and watch our backs as well."

"Bingo! My goggs and big, golden brain are telling me that there were definitely signs of life here in the past. They also tell me that someone has been here recently, carving their way around," Kei added, her expression a strange mixture of bemused and chagrined satisfaction.

"A running waterfall isn't too common in caves, right? Especially in newly formed ones," I mused aloud.

"I haven't even seen any in the ten caves I have quested in." Umbrea sat next to me.

"I see ten flat rocks here. Anyone else? Huh? Huh?" Kei left a rather snarky comment and took a seat all the way on the other side of the circle from me. Daji and Stacy filled out the middle.

"Do you guys get that itchy feeling that someone's eyes are following you every time you move?" Kei wondered.

"It's just you," I said. "Attention seekers get attention, after all."

She glared at me.

"Snack time!" Stacy chimed in, clearing the awkward silence before sticking both of her hands together in prayer. A dark circle that was the embodiment of ominous opened up over her head, filling me with the dreadful feeling of incomprehension. *Is it an enemy attack? Does she really not notice it? How can she be so calm?*

The endless void stood in the air silently. Then, with the speed and skill of a veteran archer, it spat out five metal containers. Each one floated away from her and landed in the palms of our hands, quickly and cleanly. They were big enough to need both hands to hold and weighed as much as a rock.

"Dig in! I used Kei's cooling and heating containers to keep the sandwiches I made nice and fresh. Thanks, Kei!" Her praise sounded earnest and sweet, but if you could read between the lines, then maybe...

"Huh? You did what? But those were for my specimen. How did you even get th—"

"Thanks, Kei!"

"You're welcome…" Her lips were quivering under Stacy's reproachful gaze. I wasn't even facing her, and yet I could feel my body tremble ever so slightly.

There were eight in total for each of us, but despite my hunger pangs, I decided to only eat two. I would make it up to Frosty later with the money from this quest.

I tossed away the worries of my wolf and eyed my food with voracity. "Mmmm! Is this that peanut stuff I've seen on menus from time to time? Oh, there's something else, too!"

"That's jelly and yup, you solved it—it's peanut butter. I call it a peanut butter sandwich or pb and j for short."

"It's amazing!" I was elated. This stuff was divine.

"Yeah, I don't think I have ever had peanut butter so fresh before," Umbrea added.

"Stace woke up at dawn and put a lot of work into finding the right ingredients for us this morning. She would make a great empress or wife if she didn't always open her—Ow! Ow! Ow! My Eaaar! It's gonna tear off! Off, I tell you!"

Stacy had leapt from her seat and savagely grappled Daji's ear, while gracefully holding her sandwich in the other hand.

"Just praise me and be done with it, Daj. Let's not do this dance today. Unless your body can *handle* it, that is."

"Nope. Not in this flesh. I'm good! Y-you are right!"

After their comedy routine was done, she smoothly returned to her seat and continued to chow down like the rest of us. We finished our meals and prepared to move on. Stacy waltzed ahead and peeked into each path, most likely to see if any of them were particularly narrower or wider than the other.

"Two of these paths are pretty spacious, but the middle one seems like it will be a tight squeeze. Let's split up into teams of two and three. There's a good chance that both paths will eventually lead to the same place. If you reach a dead end or find danger that you can't handle, come back here within the hour so we can meet up and plan our next move."

Umbrea raised her hand to ask a question. "How are we going to decide on who goes with whom?" She looked over to Daji and then back to me. *I guess that's her dream team and the main reason she's asking. I respect your hustle, girl.*

Stacy winked. "Tell 'em, Daj."

He nodded and grinned with delight as he reached into the small pack on his back and fished around. You would think he would still be in the same state as Kei after how deflated he'd appeared just a few minutes back, but I guess one reason he had been able to keep up with Stacy all this time was because of his quick recovery skills.

After a minute, he finally pulled out a set of path markers. "These were supposed to be for marking where we were in the cave in case anyone got separated, but since this place is surprisingly well made, we can use them to draw lots instead. You know how it goes: whoever has the shortest one loses. I even added in two short ones to make Team Two easier to form."

He giddily turned around and messed with them before spinning back to us. "All of you, take one."

* * *

"Why do I have to be with her?!" Kei and I bellowed in unison. We had both drawn the shortest sticks and were unfortunately paired together.

Umbrea had a look of relief on her sweat-ridden face, but I could tell she felt bad for leaving me with the problem child. I would have felt the same if our roles were reversed. I really wished they were.

"C'mon you two. You have been fighting since you first met. You're both capable women, and Kei has her heat signature tracker as well. Call this team bonding, now get going!" Stacy gave the two of us a forced shove, propelling us forward.

"For your information, it's called **Spotter Skite**, and I refuse to—"

"Get. Going."

"Okay!" *Were Kei and I both squealing like mice now? No, it must have been my imagination. Only she would act that way. Yeah, definitely.*

Aaaaand, that's how I ended up with Little Miss Big Ego as we monotonously explored the leftmost tunnel. It was awful. Just the *worst*. All I could do was muster a fake smile to appease her.

I didn't want to rely on her light, so I used my fire ring to create my own. We both wandered aimlessly, walking side by side in pure silence. The passageway was paved pretty well, making it rather easy to tread. There were no stray rocks on the ground, or anything that could kill us if we accidentally fell on it. Maybe someone really had been there recently, but why? And how did they get past the rocks?

There was a slight silver lining to this whole unprecedented ordeal, though. I could finally ask her what had been on my mind since she'd first audaciously introduced herself.

"Hey! I'm sure I'm waaay off here, but I need to get this tasteless thought off my chest." I placed a hand over my heart and drew in a deep breath, wanting to be as calm as possible for this discussion. I couldn't afford to show her any more of my weak or prideful side than I already had if I wanted to get a serious answer. Even with this soothing ritual, however, I still slightly bit my lip as I continued. "Are you related to Isabella Bela?"

Kei stopped dead in her tracks. A few seconds of silence passed as we both stood in place. Her face elicited a response that told me I had hit the bullseye.

"So, you've finally done it, huh, Extra?" She turned toward me with a glare that could kill. "You've finally *admitted* it." Her voice was firm and loud, but rough.

A wave of cold caused my entire body to turn frigid under her scrutinizing gaze. My eye fell upon one of hers, then quickly switched to the other. There was nothing but contempt in them. Those beautiful amethysts were full of pure animosity and rage. *"They are connected"* was the only thought to trickle out of my frozen brain.

"S-she was a girl I met in Trident, and my first real friend. She... She showed me so much, and taught me even more."

I felt like I was on trial for my very life. I could no longer meet her petrifying gaze; it was too much for me to handle. I instead focused on the goggles that were practically dangling off her head. She was too indignant to notice.

Kei desired to clobber me for sure, or perhaps something much worse. I had never come upon such hatred in someone before, no matter the situation. Neither the Sand King nor Gilgamesh had shown this much disdain when they looked back on the past. It was unbridled fury and anguish directed solely at me, and me alone.

"So, I was right," she snarled, her tone icy. "You killed Bella! You killed my sister!" Kei smacked her metal fist into her palm, most likely hurting herself. "To think it really was some pompous E-extra like you. I can't believe I doubted myself for even one second."

"W-woah there!" I took a few steps back on instinct. This was not the ideal time to be in her line of fire. "I had nothing to do with Bella's death. There were pirates and the Leviathan—they killed her."

"Oooh? Is that so?" Her eyes were now bloodshot and wide. "You sound so superficial that it's just plain funny on the ears. Ha-ha-ha! Priceless. What splendid acting! Wipe that counterfeit smile off your face! You have been showing it to me since we met! Deep down, you felt guilty about it too! So, stop!" She made a few slow claps with her hands that were as shaky as my body. It was good to know I wasn't the only one overwhelmed by nerves. *Was I really always smiling like that around her? Did I know who she was the whole time?*

"How long did you spend rehearsing that? Do you even know what you sound like right now? Huh? HUH?! How the hell did an ugly bitch like you survive against those odds? The only option would be to sacrifice her so you could escape. You're the worst! Don't lie to me, harlot!"

What was I supposed to say? That deep down, I knew who she was? That Bella had told me all about her prodigy sister? That the moment I'd heard her name, I'd pushed all my feelings away so I wouldn't have to face her?

She was right. I was the worst. I'd owed her a proper explanation back when we'd first met. Not now. Not here.

There was no way I could reason with her in this state. I was nearing my wit's end, just inhaling the toxic fumes spewing from her. What could I do to remedy this situation? I knew her conclusion was wrong, but wasn't I just as guilty for not correcting her, nor telling her in the first place? My resolve had stood strong for some time now because of the severance of my guilt. It had drifted away along with the body of that sea monster. I'd accepted my failure and planned to make sure it never happened again, yet I still hadn't taken responsibility like I said I would. I said I had moved on, but I hadn't taken any actual steps forward. Just like Kei, I was still grappling with the past.

We both needed to accept that.

But—I had to do something, for both of our sakes.

I let out a long, wistful sigh to clear the air. It was stressful enough that she seemed to relax a bit. Then I did what I would do for anyone that I called a friend. Just like I had always done with Bella, and mostly with Umbrea, I spoke from the heart.

"Kei... I would never do anything to harm a friend, especially *her*."

I did my best to sound calm, but inside I was scared. Never had I been in a position like this before. Even if I was fed up with her, she really was just a girl, crushed under the pressure of success and praise. She was an older sister, grasping at the straws of fate. All she desired was to know the truth that had befallen her younger sibling. There was nothing wrong with that. Even though Bella wasn't my own sibling, I'm sure I had felt a similar pain at the time. Even now, I carried it like a hole in my quivering heart.

We were both suffering after losing Bella.

I continued, her silence beckoning me to keep going. "B-before I was taken by the pirates, I passed out from an attack to the head. When I woke up, everyone was gone, and the ship was sinking into the open sea. That's what happened."

She had been silent as I spoke, but soon after, she flew into a fit of rage, her voice even more hoarse than before. "Don't bullshit me!" she howled, emptying all the air she possessed into her shout. "There's no way such a convenient outcome would happen right after her demise! Tell me why! Why did you let my little sister die?! *Why, why, why…*"

Tears welled in her eyes. Her sadness had far surpassed her anger now, but remained within her like an aftertaste.

Even with all her enmity toward me, the love for her sister had shaken her heart. Right now, we were at an impasse. Would she attack me to avenge her sister, or would she break down in tears and escape from the depths of her well of misery?

The choice had unexpectedly fallen to me.

With an expression of both sorrow and compassion, I spoke to her as kindly and as gently as I could. "It may not mean much, but…" I fished through my satchel and pulled out one of my most prized possessions. Even now, my hands clamped down on it just to make sure it couldn't possibly leave me… like she had. "This was the two of us, the day before she passed. I t-treasured her as much as any friend would—probably even more since she was my first one. She meant the world to me, but I bet she meant the universe to you, so take it. I'm sure she would have wanted you to have it."

Did it… Did it work?

Kei sniffled. "S-she would?" Tears trickled down her face as she took the photo.

Kei stared at it with her tears dropping onto it like rain, staining the white background of the picture. "She looks so h-happy. She was so brave to leave home even after I made it big. I offered her a job with me, but she declined… S-she wanted to see the world for the both of us. I was too tied down with w-work…" Her long eyelashes quivered bewitchingly beneath her sagging goggles. They had nearly collided with her eyes now.

I slowly dropped to the ground in exhaustion. She did the same. "She was a great waitress," I told her. "Told me it was love at first sight."

Kei looked up at me with puffy eyes. She awkwardly pressed her lips together into a stiff, but legitimate, smile. "Really? So, she... she made it?"

"Yeah." I beamed. "She made it."

"Then why did she have to die?" she asked, sounding so lost. "Why?"

"I wish I could tell you," I replied solemnly. "Nothing in this world ever goes as planned. We all wish it would, but..."

I didn't need to finish that sentence. There was more to it than chalking it up to bad luck. *I was too weak and lonely at the time. If only I was like I was now, maybe then...*

"Didn't you try to save her? I'm sure e-even the l-likes of you could have been useful."

I didn't want to hide the new information that I'd gained, but hope can be a sickness with very few cures. *There's no reason for me to get her excited. It only leads to more pain and sorrow down the road.*

I could have broken down, just like her. I could have shown that weak side of me like I had all those years ago in the tragedy's aftermath, but what good would it do? I'd vowed to never be vulnerable like that again, and I planned to stick by it. It was more than a promise to me; it was a promise to her as well. *"Be strong for me. Okay, Lethe?"* Those were her last words.

I decided to tell her the bare minimum. My pride wouldn't allow me to expose any of my weaknesses or incompetence, even to a girl who'd just bared her soul to me. Little did I know how pathetic I truly was with upholding my ideals.

I sighed. "I tried, but there wasn't enough time. Then the next thing I knew, there was a sinking ship, and my only option was to flee. I was stranded on an island for a week and ran into a cult that was reviving an ancient, eldritch god."

"God, that sounds like one of Bella's favorite novels. She ate that shit up. Would never stop recommending these lovey-dovey series and droning on and on back when we shared a room. Such a feisty book chick."

"Totally."

"Heh..."

"Aha..."

Somehow, we both started laughing.

Kei had a genuine smile on her face. Not some stupid cocky smile, but one of pure bliss and joy. It looked good on her, but her lips were already wavering under that foreign position.

I hoped I appeared just as genuine despite the small guilt that burrowed its way deeper into my chest. I stood up, my knees aching from being pressed onto the rock floor, and held out my hand. Even though I disliked being touched, if I was the one that initiated it, well, that was different.

"Listen. I know we have our differences. You don't like me, and I can't stand you. That's alright, though. As long as we both keep Bella in a special place in our hearts and don't cause her grief wherever she is, I can be satisfied with that. The real question is—can you?"

"I think so." She took my hand. "As long as you don't tell anyone about this."

"What? Your tear festival? I don't think anyone would care about—well, there is one person..."

"The Beast."

Oh, the irony.

I nodded. "She can be scary at times. Still, I feel a lot better with her around."

"Likewise," she giggled. "She has been my protector for so long now. Despite her antics, I would be clueless without her. If I was a guy, I would no doubt have fallen head over heels for her by now."

"Oh? Is that so?"

"W-what the hell is funny about that?!" she barked, her eyes flashing in anger.

"Nothing, really. I just didn't expect you to say something like that. You sound like a maiden in love!" I couldn't hold back my laughter. I should really learn some restraint. That would have to wait till tomorrow. Somehow, some way, things were better now.

"S-shut up!" She let go of my hand and faced forward. "Let's find the end of this path already. I don't have all day. I need to finish mapping this shit!"

"You do."

She nodded, her face once again full of life and clear of tears. I could tell that what had been weighing her down had finally vanished. The raging maelstrom of Kei had finally been tamed—or perhaps—quelled.

"But first..." She pulled out a strange object from her pack and used it to flash a light at the picture for a mere second. "Here, keep it." She shoved the picture to my chest, forcing it to fall into my hands as she retreated.

"Huh? But—"

"I got a new one right here, see? Did you think only magic could make these photos? Nope! With the power of artifacts, anything is possible. An Extra like you wouldn't get it."

I pouted when I heard that. "You still think of me as an Extra after all *that?*" *And aren't artifacts still made of magic? They at least have mana. I know that.*

I wanted to say we had made some progress, even after both admitting that we weren't very fond of each other. She felt somewhat more tolerable now. Just a bit. *Ugh. Do I actually like her now? What would Umbrea say if she saw me?*

Kei saw my face and frowned. "Hmmm... You're right. What's your name again?"

"I already told you." My happiness deflated like a popped balloon slime.

"Actually, I believe I cut you off before you did." She lowered her gaze, as if feeling guilty before facing me again. "It would be, um, great if you could tell me again."

"You know, I can see why only Stacy puts up with your antics. The name is Lethe, by the way. Just Lethe—and uh... sometimes Kulu."

"Oh! You're the one that turns people into ice and sells them for cash, right? To think you were such a ruthless chick!"

"Yeah. I guess I've done that a few times. They did deserve it, though. I'm no killer."

She chuckled. "Sure, sure. And that name, Lethe, sounds like something I heard before." She snapped her fingers as her eyes widened. "Oh, right! The infernal river, Lethe. It's a place in the underworld. It is said to be able to erase memories and junk like that. I always wanted to go down there to see if it was legit. But with the Netherworld being nearly impossible to reach, and the fact that I'm not dead, it didn't really seem feasible."

"I can't say I feel the same, but my namesake is indeed that river." *Maybe I'll find clues if I go there. If there is a way to get there without dying, that is.*

"Well, now that I put a name to your plain face, we can get going."

"Uh huh…" *What part of my face looks plain? Maybe I should use the Eye of R'lyeh. I'll put the fear of a god in her. Maybe later.*

She strutted forward, paying me no mind for the first time in a while. Even after all the anger and tears, I rather enjoyed our conversation. We walked in silence for some time, but then she said something that caught my attention. "You know, I don't think you're that bad. I think I can see why those other losers enjoy being around you—just a little, okay?!"

My mouth drew into a sly smile. *Seems she feels the same way. Oh, how the tables have turned on our venomous relationship. The others will be shocked.*

It was then that we arrived at our destination.

"What is going on? W-why are these here? Grrrrr!" Kei kicked at a casket in frustration. She angrily gazed at the place after readjusting her goggles.

I took in the entire room. It was a sight for sure. Fifteen caskets were randomly scattered around the dusty, dark room. In the center sat a golden sarcophagus that looked even older than the gods. It stood out from the rest, as if it didn't belong, and gave off a frightening aura. It really rubbed me the wrong way. Not to mention that a musty smell permeated the air, assaulting both of our nostrils without warning.

Kei cringed back. "Ack! This feels unnecessarily ominous. Should we go back the way we came? Not that I'm afraid, though! I just think we should have more opinions before proceeding." *So, she wanted someone else's opinion. Now, this really is character growth!*

I genuinely agreed with Kei's suggestion. She was the artificer, and apparently a good one at that. Between the two of us, she had the eyes to decide what to do in a situation like this. *I can't believe I am actually saying this, but I tr—tru... trust her.*

"Hmmm," Kei stared at her creature locator with a puzzled expression. "I'm not getting any other flames near us, but I really don't like this. The markings on this are a lot older than anything else here. My golden brain is unnerved. It tells me that whoever refined the tunnels of this cave may have placed it here. My goggs can't even get a reading on it, which means..."

"Which means...?"

"It means that there's a good chance it was crafted back in the times of the old gods. You know, where magic was abundant, there were no countries becoming another Null after being ravaged by the Void, and there were still stars in the sky."

"So, it could be over three thousand years old then. Woah."

Cobwebs covered each of the caskets except for the golden leader, hinting at how long these things must have been stored there. Each of them gave a rather crude odor, perhaps the same odor that Umbrea had mentioned before. I wanted to leave as soon as I could, but—

"Leave no stone unturned, right? If you want to fully map this place out, we need to find out what these things are hiding. Even if it's some sort of trap!" I was trying my best to be useful when I had no experience or knowledge whatsoever. Even as an avid reader, I felt out of my element when it came to ancient history.

"Yeah." She sighed. "You're right. And since you are leading the charge, why don't you start by taking the tops off? If I'm killed by whatever is under there, it would be a grand loss for the world." She shook her head as if to say: *"It's simply impossible."*

"Can't argue with that logic. I guess." I moved forward. "Let's see... I'll start with this one."

I gripped the sides of the stone casket tightly with both hands. However, my effort was wasted. *It's really not as heavy as I thought.* I brought it back about halfway before I stopped and peered inside.

"What do ya see?" Kei asked curiously, her eyes practically sparkling as she stood safely near the entrance. "Anything dangerous—or cool?"

"Ehhh. It's a skeleton with some old jewelry."

Kei appeared at my side in an instant. *She's fast!* "Really?!" she cried. "A skeleton with a family heirloom? I wonder what era it's from and if the quality still holds up. I don't wear jewelry, but maybe it would bring out more of that sex appeal the guys at work keep going on about. Let's check the other coffins. Quickly!"

She raced off, fast as a horse, to pull off the other covers and elaborately inspect their insides. The results were similar. They all contained skeletons with some kind of jewelry. *So much for being cautious,* I thought as I watched her act like a child in a candy shop. Within a few minutes, the only one untouched was the archaic golden sarcophagus. We both gazed at it with curiosity.

"Pull it off together on three?" I asked.

"Psh. Like I need help. Watch and—Hrrrgh! Work dammit! Come... on! Ugh... Okay, I might need just a tiny bit of help. That's all."

I rolled my eyes. "Alright," I replied with a smirk.

After watching her struggle, she graciously allowed me to join her on the other side. Together, we removed the top and pushed it onto the floor between us. It knocked dust into the air on impact, which caused us to both cough for a few seconds. Skeleton dust sure wasn't tasty.

When we both got a look at what was inside, a wave of unease washed over us.

"Uh, did we really stumble upon something from an ancient civilization?"

"Well, for starters, I don't 'stumble' across anything. This place was discovered with my genius intuition—even if it was placed here after. It was placed for me, after all." Kei tapped her forehead with a finger and crossed her arms. "But this seems really fishy."

"Yeah... That's a lot of jewelry." I sized the body up and down. "And that crown... That's gotta mean he or she was a king or queen, right?"

There is definitely some magic trapped in those gems.

The skeleton lord we'd discovered was dyed as black as night. On its head sat a golden crown with three gems placed within small sockets. The center crystal was a dark shade of red, while the others were both bright blue. A thick, gold necklace was draped below its neck and reached all the way down to the breast, while displaying more gems—this time all black. I could smell the noxious stench of death trailing off the body and crawling up my nostrils. The pungent smell was the worst I had encountered in the cave by far.

Kei analyzed the skeleton, giving it a good scan from head to toe. "Hmmm... I don't like it, but I just can't... I can't *not* remove that crown. Who knows what could happen! It could contain the lost magic I have been searching for. Then, I can... Anyway, I must know!"

As a prodigy inventor, she must have always been pushing the boundary on what was possible. I hadn't noticed it before, but her eyes always seemed to radiate curiosity. It was just usually hidden behind an ugly scowl.

As seen with her teleportation gate, she was eager to throw away caution to get immediate results. *I can see how she lost her arm and got over it so easily.* Her intense drive was both her greatest weapon and worst weakness.

I knew there was no way to stop her—I saw it in her expression. It had been the same for Bella when she wanted me to read a book or try something new. Her interest in a subject had overwhelmed me every time.

That's why I said, "Why are you even looking for my approval? You're going to do it, anyway, aren't you?" *I want to know what lies in those gems too, if I'm being honest.*

She nodded so vigorously that I honestly thought her head might fall off. "Yup, yup! You sorta get me! No way am I going to let this chance pass by.

Who knows if this crown can grant special powers or even get all these bags of bones to rise once more. Just the thought of it is making my bottom half uncomfortably warm."

Does she have to go right now? Now that I think about it, I also kind of have to go... There was a chance she was talking about something a lot lewder, but there was no way I planned on finding out.

She's drooling! Gross! And why is she panting like a dog in heat? This can't be what she's into, right? I looked away with disgust and valiantly stood guard to face whatever she would undoubtedly unleash. *There's a good chance we get attacked here. I hope she's prepared to fight.*

"By the way," she said, her eyes still focused on the skull. "Why haven't you ever gotten that eye of yours healed? I have the tech, but there are many healers out there that can regrow limbs and whatnot for the right price."

I sighed. I'd expected that kind of question from Umbrea, but not her. "My grandfather tried. He had a lot of discarded items that should have been able to restore something small like this, but nothing worked. From my understanding of healing and restoration magic, it's supposed to bring back the part of you that is gone. If it fizzled on me, then my eye must not belong to me anymore."

"That sounds ridiculous."

"If only I could remember how I lost it."

Kei turned toward me. "You know, I could always give you a fake one, just like my arm."

How nice of her. Are we actually becoming friends?

"Thanks, but I got this patch from someone special and, on the off chance I do get my eye back, I don't want to deal with complications." *Plus, if C.T. says her blessing dwells in that eye socket, will it go away if it's replaced?* It hadn't been useful so far, but that could change down the line.

"Check this out." I focused really hard on my left eye, putting the same passion and fire into it that I did with my Eternal. Okay, maybe not the *same* amount, but you get the point.

"Oooh! That's kinda neat! It's green and... now I want to run away? And I might have"—she glanced down at her shorts—"Shit! Well, not shit, but—"

"Sorry! I forgot it could do that." *That was a lie. I would never forget something like that.*

She waved her hand. "Don't worry about it. It's cool and a little shocking that a green flame can be that menacing, even with my fear resistance. But what can you do?"

That fear resistance didn't seem to work against Stacy, did it?

"Anyway, I can dry it and extract the liquid in no time, but that's not important right now. I think I have finally found the right spot to avoid this thing reacting. Yup, this is it! Show mama what ya got!" She reached for the necklace. The moment she touched it, the room's temperature plummeted.

Umbrea

Soon after we separated from the other two, we reached what must have been a mausoleum. At least, that's what Stacy called it. Withered bodies filled the entire atrium, either on the ground, in wall cubbies, or suspended in the air with strange magic. *That's so damn creepy!*

"They still have flesh on them. Be on guard; this isn't the first time we've been attacked by the dead."

"I told you, Stace! I told you there would be undead here! Leave it to the mighty Daji to—"

"Will you shut up?" she hissed, taking the words that were about to leave his throat and shoving them back down. "What if they respond to your boisterous and obnoxious voice? Can you not smell the death magic on them?!"

"I just wanted to fight them." Daji backed down and lowered his head. "R-right… I wasn't thinking. Sorry."

I chimed in, "Do you think we should head back or go through there?" I pointed toward the wall in the back. It had a gaping hole in the middle. Even with the dim lighting from the floating lanterns of the room, it was still easy to make out the pathway that led into a deeper section of the cave.

"That is an option. This area is a lot more dangerous than it looks. Someone is playing with us," Stacy said before pressing onward, doing her best to step around the bodies.

While the undead were scary, not having a light source—besides our own—sounded utterly terrifying. I didn't talk about it a lot, but I really hated the dark. No, seriously! I hate it a lot!

I hesitantly pushed forward, keeping the two of them in my line of sight. With every step, I felt the sense of dread creeping deeper and deeper into me. It was a familiar feeling; the same sort of feeling I'd felt when I confronted the shadow in the lamp with Lethe. *At least it's not dark!* The apprehension I felt now was ten times worse than that, and it wasn't getting any better. *I have to be on guard… I also wonder how those two are doing? I hope Lethe can handle that really mean girl. I wish we got put together, instead!*

"Yo, Umbrea, you coming?" Daji asked, sending my thoughts scattering. It didn't help that I wanted more than anything to be by his side. But I didn't deserve it—not yet.

"Yup! Coming," I quietly called back. "This room reminds me of a place I wasn't too fond of in the past."

Daji and Stacy both turned back to me, clearly interested. *Aren't we supposed to be on high alert?! What gives?!*

"Seriously? What was it like?" he asked, pounding his fists together with excitement. He seemed genuinely interested to hear from me, which warmed my heart. Stacy also wanted to know. *Cool.*

"Yeah, if you have any relevant info—that would be great. We have more experience with living enemies, especially long-lived ones."

What? Like elves or something? That sounds way more interesting than anything I have experienced.

"I see..." I gazed down at the bodies all around us and twisted my lip upward. "This place reminds me of the Great Tomb of Ateus."

Both of their expressions screamed ignorance. They really didn't know what I was talking about. *Seriously? And here I thought it was a pretty famous tomb among adventurers. Guess no*t.

"It's a cave that leads deep into the ground in the old Republic of Hakon. It's down near the Null. An ancient king and his subjects were buried there after being killed in a rebellion. I still don't know why, but when we entered the tomb where they were buried—they had all risen from the dead."

Stacy snapped her fingers. "Zombies, right?"

I shook my head.

Daji squished his fist into his other palm. "Skeletons?"

I shook my head again. "While those are both common undead in those kinds of places, I don't think that's the case here. Just like back then."

Stacy crossed her arms and moved closer to me. "So, what do you think then? All this beating around the bush is getting me pretty curious. You better not be pulling my leg here."

"Umm." I nervously scratched my cheek, doing my best to avoid her intense stare. It was a bit unsettlingly intimidating. "Um... No. I'm being serious."

I'd always had trouble looking most people in the eyes for more than a second. It was too nerve-racking. But on one of my quests, with a party of four and one loner like myself, I'd learned something that helped me a lot. One guy had told me that I never had to look someone in the eyes, only make them think I did. Instead, I should focus on the center of their nose.

He's a genius! I had been using this method ever since, allowing me to keep up with and take part in a conversation. It was sweet!

I stared at the tip of Daji's nose and nearly opened my mouth, but the words got caught in my throat. The combination of conveying important information and speaking to the guy I sort of liked was too much for me to handle. I'm sure my cheeks were the color of peaches as well. *Just great.*

Alright. On to Stacy! This time, I focused on her nose. When she saw me gazing so intently at her, the corner of her lips turned upward into a satisfied smile. There were a lot of things you could notice from looking at someone, like the faint freckles that were randomly sprinkled across Stacy's nose or the slightly rosy complexion of her cheeks. *Wait! I'm getting distracted!*

"Have you two ever heard of *draugr*?"

They both seemed puzzled.

"Nope."

"Don't think so."

"From what the people I partied up with told me, they're a cross between zombies and skeletons. Children of The Breathless King from a long, long time ago—when there were still stars in the sky. They are, like, waaay stronger than either of the other two and smell way worse. They're relentless and won't die till all their parts are smashed into pieces or burned to nothingness."

Daji didn't seem concerned in the slightest. On the contrary, he actually looked happy. "That sounds kinda cool. Can we fight one?"

"I would hope not! The more ancient they are, the stronger their aura. One touch is all it takes to snuff out our lives."

I broke away from the two of them and examined all the bodies. They definitely looked similar to the ones I'd faced before. There were at least thirty of them that I could see. How could we fight them all in a cramped room? *No, there's only one way to get through this.*

"The thing with draugr is that there's usually a requirement to stir, unlike other undead. Usually it's some kind of goal, like protecting treasure or gateways to their king's resting place." I stopped in front of a row of bodies. "As long as we don't trigger one of these conditions, we can continue safely. The Breathless King was a pretty strange creature, from what I read."

"But that would require us to go back the way we came. Or else there's a chance that this next pathway could lead to their king."

I nodded at what Stacy said. "Y-yea, that's very true. I think I have a way to check, though." I stuck my pointer finger toward the door, like I was holding a bow, and bent my hands upwards as if firing. A dark beam flew out from my finger and into the new passageway.

"What was that?" they both asked in confusion. I guess it startled them to see my magic. I really couldn't blame them.

"A piece of my shadow," I said with courage before closing one eye. "It will let me see exactly what is in the other room. Oh, it's entered—lemme see— Oh!"

"What is it?"

"I seeee... treasure! I think? There's a bunch of chests sticking out of something that looks like sand—Eek! There are skeletons all around the mound. Their gear is super outdated, but they all look like adventurers!"

I called back my shadow fragment. "I think we should—"

Stacy nodded. "Not push our luck? Yup. We are heading back."

"But I wanted to—"

"Zip it. I don't want to see you get your ass handed to you by a bunch of chicken-boned zombie fiends. We were lucky to not have triggered this death zone when we came in here. It's a good thing we found this place first. We would probably be fine if it was a normal trap, but I get the feeling that it's more than that. Without caution, it could become a bloodbath."

"Oh, wow!" My eyes went wide. "You knew about the soul rending area too? I didn't want to bring it up and worry you guys, but..."

"Don't worry about it. Not the first time we've had to deal with something that takes the lives of more than just mortals. Let's be on our way."

She was right. Anything *that* malicious was none of our business. We were just adventurers.

"Yeah, let's head back and wait for Lethe and the mean girl," I said with a bit of scorn.

"I second that, including the mean part." Stacy nodded after letting out a giggle. Daji's head had been in the ground, but he perked up pretty quickly.

Was it because I mentioned Lethe or going back? I hope it was the latter for my own tiny, maiden heart.

But it seemed our luck had run out. Because the second we reached the spot from which we had entered, the bodies began to stir and rise from their long slumber. Their desiccated flesh and bones creaked and snapped as their heads turned to us. Then a chorus of moans grew to a roaring growl.

"Shit!" Stacy yelled. "Run for it!"

As the dead began to sprout up all around us, we sprinted for the hole in the wall, hurtling us back into the dark tunnel. We didn't stop running until we reached our break spot, each of us nearly out of breath. However, we soon realized we had bigger problems. I had a feeling it was likely related to our own plight.

That big meanie, Kei Bela, was there with a nonchalant look on her face as she was surrounded within a circle of horrifying skeletons, wreathed in a dark aura of death, while Lethe had been pushed to the ground. There were cuts all over her body, revealing skin on her shoulders and legs. A dark, fleshless foot was pressed over her chest. I followed it all the way to the head, where I gazed upon a black, skeletal face with a crown of jewels. In his arm was a golden scimitar, and he was ready to let it feast.

Lethe

"Why did you try to pull it off if you knew this would happen?!"

"I did it for science, dammit! I have no regrets!"

"Well, I do!"

Kei and I screamed back and forth as we fled from the room of skeletons and into the tunnel. The moment she'd reached for that large necklace of jewels, a ghastly ball of flame had appeared in each of the black skeleton's eye sockets.

The animated body had firmly grabbed Kei's hand while rising out of its sarcophagus with a golden scimitar with strange letters written all over it. Kei screamed like a baby, forcing me to help her by firing a few blasts of fire to draw its focus to me. It was just enough for her to squirm free of its grasp.

There was a dark aura surrounding it, but luckily, her fake hand was the one it had grabbed. I wonder what would have happened if it had been the other way around?

Around that time, the other skeletons returned to life and ran toward us. Our only option was to flee with so many enemies in pursuit.

We made it back to the break spot to catch our breath. I could hear the sound of bones against rock echoing from the tunnel, and it wouldn't be long before they reached us.

"The great Kei Bela never runs from an enemy!" She grabbed her goggles with both hands and fastened them over her eyes. "Let's do this."

Uh, didn't we just flee, though? Have you already forgotten?

I brought my hand up to my face and examined my rings. *Should I use fire, ice, or Ashardna?* Ice could be more useful, but I had heard that undead aren't affected by the elements as much. This couldn't be a worse match up for me. Something like fresh undead would be easy to burn, but not skeletons. Ashardna would have to do, even in a rather tight area.

I glanced at Kei. She was messing around with her metal hand again. "I got something, but it's going to take a bit of time to charge. While I'm at it, I'll analyze that skeleton king's weapon. There's a chance it could have a scary and super sweet enchantment that I could then replicate for my other creations if I got my hands on them."

She's drooling and panting again. What a weirdo!

I imagined my gauntlet appearing, invoking the summoning ritual in my mind.

But—

Nothing happened.

I tried using ice magic, and then fire. "What the—My rings aren't working. Neither is Extinctathon!"

The sound of elder bones was almost upon us. I was next to defenseless. *Would the eye work? No, she said only living creatures, and this messenger of death is certainly not alive!*

"Here, take this. Your signals are getting jammed. From what I've researched on Eternals, anything below the colored ones is susceptible to it just as much as any artifact." She tossed me the device that showed flames on a display and a dagger. There were thirty or so red flames closing in on us from the north. They would be there in under a minute.

"Signal? Jammed?" I asked, puzzled. "What do you mean?"

Kei was still messing around with her arm's inputs. "Every artifact, and I guess, Eternal, has a mental connection with its user. If the connection gets disrupted, then it's temporarily suspended as if it was severed. My golden brain is telling me that each of the gems on the crown and necklace has some sort of magic imbued within them. And one of them, that must have only just been activated, has some sort of jamming magic. Guess your Eternal really isn't up to snuff."

"The Silver King is probably not a fan of your words. It's from an ancient god, you know, and wait—why do all your artifacts still work then?"

Kei continued to give all her attention to her arm. "It's simple, really. My artifacts don't run on a magical-mental connection." She tapped her forehead with her normal arm. "A while back, I installed a metal chip inside my skull, giving me a direct connection with any artifact I touch. It's less like a mental connection and more of an extension of myself. It's just like using an extra leg or arm. A jamming spell can't do shit against someone's body parts. As for why your Eternal isn't working, it's likely that the artifact the skeleton guy was wearing was placed with him after he was buried so no one could stand against him when he stirred. There are some strange things about this world that even I don't understand. Just bear with it for now, 'kay?"

I stared at her in disbelief. "Have you encountered either of those kinds of magic before?"

"Nope," she said nonchalantly. "I just wanted to have artifacts that could keep up with my brain processing speed and commands. Every person can only control a few artifacts at a time, but after I installed it, I can easily use over ten. The mental strain is non-existent. I don't know too much 'bout Eternals, but this stalker must be pretty powerful to interfere with a god's gift."

Great. Looks like I'm dead in the water. "I see," I muttered. "I guess that—"

"They're here!" she screamed. "Don't come near me for a bit. I'm deploying a stunning field in a two-foot radius around me until"—her voice changed into one of seduction—"**Big Daddy** comes online. He's a slacker, that one. Always loves to sleep."

Again with the stupid, sexy voice? What is with this girl?!

"But I can't fight—Oh, thanks."

"Don't mention it. Oh shit! That enchantment! Don't get sliced by that scimitar, my goggs are telling me it can rend souls from their bodies! That dagger should also protect you from its death aura. You can't see it, but there's a holy shield already shaped around your body."

"How are you so prepared?"

I didn't get an answer from her. The skeletons spilled out of the darkness of the tunnel like rodents, armed with stony blades and daggers. The black skeleton emerged more slowly, the blazing balls of flame in its sockets directed straight toward me.

Sheesh. What did I do? Kei was the one that woke you! Go for her instead! Sadly, my complaints were ignored. The skeleton king kept coming.

I clutched the thin blade that Kei had tossed me. How did she expect me to fight off the horde of skeletons and their king with a flimsy baby sword and a little magic shield?

The first skeleton's body creaked as it lunged at me with both hands.

"Ahhh! Back off!" I slashed at it horizontally with my pathetic dagger. Surprisingly, it tore right through the bone, shattering the skeleton to pieces.

"Hey, Kei, it works! It actually works!" I turned back to see several skeletons gathered around her, strangely unmoving. *Must be her stun field at work. I wish I had one too.*

She spent the time she bought, glancing back and forth between something in her hand and the black skeleton accompanied by two lackeys. *How are they so damn fast?*

Kei set her sights on me and puffed out her chest. Even in this situation, she needed to act like a big shot and flaunt her goods at the same time. I really had to give it to her. I could never be that cocky.

"You betcha! This bad boy, **Deep Wave**, deploys a shockwave every few strikes. It doesn't require a connection with the user, so it gets around the jamming, even with your hands. I'll kill ya if it breaks, though!"

Right. I backed up closer to the wall as more skeletons poured in from the tunnel. Unlike the king, there was a plume of death surrounding each of their bodies. There was a good chance they could wither and destroy my flesh with a single touch. Boreas fought something similar in the past and it cost one of his allies their life.

I tilted my head down at the black blade that I'd been given. Maybe I could do something with this after all.

The skeleton king—or whatever he was—eyed me from the other side of the rock formation. It was the same spot where we had eaten lunch just half an hour prior. His pace had slowed down, instead sending skeleton after skeleton in my direction. Truly befitting of his king status.

"Hyaaa! Die!" I shouted as I swiped the blade with unsteady hands toward any skeleton in my vicinity. *Don't touch me... Don't touch me. Don't touch me!*

A surgeon would be appalled by my lack of technique, but I didn't care. Did I mention this was the first time I had ever held a blade? Not the best way to get started, but after toppling a few skeletons, I was quickly getting used to it.

I shouted more meaningless cries as I kept my defense up. Somehow, it was going well. "Kei, how much longer on that, um, Big Daddy?"

"Grrr. These shitters are trying to resist my stun field, which is interfering with my work! Damned death magic! How unfair! I'll need at least two more minutes. But don't worry, it will fix everything. You have my word as the great Kei Bella! Leave it all to me!"

I hope that's more than just big talk!

Piles of bones crunched beneath my boots as I moved backwards, my arms already tired. Still, confidence was swelling in my chest. I could do this. *I totally can.*

My breathing had become staggered, and a few claw attacks had given me enough scratches that if I received cuts in a few more places, Daji would have a field day with all my exposed skin. *At least it was their stony blades and not bones that touched me.* Their evil aura didn't seem to extend to their weapons.

I smelled the iron of my blood and anger coursed through my veins when I noticed that my new gear, which I had purchased from the Tribunal for a pretty penny, was getting unjustly assaulted. At least C.T. could repair it as long as I made it out. One of her jobs was apparently being a great tailor. *Why did I even pay extra for those enchantments? What a scam!*

The number of skeletons began to dwindle. Only a few surrounded the skeleton king now, while the ten or so near Kei continued to stay rooted in place.

The skeleton king finally made his move. He stomped toward me, roaring, and held out his ebony hand as if to grasp something. One of the blue gems on his crown gleamed like a corrupted diamond, dazzling in the darkness. A sudden gust picked up, sucking me forward in a whirling vortex.

Oh no! What the heck is this?!

I lost my footing and flew through the air, dropping my weapon. "Woah, woah! Heeellp!" My body collided with the black skeleton, and they smacked me out of the air with the force of a mighty fist.

"Aagghhh!" My body struck the hard ground, sending me into pure pain. My already staggered breathing had become ragged. I may have even heard something crack inside me. That couldn't be good.

"Keh, keh, keeeh," said the skeleton king. Was he laughing? I couldn't be sure, since skeletons couldn't exactly change their facial expressions. He triumphantly planted his foot on my chest, crushing me even without a lick of muscle. It was getting harder and harder to breathe. It raised its soul-shattering sword, but before it could attack me, a scream filled the cavern.

"Leeetheee!" squealed a familiar voice. "Take this!"

A deluge of shadows pelted the skeleton king with the force of a warhammer. It shoved him completely off of me.

"My turn, now." From the corner of my vision, I saw Daji leap out and slam his fist into the ground. The force shattered every skeleton in the vicinity in one fell swoop, reducing them to piles of bones. A crater oozing with a dark aura had been formed in his wake.

Daji smirked and cracked his neck. "Too easy. Was that all of them? I sure hope not."

"Idiot! Who do you think we were just running from? That black skeleton is still kicking, too. Get him, but don't let him touch you until I prepare a holy ward!" Stacy ordered as she conjured up a spell.

Daji leapt toward the downed king while Umbrea released another volley of shadow arrows next to Stacy. Before either of them could land, the skeleton disappeared from sight, reappearing behind both Stacy and Umbrea.

"Look out!" I yelled from the floor, still wincing in pain. "He's behind you!"

The faint blue glow of the gem in the crown gave away its position in the darkness, but both Stacy and Umbrea hadn't seen it. What could they even do after hearing my warning? Well, apparently, they could do quite a lot.

The skeleton king's sword flew down at Stacy's back but was met with a jade barrier that appeared from thin air.

"Sneak attacks only work on those that are not prepared," she replied curtly. "Umbrea!"

"R-right!"

Umbrea's shadow massively grew, consuming both of them. It disappeared and then reappeared right by me. Now, what kind of black magic was this and why hadn't she used it earlier?

Stacy held out her hand. "Looks like you might need some healing. We have a lot of draugrs heading this way, so be prepared. A single touch can spell death."

Great. More death. I took her hand and coughed. "Gah! It hurts. Wait. What's a draugr?"

Stacy sported an impish grin. "You'll see. Now stand still." A green light washed over me, warming me to the core.

Meanwhile, Daji and Umbrea stood ahead of us, blocking the skeleton king's advance.

"H-hey! Where did all those bony guys go?" Kei glanced left and right in confusion. Then, in a sultry voice, she said, "**Big Daddy** is hungry! I can't put him back without feeding him." She grimaced.

"Don't worry. They should be here… soon," Stacy assured her.

The skeleton king must have known it as well because he disappeared into the third tunnel, the one that the three of them had tumbled out of. I could hear the stomping of many feet, far more than the skeletons before. This might be too much for any of us to handle.

An even more intense stench of death reeked as black, decaying corpses limped out from the darkness. Unlike the skeletons, they were far more frightening. The draugrs looked like what you got when you crossed an ancient dead body with a rotting corpse. They seemed semi-mummified. Their faces had skin, but they were so old and bleached that you couldn't make out their features.

More and more flooded out of the tunnel until the majority of the room had been taken up by them. Not a single one moved once they settled in. They were frozen in time, awaiting commands from their leader. That's when the skeleton king brazenly walked back in.

Even though they were separated in death, these were his true subjects. I had been tussling with the normal, souped-up undead this whole time! How could I fight for my life against instant death? Withering was bad enough, but this didn't even give me a fighting chance! The odds were stacked heavily against us, even with my body once again in fighting condition. There was no way we could take on nearly a hundred of them at once, plus their king mixed in.

We all gathered in front of Kei and attempted to piece together a decent plan. "I can't use my rings, so all I can do is fight with a weapon."

"I'll protect you, Lethe. I swear!" Umbrea beamed, stepping in front of me.

"I can take... maybe half?" Daji mused. "But I need you all to deal with the stragglers."

"Half of them shouldn't be considered stragglers, Daj. Anyway, the ward is good to go. If only I could give it to more than one person at a time."

"It's fi—" Umbrea tried to say before a new voice overtook her.

"Fools! Let your fearless leader, the magnificent Keidana Bela, take on this task!"

Oh, so that is her full name. It almost sounds like a guy's name. No wonder she keeps it short.

"Fearless?" I questioned.

"Leader?" Stacy echoed.

"Just shuddup, step back, and watch me go!" Cradled in her arms was a hand-held weapon. It had a large muzzle at the end and a place to pull and release a trigger. The weapon she was holding reminded me of a specific type of shark, but was both as sleek and black as the abyss instead of pearly white. A metal cord stuck out from the end and snaked all the way around her form and inside her pack. It took the strength of both her arms to even balance the weapon properly.

"**Big Daddy** was born to me when the concept of a weapon destined to be made in the future came to light. It was called a flame-thrower since it spewed out flames like no tomorrow. I decided to one-up that theory. By capturing the flames of multiple enslaved elemental dragons and incubating them, I was able to whip out this baby. The design is after one of my favorite creatures as well. Cool, right?" She gripped its body with one hand and the trigger with the other. "Feel the wrath of five ancient dragons all harnessed together into one thick, solid beam. Get 'em, **Big Daddy!**"

As Kei finished her speech, the skeleton king commanded his army to move up on us. The ultimate battle between metal and flesh was now upon us.

"I said to move outta my way!" She cackled like a sadistic villain out of an action novel.

We all ducked behind her, cowering in fear—not from the undead, but from our trigger-happy artificer that seemed prepared to light up the stage with anarchy.

Then she firmly squeezed the trigger.

Shrooooom!

"What is that?" I yelped in disbelief.

The beam was something else. It was otherworldly, or even godly. A thick, rainbow beam blasted from her weapon at the wave of draugrs. When flesh and augmented magic collided with each other, it was clear which one would be the victor.

"My god... She was carrying that with her? Unreal," Daji said in awe. "That thing might be able to kill even me!"

"I sure hope so," Stacy added—sarcastically, I think.

The dragon beam tore through the draugrs like child's play, obliterating their bodies from existence. They tried their best to charge at her and overtake her with numbers, but the power difference was overwhelming. Anywhere the beam went, death and carnage followed, scouring their essence to the worlds beyond. Team Flesh lost by a landslide as Kei's weapon finished slashing down their ranks with blinding speed. The almighty skeleton king himself couldn't stand long against her weapon.

Not even the dead were safe from the true reaper.

"So this is why she called herself a genius. I'm really glad she's on our side." Umbrea glanced at the fight with a mix of wonder and fear.

"Yeah, Kei isn't a big shot for nothing. Or else I wouldn't put up with her childish attitude. That beam was also super gorgeous, right?"

As long as you are not on the wrong side of it, Stacy.

"*Phew*! Killing all these undead really works up a sweat. Don't 'cha think?" Kei casually placed her goggles back on top of her head and dabbed the sweat from her brow with a handkerchief. Her weapon of mass destruction had already been safely tucked away inside her backpack to recharge. Silence had been restored, and with not an enemy in sight.

The bones and flesh had all but disappeared. The only remaining reminders of the undead were two pieces of jewelry and that special sword.

"Dibs!" Kei cried as she scampered to pick up the malicious weapon that had nearly ended me. "This one is coming back with me for some testing!"

Daji picked up the necklace, and after some deliberation, Umbrea took the crown.

"From what we saw down our path, all that waits at the end of this cave are traps and treasure. It would be safer to seal off, permanently," Stacy said.

"That sucks. But if you think so, Shepherd, then I agree. Someone already looted this place, anyway. You can tell that those creatures were not supposed to be mixed in with the skeletons. But who cares! I already got something worth taking back with me, as well as collecting field data for **Big Daddy**. Just let me be the one that blows this place to kingdom come, 'kay?"

"Just don't do it when we're around," I replied with a small smile.

We all laughed, which caused Stacy to raise an eyebrow. "When did you two get so close? I thought you hated each other's guts."

"We still do. Well, kinda. She did save my life with that knife."

"Indeed. My tech never fails!"

"And w-what caused this sudden change?" Umbrea inquired.

I chuckled. "Well, we had someone that brought us together, and she wouldn't want us to fight."

"I agree. My little sis would haunt me if she saw how I was treating a friend, so it's cool now."

I was still shocked by her kind words, but it made me happy to hear. I looked around at my party. Without them, I would have been dead. All I'd done was kill a few skeletons with Kei's artifact. Yeah, that was all I did.

My chest burned, but not with guilt. It was something I wasn't used to. It made me feel... icky.

I smiled through the alien pain. "Yeah... Thanks."

"G-good for you two!" Umbrea praised. "Now, can we go dump this crown? It's rumbling between my fingers like a miniature earthquake."

* * *

We made our way to the outside of the cave. No one was eager to chat besides our resident greed lords, Umbrea and Kei. I had expected to be attacked by the one who had forced those evil undead upon us, but it never happened.

"The enchantments on the crystals could give my babies the power boost I've been searching for. The sword is also the key to my artificer block!" Kei was super pumped and—was that drool coming from her mouth? Again?!

Umbrea was nearly as enthusiastic. "I just need a cut. Just half—or even a fourth! I just need money! Anything to get the scary loan men away. I'm sure even without the crystals, it could be pricey. I mean, look at all the gold!"

They were really hitting it off. *I guess money and power can bring even the strongest of adversaries together.* Besides their fruitless chatter, everything was all fine and dandy until we heard:

"Hand over all your valuables. Or else."

Huh? Seriously? Where did you guys even come from?!

A group of nearly fifty people had the canyon blocked off. Kei had planned to destroy it at a later date since there was paperwork to fill out first.

The gang was filled with kids and adults of all shapes and sizes. You could tell they were running with little sleep because of the massive bags beneath their eyes. It was also clear that they hadn't eaten a good meal in quite some time, judging from their unhealthy complexions. Most of them had some form of long-ranged weapon, be it a crossbow, staff, or bow and arrow. We would be at a complete disadvantage if we wanted to fight.

"Hell no! This is the rightful property of Bela Labs now! Step off, hoodlums, or face my wrath!"

"Actually, it belongs to the guild you work for and the Tribunal who funds you, but..." I trailed off. Umbrea had a look in her eyes that I hadn't seen in some time. It was proof that she'd made up her mind about something.

"If you want this, come and take it! Haaa!" She tossed the crown in the air above them, diverting all of their attention away from us. "Now, get next to me!" she shouted.

We grouped up, not asking questions despite Kei who was thirsting for round two. The shadows below us enveloped our bodies and transported our forms to a completely different location. As we shifted away, I heard the low growl of someone cursing behind us.

Then, once more, that sweet voice invaded my mind.

The Silver King howls with laughter at the pitiful Crimson Emperor. He hopes you humiliate them again in the future.

Ah, yes—more cryptic names. And this time, I don't even know what I did to incite a reaction from him. Welp! I'll think about it another time. After all, we just earned ourselves a sweet victory!

* * *

"The crooooowwwn! My rewaaaaaard!" Stacy wallowed in anguish. She took a long swig from her cup, the festive tavern lights doing little to lighten her mood. I really didn't expect her to be so bummed out. Umbrea? Sure. But Stacy?

Utterly crestfallen, she let out a long, wistful sigh. "We only ended up with half the amount we should've." She took another large sip from her mug; it was the largest one at the table, or maybe even the entire tavern.

Umbrea gave a loud sigh as well, but rapidly perked up as she spoke. "That thing felt pretty sinister when I was holding it. I could sense myself getting corrupted the more I held onto it. I think those bandits really did us a favor, don't you think, Lethe?"

"Hm?" I was innocently sipping down some fantastic hot chocolate. "What was that?" I asked, obliviously. *I would prefer it if you left me out of this while I'm drinking.*

Sadly, I chose the wrong person to rely on reading the room. "I said, don't you think they did us a favor by taking that evil crown away?"

Sighing, I put my cup down and folded my hands over each other. "Hmmm... I guess so. I just hope we don't have to see it ever again. That magic was really a pain to deal with."

"I could have beat him down, you know." Daji loudly drank from his cup after cutting in. "I wish I showed up sooner. There were already so many dead skeletons. I really wanted to fight lots of undead..."

"I wish you were there sooner, too. Then I wouldn't have had to use an actual sword."

"His name is **Deep Wave**—remember that! Plus, he's a dagger, not a sword. And he performed splendidly for his first test run. Not as much as **Big Daddy**, though. He did great work for you. Can a mama be prouder?"

During a pause in the conversation, I said, "I'm gonna miss you guys. Like, *really*. I don't think I've ever had so much fun in a party before. Thanks."

"Don't mention it," Stacy said with a wink. "I'm just glad to see you're still kickin'. Maybe now we can actually have that girl time."

"Oh, right. That! I still don't know what that really entails, but I am all for it."

"Is it alright if I j-join?" Umbrea asked meekly.

"And me as well!" Kei said with pride written across her red face. She was very smashed, but maybe watching someone be on a bender would convince me to try drinking or stay away from it for good...

"And—" Daji started.

"Nope."

"Negative."

"Ehhh?!"

Stacy shook her head. "Sorry, Daj. No dudes, or whatever you call yourself these days, allowed."

He dropped his head, looking beyond despondent. "I really need to get some guy friends and ones that aren't sharks or maniacs. Oh well. I'll check on our objective while you're away."

"Yes, do that. Thanks, Daj."

"Heh-heh." He brought a finger back and forth under his nose. "No worries."

I recalled them talking about a seal or something in the past, but I didn't want to press them at a celebration. It sounded important, after all. It wasn't really my business, no matter how curious I was.

* * *

It was fun learning more about Kei, just like I had with Bella. We ended up hanging out on the wooden floor in Stacy's apartment. The problem came after I was a few drinks in. To preface, this was my first time drinking anything strongly alcoholic. Needless to say, I exposed my true feelings for the whole gallery.

"Y'all are so... ahead of me. It's not faaair," I whined.

Umbrea turned to me, her cute face overcome with confusion. "Lethe, it seems you are a pretty big lightweight if you got drunk from only a few drinks. And what do you mean by that? You're waaay more ahead than I could ever hope to be."

Kei and Stacy also turned toward me.

I gazed at them, my eye unfocused. "You all are like shining stars: pretty, wonderful, rare, and strong. I'm like a moth. Something that will attempt to fly up to the moon to reach you but will never get there—no matter how hard I try. I'm a girl lost in the darkness. I can't find my way."

I could tell Umbrea wanted to say something, but she kept quiet, wanting me to continue. I didn't even know what I was saying, but it felt like a load had been removed from my shoulders the moment the words came spilling out. Now this was truly speaking from the heart.

"Umbrea, you are talented beyond compare with your magic and are as sweet as candy. Kei, you may be annoying, but you are a true genius—a master of your craft. And Stacy, you seem so mysterious and understanding. I feel like I can tell you about all my problems, but you also always save the day with your magic. Every time I saw you all do such amazing things, my heart would ache with agony. Jealousy—that's probably what it was. To have a talent, a skill, a brilliant mind—I lack it all. I have to rely on these flimsy rings, this cursed eye, and a godly gift that banks on the power of an extinct hedgehog wolf. I can't do anything alone. I'm so... pathetic."

While the drink may have dulled my wits, my heart felt clear. I wasn't sober, but I didn't really feel anymore, either. I was just expressing what I had hidden for some time. The quest had made it abundantly clear how little I could do without others around, but I had been thinking about it since our fight with the Leviathan.

"Lethe..."

"So that's how you felt."

"So, you admit it? I truly am a—OW! My bad..."

I dropped my empty drink, watching it roll on the floor. I felt the same way as that bottle, rolling aimlessly on the ground of life.

The other three looked as uneasy as I felt.

Stacy was the first to open her mouth. "Lethe... Life isn't all about talent, prowess, and power." She scooted closer, her eyes never leaving my own. "Sure, there are a multitude of benefits that come with being smart or unique, but everyone is different in their own way. That's a fact."

A wry smile formed on her face. "Where Daji and I are from, we were known as laughing stocks in comparison to the skill, power, and even the looks that others around us possessed. We couldn't compare. I know that may seem too distant to your own situation, but it all comes down to a matter of perspective."

"Perspective?" I repeated, as if lost in a trance. I was absorbing each and every one of her words.

She nodded. "One reason Daji and I departed was because of the enormous weight that had been unjustly dropped on our shoulders. Well, it's not like it disappeared, but we were able to take it with us—make it our own. We brought it to a place where we felt like we actually belonged."

She took a sip of her drink and continued. "Just like us, or Kei, or even Umbrea, you have your own unique qualities, talents, and especially— experiences. We may have traveled for a long time, but your knowledge of the world easily trumps either of ours. I doubt these other two know more, either. Kei's sister may have been a big reader, but she, herself, isn't any kind of bookworm."

"That's true. I love figuring things out for myself. It's more fun that way," Kei chimed in.

Umbrea smiled thoughtfully. "I'd say that I also have a good understanding of the land beyond, but that would be a lie. Even after half a year, I've learned little about what lies beyond myself and my magic. But you gave me the exact reason to leave and create a path of my own. A reason to venture out into the world and see what you see. I'm grateful for that."

I didn't know what to say.

But Stacy did.

"And it doesn't matter if you rely on artifacts to use magic. Did you forget that most people can't even use those without Kei's help? And that dog you summoned is of a unique origin. I'm sure it, and your own gift, will develop as you grow. I also can't believe you are contracted with an actual god! Not just anyone can do that, you know!"

She threw herself on me, giving me hug upon hug. I couldn't even complain about being uncomfortable. I was already so filled to the brim with warmth there was no way I could feel cold.

"There are many more things that make you, well—you. So never forget that. And don't you ever compare yourself to anyone else!"

She glared at Kei, who turned her head away in embarrassment.

I wanted to cry, but because of either my vow or the alcohol, nothing came out. I did stay in her embrace, though. It wasn't long after that I dozed off.

"Thank you, Stacy," I said gratefully as my consciousness drifted away. "Thank you so much. I really needed that..."

Her tender smile was the last thing I saw.

* * *

The next day, they all saw me off.

"That really was a crazy experience for you, huh?" Stacy asked as I mounted Frosty.

"Yep, that it was. Thanks for the fun last night. I can't say I will forget it."

"You better not, and I hope we can meet again somewhere."

"Likewise."

Umbrea hovered behind her and piped up, "I'll miss you too, Lethe."

"Umbrea. You have done well for yourself. Just, you know, don't go taking stuff with that shadow magic like you did before."

She blushed to the tip of her ears. "You know I don't do that kind of stuff anymore, right?"

"Y'all are yapping a bit too much. Let the chick leave already. And here," Kei came forward and pressed something wrapped in white bandages to my chest. I quickly grabbed it and stored it in my satchel.

Earlier that morning, my clothes had been repaired by C.T., who was happy to see me get a win for once in my life. Was she really an ancient, evil, forgotten, eldritch god of madness that wished to tear the world asunder?

Daji awkwardly itched his nose. "Keep up the stunning looks and don't fall off a ship again."

"Noted."

"Just get out of here before Stacy starts crying." Kei sniffled.

"Huh, me? Kei, what are you even saying?"

I gave them all a cheerful salute. I would have liked to wink as well, but you know how that would go. "Alright, then. It was a pleasure, really. I hope to visit again when I need money. Please carry me again."

"Psh! It wasn't like that at all," Umbrea said. "You helped." She didn't meet my gaze, but that was common for her. It seemed she could adequately look the others in the eye now, though. That really miffed me for some reason.

"Anyway, thank you all. Take care."

"You too!" Stacy shot back.

"Till we meet again," Daji added with a cheeky grin.

"I really can't go with you?" Umbrea asked in desperation.

I'm not shouldering your debt!

"You can tell people you know me to increase your street rep. I wouldn't mind." Kei had snot dripping out of her nose and tears welling up in her dewy eyes.

How un-charming. For such a hot-headed big shot, she sure had an unexpectedly soft side.

I shook my head toward Umbrea and thanked them all one last time before setting off. The last thing any of them said was, "I wonder what happened to that crown."

* * *

I ended up coming back a few days later, mostly to ask C.T. what she thought about the situation back in the cave. She was laughing to herself while her eyes were glued to a newspaper. "Now would you get a load of this, Kulu! Those blood-sucking bandits had it coming. Don't you think so?"

I grabbed a paper off the stand next to the door of the guild and took a look for myself. I didn't think I should be as happy as I was, but my mouth did indeed draw back into a nasty smile.

"Serves you all right for stealing part of my pay!" I shook my fist in the air, causing C.T. to crack another laugh.

[Bandit City Overrun by the Undead]

Watch out for the skeleton horde near the vacant town of Hesta. The leader is a black skeleton with a golden crown. Do not engage if you come upon it. The name it has been given is the Crown of Despair. If found, please return to the guild to be fully compensated. Adventurers will be dispatched shortly.

If that isn't ironic, then I don't know what is.

C.T. seemed to get a bigger kick out of it than I did, but soon her face grew more tense than I had ever seen it. "I forgot to mention this before, but there might be a way for you to save your friend. I read about it in our archives. Go have a look for yourself. Here's the location."

* * *

A lone individual appeared from the rocks within the cave. Irritation was written all over their faces. At times, they were small, while at others they became refined and menacing to all—just like in the ancient days following Ragnarok. Their long, crimson hair shifted frantically from left to right as they seethed with rage.

"Those fiends! So even that wasn't enough to take them out. What artifact or Eternal could protect against the instant-death aura of a draugr? I even improved those basic skeletons, too! That should spell the demise of humans! Especially with a Skeleton Lord to lead them! What the hell!"

Just how many days did I waste digging for those breathless spawn?

A fist slammed into the rocks, causing it to rumble before caving in. *Why must I watch from the shadows? Why won't he let me use my power to turn it all to oblivion? I'm no coward! Stalking from the sidelines is not in my job description!*

"They even took the jewels I so carefully prepared! No matter... As more stars return to the sky, his bindings will grow weaker. It won't be long now..." They stared up at the midnight sky, adorned now by a single constellation. It appeared to resemble an ancient mythical beast. Perhaps more would follow, leaving their hiding place.

The individual thought back to what they witnessed while concealing their presence within invisible flames: a party working together to overcome a threat even if it was hopeless. It was supposed to be, anyway, but that annoyingly brilliant artificer had other plans. "A weapon so powerful that it devoured all life it touched. Now, why won't he let me fight that?"

They let out a long sigh.

"If I want to track down the other seal-bearers, I need to place them into the most desperate of situations. Then at last, I will finally be free from this putrid mortal flesh! How mortifying to be brought here in this wretched fashion. How do the others live with it? How could any divine being? It doesn't suit a superior archon like me. I JUST WANT TO BURN IT ALL DOWN!"

"But I can't. Not until our options are 'exhausted' as he would say. That scaly schemer! I may lack his intellect, but my wrath is second to none. Yet, I have to use the one with more mental damage than a Cthulhu cultist! At least he is supposed to be strong. I can fight him and prove my power after the girl and the seal bearers melt and rot!"

A small smile creeped across their face. Their body had become small once more, but they either hadn't noticed or chose to ignore it. "And I know just where to find him."

Epilogue

Powers Akin to Gods

I'd spent more time combing through documents than I'd expected. After a few hours of thumbing through containers, my hands were tingling with numbness, but I had finally found what I was looking for.

Currently, I was at a branch of the Tribunal. In the past, I had thought of searching for a way to resurrect the dead, but quickly dropped the idea. I had seen my fair share of the undead and shivered at the thought of Bella joining their ranks.

When I had first joined the Tribunal, I was told they held one of the largest databases of artifacts, creatures, and deities in the world—the biggest of them being in the academic country of Archivieara.

That wasn't where I was, unfortunately. I was in the nation of Athello, one of the biggest subsidiaries of the High Tribunal. I came there to find anything that could help me break Bella out of her eternal slumber. Nothing natural had worked, and so I'd drifted toward the unnatural for a solution.

I smiled as I looked down at the file I held in my slightly trembling hands. "Eternals..."

Eternals are formed in two different ways. The first is to be created by gods to sponsor champions in a realm now past their grasp via bestowing them part of their soul as a summonable object. The second is to be birthed onto the land by the death of a deity or ancient being and forged into whatever form the one who slew or came upon them desired. Eternals are the manifestation of the soul; a supernatural existence given physical form. They can appear as clothing, armor, weapons, or even rarer shapes. Eternals can even imitate their creators if enough favor has been bought, as long as they are still alive, anyway.

"Mm. Lines up with what C.T. mentioned."

I continued reading, falling to my butt on the dusty floor because standing seemed like a pain after being up for so long. A wave of anticipation rose within me as I read the next few lines within the section labeled "The Most Dangerous and Powerful Eternals Recorded Over the Last Millennia."

Most of them only had a name, but some were simply leagues stronger. They were called the "Colored Series."

The fifth on the list instantly caught my interest. It was named Frozen Legion, the White Eternal. Its sponsor was unknown. What was known was that it was nicknamed the Frost Dragon Calamity and could leave entire cities encased in frozen tombs for decades. How terrifying. It was nice to see documents about another dragon besides the Cursed One. *I wonder if the sponsor is a dragon as well. A dragon god! Now that would be a sight to see!*

Its last known whereabouts were in a place I'd read about a while back, the Azure Mountains, but it had never been found. It hadn't been sighted since 1004 P.E. (Present Era). *It's been nearly 400 years since it was last seen!*

Its natural form was a spiky set of armor the color of frostbite. There was also a section on its last host, but that was left blank. *If that's number five, then the others have to be world-shattering! I hope the excitement isn't getting to my head. It must have been created by a crazy frost god and an even crazier champion.*

The next one I was rather familiar with. Just the thought of his bitter smile sent shivers down my spine. Number four on the list was known as the Golden Eternal. Sponsor: Tiamat, known as the Brood Mother of Creation, and said to hold the most robust and dangerous powers within her grasp. Natural form: unknown.

I recalled Gilgamesh and his desire to collect "gifts" like the magic of that unfortunate king of the sands. This thing gave him the power to do just that. He was her Chosen.

Strange how none of the other top five have their sponsor included besides him. I was already two in, and the powers seemed nearly god-like, just as expected from a god's creation.

The Golden Eternal's last known location was Uruk. It was last sighted in 405 P.E., nearly a thousand years ago. What kind of power did a demi-god hold? He had said he was immortal, but did that really bypass aging as well? Well, we know where it was actually last sighted.

I should let the Tribunal know. Oh! His name is also written right here under "Host."

"King Gilgamesh? Just as I expected." *I really hope to never see him again.*

I looked past the next two, who frankly should have belonged in the realm of the gods. One of the two was a trident the color of the deep sea and had been taken from its champion's tomb by an ancient cult. That rang a bell, but I had no reason to chase after such a dark and evil-looking weapon capable of only slaying immortals. Besides, I was sure it had fallen into somewhat capable hands a few years back. *I do fear what she could do with it if she really planned on destroying the world, though.*

Anyway, the last one was exactly what I was looking for.

Grand Paradox, the Silver Eternal. It was the unknown specter that wielded nearly omniscient power over the past, present, and even future. Reading that filled me with confusion and panic.

Could this information be forged? There's no way something that powerful can exist. Surely this must be a farce. Either way, I continued reading.

There wasn't much information. Sadly, the Grand Paradox had the least information of them all. "Last known whereabouts: unknown; Natural form: unknown; Sponsor: unknown; Host: unknown... What *do* they know?!"

They know nothing about it, so how do they know that it even exists?

I looked through the rest of the papers, flipping back and forth to make sure I hadn't missed anything.

I sighed. "There's nothing else about it here anywhere." I hastily shoved the papers back in the order I thought they probably came in. As I did, I glanced at one last document that stuck tightly to the wall. "The list of the current Ten Conquerors, huh? Now that's a good place to start."

As I left the facility, I could feel my confidence growing despite knowing next to nothing about my target. *I just need to find it and use its powers to reverse Bella back to before she fell, and who knows, maybe I can even recover my memories.*

My pace quickened, my form illuminated in the faint light of a single lamp post hiding within the hazy night. I smirked. Even on the darkest nights, there's always a light to lead the way. You just needed to know where to find it.

* * *

In a dark forest, a colossal beast pushed through every tree, rock, and organism in its path; its body shrouded in darkness. Whenever a bear or some other alpha spawn of wildlife would get in its way, a flurry of dark matter would shoot out from its body, skewering the animal for sport. At will, its long tail could extend double its range, and its flexible joints made hunting all the easier.

Nothing could stop it on its path to the main city, though many had tried.

It opened its jaw, revealing rows and rows of sharp fangs and a wickedly forked tongue. Its nostrils flared and its body ceased movement, taking in the sudden silence.

"Mmmmmmm. I smell one. The Demokai and its master. It's close! The rotting man of old is here as well. Oh, joy! It seems we have similar values—to fight one of the Ten, or maybe even *two*! Peeerrrfeeect!"

Night had slowly set, but the apex of predators was far from done feeding. Its massive maw could unhinge wide enough to swallow an elephant in one swift gulp and still have room for much, much more. Nearly nothing could satisfy its ceaseless hunger—not now, or hundreds of years ago in the past. Even its user could barely contain its true power, instead deciding to submerge themselves within it.

It only had one goal as of now: find the Demokai and other beings that shouldn't exist in its world, and devour them—just like it had done to those in the past.

The fiend could clearly see a small country, even at night.

"TIME TO FEAST!"

Extra Stories

An Unlikely Duo

"Hey, Umbrea. You know following me around all day isn't healthy for a growing girl, or really a person in general, right? I'll be leaving this place real soon to continue on my life journey. You should figure out your own. Plus, it's kinda creepy."

—Lethe

"Ughh... Why did everyone have to get up and leave me?" Tears trickled into my drink. It wasn't enough to ruin the taste, but it was enough to notice. I had been crying into my drink like a damn child! "Ahh! What am I even doing with my life?"

It was quite ironic that I was in such a state after witnessing someone who was actually suffering from imposter syndrome. Just the other day, I had a glorious adventure with my newly made friends. We'd delved into a deep crypt of darkness and terror, filled with both skeletons and the deadly draugrs. My best friend in the entire world, as well as one of my lovers, Lethe, nearly died during the exchange. If I, the great Umbrea, hadn't been there to save the day, then who knows what could have happened?

Wait! I sound like that mean girl, Kei. Now! I'll stop.

Alas, after all the dust settled, my precious Lethe left me the same way my mother did when I was young. Well, er, that's not exactly accurate; Lethe actually gave a pretty heartfelt goodbye after sharing her burden with us the night before, yet she still hadn't let me tag along! Why must my fate be so cursed?

After she left, the coolest guy I had ever seen, Daji, and the scary girl that accompanied him, Stacy, departed for a duo quest. Tha left me and the foul-mouthed girl, Kei Bela. She still scared me to tears, despite having grown more tame. Just not as much as Stacy.

Wait, don't tell her I said that! It was a joke! Joke I say!

Anyway, even Kei had to get back to her lab to analyze the goods we had recovered. Speaking of goods, the golden crown I took nearly consumed my soul. At least, it felt that way. It was scary as all hell! I was more than glad to make the hero play and toss that wretched thing toward those frightening bandits. Who knows what might have happened to me and everyone else if I held on to it?

A faint image of an undead version of myself danced through my mind, sending shivers across my whole body. Yeah, no thanks. Anyway, that's all over now. I received a good amount of money for completing the quest. However, eighty percent of that money was painfully taken away to pay off my debt to a certain museum. Now, here I was, by myself in a tavern, drinking away my sorrows with cheap alcohol. Could it get any worse? My life was so much better when Lethe was around. How did it come to this?

"I'm sooo saaaad…" I blurted in anguish to the empty table. My heart felt a lot heavier than my drink at the moment. *What am I going to do with my life?*

I sighed. My arms slumped onto the table, nearly snapping my glasses that I had set aside while I drank.

If only Lethe were here. Then I could enjoy another fun quest with her. All the stuff around here is too hard for me to take alone, and without doing recon, there's no way to be sure I can get into Daji's party again.

"Oh, now what do we have here?" called out a voice behind me. "You smell... *familiar.*"

I tried to reply, but I'm pretty sure that the words I said made no sense. Perhaps I was a bigger lightweight than I'd thought. *Can't use that as a bragging right anymore then. That feels bad.*

"If this seat is free, allow me to accompany you."

"Mrrrrrp."

"I'll take that as a yes." She had a voice as sweet as honey, yet I could only imagine her as one of those plants that gulped down bugs unlucky enough to come across her.

Yet, I easily lowered my shields. I was too smashed to think straight. "Dooo ash you like. I'm Umbreaaa."

"Someone has had a little too much to drink, haven't they? " The woman giggled before taking a seat. Her outfit seemed rather familiar, but where had I seen it? *Eh, who cares? Jus' gimme more booze!*

A waiter rushed over to the refined, older woman and took her order with a genuine smile, as if serving her was the most important thing in the world. The same couldn't be said for my service... *What is with this discrimination?! They just looked at me with an expression full of pity!*

Just gazing at the beautiful woman was enough to fill me with envy. Perfect proportions, curves in all the right places, feminine charm, slim waist and big brea—you get the point. She was wearing a guild outfit as well. *That's why I recognized it.*

"I'm jeaaaaalous!" I divulged honestly in my drunken stupor before burping. The lady cracked a bright smile at my sad display. "Mmn? Why thank you."

"Not really humble, are youuuu?"

"Ha, humorous. Would you be in my position?"

"That's a fair point…" I had started to sober up now that she'd arrived. *But that means I have to deal with the real world! Lemme go back! More booze! Oh, wait. I have no more money.*

I noticed my glasses were awfully close to falling off the edge of the table. Therefore, I snatched them up, like a warrior donning her armor. *It seems we're gonna have a conversation.*

"What's your name again? I feel like I've seen you around before."

"Oh?" She adjusted her own glasses and smirked. "I'm the beautiful and most popular guild attendant in this city. You have probably even seen me at the top of the rankings for *Markarth's Most Popular Women.*"

"There's no way something as ridiculous as that exists!"

She grinned. "Oh, my dear, but it does."

She sounded so pretentious while saying that, and I wasn't sure how to respond. I ended up puffing my cheeks like a seething child.

Then a question popped into my head. "Anyway, why are you here? Can't you see I'm trying to drown in my despair?!"

The guild attendant placed a hand to her chin, relaxing her shoulders in the process. "Ah, yes, *that.* I noticed you needed some new quest to combat your adorable sense of loneliness. I think I might have just the thing for you. By the way, I'm C.T., if you didn't know already."

"I-I'm not lonely!" I stammered. "My motivation is just…" *Shit. What was I thinking about again?*

"Right. Oh, thank you. You're such a good boy, Russel."

In the middle of our talk, a bearded man had come by the table and dropped off a few plates of food. He had a stern look, but he practically melted when C.T. flashed a smile at him. It was unnecessarily seductive. *Were guys always this easy? I glared down at my own weak points. I guess only for the strong.*

The food set in front of her made my stomach grumble like I hadn't eaten in days, which was somewhat true. It was far too much for one person. Well, I knew one girl that could most likely finish it.

God, it's so tantalizing.

C.T. was enthusiastically eyeing her grilled fish when something snapped her attention toward my gluttonous gaze. "My, my, is the little kitten looking for a free handout? All you have to do is ask."

"Ehhhh."

I believed she was testing my pride, gauging what kind of person I was. My merchant father had taught me that there was no such thing as a free meal. Everything had its price.

C.T. had conveyed her interest in me from that small talk alone. She continued drinking not only her beverage but my serious expression as well. "If you can't then that's—"

"Please give this little kitten as much as you can spare, I beg you!" I quickly tossed away the last shred of pride that remained in exchange for something a lot more tangible. She passed me a few plates, assuring her victory and my defeat. *Whatever. Everything tastes better when it's free, anyway.*

"A bit unexpected, but you do really remind me of her."

I stopped mid-munch on what she said. C.T.'s scarlet eyes had a dreadful glint in them. Looking at them too long gave me the creeps. *Does she want me on the menu?*

"My favorite and only follower, Lethe—better known as Kulu—of course," she said with a coquettish grin.

I nearly choked on my food. "Ack! You know Lethe?!" Like an addict catching sight of her favorite drug, I was helpless when it came to Lethe. *I will not allow this chance to gush about her to go by!*

* * *

After we exchanged stories, I patted my full stomach with satisfaction. I felt a tiny-bit guilty about abandoning my father's life lessons at the mere sight of something delicious, but eh, that's just life.

The words I'd heard from C.T. were quite troubling, but if she really was an ally of Lethe, then I had nothing to worry about. She wouldn't eat me. *I think.*

Even though it was suppressed, I could sense an unholy aura emanating from her sublime form. It paired up with her declaration of godhood pretty well. One glance at her shadow was all I needed to measure her strength. Not too long ago, I'd developed the ability to view someone's true strength and power from the size of their shadow. Most people were pretty normal, while a few others could be quite big. But for C.T., I couldn't even see her shadow in this gigantic tavern. That meant it was much larger than I could imagine.

"Sooo…" C.T. intertwined her fingers together on top of the table. "Would you like to accept my request? It pays well, and I can tell you are no weakling. A lot of mana is required."

I shuddered. *A lot of mana? That sounds suspicious as hell!* What if she used me for some kind of blood ritual or stole my soul? This could be really dangerous! It could even cost me my life. I had to play it safe.

"Uh… How much do you really plan to give me?"

"Double what you made from the artificer's request."

I vigorously slammed both hands on the table, my pupils morphing into temporary gold coins. "Where do I start?! Who do I kill?! I haven't done it yet, and promised my first time to someone special, but that can be overturned!"

All heads turned my way, resulting in my face becoming the color of a peach. I softly settled into my seat, doing my best to become as small as I could.

Ahhh! I want to diiie!

C.T. could only laugh at my unexpected performance. "I feel like we will get along fairly well."

* * *

The full moon illuminated my body like a spotlight as I continued my grueling task. While really putting my back into it, I thrust my shovel into the dirt. Three shovels created entirely of shadows supported me in my endeavor, quickly removing more and more dirt from the hole.

I really appreciated the light. If not for the moon, I would be quivering in my boots at the fear of being enshrouded in the darkness, unable to use my powers. *I really hate the dark!*

"Whoo..." I briefly dropped my shovel. "This really works up a sweat." I grabbed a rag from the pack at my side and wiped down my forehead. It was rather humid for summer, leading to multiple stains of sadness showing up on my tank top and shorts.

I tilted my head toward C.T. "Is this even legal?"

C.T. laid idly on a long, white reclining chair, basking in the rays of faint moonlight. She wore shades to block out the... moon? Scantily clad in a dark green, two-piece bikini with frills all over, she watched me labor away, casually sipping from a fruit drink in the shape of a—I think they were called—coconut. Did she think we were at a beach?

Unsurprisingly, that was not the case, though I wish it were. After all, this was a graveyard, and I was digging right in front of a multitude of tombstones. *Is this what it's like to disgrace your ancestors? I can really feel it. I'm going to the Netherworld for this, aren't I?*

"Hmm? Of course, it's legal," she said. "There are no actual bodies beneath these tombstones; I checked in advance."

How convenient. A boneless boneyard!

"Just keep digging."

"That's not what I meant!" *I really hope we don't get caught.* I'll never be able to pay my debt off from jail.

I retrieved my shovel once more and inspected the progress my little buddies had made. The hole was nearly five feet deep now. Just how far did she want me to dig down?

"The barrier between worlds is weaker the deeper you dig. Once you reach ten feet, we can begin the ritual."

"What does any of that even mean?!" I yelped, despite continuing to dig. Money was on the line, after all. "We better not be summoning a demon or something nefarious like that."

"Well..." C.T. looked away from me, unable to meet my inquisitive gaze. "I can't say it's better."

"Oh god, please no!"

"Relax. Just keep digging. It's the boss' job to worry about the problems. Besides, no demon would dare try to steal my spot if they valued their lives."

I gulped. I solemnly continued my work without another peep.

* * *

"Finally!" I shouted from my spot in the dirt pit. "It's done!" The hole was ten feet deep and around six feet long. It was surely big enough for a few people to fit, but C.T. still wouldn't tell me what it was actually for.

"Splendid. You can come up now. We have to begin the next sequence."

"Ugh..." My back ached, and the energy had all but left my weakened body. Still, I needed those coins. My shadow shovels transformed into a set of wings and attached themselves to my back. With them, I could easily leave the hole. When I made it back out, C.T. stood before me, arms crossed, and glasses now replacing her shades.

"Um, I was going to ask this earlier, but why are you in a swimsuit?"

C.T. appeared to be in rather deep thought, but was brought back to the real world by my burning inquiry. "Ah, that. Well, it makes me look pretty hot, does it not?"

I was somewhat baffled. "Yeah. I guess it does." But it was difficult for me to not agree.

"But the real reason is so I can absorb as much mana from the dead as possible. If my clothes are too thick, I won't be able to get the max value."

"I thought you said earlier that there were no bodies here!"

"Well, there aren't anymore. They dwindled into nothingness after I feasted on them, but the stench of death remained."

"Oh... Wait, you did *what*?"

"I also would have preferred to wear nothing, but I worried what it would do to your health if you were to see me that way."

I was getting more dazed by the second. "What? Why?"

"Mortal minds can only process so much, after all."

Was she seriously saying I wouldn't be able to process what I saw just because she was nude? What does she take me for, anyway?

"Never mind that. I need your hand."

"Huh? Like this?" I thrust out my right palm to her. She was a bit taller than me without her heeled shoes, but I could feel that the difference between us was as vast as that between the sky and earth. Who was I blindly giving my body to? *Wow, that came out wrong.*

"Exactly. You're going to act as a catalyst and anchor to this realm while the ritual takes place. Know that if you run out of mana during it, I will have to use your life force as a replacement."

"Uh... *What*?"

"Just do your best to keep the mana flow up during the summoning." She gave me a heartwarming smile without a hint of malice. That only made me more scared to mess up.

"Summoning? What could we possibly be summoning—Ahhhhh! I feel like my soul is being sucked out!"

"I haven't even started yet. Cease your whining. It's really time now. Let us begin."

C.T. began to chant something that couldn't have been made with the human tongue. It was more screeching than speaking. Hearing those ungodly syllables filled my entire body with icy dread.

The ground around us rumbled, while a pale green light oozed ominously from the hole. C.T. calmly continued her chant, while I experienced what it would be like if someone was sucking the air I was about to breathe right before it could reach me. Every time my mana reformed, it was immediately sucked away once more.

C.T.'s body gained a faint green tint, while the eyes that hid behind her glasses burned bright crimson, like a predator in the dead of night. I avoided eye contact at all costs. If I didn't, I would end up paralyzed from the intensity.

"Here's where I come in. It's been eons since I have had to play defense, but these guys never change, do they?" I couldn't tell if she was talking to me or to herself. In the end, what really mattered was what happened next.

Dark humanoid shadows coalesced around the pit. All I could feel from them was pure evil and eternal darkness. Why had they been drawn here?

"Back off! You conceded your throne the moment you left for the other world. Now, return whence you came!" C.T. thrust out her free hand, a green flame flying from it and splitting into smaller flares. Each of them found its target, erasing the dark shadows like one would erase a mistake with an enchanted rag.

This is freaky as hell! I WANNA RUN!

As I was nearing my wits' end, she released my hand. "Glad they went away so easily. You have done great. Just sit down and watch the rebirth of my former glory."

I had no idea what she meant, but I followed her advice and took a seat on something that was most definitely a shattered tombstone. I ended up sitting idly a few feet away, watching as C.T. held out her hands and commanded the aura emanating from the pit.

Rough, silver matter spawned into existence and took the form of a bipedal squid with wings. It was leaning on a pedestal that jutted out of the pit. What the hell was this?

"It's here! At last! My triumphant return is near!"

Oh, hey. That rhymes!

Tears welled in C.T.'s eyes. She removed her glasses, her gaze hungrier and more piercing than ever before. It seemed this large idol or statue meant a lot to her. It was a little gross, but the aura that radiated from it was eerily similar to C.T.'s.

"What is this?" I asked with a trembling body. "Looks like a scary monster from nightmares."

"Why, thank you. Though it has been sometime since I've entered the minds of men looking like that."

Did she think that was a compliment?

C.T. noticed my glum look and crossed her arms. "No need to fear. This is the newly made shrine of my true form. Isn't it amazing? Godly, even?"

"Y-yeah..." I could only nod my head in agreement. This "shrine" was clearly something beyond my understanding. At least the ominous air around it had begun to dissipate. Now it only looked like a creepy statue the size of an adult bear.

"I must say, I really do look amazing. With this shrine, I can once again amass a following. The other 'me' should be doing the same thing, given enough time and mana." She moved very close to me, indulgence leaking from her eyes. "I can't thank you enough for helping a lost god finally reclaim her shrine. When I take over this world, I'll make sure to grant you a good plot of land to live out your days in solitude and bliss. Oh, I can't wait a few hundred years to finally be at full power again. **The reign of Cthulhu will return at last!**"

Her fervent gaze was beyond overbearing to a weakling like myself. The grand words she spouted also did nothing to reassure me. *What did she even mean by "a few hundred years"? I wouldn't even be around by then!*

"Right. Well, anyway," I said while trying to get out of her sight. If I stayed any longer, I felt I would witness something that could not be unseen. It already was way too bizarre for someone like me to handle. "I'll come to pick up my reward tomorrow, so I must be going!"

As I turned to leave, a well-manicured hand grasped my shoulder, rooting me in place. "Where are you going, disciple number two? Just because my shrine is finished doesn't mean everything is over. Without you, I won't be able to lay claim to this idol when the others come. It was a shame that Kulu had to leave, but you will do nicely."

Ah, I did it again. Now they will never take me seriously!

"Ugh... Okay." My shoulders sagged and my back ached. I was going to have to meet whatever "others" C.T. was referring to. *Please don't eat me! I don't taste good at all!*

Soon after, the world around me became ensnared in perpetual darkness; I couldn't even see my feet. The only light in the vast shades of black were three sets of eyes: a pair of scarlet red, two that were bright yellow like a lantern, and ominous, jade eyes like the flames C.T. had produced earlier.

Ahhh! Can't see anything! Heeelp! Light. I need light!

I panicked and brought out the spare lantern I always kept in my bag, pumping mana into it to spur it to life. I breathed a sigh of relief and stopped quivering, finally able to focus on the conversation... or at least try.

"So, you have arrived, and in such a conspicuous form," C.T. called out from somewhere near me, her tone neither playful nor filled with anger. "It's been a while."

"Indeed, it has, my little 'Thulhu. I only wanted to match your new look, nothing more. It is fitting enough for the Crawling Chaos, is it not?"

I would prefer if she didn't crawl in the cemetery. My heart wouldn't be able to take it, for a myriad of reasons.

The one who spoke had a refined manner of speaking—a facsimile of how C.T. spoke—yet it somehow suited her all the more. Every word was jammed full of both feminine appeal and sweetness that reminded me of a rose. I just couldn't tell when the thorns would come.

Her malignant, verdant gaze was nothing but terrifying in the vast sea of darkness. It contained a vast well of pride and condescension. If I were to put the two of them together, this new voice would give off the air of an older sister. She simply sounded a lot more experienced and down-to-earth than Cthulhu. Of course, I could be talking out of my ass, but I trusted my analysis.

"Jealous were you, not only of my new vessel, but also my shrine? Why else would you be here, you conniving thief! This shrine has already been claimed!"

"C.T., w-what's... happening? I can't s-see a thing." My words chilled me as they left my tongue, making it seem near impossible to complete a sentence. "Oh, sorry, my follower. You can't see in Nyarla's veil of darkness, can you? Give me a minute, while I make this homewrecker back off once and for all."

I gazed towards the yellow eyes that sat close by the clashing noises. I knew there was another existence there, and yet it said nothing as the two women continued to verbally assault each other.

"I didn't plan on taking this shrine, anyway. I just wanted to see how you were doing. How long has it been since you were last awoken from your slumber in the other world? A thousand, no, two thousand years? You really missed a lot in that time. Oh, the joys of being able to walk this earth in bliss!"

"I'm doing fine. I have already acquired two true followers."

I felt a hand pat me on the back.

"Oh? Is that so? And what of the cult that spent generations in R'lyeh to bring you back from the brink of nothingness? Were those not your high cultists?"

"Shut up! They couldn't even manifest me! What kind of cult can't imagine what their ruler looks like in the flesh? I have many idols shaped in my likeness! I had no choice but to dispose of them for their insolence!"

C.T. seemed *very* riled up. From being around her, I'd pegged her as a more relaxed and confident type. That facade seemed to peel in the face of this newcomer's provocations. It's as they say, "There are always bigger fish."

Around that time, my vision suddenly became awfully clear, exposing me to a gathering that no mortal should have seen.

There was C.T., arms crossed and flustered as one could be. Past her stood a woman, her skin the color of caramel—and just as smooth. She was both beautiful and healthy enough that she could have been in her early or late twenties at the same time. Her hair was long and luscious, black as night, with golden highlights woven in. Her long eyelashes and violet, glossy lips matched C.T.'s charm when it came to enthralling others, while her slender waist and large bust (that I totally wasn't staring at) directly mirrored or even slightly surpassed her. *Any woman would certainly be jealous of her. Not me, though. I have my own charm. That's what my dad always said, and he made lots of money!*

Everything about her was sinister. Her height was also slightly taller than C.T., which made even more of a difference with her booster shoes—I mean—heels. It was like she had been specifically engineered to be just slightly better than the original in just about every way—and she kinda was. Even her attire shone brilliantly against C.T.'s lackluster swimsuit. The copy had now surpassed its original.

She wore a sultry evening dress that sparkled in the faint moonlight, and had stardust-colored shoes that clacked as she majestically moved around C.T., free of spite.

She was breathtaking, cosmic brilliance just flowing out of her like an escaped light. It wasn't divine radiance like a god, but resembled something similar. *Someone just like C.T.? That's pretty interesting! I wonder what she really is!*

Even as a woman, I was beyond captivated by her elegance. *Maybe I really do swing both ways because my heart is pounding so hard that it's nearly bursting from my chest.* Was it adoration... or fear?

"Don't be entranced by her looks! She has a thousand faces and yet she's still a copycat!" C.T. hissed in outrage. "Don't try to take my follower from me with your seductive charm, Nyarlathotep!"

Well, we were both girls and all, but I could see where she was coming from. There was definitely some seducing happening, and I was all for it. *Don't worry Lethe and Daji. I seek the sacred harem ending!* Then again, I thought "seductive" fit C.T. to a T.

"Oh, my. Someone's got their panties in a twist. Hastur and I just wanted to check on how you were doing after all these centuries. The shrine's aura led us right to you." Nyarla strutted forward, a single tan finger on her chin.

C.T. responded in kind, accepting her challenge by advancing forward. "I know you well enough to realize that can't be the only reason you two came. Spill it or prepare to face the wrath of The Great Dreamer!"

The air around us grew cold once more, each side refusing to back down. I timidly stood behind C.T., nearly covering my eyes to avert my gaze.

The lone, lantern-eyed person I'd seen in the dark earlier sat behind Nyarla, drawing what looked like ancient symbols and hieroglyphics in the dirt. He wore a bright yellow overcoat with a hood that hid his face. Under it were those bright yellow eyes, clouded in darkness. *How unnerving.*

His body was small, resembling that of a child only twelve years of age. He seemed neither interested nor in the mood to deal with the quarrel of the older women. *So then, why is he even here? Ah, you must have been dragged into it. Just like me. Poor thing.*

"Alright, alright, you caught me. The real reason we are here is—"

C.T. stared daggers at her, while I watched with bated breath.

"—to find work."

"Huuuuuuh?!"

We were both flabbergasted by her declaration. C.T.'s eyes were nearly bulging out of their sockets. As a fellow person of poor sight, I felt bad for her glasses.

C.T. held her head in embarrassment. "W-why would you come to me f-for *that*?! Such an idiotic statement can hardly be true."

"But it is." Nyarla took a few steps back. "You already know that the male versions of myself rein in many popular positions throughout this world. However, I have been unsuccessful in landing this form in a higher position like the rest, no matter how hard I try. It's pathetic, really."

You can't be serious. That's the reason? Sooo lame! Let me leave now!

Nyarla continued, while C.T.'s expression eased into one of curiosity and interest. "I know of your position within not only the guild, but that other troublesome place as well. Please show me the ropes so I can ascend the ranks just like you." She knelt down, slightly dirtying her magnificent dress in the process. "Hastur's child form also needs a place to live and grow, but all the other deities and workers think he is... 'creepy.' Won't you please take us into the guild?"

Plot twist! Am I reading a book right now?

This was not what I had expected at all! And from C.T.'s look, she'd never even dreamed of it! However, it took her all but three seconds to return to her normal, mature self.

"Mm? Is that so? Well, I can't just send you running back like that, but first you must say what you told me to say in the past when I sought your assistance. Surely, the great Nyarlathotep hasn't forgotten, has she?"

"Ugh..." Nyarla winced in pain. "Alright, alright. 'The great Cthulhu is the most supreme of all the Great Old Ones. No one can surpass the Great Dreamer even if death dies. All will go mad against his power.' That was it, right?"

"Close enough. I'll start you off as my assistant. You have a long way to go before I can take you to my other job. Hastur, on the other hand, will make a great mascot and bodyguard for warding off pesky adventurers that also want to take me out."

"Like, kill you?" she asked.

"Like a date," she replied, miffed "I'm not sure how long it has been since you have manifested in that form, but being a guild attendant that is both well-endowed and good-looking is something you will need to get used to. You're going to have to do something about the aura of darkness that lurks behind you as well. Can't have you scaring my victi—I mean—adventurers away."

"Please teach me, Miss 'Thulu."

Hastur approached them and nodded as well. A small, pointless flame ignited within my chest and burned away some of my fear. *You traitor! What happened to being here against your will?* I felt like a fourth wheel in their conversation, simply watching idly as the devil gods planned to work and integrate into my town like foreign refugees. Why was I even here? Seriously. She could have let me leave the moment it became night everywhere.

In the midst of my uneasiness, a hand reached out to me. Of course, it was C.T.'s. "Sorry about making you sit through all of this. I didn't expect to reconcile with these two. If you want, I could also get you a job at the guild. It probably pays better than the bottom barrel contracts you are doing at the moment."

"Hmmm."

"It would be my pleasure. Allow me to bestow this blessing onto you as well, just like the one you covet."

Nyarla chimed in. "I too am interested in the child that assisted with summoning this shrine. Perhaps there's more to her than meets the eye."

Child? I'll have you now that I'm turning seventeen this year, lady! I'm well past the age of marriage... which is kinda messed up if you think about it. The time I've lived can barely be called a life. And I've never had a partner either... God, maybe I am a child.

Putting my inner turmoil aside, Nyarla had consented to C.T.'s idea, further propelling me to choose my path right there and then. Would I join these forgotten gods, or would I be on my own again like I had been for most of my life?

C.T. noticed my concern and clearly addressed it. "Our guild has many locations throughout the land and would have no trouble sending you to another city if need be."

That was exactly what I wanted to hear—a proper job with people I could rely on, and a chance to meet up with Lethe and even Daji once more. *Dad, your little girl might have finally found a way out of her fruitless life. Just watch me grow!*

I couldn't believe that this sketchy quest had ended with a job offer, of all things!

I took in the dark atmosphere around me. I stood before two dazzling women and a young child that could be the villain in an old kid's book. C.T.'s hand was outstretched, beckoning me forward. I wasn't as weak as I used to be, but I still had a long way to go before I could reach the level of Stacy, Daji, and Lethe.

So what? The next time they saw me, I would either be successful or struggling along the way.

"I accept your challenge."

I took her hand.

I hope Lord Harrow forgives me for two-timing... Or perhaps three-timing.

And then I stepped into a whole new world.

For once, I had no regrets.

The Sand King's Soliloquy

A boy as poor as stones, life for him was tough.
But when his magic developed, he shone like a diamond in the rough.
Merchants praised his weapons; children praised his toys.
Mothers asked him to create animals for all the girls and boys.
Through his hands breathed life into the sand down below.
His methods were superb, but his work became slow.
The kingdom adored him and put him on the throne.
They called him the Sand King. He brought prosperity to all.
Heralded as the next to join the great Ten Conquerors.
With him on the mantle, Rima would never fall.

There was a good reason Rima had become the talk of the world. Its economy had risen from nothing and grown massive with its wild products, crafted from creatures exclusive to their biome.

The founder had been an exiled prince from an island nation in the far east. He used his hunter's knowledge, as well as his experience as an apprentice craftsman, to slay many species native to the desert and turn them into everyday clothes, jewelry, and even weapons. It greatly helped that the well-preserved remains of the great demon scorpion, Anorok, had been scattered across the land years prior. Merchants flocked in droves to get an early edge on the booming industry that he had created, which resulted in exiles and refugees from nations that had become Nulled, to join under his new banner. That was how the unique desert country of the north, Rima, had been born.

That was only the start of their monumental history.

Two generations later, the Sand King was discovered. Even as a child, his special power was all that was required for their renown to burst through the roof. Everyone wanted to witness the Sand King's miracles, and everyone wanted to go to Rima to see him in action. Tourism was already popular in

Rima because of the strange lizards and insects that could only survive in the desert environment. Hunting was allowed in moderation as well. Yet now, everyone in the nation only had one individual on their mind.

The exiled prince, Manorus, had dedicated his new life to serving Ra—who supposedly had led him to the barren desert that brimmed with opportunities. He invited others from other nations who served the sun god to help him spread the religion over his young kingdom. With the mass spread of Ra-ism, so did the fable of his son, the god of the desert—Ziir.

With the ability to create sand from nothing and control it like magic, Ziir was the symbol of the people of Rima. Many stories were archived of his struggles, but unlike his father, he had never been glimpsed in physical form.

It was an easy decision for the people of Rima, and those who had heard the religion's tales, that this young boy was the incarnation of Ziir. Years and years of prosperity passed in Rima, much to the dismay of the countries near the desert kingdom. When the Sand King was in his prime, around thirty years ago, he'd been summoned by the neighboring nation of Orellia to meet their grand bishop.

This was the very first time someone from Rima had been invited outside their country since its creation, as well as the first time the Sand King himself had ever set foot beyond the borders of Rima. He was welcomed with open arms and planned to spread the word of Ra with his miracles of sand.

The Sand King didn't return home for nearly forty years.

A few days into his trip, the grand bishop's clergy captured him and ordered to create sand creatures for their army. His creations were strong and would be nearly unkillable in the fight against metal and stone. Now, the bishop's country could not only take over its competitors, but steal Rima's fame as well.

"You could be a part of something great," the bishop had said. *"It's far bigger than some upstart kingdom that worships the grains of sand they tread upon."*

Of course, the Sand King refused to do it. He was a strong and just king, who would have little difficulty escaping on his own. But with his capture had come a warning. If he escaped, his country would fall to ruins by one of the grand bishop's most dangerous spells.

It was a country that was governed by the strong, as per their goddess, Hestarte's, wishes. She was a desert deity of mystical power. He knew that the strong, but small, infantry of Orellia could shred his proud country to pieces in his absence.

"Here. Allow me to demonstrate why the king lets a simple, pious mage run the show."

The bishop's cruelty blew the Sand King away. *He could use his power for his people, yet...* After seeing local criminals succumb to the sickness the bishop had spread during an execution day, he started to worry greatly.

Days became months, and months became years, for the man said to be the son of the sun god. Before he knew it, he'd forgotten his home and the reason he'd come to Orellia. He held onto the heart of Rima as if it were his own heart—the people. That was what grounded him. That was what caused him to resist every time he was asked for his service.

His once daily visitor, the grand bishop, didn't offer him any solace. Thus, he stayed secluded and alone, with not even a window to peer out of. He did not find any solace from his one daily visitor—the grand bishop.

"Your country indeed worries about your health, but I have assured them that you are accomplishing great deeds here in the name of Ra. Your son has taken up the mantle in your stead. You have no need to worry, so why don't you just comply?"

The lying priest! How dare he!

The Sand King cursed internally at the grand bishop's red robes. Still, he was getting weaker and weaker by the day. It wouldn't be long before he caved.

The bishop was his only communication with the outside world. He fed him information that he couldn't verify about his country, and eventually there were rumors that Rima would be invaded by another desperate kingdom in the near future.

Every day, he grew weaker until his resistance felt futile and pointless. He had nothing to hold on to anymore. *The heart is the people? What a joke. No one has ever helped me. They only take and take. They never give!*

The Sand King had become increasingly bitter, his mind deluded and tainted by the lies of the bishop and his own crumbling heart. But he didn't care. He just wanted to see the sun. He wanted to see his 'father.'

It was far easier to let go.

At long last, his mind rotted the same way his body had in that tarnished cell. His meaningless existence was as a tool to serve the grand bishop. He was no longer Ziir, the Sand King. Only a lost soul, seeking truth from the sun, who had already forgotten his birth name long ago. Now, he had forgotten his god's name as well. The great Sand King had finally cracked, crumbling to sand like his creations after time sank its cursed teeth into their soft flesh.

The lost soul helped the bishop create an endless number of soldiers to wage war on other countries in the area. His creations conquered them within a day. Long ago, he'd been promised that no harm would come to his country as long as he complied. The grand bishop had said he always kept his word. The promise seemed fruitless now, yet he still clung to it like a lifeline—a rope out of the quicksand of his futile life.

It was all that let him live with himself at night when he regained enough energy to notice the destruction his mindless children caused. So much death and destruction—the opposite of the wonder and happiness he'd so easily provided back home.

"You have followed your destiny. You were born for war, nothing else. I'm sure your god would be proud," the grand bishop had said with a smile after the former Sand King had been rewarded by the king of Orellia.

Who would be proud of a murderer who slaughtered thousands?

Then one day, he decided that he'd had enough.

He dissolved his sand creations and created his own escape out of Orellia by building a massive spire into the sky and making a bridge that spanned multiple miles away.

He could have retaliated against the country that had imprisoned him for so long, but he didn't have the spirit nor the energy for malice at his tender age. He'd become an old man. All he wanted was to settle down in his country and be at peace once more. He never wanted to fight again—not for anyone. War, terror, and despair were nothing more than thoughts of the distant past for him. At least, that's what he made himself believe.

After nearly forty years, he arrived in Rima only to find his people and his country in ruins.

A few days prior, a horrible plague had washed over the entire kingdom, infecting every single citizen with an incurable blight. He tried his best to save who he could, but even those people perished within his grasp. One by one, the citizens died in horrible pain, leaving him entirely alone once more.

He cried, he screamed, pounding his fist on the barren sand—but no one could hear him. How could they? He was the sole inhabitant of Rima. The searing sun shone down on him like in his early days of ruling, yet now it was as pointless and empty as his escape.

If only I stayed away forever. If only I always complied...

He lamented his cruel fate for days on end, until an idea sparked within him and pulled him out of his stupor. He used his loving memories, the pride and joy of his country—the heart of Rima—to give birth to his greatest creation yet.

The sand people—that's what he called his new children. Each was crafted with the memories and image of every citizen the Sand King had ever met. Once again, his country would prosper. Like the sun of the desert, Rima would rise.

A few years went by. His newly born citizens lived in harmony with each other, not knowing the dark truth of their former selves. During that time, travelers ceased to visit, and business with other countries ground to a halt. They were all too frightened by the new Rima and her people. Word never left the north without it spiraling into over-exaggerations that no one believed. It was the reason I'd never learned the context of what had happened here until now.

Glossary

Anorok: Ancient scorpion beast from the Netherworld that was killed by a sun god and used to build Rima. Its offspring are said to live in the desert to this very day.

Archivieara: The country of magic scholars and research. Creator of the Ten Conquerors list, it never stays in the same location, and moves with the mist that surrounds it.

Ashardna: Born from an ancient species of wolf known for their spikes and nimble bodies. Ashardna was the most renowned of them and was the chosen summon for Extinctathon.

Boreas Tyrel: A famed hero missing for decades after publishing his exploits.

Breathless King: The father of Draugr, collector of many things, and a scourge to humanity in the far past. Some say his large stash of treasure held inside him through a magical storage can be breached within his hidden cave, leading to many adventurers traveling into tombs of the death gods to find it.

Cthulhu: The resurrected old god reborn through Lethe's vision. Nicknamed C.T., she plans for world destruction as she works her way up the job ladder.

Eternals: Items forged from fallen gods or deities who have chosen a champion. They are manifested from the soul into a physical form and bound to someone for life and taken by the slayer in death.

Extinctathon: An Eternal that can summon a famous creature from the past after bonding with their descent.

Harrow: A god of parting, death, and despair. Often worshiped by outcasts or those looking to become a solo adventurer.

Intrathon: The continent of giants, mutated creatures, and monster hunters. Many unique species originated from there, while others that dwell within its biomes are older than the land itself.

Netherworld: Alternate dimension where demons come from. Humans who are deemed unfit to reside in the land of the gods are sent here after their demise, cursed to be tortured for all eternity. Every now and then, gateways will open up and allow them to escape into the world, but most of the time, they are summoned to form pacts.

Rankle: A bounty hunter and monster slayer from Intrathon. Being infected by a crystal infection has allowed his body to stay young for a *very* long time.

Rima: A desert country and home to the Sand King.

R'lyeh: A sunken city used by cultists for annual meetings and summoning their lord every few hundred years.

***The Adventurer's Journey*:** An autobiography of Boreas Tyrel's exploits during his youth and young adult years. To some, it is but a fable. But to others, it is one of the greatest documentations of mortals and gods interacting.

The Cursed One: One of the few named elder Dragons. He is the creator of golems, a fan of grand machinations, and one of the Ten Conquerors who was banished to the Netherworld and stripped of his very name.

The Null: Any place that is taken over by the Void, becoming desolate, corrupted with strange flora and fauna, and painted vermillion.

The Ten Conquerors: The ten strongest beings in the world that aren't gods. Measurements used to determine their strength are unknown, but it is monitored by the research country of Archivieara. The current conquerors of the era are:

> **The King of Heroes:** Gilgamesh
> **The Cursed One:** Aboleth Murrain
> **The Lord of Rot:** Ashborn
> **Devourer of the Cosmos:** The Starscourge
> **The Apex Predator:** Clade Rancor
> **Sovereign of Dusk:** The Revenant King
> **The Void Empress:** [REDACTED]
> **The Elder Primal of the Nightscape:** Ashior the Ever-Dream
> **The Sire of Monsters:** Behemoth

The High Tribunal: One of the leading organizations of peacekeeping around the world. They police cities, investigate crimes, and take and/or even kill dangerous individuals.

The Silver King: The Father of all wolves and ancient constellation god. Has chosen Lethe as his Champion.

The Starscourge: A serpentine beast that devoured the constellation gods of the sky and sent others into hiding. It is currently sealed away, thanks to the mortal realm and one other, but the seals are beginning to wane.

Trident: The "City on the Sea" and one of the home bases for C.T. as a guild receptionist.

Umbrea: As a wielder of shadow magic, there are many things she can do. Not one of them is getting out of debt, however.

The Void: An alternate dimension full of creatures filled with gluttony and the urge to assimilate all into their hive.

Rock-Howler: Lethe's adopted grandfather and one of the few golems in existence. He resides in the Bretha Tundra and is the last remaining crystal golem. Rock was appointed to guard and preserve the knowledge he has accumulated for all eternity.

Vorax Cruciator: An ancient, four-armed demon known as one of the Abyssal Lords. His immense mana is what makes a pact with him so enticing. He is currently bound to a host, only sprouting up at opportune moments as he bides his time to strike.

Afterword

Hello! My name is Ivern and I hope you've enjoyed the first volume of River Lethe. It's been something that I have been working on for a few years and I'm so happy to finally get it out to you all! There are many things that inspired me to write this book, but the main one had to be *Wandering Witch: The Journey of Elaina*. The episodic nature of the series, mixed with the unique and assertive main character, were my favorite characteristics of the novels. Besides that, I'm just a huge nerd for fantasy! I wanted to do my best to build a unique world filled with gods, monsters, and weirdos that feel diverse and interesting. I have a lot planned for this series, so I hope you'll stick around.

I would love to thank my illustrator, Shouu-kun, for the amazing work they did, especially when bringing my characters to life. I would also like to thank the cover artists at Light Comic Studio for creating an amazing cover that perfectly captures Lethe. It all looks great. Big thanks to my editors, Jyorin and Ren, for taking the time out of their busy days to read through my work and help improve it a lot.

Thank you to my friend, Boat, for being my first fan and someone I could brainstorm with. To my role model, Papa, it means a lot that you were my first reader, and I'll always look up to you and your writing. And last, my deepest thanks to you—my readers. The support you've shown me by purchasing *River Lethe* is more than I could ever ask for. I sincerely hope it has made your day even the tiniest bit better. It's been a dream come true!

—Ivern, July 2023

Thank you for reading a MoonQuill original novel. To experience more exciting stories, visit us at <u>moonquill.com</u>

To know when we release new books, join our <u>mailing list</u> from our site and receive three books for free!

We will never spam you!

To talk with other members of the MoonQuill community, check out our community <u>Discord</u>.

Finally, we would really appreciate it if you could take a moment to review the book. Every review greatly helps the author and supports their ability to continue writing fantastic books for us to enjoy.